HIGH PRIESTESS

A Solstice Coven Novel

Wendy Hewlett

High Priestess
Wendy Hewlett
Copyright © 2019 Wendy Hewlett
All rights reserved.
ISBN-13: 9781999262617
ISBN: 9781999262600 (eBook)

To my sisters ~

A sister will always pick you up when you fall, as soon as she's done laughing.

Chapter 1

Detective Constable Raven Bowen slid her hand across the bed in search of her lover's warmth and was met with cold, desolate sheets. With a groan she curled into the fetal position and pressed her face into the pillow. One of these days she'd stop reaching for Riley in the night. Wouldn't she? She groaned again at the piercing ring of her cell phone and grabbed it off the nightstand.

"Bowen."

The Ontario Provincial Police dispatch officer gave her an address, ordering her to report to the scene of a DB - dead body.

She didn't think of only being in bed for a couple of hours, most of that time spent tossing and turning, thinking of Riley and trying to ignore the heat of desire flooding her veins. She just reacted, throwing off the duvet and jumping out of bed.

The drive to the crime scene took ten minutes and deposited her in the middle of nowhere – a little-used dirt road on the outskirts of the small town of Solstice in Central Ontario.

Raven parked her unmarked, a black Dodge Charger, on the shoulder behind two Ontario Provincial Police black and white squad cars with their red and blue lights beaming out over the snow covered expanse of farmers' fields like a laser light show. She exited her vehicle and the wind sliced in from the north, the damp air cutting through her extra layers of clothing, seeping into her bones. Ducking her head, Raven made her way to the closest squad car.

The officer in the driver's seat rolled down the window.

"Evening, DC," he said. "Nice bed head."

"Closer to morning, Tate," she growled back, absently running a hand through her unruly short black hair. Probably should have glanced in the mirror before running out the door, she thought. "Want to show me where the body is?" She didn't want to spend any more time with Constable Darren Tate than necessary. He was one of the most annoying people she'd ever met.

He pointed toward the ditch on the other side of the road. "Snowmobilers found her. Guy stopped to take a piss and nearly shit his pants." Tate's head rolled back with laughter.

Constable McHaela Warren, who sat in the passenger seat, no doubt enjoying the heat blasting out of the vents, leaned over Tate. "Sorry to hear about your mom, DC Bowen."

"Yeah, thanks." Raven wasn't close to her mom. Losing her, making the funeral arrangements, and surviving the horrid day of the funeral hadn't bothered her nearly as much as what her mother said to her from her death bed. And how she said it, because Raven hadn't been anywhere near her mother's death bed at the time.

Raven's mom, Ena Amaris Bowen, was Wiccan, which is how Raven ended up with the embarrassing name Raven Sage. It was bad enough having to live her life as Raven Sage never mind the whole town knowing her mother was a witch. And not just any witch. Ena was High Priestess of the Solstice Coven. Or, as Raven like to call her, HWIC - head witch in charge. Raven had been rebelling against all of that hokey crap since her early teens.

On the night of Ena's death, Raven had clearly heard her

mother's voice inside her head.

You have great powers, Rave. You've only to open yourself to them.

"Yeah, right," she said to herself as she crouched down at the edge of the ditch, her flashlight illuminating the pale form below. This poor girl had been here for some time, preserved by the icy temperatures, her upper body revealed with the spring melt. She was face down, left arm extended up over her head. Long, red hair fanned out around her, tangled and matted. At a glance, it could have been Riley lying there and that thought chilled Raven to her already icy bones.

"I don't know who you are," Raven whispered. "Or who hurt you..." And threw you out like garbage, she thought with a shake of her head. "But I promise to do my damnedest to find out."

At the sound of crunching gravel behind her, Raven glanced over her shoulder, surprised to see Constable Warren approaching in her dark blue uniform and shiny, black boots. She was relatively new to the Solstice Detachment. Probably her first murder scene. Warren's curvy figure crouched next to Raven, her wavy blonde hair tucked up into a black toque. Her warm brown eyes saddened as she perused the scene in the ditch.

"No outstanding missing persons reported in Huntsville in the past six months."

Raven smiled ever so slightly. It was the first thing she would have checked. "Tell me what you see here."

"Appears to be naked and frozen solid."

A low rumble of laughter quickly blew away in the arctic wind. "That's it?"

"Ligature marks on the left wrist."

"You're only telling me what you see with your eyes." Raven thought again of her mother's words. Was the old bitch right? Had she been using her *powers* all along?

"She's been there for a long time. Is that what you mean?" Constable Warren's big brown eyes settled on Raven's icy blues. At a nod from Raven, she continued. "This was just the dump site. She wasn't murdered here. But, we need to see what's beneath her, what's buried in the snow."

Raven looked over her shoulder again. Tate still sat on his butt, staying warm in his squad. "I don't suppose he called in forensics?" Solstice had a small OPP Detachment, so the forensics unit came in from OPP Headquarters in Orillia when required.

"They're on their way. They should be here within the hour."

"You called them in?"

"Wasn't I supposed to? I asked dispatch to call."

"No, you did good, kid." Raven rose to her full height, stretched her back. "I'm going to stay with our vic until she's safely on her way to the morgue." It wasn't that she didn't trust the forensics team to do their job, she just felt like she owed it to the victim. Plus, she wanted to be there to take notes for herself. "You up for a long, cold night, Constable, or are you going to sit on your ass in your squad staying all warm and toasty?"

The edge of Warren's full mouth curled as she stood. "Oh, I'm up for it. I'm no pussy, like Tate."

For the second time in the span of a few minutes, Raven laughed a deep, throaty laugh. It was the first time she'd laughed in weeks. Maybe, just maybe, she was beginning to get over losing Riley. "Well, at least he's good for one thing. I'm sending him for coffee." She grinned at Warren. "Can I buy you one, Constable?"

* * *

After hours under a makeshift tent while the forensics techs delicately extricated the body of the young woman from her icy tomb and collected what little evidence hid under the snow and the body, Raven drove to her mom's house. It had been years since she stepped foot inside this house, yet it seemed like yesterday. Nothing had changed. Dried flowers, plants, and herbs hung above windows and down from the ceiling all over the kitchen emitting a spicy floral aroma. The morning light spearing into the room brought back a flood of before school memories of breakfasts gobbled down at the huge kitchen island, now littered with books, pestles, bottles, and pots as if her mom had been cooking. Except it wasn't meals her mom cooked here - it was spells and potions.

What would she do with this place? A lot of work would be involved to get it ready to be sold. And time, which she didn't have to spare.

It's yours now, Rave. Please, don't sell it.

Raven scanned the room, half expecting her mother to appear. Was her mother talking to her from beyond the grave? Creepy. She turned towards the door, intending to leave, but her curiosity got the best of her. What had Ena done with her old room? She padded up the creaking wooden steps that had made it impossible for her to sneak in late back in the day.

Peeking around the doorjamb, she found her room exactly as she left it some twelve years ago, right down to her grade ten math textbook sitting on the desk. The sick roiling in her belly reminded her why she despised this room. Why the hell didn't Ena convert it into something else?

Oh, sweet angel. Because I love you.

"Stop doing that?" Raven spun around, looking up and down, fists clenched at her sides. She stood surrounded in the suffocating silence for a few minutes before she decided her imagination was running wild. People didn't talk to you after they died. She plodded into her childhood room with its bubble gum pink walls and white canopy bed. It was like walking into a deranged fairy tale doused in Pepto-Bismol.

The pink, princessy theme sickened her. Sports were her thing growing up, not tea parties and frilly dresses. She still couldn't stand dresses.

She dragged a finger across her dresser and examined the tip. Not a speck of dust on it. Why would her mother still be cleaning this room?

Because I always hoped you'd come back.

"Stop that." Raven slapped her hands over her ears like a bratty child.

You asked.

"I also asked you to stop it." She must be stark raving mad talking to a ghost. Quick stepping to the stairs, she fled down them. Before she could get out the door, her mother's voice rang in her head once more.

Check Orillia for missing persons.

* * *

Raven sat down at her desk to wait for her computer to boot up. Sleep. That was the problem. She'd put a few hours in at the office and then try to get a couple of hours of shut eye. She was just about to lean back in her chair and pop her boots up on her desk when Constable Warren's head appeared in the doorway.

"Got a minute, DC?" Warren asked.

"Didn't your shift end hours ago?"

"I wouldn't have been able to sleep, so I figured I'd just keep checking missing persons." She held up a file folder. "Seventeen year old Emily Kathryn McMurtrie. Reported missing last November. Out of Orillia."

Told ya.

"Did you hear that?"

"Hear what?" Warren raised her brows, perked up her ears.

Oh, sweet baby Jesus. Her mother was inside her head.

"You okay, DC Bowen? You're looking a little pale."

Raven rubbed her hands over her face then shoved them through her hair. "Yeah." She sounded a little breathless even to herself. "Just need some sleep is all. Let's take a look at that file."

Warren brought the file over to Raven and took the seat next to her desk. Emily McMurtrie was last seen leaving her boyfriend's house at 22:15 on November twenty-first. She was supposedly walking home, which was about two blocks from the boyfriend's, to make her 22:30 curfew.

"Beautiful girl," Raven said. "Even in her driver's license photo."

"She was a model, according to her file. She had a contract with some big agency in Toronto."

And that could make for a multitude of leads to follow up on. Raven closed the file with a long sigh then tapped it on her desk as she got to her feet. She took the file to the Detective Sergeant's office and talked him through what they had so far.

DS Grayson LaCroix's dusty grey eyes stared up at her as he rubbed his thumb and forefinger back and forth along his jaw. He'd taken to shaving his head to hide his receding hairline, but he was one of those men who looked great bald.

"I want you to work with Constable Warren on this," he said.

Raven narrowed her eyes at him. "I work alone."

LaCroix laughed. "Come on, Rave. Warren needs the training and there's a lot you can teach her."

Raven liked Warren, but that didn't mean she wanted to take her under her wing and she thought she had an understanding with LaCroix. "I'm not a freaking training officer, Gray."

"Look at it this way, you'll have someone to do the grunt work."

"No."

LaCroix stared at her for a moment, tenting his fingers and tapping them against his chin. "It wasn't a request. You've got Constable Warren for a week and then we'll reassess." He spun in his chair, giving Raven his back.

Raven stomped back over to her desk and sent Warren home to get some sleep with orders to report back to the detachment at fifteen hundred hours. She filed her report and then headed home to get a few hours of sleep herself.

Letting herself into her little cottage, she headed straight to her bedroom, stripping off two layers of clothes as she went. She didn't even stop to take in the view of Fairy Lake from the living room window. She hadn't heard Ena's voice for a while and she was praying it would stay that way. She didn't want to talk to her in life, what made Ena think she wanted to talk to her now?

Did you really hate me so much?

Raven stopped undressing with one foot pulled out of her long underwear and one foot still stuck in the leg. "Why are you doing this? Can't you just go on to wherever dead people go and leave me alone?"

Do you want rid of me that bad, Rave? Do you still hate me, even after all these years?

"Gah." Raven flopped down onto the edge of her bed and fisted her hands in her short hair. She couldn't tell her mother that she hated her. That wasn't the right word for what she felt.

What is the right word?

"Stop it already. What do I have to do to get you the heck out of my head?" She pulled the long underwear from her leg and threw them across the room. Then she literally heard Ena sigh in frustration. She could picture her frowning down at her with her hands on her hips.

I will leave you alone on one condition.

Raven narrowed her eyes. "What condition?"

Find my killer.

Whoa. Totally didn't see that one coming. "I thought you died of cancer."

I didn't have cancer, Rave. I was poisoned. Please. Look into it, find out who killed me and then I'll leave you be.

This couldn't be happening. She must be having hallucinations from severe sleep deprivation. A few hours in the sack and she would be laughing about this. Except she couldn't sleep. She tossed and turned, her mind reeling, asking herself if cancer could be mistakenly diagnosed. Ena hadn't gone to the doctor until she was hours away from death. Did they just give her that diagnosis to explain her quick decline from healthy to dead? If she was poisoned, wouldn't the coroner have caught it? It wouldn't be difficult to run a toxicology report. Raven flipped from one side to the other then kicked and punched her duvet until it was on the floor. She sat up, huffing.

"You couldn't have waited to lay that on me until after I got some sleep?" she yelled.

The silence mocked her. "Yeah, great. Don't answer." Raven got out of bed, kicked her duvet and stomped into the bathroom to turn on the shower. "The bitch is probably having a nice nap somewhere."

Chapter 2

It was shortly after noon when Raven pulled her Charger into Adara Kirby's driveway. Adara had been Ena's best friend until she took Raven in when she'd left home at the age of fifteen. She'd taken care of Raven and become her closest friend. But, Adara hadn't left Ena's coven and that made her the best place to start asking questions about Ena's passing.

You can't tell Adara what you're doing. You can't tell anyone.

"Are you crazy?" Jesus. I'm talking to a dead person and I'm asking if *she's* crazy?

Everyone in the coven had reason to kill me, including Adara.

"Again, are you crazy? Adara wouldn't hurt a flea. And why would every coven member have reason to kill you?"

There are those who covet the High Priestess title.

"If that's why you think someone killed you, why now? You've been High Priestess for as long as I can remember."

I don't know. Someone sent me a gift a few weeks ago. Along with the flowers there was a beautiful silver chalice. I was using it daily for my rituals at home. I think the poison was in that chalice. If indeed that was the source of the poison, it would have to be someone in the Wiccan community.

Not necessarily. Anyone could look up Wiccan rituals online and learn the tools of the trade so to speak. It wasn't a secret Ena was Wiccan. The entire community knew. Raven had suffered through ridicule and bullying throughout her school years because her mother was a witch. It was one of the reasons Raven had suppressed her own powers. But, would someone outside the coven want her dead for it?

"Was there a card with these flowers? Do you know what florist sent them?"

There was a card with a poem on it and it was signed from an admirer. It will be in the left drawer in my desk. The chalice is on the kitchen island.

Raven put the car in reverse. If she couldn't talk to Adara about what she was doing, there was no sense being there. She drove to her mother's place for the second time that day, entering through the side door into the kitchen again. The sun wasn't streaming through the window at this time of day, shrouding the room in shadows. She scanned the island, but saw no chalice. There was a white marble mortar; a black-handled athame with a wavy silver blade polished to a shine, a triple moon at the hilt and a pentagram at the base of the handle; Ena's massive leather-bound Book of Shadows which contained all of her spells and what-not; jars and bottles containing God only knew. But no chalice.

She crossed the room to Ena's office and opened the drawer on the left side of the desk. Apparently, Ena received flowers on a regular basis because there was a massive stack of those little cards florists provide. Raven rifled through them and although the handwriting differed, each one was signed with a little heart and the letter K. Wow. Had Ena finally settled down with just one lover? Interesting. It took a while to scan through all of the cards, but she didn't find one signed from an admirer. Was Ena yanking her chain?

No, I'm not. Someone must have taken them. And must you call me Ena?

"What would you prefer I called you? Slut?" Raven dropped the cards back into the drawer and slammed it shut.

Not that it's any of your business, but when I take a lover, I'm monogamous as long as that relationship lasts.

Raven snorted. "And that's usually a whole night."

If I was in my physical body right now, I'd slap you for that.

"Well that hasn't changed in twelve years then. Blame Raven and defend your flavour of the night."

Is that why you hated me so much? You were jealous of my lovers?

Heat surged up Raven's throat and flamed over her cheeks. Her hands were tight fists desperate for a target. "Jealous? Are you freaking kidding me? I was a kid and I was all alone. I had no one in my corner. It was always you and your lover du jour against me. You were blind to me. You didn't see me. All you cared about was getting laid." Raven stormed across the room and out the door, slamming it shut as hard as she could and hoping, praying her mother didn't follow.

She stomped past her car then picked up her pace to a quick jog. She needed to expel some of the rage coursing through her veins and tamp down the memories their discussion had conjured. She was so charged up she felt like she could flick her fingers and electric blue sparks would shoot out of them. If Ena got in her head right now, she'd know exactly why Raven ran away from home and never went back. There was no point in Ena knowing the truth. She was dead. Gone. She'd been dead to Raven for twelve years.

She'd had a rip roaring fight with Ena on that night twelve years ago when she fled the house and sat in the park, hoping her mother would come to her and apologize for not seeing what was going on under her own roof. Stupid. Her mother never stopped thinking about herself long enough to concern herself with what was going on with her daughter. Ena never came for her. If it hadn't been for Adara, she would have been Solstice's only street person. Yay.

When Raven returned to Ena's house, she circled it,

checking for signs of a break and enter and found none. If someone stole Ena's card and chalice, they had a key or they were very good at picking locks.

* * *

Her next stop was the local hospital where Ena had been taken hours before her death. Raven walked through the sliding glass doors and caught sight of flaming red hair in the triage office to her right. Her heart fluttered and she skidded to a halt. This whole thing with her mother had her so distracted that she hadn't even given a thought to the fact that Riley might be working. She was just about to spin around, resigned to coming back the next day, when Riley's voice drifted across the hall.

"Rave? Everything okay?"

Riley's hair was tamed into a tight twist and her pale green eyes hid behind the black-framed glasses resting on her lightly freckled nose.

"Yeah. I'm not, um … here for me. I'd like to speak to the doctor who saw my mother when she came in last week."

"Oh." Riley's face flushed. "I'm sorry about your mom, Rave. I know you weren't close, but still."

"Yeah, thanks." It still felt awkward responding to people saying sorry about her mom, even coming from Riley. She'd been closer to Riley than anyone else in her entire life until Raven screwed up. She didn't blame Riley for ending their relationship, but she wished there was something she could do to fix it, like turning back time and making smarter choices.

Riley held up her finger and disappeared around a corner. Raven stuck her hands in the pockets of her jeans and leaned against the door jamb while she waited. Now that the adrenaline had worn off from her rant at her mother and her run, her eye lids felt weighted. She yawned just as Riley stepped back in.

"Dr. Tang. He's scheduled to work in the ER again tomorrow afternoon, or you can catch him at his office. I wrote the number down for you." Riley handed Raven a yellow post-it note.

"Thanks," Raven said as she accepted the note, pushed herself off the door jamb and started towards the door.

"Hey, Rave?"

Raven turned back, her heart leaping in her chest, hoping Riley was going to say she'd made a mistake, that she wanted Raven back.

"Get some sleep. You look like shit."

A soft smile appeared on Riley's face and Raven's heart sank. It was like losing her all over again. She tried to smile, but couldn't quite pull it off. "I'll get right on that." Riley's smile had the power to weaken her knees, so she was proud of herself when she managed to make her exit without falling on her face.

* * *

"You drive." Raven tossed the keys to Warren.

"Sweet. Nice ride."

Raven settled into the passenger seat. She didn't trust herself to drive all the way down to Orillia when she was this sleep deprived. While Warren adjusted the driver's seat, Raven tilted her seat back as far as it would go with the partition behind her.

"Didn't get much sleep, eh?"

Raven opened one eye to look over at Warren. She was driving with a smile on her cute, heart-shaped face. "You got a first name, Warren?" It just sounded too weird calling the woman Warren.

"You know I do. You would have checked my file by now."

At least she could take some pride in pegging this kid as smart. "Yeah, I read your file, but it didn't tell me how to pronounce your first name. Michaluckachucka. Or something."

Warren laughed as she pulled onto Highway 11 to begin their journey south. "It's McHaela, but my friends call me Mick."

"How much sleep did you get, Mick?"

"Oh, about four hours, I guess."

"That's about four more than I got, so I figure shutting my eyes for the next hour wouldn't hurt."

"Absolutely. I'll wake you up when we get to Orillia."

The next thing Raven knew, Mick was yelling, "DC Bowen?"

It jolted Raven awake. The view through the windshield was the OPP Headquarters building. "Crap." Raven swiped her sleeve over her chin. God, had she been so out of it she was drooling?

"Sorry, DC. I tried to rouse you a few times, but you wouldn't wake up. I got you a coffee though." Mick picked up a large coffee from the console and handed it over to Raven.

Raven rubbed the sleep out of her eyes and ogled the cup. She took it and smiled at its warmth in her hands then closed her eyes as the aroma drifted up to her. "Thanks."

"No problem."

"Mind if we just sit here for a few minutes while I drink this and wake up a bit?"

"Not at all." Mick took a slow sip of her own coffee and turned to Raven. "Let's play a little game in the interest of getting to know each other. Three questions. They can be anything, but you have to answer honestly. You can go first."

"You can't be serious," Raven said with a raised brow. Damned if she was going to play some stupid game. She had no interest in getting to know McHaela Warren.

"I've been at the Solstice Detachment for over a year and I've never had a conversation with you before last night. I thought it would be nice to get to know each other since we'll be working together."

Raven sat up straighter in her seat. "Let's get something clear. I work alone. The only reason you're here is because LaCroix didn't give me a choice."

"Wow, that was ... cruel. I guess it's true what they say about you."

Raven didn't have to ask what Mick was referring to. She knew people thought she was a loner with a bitchy attitude and that was fine with her. It kept people from bothering her. But, she felt bad about hurting Mick's feelings. "One question. That's all you get."

"Why aren't you involved in the coven?"

Whoa. Raven totally wasn't expecting that one, nor was she sure how to answer it. "It's just not my thing." Mick raised her eyebrows and stared at Raven, waiting, but there was no way Raven was going to elaborate. She'd answered the stupid question, hadn't she? "How did you know I used to be a member of the coven?"

Mick grinned. "Is that your question?"

Raven rolled her eyes.

"I should probably tell you that I knew your mother," Mick said. "My mother is Wiccan and she was a single mom, so she took me to a lot of the gatherings and ceremonies."

"Apparently we didn't need three questions to get to know each other better. At least, you didn't." She wondered what else Mick Warren knew about her. "Are you Wiccan?"

"No, I'm not Wiccan. I may go that route at some point, but I'm focusing on my career. It's what is important to me."

Now Raven was desperate to ask why policing was so important to Mick. What catastrophic event pushed her toward seeking justice?

"You have a reputation for being the best at what you do, DC. I was hoping that you would take me under your wing, but … I guess that's not going to happen."

She supposed it was a compliment that Mick thought she was good at her job, but she wasn't interested in training anyone. Ever. "Look, Mick, I don't want to offend you, but I don't have a partner for a reason. I prefer to work alone. That's just the way it is." She turned to stare out the passenger window so she wouldn't have to see the hurt on Mick's face. For some reason, this kid wanted to work with her specifically. Raven didn't understand it. Maybe she had an ulterior motive, something to do with the coven perhaps.

* * *

They crossed the lobby of the OPP Headquarters building and Raven introduced herself to the desk Sergeant. "We're here to see DC Sawicki."

"Right here."

Raven turned and watched a very good looking man she judged to be in his early thirties walking across the lobby towards them. His dark blonde hair shone under the florescent lights. A brown leather jacket accentuated his wide shoulders and slim hips. Smiling, he extended his hand and Raven clasped onto it, studying his hazel eyes all but twinkling at her.

"I'm Detective Constable Bowen. This is my partner, Constable Warren. Thanks for meeting with us."

When he didn't let go, Raven pulled her hand out of Sawicki's and he offered it to Mick, but kept his eyes on Raven's.

"I was just going to head over to see Dr. Maxwell. He's our lead pathologist," Sawicki said.

"Why don't we follow you? What are you driving?"

"Black Chevy Suburban. You can't miss it," he said and flashed a cocky grin.

Raven and Mick laughed. Every other OPP unmarked vehicle was a black Chevy Suburban.

"Why don't I meet you out front?" he asked.

Raven and Mick walked back to Raven's car and Mick handed her the keys.

"Keep them," Raven said with a wave of her hand. "We're just going down the street."

"Those were some serious sparks between the two of you," Mick said as she settled into the driver's seat. "I thought you were gay."

"What sparks? And why are we talking about my sexuality?" If there were any sparks, they were totally one-sided. Raven wasn't attracted to men. She liked women. One in particular.

Except she'd slept with Jaxon. Jaxon and Raven had been friends since they were toddlers and Jax's mother was a member of the coven. She knew Jaxon loved her, but she'd never felt that way about him and she'd been honest with him about it. Why she'd slept with him that night was beyond her. She'd rolled it around in her head countless times and still couldn't get a handle on it.

"Because there was definitely something between you two in there. He couldn't peel his eyes off you," Mick said with her eyebrows bouncing up and down.

"Exactly. *He* couldn't keep his eyes off me. It wasn't reciprocated." Sawicki pulled up by the front doors and flashed his lights and Raven pointed out the windshield. "Drive."

"He's hot though, right?"

"Seriously?" Raven rolled her eyes. "If you think he's so hot why don't you make a play for him?"

"He only saw you, DC."

"If you're going to talk about my sex life, you can at least call me Raven."

"Okay, Raven." Warren pulled into the parking lot of the forensics building and parked next to DC Sawicki. He stepped out of the Suburban and leaned back into the car for something. "See? Totally hot. Look at that ass."

Raven turned to look out her window and said ass was right in her face. She turned her head back and glared at Mick. "Oh. My. God. Can you shut up about Sawicki already?" So what if the guy had a supreme butt? He was probably all muscle – ripped abs, tight ass, strong back. Jesus. Now she was picturing him naked. "I'm not interested in Sawicki."

Damn Ena and the genes she inherited from her. Ena used to tell her the Bowen women were sexual beings, as if that were all the explanation she needed to explain her raging hormones in her teenage years. Hell, even at twenty-seven she had raging hormones. But, they had never extended to men until she slept with Jax a month ago, and ruined everything good in her life.

It wasn't like she just had a quickie with him, either. They'd gone at it for hours before falling asleep, exhausted. Then Raven woke before dawn and rode him like a cowboy in a rodeo. She wasn't a woman with inhibitions, but just thinking about that night made her feel ill. What the hell had gotten into her?

Was she getting worse? She was always more aroused on the full moon, as it was on the night she slept with Jax. Was her sex drive so out of control she would sleep with anyone? Was she destined to become a slut like her mother? "Can we start thinking about the reason we're here?"

Mick's smile vanished. She pulled the keys out of the ignition and opened her door. "Yeah, sorry."

"Have you ever been to an autopsy before?" Raven asked before Mick got out of the car. She'd never been more relieved to be going into a morgue in her life. She could think about DBs instead of sex.

Mick looked over her shoulder at Raven, her mouth agape.

"We're going to see Emily's autopsy?"

"It's possible. I just want to make sure you're prepared."

"Awesome. Let's go."

Raven stared dumbfounded as Mick pretty much bounced to the front of the car. She shook her head then joined Mick and Sawicki on the walk across the parking lot, trailing behind a bit so she didn't have to talk to Sawicki. He led them down to the morgue which was decorated in white ceramic tiles and stainless steel. Formaldehyde was the prevalent scent, although it did little to mask the unmistakable odour of death.

Emily McMurtrie lay on a stainless steel table, a crisp white sheet folded over at the base of her neck, her red hair a tangled mess.

Dr. Maxwell was well into his sixties. He walked into the suite wearing light green scrubs, a white lab coat, and navy blue crocks. Smiling, he pushed his wire framed glasses up his nose while Sawicki made the introductions. Then Maxwell picked up a clipboard from a stainless steel counter and began his report.

"We're holding off on the autopsy until tomorrow morning to give Ms. McMurtrie's body time to thaw out, but we've done some preliminary tests. I can tell you she was raped prior to death. There is vaginal and anal tearing and bruising. We've sent swabs to the lab.

"Cause of death appears to be drowning, but we will have to confirm that with the autopsy. Time of death, however, will be next to impossible to determine. The outside temperatures over the past several months have preserved the body and, hopefully, evidence. X-rays show a fractured right forearm which appears to be a defensive wound, a blunt force trauma. There's not much more I can tell you at this point."

"Is it safe to inform Emily's parents of the cause of death?" Sawicki asked. He stood next to the body, arms crossed over his chest and feet shoulder width apart, like a sentry guarding his princess.

"Yes, of course. If they would like more information, I would be happy to speak with them after the autopsy."

"Thanks, Doc."

Raven stepped forward and offered Maxwell her hand. "Thank you, Dr. Maxwell."

"You're welcome."

They walked out to the sterile hallway, making their way to the exit.

"So, did you ladies want to join me on my visit to the McMurtries? They don't know Emily has been found yet," Sawicki said.

"Yeah," Raven answered. "That's one of the reasons we made the trip down."

"Great. They don't live too far from here. You can just follow me again."

In the car, Mick was unusually quiet and she kept tapping her fingers on the steering wheel. Raven figured she'd never done a death notification and, instead of questioning her lack of conversation, she used the time to prepare herself mentally for what they were about to do. This was the worst part of the job, but she figured in the McMurties' case they would be relieved to have their daughter back. They probably knew a long time ago they'd never see her alive again.

They pulled up in front of an old brick home with a huge wrap-around porch. It was just past dusk and the warm glow of lights from the main floor windows made the home warm and inviting. Raven got out of the car and stood studying the house. It was deceiving. There was no hint of the turmoil this family suffered through every day for the past five months. Two cars sat in the driveway – a navy Dodge van and a silver Hyundai sedan.

Raven started up the path as Mick and Sawicki hung back,

letting her take the lead. She rapped her knuckles against the door, three solid knocks.

"Mom. Door," a young boy's voice rang out from inside.

Raven's stomach roiled as she listened to heels on hardwood approaching. The door swung open and Caroline McMurtrie shouted over her shoulder for someone to turn the TV down then looked up at Raven with a smile and kind green eyes, red curls hanging loose around her shoulders.

"Mrs. McMurtrie? I'm Detective Constable Bowen with the Ontario Provincial Police."

The smile dropped away, the eyes became weary. Caroline McMurtrie's entire body seemed to sag. "You've found her. You've found our Emmy."

"Yes, ma'am. May we come in?"

Caroline's knees buckled and Raven reacted quickly. She shot her arms under Caroline's and supported her weight. Sawicki stepped up just as Caroline got her feet under her again. "I'm okay. I'm alright. Steven. Please, someone get my husband. He's in the kitchen."

Raven kept an arm around Caroline's waist and escorted her to the sofa in the front room, easing her down then sitting beside her. Sawicki stayed by the door while Mick went to find the husband.

Steven McMurtrie was a good foot taller than his wife and lean like a runner. His dark hair was slicked back and greying at the temples. He wore black dress pants and his crisp white shirt was open at the collar, the sleeves rolled up to mid forearm. "Is this about Emmy?" He paced back and forth, twisting the tea towel in his hands.

There was never an easy way to do this. Quick was best, so Raven jumped right in. "I'm sorry to inform you that your daughter, Emily, was found dead last night in Solstice."

"Solstice?" Steven asked. "That's up near Hunstville, isn't it? What was Emmy doing up there?"

Raven didn't answer his question. How do you tell a parent it was the dump site? "Late last night snowmobilers found her body near a trail. We believe she'd been there since her disappearance last fall."

Caroline sobbed and Steven sat next to her, wrapping her in his arms.

"Did she … did she suffer?" Caroline asked.

Raven looked her in the eye, hating this question. All mothers wanted to know their children hadn't suffered when they passed. "I want to tell you that she didn't, but it's better if you know the truth. Emily was raped before she died."

Caroline howled, dropping her head into her husband's shoulder. His free hand cupped the back of her head.

"It appears that her cause of death was drowning," Raven continued. "The coroner will confirm that when he does the autopsy."

Back outside, Raven turned and looked up at the house again. It still looked warm and inviting. "I'd like to go and talk to Emily's boyfriend."

"I know Emily was found in Solstice, but the case is still ours, Bowen."

Raven glared at Sawicki. "You used us to do your dirty work and now you want us off the case?"

"I invited you along as a courtesy." His arms crossed over his chest again.

Grabbing the keys from Mick's hand, Raven walked to her vehicle, got in and shut the door.

When Mick settled into the passenger seat, she said, "He can't do that, can he?"

"We'll see what DS LaCroix says in the morning." She wanted to stomp on the gas and squeal down the street, but managed to refrain. She wasn't about to give Sawicki the satisfaction of seeing how much he'd pissed her off.

Chapter 3

A pizza in one hand and a six pack of Coors Lite in the other, Raven took the stairs to the third floor of the three story yellow brick apartment building. She used her boot to tap on the door of apartment 306. It had been a crap day and she didn't want to be alone for once in her life. She wanted to be with someone who understood without judging or thinking she was crazy.

Riley opened the door a couple of inches, leaving the security chain in place. "What do you want, Rave?"

"I just want to hang out. Have some pizza and a beer with me then I'll leave."

Riley shook her head as her pale green eyes glistened. "I can't do this anymore."

"Then take me back, Ri."

"Rave."

Knowing that she was responsible for the pain so evident in Riley's eyes seared Raven right down to her soul. "I made a terrible mistake, but that mistake taught me that I don't want anyone but you, Ri."

"How many people have you slept with in the past month, Raven?"

"None." Raven felt like she'd just been slapped. Riley really had no trust left in her and she couldn't blame her. She leaned in closer to the gap in the door, her lips inches away from Riley's, hoping Riley would see the truth in her eyes. "I don't want anyone else, Ri. I only want you."

Riley shook her head again, her soft red curls bouncing over her shoulders. "There's more to it than you sleeping with Jaxon. I can't do this anymore, Rave."

"Can't do what? Talk? I thought that's what you wanted."

"But, you don't talk. You tell me you slept with Jax, but you won't tell me why or how you're feeling. You're so closed off I'm not sure I know you at all."

Raven leaned her head against the doorframe and whispered, "You know me better than anyone."

"We were together nearly four years and you won't even think about moving in together. We can't build a relationship like this. *I* can't be in a relationship like this."

"Riley, I love you. I need you."

"Do you? Then why did you sleep with Jax, Rave? Talk to me?"

How could she explain something she didn't understand herself? She dropped her eyes, trying to think of something to say, but she had no explanation for her behaviour.

The door closed in her face. Gently. Raven stood there staring at the closed door and huffed. "I just wanted some company." She thought about sitting down on the floor right there in the hall and eating her pizza. How sad would that be?

She got back in her car and drove a few blocks to Front Street, to a small bungalow with white clapboard siding and green shutters. She pulled into the driveway behind Jaxon's black Dodge Ram. The living room lights glowed around the edges of the drapes as she walked up the path. Balancing the pizza box and beer in one hand, she knocked on the door.

Jaxon Lang opened the door wearing faded blue jeans and a white t-shirt stretched tight across his wide chest and bulging biceps. Jaxon had nordic blonde hair, straight as a ruler, and brilliant blue eyes.

"Hey, Rave."

"Hey yourself. Hungry?" She raised the pizza box. "I've got beer."

Jaxon crossed his arms over his chest and asked, "What's on it?"

"Pepperoni and cheese."

"That's it?"

With a laugh, Raven asked, "Do you want some or not?"

He exhaled an exaggerated breath. "You're doing my head in, Rave. You know I want more. I've always wanted more with you."

Raven stared into Jax's sad blue eyes. "Please don't tell me I've screwed up our friendship, Jax. I can't lose you, too. I don't think I'd ever forgive myself."

"I don't regret making love with you, Rave. For a few glorious hours I had everything I've ever wanted. But, you regretted what happened between us from the moment you left my bed and, in that moment, I lost everything."

Jax loved her, but she just didn't have the same feelings for him. Her heart belonged to Riley. When he just stood there looking lost, she decided to save what little dignity she had left. She started back to her car. He called after her, but she didn't turn to him. She had ruined her relationship with Riley *and* her friendship with Jax. Now she had no one. She lost everything that mattered, too. All for a few hours of passion.

She walked into her little cottage on Fairy Lake, put the beer in the fridge, and left the pizza on the counter. She picked up the clothes she'd stripped out of that morning and put the duvet back on the bed. Then she just plopped down on the edge of the bed and dropped her face into her hands.

You can talk to me, Rave.

Her head shot back up. "I thought you were gone." Silence.

"You've got a hell of a lot of nerve saying that to me now. Fifteen years ago I needed to be able to talk to you."

Fifteen? Raven, you were only twelve years old then.

At twelve years old her jet black hair hung down past her waist and she'd taken scissors and chopped it all off. Ena barely noticed.

I noticed, sweetie. I just thought making a big deal out of it would have been traumatic for you. It broke my heart to see you cut off all of that gorgeous hair.

"Get. Out. Of. My. Head." Her hands sank into her still short hair and fisted. She was too beaten down to mask what was hidden in her mind and she couldn't risk Ena discovering what was buried there - like the reason she'd chopped off her hair.

I'm sorry. Figure out who killed me and I'll be gone from your life, and your head, forever.

"Did it ever occur to you that being in my head is a massive invasion of my privacy?" It wouldn't have, because Ena only ever considered her own needs and wants.

There was no response and Raven considered it was when she hurt Ena's feelings that she left her alone. She'd called her mother a slut, but Raven was the one who cheated on her girlfriend. Could she be any more of a hypocrite?

She spent the night tossing and turning, thinking about the way she treated Ena and trying not to think about being rejected by both Riley and Jaxon in one night. Things would go smoother if she was able to deal with her mother without all of her resentments getting in the way, but she just didn't seem to be able to help herself. As soon as she heard Ena's voice, her back went up.

* * *

At eight o'clock in the morning, Raven was in Detective Sergeant LaCroix's office reporting the details of their trip to Orillia and requesting to stay on the case. He put in a call to

Sawicki's Sergeant and they agreed that Raven and Sawicki would both work the case in the interests of solving Emily McMurtrie's murder quickly.

Raven and Mick filed their reports from the previous day and headed out to Raven's car. The sun was shining and the temperature approached the mid-teens. Raven tilted her face up to the sun for a moment, enjoying it's warmth. The winters were long and cold here. It really made you appreciate spring and summer. She slipped on her aviator sunglasses and headed for the driver's door, clicking the door remote. "I've got a stop to make before we head down to Orillia."

"Sure you don't want me to drive? No offence, but you look like you still haven't slept."

"Is that a polite way of saying I look like shit?" Raven slid into the driver's seat. Despite the restless night, she didn't feel too bad. Still, the first place she was going was the Solstice Café for her second large coffee of the day.

"Well, you do." Warren adjusted her duty belt before doing up her seat belt. She wore a long sleeve uniform shirt, but no jacket, her aviator sunglasses almost identical to Raven's.

"Thanks."

"Don't take it as an insult. If I looked like you do right now on my good days, I'd be ecstatic."

Raven grinned. "Are you coming on to me, Constable?" She glanced over at Mick and her face was turning the colour of Santa's suit. She was sure Mick was straight, but maybe she had a bit of a girl crush going on.

"Ha, ha." Mick shifted in her seat. "Oh, coffee shop. Yay."

With their caffeine fix satisfied, Raven pulled up to the entrance of the Solstice Medical Centre. She put the car in park and handed the keys to Mick. "I shouldn't be too long."

"Oh, okay." Mick studied her as if she was looking for something. "Does this have to do with why you're not sleeping? I mean, are you okay?"

Raven laughed. "I'm not seeing a doctor. I just need to talk to someone." Mick's eyes widened. "Not about me," Raven added. "There's nothing wrong with me."

Mick nodded and Raven got out of the car rolling her eyes. She found Dr. Tang's office on the third floor. The grey-haired receptionist sat behind a grey counter and stared up at Raven through thick white-framed glasses. Raven held up her badge and ID. "I'm Detective Constable Bowen. I need to speak with Dr. Tang for a few minutes."

"He's booked up today. If you want to have a seat, I'll try to fit you in."

Raven glanced over her shoulder at the empty waiting room. "Is he in the office? I just have a few questions about my mother, Ena Bowen. She passed away just over a week ago and Dr. Tang saw her when she was brought into emergency at the hospital."

The big blue eyes behind the glasses softened. "I knew your mother, dear. I was so sorry to hear she passed. She was too young."

"Yeah."

"Let me see if Dr. Tang has a few minutes," she said and disappeared behind a wall.

While she waited, Raven checked her iPhone for messages. Nothing from Riley or Jaxon, but that wasn't a surprise, just wishful thinking. There was a missed phone call from Adara and that was it. She stuck her phone back in her pocket and leaned her elbows on the grey counter. The receptionist stuck her head around the wall and waved Raven back. She followed the woman into Dr. Tang's office. The young, Asian doctor sat behind a big mahogany desk with his phone at his ear.

Raven took a seat facing the doctor and the view from the window at his back overlooking the downtown core of

Solstice.

"And you're sure no tests were ordered? None?" Dr. Tang's brow creased. He glanced at Raven then averted his gaze. "Could you fax the file over to me, please? Thank you." He hung up the phone with a frown.

"Dr. Tang? I'm Detective Constable Bowen. I'd like to ask you a few questions about my mother's passing. You saw her in emergency the day she died."

"Yes, I've just been on the phone with the ER. There seems to be some sort of error here. The diagnosis on your mother was stomach cancer. She became ill very recently and went downhill fast."

Raven leaned forward. "What's the error?"

"I don't know where that diagnosis came from. There's no mention of your mother seeking medical attention prior to coming into the hospital. I would have run tests, but there were no tests ordered. I don't understand." Tang scratched his head, staring off into space.

"Do you remember treating her?"

"Yes. We made her as comfortable as possible. We treated her as if she was in the final stages of stomach cancer, but I wouldn't have done that without running tests to confirm the diagnosis."

"Had you seen Ena as a patient before she came into the ER?"

"No."

"You asked the hospital to fax you something. What was that?"

Dr. Tang stood, rubbed his hand over the back of his neck with his eyes focused on the carpet. "I think I should contact my lawyer."

Because Tang was standing, Raven rose to her feet. He was a good head shorter than her. "I'm not looking to file a malpractice suit or press criminal charges here, Dr. Tang.

What I want to do is confirm if my mother had cancer, or if it's possible she was poisoned. Was there an autopsy or a toxicology report?"

Tang's eyes flicked up to Raven's and back down again. "I really think this needs to go through my lawyer. I don't understand how this could have happened." He dropped into his chair as if his legs couldn't hold him up any longer.

"You're not in any trouble, Dr. Tang. I think there may have been foul play involved. I think someone may have murdered my mother."

Tell him it wasn't his fault, Rave. I think someone hexed him.

Oh, Jesus. Great. Now we've got hocus pocus involved. "Dr. Tang? Would I be able to have a copy of Ena's file?"

"I'm sorry. You'll need a court order." Tang answered, dazed, as if he was somewhere else.

"Do you really want to play it that way?"

His eyes were slow to move up to Raven's and then he nodded slowly. Raven pursed her lips, her brow pinched. There was nothing she could do except to try to get that court order and really, she had nothing to support it. She made her way back down to the car, sat down in the driver's seat and then just stared out the window. She didn't have proof. Not yet. But, she knew. Ena was poisoned.

"Is everything okay?" Mick asked.

Raven shook her head and started the car. "No. It's really not." Her eyes burned and she told herself it was the lack of sleep. Slipping her sunglasses on, she said, "We've got to go back to the detachment. I need to try to get a warrant."

"For?"

It was time to bring Mick into this. She would find out soon anyway. "For Ena's medical records. That will hopefully be enough to get her body exhumed and autopsied. She didn't have cancer."

Mick's mouth dropped open. "Oh, um … I'm not sure I

follow."

Be careful, Rave. McHaela's mother is a member of the coven.

Raven ignored Ena's warning. As hard as it was for her, she had to trust someone.

"I think she was poisoned. They didn't run any tests to confirm that she had cancer. The doctor doesn't even know where that diagnosis came from. They just made her as comfortable as possible and let her die. The doctor's in shock, scared shitless, and crying for his lawyer."

As she drove, Raven tried to figure out how she was going to spin this. She couldn't say her mother told her posthumously about the chalice from an admirer that had gone missing and that it somehow was the source of the poison that killed her. When she got to the detachment, she beelined to LaCroix's office with Mick quick stepping to keep up with her long strides.

"What about Emily McMurtrie? Are we still going to talk to her boyfriend?" Mick asked.

"Let's get the ball rolling on the warrant and we'll head down to Orillia."

LaCroix wasn't in his office. Raven scanned the room. There were only a handful of desks in the bullpen area of their small detachment. Down the hall was a squad room and a bank of computers the patrol officers used for investigating and filing reports. They had a secure evidence room, a small booking office, and two cells for holding prisoners for transport or until they could be bailed out or released on their own recognizance.

Instead of hunting LaCroix down, Raven cornered his admin, Kelsey Resiewski.

"Kels? Where is he?"

Kelsey flicked her long brown hair over her shoulder and snapped her gum. "He had to go out. He should be back within half an hour." She barely looked up, her fingers flying over her keyboard at an impressive speed. Every officer in the detachment tried to get Kelsey to type their reports for them at one point or another and no one had succeeded.

Raven crossed to her own desk, her mind on the report she was about to type. Everything she had was hearsay and, therefore, not worth a crap. She may be able to wring circumstantial out of the flowers and the chalice, but she had no proof of their existence. She linked her fingers together, stretched her arms out in front of her to crack her knuckles then settled them over her keyboard. She wasn't as fast as Kelsey, but she had skills. She wrote up the report as if Ena had told her of her suspicions before she died. When she finished, she typed up a request for a warrant to obtain the medical records from the hospital and Ena's family doctor.

Perfect timing. Just as she printed out the documents, LaCroix came in.

"DS?" Raven jumped out of her seat and crossed the bullpen, documents in hand, before he made it to his office door. She placed the documents on his desk and laid out what she had.

"It's weak, but I think you've got reasonable grounds." He signed the request for the warrant. "I'm sorry, Raven. I know you and your mom weren't close, but if you're right about what happened, she deserves justice."

"Damn right, she does." She may have her issues with Ena, but no one deserved to have their life taken from them. And by the sounds of it, Ena had suffered greatly over the last few weeks of her life. Raven took the warrant request and faxed it off to a local judge. All she could do now was wait.

* * *

Orillia Secondary School had seen better days. The red brick building almost looked like a dilapidated old warehouse. The halls smelled like every high school Raven had ever been in with the addition of a musty odour. Raven and Mick waited in the office for eighteen year old Hayden Stoles. When he arrived, Raven's first thought was 'jock'. This guy was all muscle with the sweetest baby face. Dark hair and bedroom blue eyes sealed her opinion of him as a hot commodity around Orillia High School. Raven was pretty sure his tooth sparkled when she introduced herself and Mick. She should have kept her sunglasses on.

"You've heard that we found Emily?" Raven asked, studying his reaction.

His face sagged and he took a step back. "What do you mean you found her?"

Raven put a hand on his shoulder and guided him to a bench to sit him down. "We found her body, Hayden."

The colour drained from Hayden's face and then it flushed red. "So, she's … she's gone? Dead?" He stared down at the floor, rubbing his palms up and down his jeans.

"That's right." Why the hell hadn't Sawicki been to see Hayden to tell him the news and question him again? "Do you think you can tell me about the night she went missing?"

"I've already told the police everything I knew. She had a ten thirty curfew on school nights, so she left my house at ten fifteen. That's the last time I saw her."

"You don't remember any strange cars parked on your street or anyone paying attention to Emily? Anything out of the ordinary?"

"No. She was supposed to text me when she got home, but she never did. I never heard from her again." His blue eyes filled and slow tears slid down his face. "How did it happen? Was she … hurt? Did someone hurt Em, r-rape her?"

Quick and honest, Raven thought. "Yes, Hayden." Hayden wailed like a wounded animal and Raven wrapped an arm around his shoulders.

When he'd recovered enough to be coherent, he said, "We were waiting until we were both eighteen before we went all the way. Em was a virgin and someone … oh, God." Hayden leaned into Raven's shoulder and wept.

"Is there someone I can call for you, Hayden? I think you need to go home and you shouldn't be alone right now."

"My mom." He hiccuped as he spoke. "She's at home."

Leaving him with Mick, Raven asked the secretary to call Hayden's mother then she sat next to him again. "Who were Emily's friends, Hayden? Who did she hang out with?"

"Her girl friends, you mean? Em and I hung out a lot, just the two of us. But, her best friend is Sarah Jensen. They hung out a lot at school."

"Is there anyone else she was close to?"

"Her mom. I know that sounds stupid. Of course she's close to her mom, but they weren't just mother and daughter, they were friends. They enjoyed each other's company."

Must be nice, Raven thought.

She took Mrs. Rebecca Stoles aside when she arrived to pick up her son and explained the situation. It was easy to see where Hayden got his looks. His mother shared the same dark hair and hypnotic blue eyes. She was tall, slender, and walked like a runway model in her stilettos. Why on earth would she be dressed to the nines at one in the afternoon if she was just hanging out at home? Sweats and fuzzy slippers, she could understand, but a slim, fitted skirt and heels seemed like torture to Raven.

Rebecca stated that Hayden and Emily had been high school sweethearts and Hayden had been devastated when she went missing.

"Do you remember the night she disappeared? Were you home that night?"

"Yes. Emily came for dinner and then Hayden and Em worked on their homework, watched some TV. Hayden said goodbye to Em on the front porch and then he went up to his room."

"How long were they out on the porch for?"

Rebecca's hand cupped her forehead. "Oh, I don't remember. Ten, fifteen minutes maybe."

"Hayden said he was waiting for Emily to text him that she got home safe. Did he say anything to you that night about her not texting him?"

"Emily's mother called at about twenty to eleven and asked if she left yet. Hayden said he'd been trying to text and phone her, but wasn't getting any response. We all went out looking for her. It was horrible not knowing where she went or what happened to her. It was just horrible." She fished through her oversized purse, pulled out a tissue, and dabbed under her well made up eyes.

Raven gave Rebecca her card and asked if she or Hayden thought of anything that might help them find who hurt Emily to please call.

"God, that sucked," Mick said. "Do you think he had anything to do with Emily's disappearance?"

"I'm not ruling him out."

"Really? You think he might have done it?

"It doesn't look like he left the house after he saw her off, but I'm not ruling him out yet." Raven returned to the counter and asked the secretary to have Sarah Jensen sent to the office to meet with them.

The mousey haired secretary frowned up at Raven with pursed lips. Even the colour of her eyes seemed to lack any life - a dull brown with no spark. "How many of our students do you plan on upsetting today, officer?"

Raven offered the secretary her best smile. "Detective Constable. And, as many as it takes."

The secretary huffed, returned to her desk, and picked up the phone. When Sarah hadn't arrived in the office twenty minutes later, Raven was on her way back to the counter to hassle the secretary. The door burst open and a flush faced teen rushed in wearing gym clothes. Or, a team uniform as the sleeveless top had a number ten in burgundy against a white background and the shorts matched the colour of the number. Long, lean legs gave way to a glowing white pair of Nikes that squeaked as she came to a halt. "You wanted to see me, Miss Reynolds?"

"Not me," Reynolds replied and nodded towards Raven. "The cops."

"Sarah Jensen?" Raven took a step towards the girl. "I'm Detective Constable Bowen. I'd like to speak with you about your friend, Emily McMurtrie."

Sarah fisted her hands on her hips. "It's about time someone looked into Em's case. She's been missing for months."

Raven took another step closer to Sarah, just in case. "Emily's body has been found."

The flushed face lost its colour in a wave, from top to bottom, like an Etch A Sketch being wiped clean. Her eyes widened, pooled, and then she teetered. Raven placed a hand on her elbow and guided her to the bench where she sat in a fluid motion and leaned right back. "Em's dead?"

"Yes. Can you tell me what you meant by it being about time someone looked into her case?"

Sarah stared straight ahead, the tears in her eyes holding there, ready to spill out at any moment. "After the initial search, there was nothing. It seemed like it to us anyway. No one came to ask us questions and we thought they would have, you know?" She turned to look into Raven's eyes.

"Who's 'we', Sarah?"

"Myself, Kristie, and Aurora. We were the fab four, but without Em it's just not the same." She closed her eyes and a tear ran slowly down her cheek. "It will never be the same."

"If the police had come to question you, what would you have told them?"

"Everything Hayden hadn't." She laughed, sort of a half laugh and half huff. "Em was trying to break off their relationship, but he wouldn't have it. He wouldn't accept it. Em went to his house to talk to him about it and no one has seen her since. Er, at least, you know. Until you found her, I guess."

"Do you think Hayden killed Em?"

Sarah placed her palm over her stomach. "I don't know. Dude was so demanding and controlling. He hated Em hanging out with us, but it got worse last September when we came back to school. He literally forbid her from hanging out with anyone except him. Em felt crowded, like he was mauling her all the time. He didn't give her any space."

"When was the last time you saw her?"

"That afternoon. She was on her way to Hayden's to talk to him and we kind of gave her a pep talk. Like, 'You don't have to put up with his crap. You go in there and tell him it's over.' Did we make a mistake?" She took Raven's hand and squeezed it, screwing her face up as if she was in pain. "Did we cause her death?"

"No, you didn't. Don't you feel guilty for empowering your friend."

Sarah nodded, her straight blonde hair bouncing down her back, but she still looked like she was in pain. She refused an offer to go home for the rest of the day and went back to her gym class. Raven got Kristie's and Aurora's last names from Sarah and had them sent down to the office one at a time. Their stories corroborated Sarah's.

"Now I see why you didn't rule Hayden out, but how do you figure out who's telling the truth and who's lying?" Mick asked. "They all came across as genuine to me."

"Because they were genuine. They all believe their stories are the truth. What we need to do is hash out the truth from everyone's different perspective. But, to do that, we need to question as many people as we can who knew Emily. Who would you talk to next?"

Mick answered quickly and confidently. "Her mother."

"Yep." Raven smiled and drew the car keys out of her pocket. "I wonder if Caroline McMurtrie wears six inch heels in the middle of the day."

"They weren't six inches," Mick said. "Three, maybe."

"Still, you can't tell me they're comfortable. Why do that to yourself?"

"They're sexy."

Raven cocked her head and regarded sweet faced, curvy Mick Warren, reams of curly blonde hair forced into a neat twist, in her starched uniform and tried to picture her in heels. She just couldn't get there. She was getting images of Mick wearing black paten leather stilettos with a pretty suede bow above the toe in her police uniform and it looked utterly ridiculous.

Mick pursed her lips and narrowed her eyes at Raven. "Maybe, if we were all built tall and slender like you, we wouldn't feel the need to wear shoes like that."

"I'm calling bullshit on that because Rebecca Stoles is about five foot eight without her spikes. It's usually the tall, slender types who you see wearing killer shoes like that." Ha, score a point for Raven. Mick's big brown eyes were like a puppy's.

Raven slipped her sunglasses on as they walked to the car. It was easy to forget the situation with Ena and the pending warrant for her medical records when she was immersed in another case, but before she got in the car, she checked her cell phone for news on the pwarrant. Finding nothing, she stuck the phone in her pocket and settled into the driver's seat.

"Nothing yet?" Mick asked as she fastened her seatbelt.

Raven added observant to Mick's list of attributes. "Nope."

Without looking at Mick, she fastened her own seatbelt and put the car in gear. She didn't drive to Emily's parents' house. She drove to Hayden's. Even with one parent working outside the home, the Stoles' had the most prominent house on the street. "Three people live in that, don't they?"

Mick nodded as she gaped at the house. "Mr. and Mrs. Stoles and Hayden. He's an only child."

"You could probably go weeks in that house without running into another person."

Mick laughed, but Raven was wondering if it was possible that Rebecca Stoles only assumed Emily was in the house until ten fifteen.

They walked from the Stoles house, following the route Emily normally took home, according to Hayden. There were plenty of street lights along the route, so it should have been well lit at ten thirty at night. She could have been offered a ride by someone she knew. Orillia wasn't a very big town. Emily probably knew a lot of people here.

"Someone must have seen her walking home that night." Raven turned in a slow circle, scanning the homes lining the streets. It was an older neighbourhood with large brick houses and welcoming porches. The further they walked from the Stoles', the less opulent the houses seemed, until they arrived at the McMurtries', which was large enough, brick construction with the wide porch. Bicycles leaned against the side of the house and a basketball net stood sentry in the driveway. It was a family house. Lived in and alive.

Caroline McMurtrie didn't wear heels in the middle of the day. She answered the door wearing jeans, a cream, cable-knit sweater and slippers. Dark circles hung below faded green eyes. Her face appeared gaunt with her red locks pulled back in a ponytail. "Officers?" Caroline stared wearily at Raven. "I'm sorry, I can't even think of your names right now."

"Detective Constable Bowen and Constable Warren,"

Raven said. "I'm sorry to bother you, Mrs. McMurtrie, but we have a few questions we'd like to ask you."

"Why?" Her whole body wilted, slumped. "I told the police everything I knew when Em disappeared."

"I know." Raven removed her sunglasses. "I know this is difficult, but everything you can tell us could help us to find out what happened to Emily that night. There may be some small detail that ends up being the key piece of the puzzle that we're missing."

"I understand," Caroline said and motioned for Raven and Mick to come in. They sat in the front room again. Caroline sunk into a plush chair that made her look small and frail. "I couldn't make myself go to work today. I just couldn't."

"I'd like to tell you it gets easier with time, but I'm not so sure that it does," Raven offered.

"It does," Mick said. "It gets easier, but you never forget."

Raven turned to stare at Mick, wondering who it was she lost. Not the time, she thought, and turned back to Caroline. "Can you tell us a bit about Emily? What was she like?"

Caroline smiled at Raven's question. "She was beautiful and smart. She wanted to be a doctor and was planning on studying at the University of Toronto. She signed with a modelling agency to help pay for her education. She didn't need to. We would have helped her as much as we could, but she wanted to pay for it herself. She didn't want to be a burden on us." Caroline waved her hand in dismissal. "She was never a burden."

"You were close?" Raven asked.

"We were a lot alike. We liked the same things, like shopping for clothes or watching episodes of the Bachelor together. She helped me a lot with the boys. She was so good with her younger brothers. She would have been a great mom." Caroline's hand flew up to cover her mouth as her eyes pooled and she began to weep, quietly at first and then her chest heaved and she sobbed. Raven moved over to sit on the arm of her chair. She put her arm around Caroline's shoulders and just waited.

Mick left the room and came back with a handful of toilet paper, placing it in Caroline's hand. "Sorry. I couldn't find any tissue."

Caroline dabbed her eyes then blew her nose. "I'm sorry."

"Don't be," Raven said. "Can you tell me about the night she disappeared?"

Caroline hiccuped as she took a deep breath. "She wasn't home by twenty to eleven, so I called over to Hayden's to see if she'd left yet."

"Was she always home on time?"

"Always. When Rebecca said that she'd left at ten fifteen, we were worried. It should only have taken her ten minutes at the most to get home. I stayed home with the boys and Steve went out looking for her."

"Did the Stoles help you search for her?"

"Yes. Both Rebecca and Hayden." Caroline scratched her head, messing her hair. "I think Matt was at work. He's always at work."

"What was Emily's relationship with Hayden like? Were they happy?"

"They had been. They were inseparable last summer, but when they went back to school, Hayden was a little controlling. He didn't like Em hanging around with her friends. He wanted all of her attention, you know? It was smothering and Em wanted to break it off." She glanced up at Raven. "It was too intense for a young girl who still had her whole life ahead of her. But, she was still in love with him. She called to tell me that they talked and worked it out. Hayden listened to what she had to say and he was going to give her some breathing room. That was the last time we talked."

Raven timed the walk back to the Stoles residence. It took exactly eight minutes and forty-three seconds. She looked at the mammoth red brick house for a moment, counting eight windows on this side of the house alone. Hayden could have killed Em and stuffed her in the trunk of his car long before she was supposed to leave. Rebecca probably hadn't seen her since dinner. She'd just assumed she was still in the house. Or, someone could have gotten to her on her way home.

"We've got a hit on ViCLAS," Mick announced, holding her cell phone in front of her. ViCLAS, Canada's Violent Crime Linkage Analysis System, matched similar crimes. "Three women with long, red hair and green eyes have been found in ditches in Central Ontario in the past year. All raped and drowned."

"Shit," Raven said. So much for the Hayden theory. Sawicki would have received the ViCLAS hit, probably long before they had as he worked out of Headquarters where their ViCLAS database and analyzers were housed. It was probably why he hadn't bothered to re-interview Hayden or the McMurtries. And it meant he was probably way ahead of them on this investigation.

She tossed the car keys to Mick, the lack of sleep catching up to her again. "Let's head home, kiddo." She slumped in the passenger seat and pulled out her own phone to check the status of her warrants. When there was no notification, she used the Charger's onboard computer to look into the other two murders from the ViCLAS hit.

The first victim, twenty-five year old Charlene Brock went missing from Gravenhurst in September. Her body was found a week later in a ditch just outside of Solstice's jurisdiction, on Savage Settlement Rd., just north of a town called Novar. The last victim, twenty-two year old Sandra Kelway, was reported missing from Barrie two months ago, in February. Her body was also found just outside of Solstice's jurisdiction on Peter St. in Novar two weeks after her disappearance. Raven opened Google Maps on her phone and zeroed in on the locations the bodies were found. Another two hundred yards south and Sandra Kelway would have been Raven's. Charlene Brock was only another few kilometres north east. All of the victims were found within a five kilometre radius in easy access of Highway 11.

"He's travelling to find his victims and dumping them close to home." He was taking his victims somewhere, to his home maybe, and spending some time with them before he dumped them. It was worth travelling the distance to abduct them, but not worth travelling any distance once he was through with them. Raven continued to stare at the map. Where was he finding the vics? He wouldn't be travelling all the way down to Barrie unless he had a victim established. He had to be finding women meeting his criteria – the red hair, green eyes, slim builds – in a common location and then travelling to stalk them. Facebook or a dating site was Raven's guess.

Your warrants are in.

"Jesus." The voice in her head startled her out of a deep concentration.

"What?" Mick asked.

"Nothing." As if on cue, Raven's cell phone chirped the arrival of a new email. Sure enough, it was the confirmation her warrants had been issued. "Warrants are in. Let's pick them up."

Mick glanced over at Raven and offered a thin lipped smile before turning her attention back to the road. "You okay?"

"You're not going to be one of those people who are constantly asking that question, are you? Because it's really annoying." Of course she was okay. She leaned back and rested her head against the headrest. She probably shouldn't have snapped at Mick. The kid was just being compassionate.

"Look, I'm probably a bit grumpy from lack of sleep. Forget I just said that, would you?"

Keeping her eyes on the road, Mick gave a short laugh. "If that's your way of saying sorry, apology accepted, DC." Mick spared another glance at Raven, but her eyes were closed, her chest rising and falling rhythmically. "Okay then." She shook her head and laughed again.

Chapter 4

Raven's first stop was Ena's family doctor, Dr. Simone Wagnar. She presented the receptionist, who oddly resembled Dr. Tang's receptionist with steely gray hair and coke bottle lenses, with the warrant. Once the receptionist got the go ahead from Dr. Wagnar, she pulled Ena's file from among a wall of files in seconds. Impressive. Raven flipped open the file and scanned through the documents. The file was thin, with only annual check ups contained within. Ena Bowen was in great health right up until weeks before her death. "Was this the last time Ena was in?" Raven asked.

The tiny receptionist stood to peer into Ena's file then resumed her seat and tapped away on her keyboard. "Yes, that's right. She was last in on February tenth for her annual physical. She did call a couple of weeks ago to make an appointment. Dr. Wagnar was away, so the earliest I could get her in was last Thursday. Obviously, she didn't make the appointment."

"Did she say why she wanted to see Dr. Wagnar?" According to the file, Ena only came in on those annual visits.

"Yes, she thought she had the stomach flu or something. She couldn't keep anything down. I suggested she go to Urgent Care if her symptoms persisted."

"Do you know if she did?" Raven looked up from the file

into the coke bottle lenses. "Go to Urgent Care?"

"We would have gotten a report, so, no. It doesn't appear she did."

"Could she have gone to another walk-in clinic, or the hospital emergency?"

"We would still have been notified of the visit as Dr. Wagnar is listed as her family physician."

"Did you receive a notification from the hospital of her death?"

"Yes. Dr. Wagnar must still have it as it's not in her file yet."

Raven closed the file. "Thanks for your help. Is Dr. Wagnar available to see me for a few minutes?"

"I'm afraid she's not in the office this morning. I could have her give you a call."

Raven shook her head. She'd catch up to Simone later. "That's okay. Thanks again."

She took the keys from Mick and settled into the drivers seat, moving it back to allow for her long legs. She took a deep breath and deflated as she released it. "What do you think? What's your gut telling you?"

Mick looked over with her lips pursed, eyes droopy. "That something is definitely not adding up. I mean, it's possible for cancer to spread quickly. But, something just doesn't feel right."

Raven's smile was tight. "Yeah, that's what I'm talking about. It's not something you can put your finger on. It's just something you sense." And that was supposed to be a gift, wasn't it? One of the powers that she'd long ago suppressed. That sixth sense. Intuition. Gut feelings. Everyone had it. Not everyone tuned in to it.

Finding a parking spot at their quiet little hospital was not an issue. Raven checked the time on the dash as she parked. If Riley was on afternoons, she'd be there. She really didn't want to see her after embarrassing herself last night. She picked up the warrant and slapped it in her palm as she stared across at the emergency entrance. Nothing she could do about it. If Riley was there, she was there.

Mick sat in the passenger seat watching her. Raven supposed she should give her some kind of heads up.

"Uh, listen. This could be … um, well." Shit. She didn't discuss her personal life with anyone. Ever. Apparently not even with Riley. "The fact is that my ex, Riley, works in the ER and she could be here."

"Okay."

Raven had to laugh. Mick was so easy going. It didn't phase her in the least. "Okay." She opened her door and headed for the entrance, trying to keep her pace slow so Mick didn't have to jog. They walked through the sliding doors and there was Riley, crouched down speaking to a little girl with blonde hair that was almost white flowing down her back in waves. The girl was leaning into her mother, her arms wrapped around her leg in a death grip.

Riley's eyes flicked up and she frowned, her eyes narrowed, then she returned her attention back to the little girl. And, if Raven wasn't mistaken, her face had flushed.

"Oh," Mick said. "She's definitely not happy to see you."

Raven gave her ribs a little elbow. "Shut up."

"Okay." Mick hooked her thumbs in her duty belt and smiled.

Since running out the door wasn't an option, Raven stood stoically, waiting for Riley to finish with the little girl and her mother. The girl loosened her grip on mom's leg and she slipped her small hand into Riley's. Riley led them into the triage office and shut the door.

Raven started pacing the hall, impatient to get Ena's files and flee. Yes, she could admit that she was running away.

You really love her.

"Oh, for the love of God."

Mick reached her hand out and placed it gently on Raven's arm. "I can handle issuing the warrant and getting your mother's file for you."

Raven's hands shot up, palms out. "I'm fine. Okay? Fine." She dropped her hands, crumpling the warrant in her tight fist and began pacing again, out of Mick's hearing range. Trying her best to blank out all thoughts, she whispered between gritted teeth, "You do realize this is a gross invasion of my privacy, don't you?"

I'm sorry, Rave. I've only felt love like that once in my life. It's worth fighting for.

Raven laughed. Her mother was the last person she'd take relationship advice from.

I told you about him. Your father.

"Shut. Up." The father she'd never met left Solstice before Ena learned she was pregnant. So, he'd never known he had a daughter and she had no idea who or what her father was. Better that way if he was anything like Gregor.

What's Gregor got to do with your father?

Fire burned up Raven's neck, spreading over her face. Riley picked that moment to open the door to the triage office.

"Out," Raven growled, a little too loudly. All eyes turned to her. Her face had already been burning, so at least it hadn't gotten any worse with the attention. Her palm slapped against her temple, her fingers curling in. "Sorry. I've just got a headache brewing." As if that would cover her outburst. She didn't lie about the headache though. Her head was pounding, in rhythm with her racing heart.

Riley took a couple of cautious steps toward her. "Why don't you sit down and I'll get your blood pressure?"

"I don't need my damn blood pressure taken." She slapped the warrant into Riley's outstretched hand. "I need Ena

Bowen's records."

Riley blinked a the rumpled document in her hand then stared up at Raven. "I don't understand."

"That's a warrant for Ena's records. Everything you have on Ena Amaris Bowen."

Riley continued to stare, mouth open. Then her eyes narrowed, her back straightened and her mouth closed, forming a thin white line. "What are you doing, Raven?"

"Hey, Riley," Mick said, stepping into the mix. "We have reason to believe there was foul play involved in the death of Raven's mother. We're executing this warrant for all hospital records regarding Ena Bowen in order to try to determine her actual cause of death."

"She had cancer." Riley continued to glare at Raven. "I was here when she came in, Rave. She died of cancer."

Still in a state over the slip she made with Ena, Raven couldn't keep the attitude from her voice. "If you were here and you're so sure she died of cancer, you'd know where that diagnosis came from."

"I don't understand."

"Were tests performed to confirm the diagnosis? Did a qualified doctor give you the diagnosis? Is there paperwork, CT scans, x-rays, something to confirm this diagnosis?"

Riley's eyes widened. "Am I in some kind of trouble here?"

Really? Raven was getting sick and tired of everyone in the medical profession being more concerned about covering their own butts than trying to get to the bottom of what actually happened to Ena.

"Just get us her files."

Riley unfolded the document, scanning it instead of reading through all of the legalese. When she finished, she folded the document and addressed both Mick and Raven. "If you'll wait here, I'll get you a copy of her records." She walked away stiffly, with her head in the air.

"She thinks you're doing this to spite her," Mick said.

"Why?" She had no reason to think that. They weren't doing anything *to* Riley. She hadn't even known Riley had been here when her mother was brought in.

"I don't know. Did she do something to spite you?"

Raven turned slightly, facing away from Mick and scratched her head. "Why are we discussing my relationship – oh, excuse me – ex-relationship?" She turned back, glaring at Mick.

Mick put her hands up in defence. "Sorry," she said as she backed up a couple of steps. "Off bounds. Got it."

Did she really look that threatening? Raven didn't have time to ask, because a very stern looking grey-haired man in a slick business suit was barrelling towards her with Riley close at his heels. "Officer Bowen?"

"Detective Constable Bowen. This is my partner, Constable Warren. And you are?"

"Robert Stanson, counsel on behalf of Solstice General Hospital. What can we help you with?"

"You can help me by supplying the records named in my warrant."

"Ah, yes. There seems to be a little problem. The records for Ms. Ena Bowen appear to be missing."

The blood racing through Raven's veins felt like it had been set to boil. "Then we do have a problem, Mr. Stanson. You see, I had no intention of filing suit against Dr. Tang or the hospital. But, if this is the way you want to play it, I may be forced to change my mind. Those records were here this morning when Dr. Tang called over. So, they've only gone missing since you realized there was a problem with the way my mother was treated in this hospital."

"We treated –" Riley started, but was rudely cut off.

"Ah, ah, Miss Gallagher, not a word." Stanson actually wagged his finger in front of her face.

"Your reaction to the warrant will give me grounds for the exhumation of Ena Bowen's body in order for an autopsy to be performed. I don't even need the records you're withholding, Stanson. Your behaviour speaks volumes." Raven headed for the exit, not looking back when he called 'Miss Bowen'. Bastard didn't even have any respect for her job or her rank. She was too riled up to sit in the car, so she paced back and forth beside it, trying to get rid of some of her excess energy and anxiety.

Mick stood on the other side of the car, staring down at the ground with her thumbs hooked in her duty belt. Raven glanced at her every time she made the turn towards the front of the car again. She didn't move. Just stood there patiently waiting. It would be so easy to lash out at her, but that would be her lack of sleep and anger getting the best of her and she wasn't about to let that happen. Besides, Mick didn't deserve it.

Raven was still pacing when Riley breeched the doors from the emergency department wearing her colourful scrubs - some kind of cartoon character graced the top and the bottoms were a bright blue. She carried a manilla envelope. The records the warrant had specified, Raven assumed. The lawyer must be shaking in his boots by now. The coward sent Riley out instead of dealing with her himself.

She didn't stop pacing when Riley approached. Riley hadn't even thrown a sweater on. With the sun going down, and the temperature dropping with it, it was getting pretty chilly.

"Rave?" Riley held the envelope out.

"So, what? Ena's records have miraculously appeared?"

Riley dropped her arm when Raven didn't take the envelope from her. "Can you tell me what's going on, Rave? Am I in trouble here?"

That's right, save your ass. "Why don't you ask your

counsel there, Riley? Ask him why he's shitting bricks."

"I'm asking you."

Raven stopped pacing and turned to face Riley. Worry lines scored her forehead and that spot just between her eyebrows. And Raven was just angry enough to put a few more there. "Ena didn't have cancer, Ri. She was poisoned and instead of helping her or doing tests to figure out why she was so sick, you all fucked up. You made her 'as comfortable as possible'," Raven air quoted with two fingers. "And you let her die."

"No." Riley gulped. "No, that can't be right. The paramedics who brought her in said she was forth stage stomach cancer."

"And you didn't do any tests to confirm that diagnosis? You took a paramedics word for it?"

Riley's brow furrowed again. "No, we must have confirmed it. We wouldn't just let her lay there and die. We wouldn't do that."

"So where's the confirmation?"

Riley looked down at the file in her hand. Raven stepped forward and took it from her. She opened the flap and removed three sheets of paper. As she scanned through the pages, Riley crossed her arms over her ribs. Raven wasn't sure if she was shaking from the cold or the situation.

"You didn't run any tests. You gave her morphine and let her die." Raven looked up, meeting Riley's sad gaze. "Why?"

"I'm not allowed to talk about it."

"No, of course not. Wouldn't want you to risk your precious career." Raven stuffed the papers back into the envelope and got in the car. While she fastened her seatbelt and started the car, she watched Mick walk over to Riley and take her hand. She said something and Riley nodded her head. Then Mick wrapped her arms around her and Riley clung to her, her body shaking. Raven looked down at her lap, unable to watch any more. She didn't look up until she heard the passenger door open. When she looked out the windshield, Riley was jogging back to the entrance, arms hugged tightly around herself.

She waited for the click of Mick's seat belt and put the car in reverse, backed out of the parking spot, and made her way out to the street. "Want to tell me what that was about?"

Mick let out an audible sigh. "She feels terrible."

"Yeah, we wouldn't want that."

Mick scowled at her. "She doesn't want you to think she killed your mother."

Raven fisted her hand in her hair and suppressed the urge to scream. "Why didn't they just run the damn tests?"

"Well, that's the question, isn't it?"

* * *

Raven cut Mick loose for the night and sat at her desk to type up her report and a request to have Ena's body exhumed and autopsied. Then she went home to her cottage, glad that she still had that six pack of beer from the night before. She sat in her living room with the lights off, staring out at Fairy Lake with the bright moon reflecting off the water. There was something about the water that calmed her. Being here, looking out at that view, centred her, grounded her.

She got out of her chair and walked to the window, looking up at the moon. In a couple of days it would be full.

Sunday.

"Get the fuck out of my head." Raven glared up at the ceiling, as if she would see Ena there. She took a long swig of her beer and headed to the fridge to grab another.

Raven Sage. Is that the way I raised you?

Raven stopped in her tracks and laughed. "The way *you* raised me? You didn't even see me."

That's not true. I've always loved you, Rave. You didn't always make it easy, but I loved you.

That tore the lid of Raven's temper. She whirled around and threw her beer can across the room. "*I* didn't make it easy? Are you kidding me? I was twelve years old. Twelve."

Why can't we just get along? Why can't we have a normal conversation, Rave?

"Why can't you just get the hell out of my head? I'm looking into what happened to you. You can leave me alone anytime now." She made it to the fridge, pulled two beers out and took them with her back to the living room where she flopped down into a big easy chair, cracking the first one open. Silence. Finally.

It took about five seconds before she realized she missed having someone to talk to. Even if it was just her mother's voice. She downed half the beer and went to the window again. She'd gone off on Riley and now Ena. No wonder no one wanted her. At least she had the moon and the water.

When she finished the second beer, she pushed off the window and picked up her laptop. Sitting back in the easy chair, she opened the browser and signed into Facebook. In the search bar, she typed Charlene Brock. As expected, no one had deleted her Facebook page. Her family wouldn't be ready to let go. Raven looked through some of her photos first and then through her posts. She'd danced in some well known theatre productions in Toronto and even one on Broadway. She was vacationing at a resort near Gravenhurst when she went missing and she'd posted her location on Facebook. Raven wasn't one of her 'friends', so the post was 'public', meaning anyone could see it.

She searched for Sandra Kelway next and found her page as well. She was a student in Barrie and she played in a band on the weekends doing local gigs. The night she went missing, she'd posted that she was studying at the college's library. Again, the post was public. Why didn't these girls learn to be more cautious with who could see their posts?

She'd never understand it.

Emily McMurtie had her security settings set to 'friends' or 'friends of friends' because Raven couldn't see any of her posts or her private information. Good girl, she thought. But, it ruined her theory that the offender found his vics on Facebook. She tried a couple of dating sites before she hit pay-dirt. All three girls had bios on the Dating Pool website.

She was about to shut down her laptop for the night when she had a thought. Riley had left the security chain on when she answered the door last night. Was someone there with her and she didn't want Raven to know? Riley shared the long red hair, green eyes, slim build, and fair skin of the vics. She did a search of women looking for women, ages 25 to 35, in the Muskoka area. Sure enough, there was Riley. She'd used a picture that had been of the two of them on Raven's dock with Fairy Lake behind them, only she'd cropped Raven out of the picture and zoomed in on herself. There should be a rule about using pictures of you with an ex, even if you couldn't see her, to fish for dates. Ha.

Stupid. If she hadn't gone home with Jax that night, how different her life would be right now. She was happy. Really happy. It was one damn slip when Riley had been on a stretch of ten night shifts. She'd given up her days off to cover another nurse who was off sick. Raven was itchy. She couldn't stand the loneliness and she'd headed down to Jax's favourite pub. Stupid. She'd had no intention of sleeping with him. She never thought of him in that way.

Why the hell had she gone against everything she believed in and slept with her best friend?

* * *

A banging at the door startled Raven out of a deep sleep. She was still holding a can of beer. She set it on the side table and stumbled to the door, not because she was drunk, but because she was so exhausted and still half asleep. She flung the door open and Riley stood there, her arms still wrapped around her torso, but at least she was wearing a warm coat now.

"Can we talk?"

Raven snorted. All she'd wanted last night was to spend some time in Riley's company. Just someone who would understand the pressures of her job and maybe hold her for a while.

"What's so funny?"

"Nothing's funny, Ri. Ironic, maybe, but not funny." Raven dipped her knees and waved her hand towards the living room, inviting Riley in. "Can I get you a beer? Coffee?" Roll in the hay?

"Coffee's good." Riley bit her lower lip, her hands worrying in front of her. She took a seat on the edge of the couch with her clasped hands squeezed between her knees.

Raven put a pot of coffee on, came into the living room, and stood by the window. The moon had moved out of view, but she could still see its reflection over the lake. She stuck her hands in her pockets and just stood there looking out, waiting for Riley to start the conversation.

"When you came to my apartment last night, was it to talk about what happened to your mother?"

"Nope." She half expected Riley to stand up and leave. But she continued to sit stiffly, looking up at Raven like she was in pain.

"Rave, come on. Throw me a branch here. I don't know what's happening. You have to know I would never hurt anyone, especially not your mother."

"I'm sorry. I thought your lawyer told you not to talk about it."

Riley stood, threw her hands up in the air and then slapped them down to her sides. Then she dropped down to the couch, buried her face in her hands and wept. Raven's first instinct was to go to her and wrap her in a hug, but she stopped herself. It wasn't her place to do that anymore. Riley made that clear last night.

"I'll just get the coffee," she said and escaped to the kitchen.

She came back out with two cups and set one down in front of Riley who was still in the same position, still crying. She took her own back to her easy chair then just sat there and waited. She didn't know what she was supposed to say or do. She wasn't good at comforting people the way Riley was.

Riley sniffed, swiping the tears from her face. It reminded Raven she should offer a tissue. She scooted to the bathroom and came back with a box of tissues. Riley accepted the whole box, pulled out two, and mopped her cheeks before blowing her nose. Just when Raven thought she'd gotten herself under control, she began weeping again.

"The h-hospital's going to p-pin the whole thing on m-me." She pulled two more tissues from the box and buried her face in them in a chest heaving wail.

Bastards. Spineless bastards. Raven sank down on the couch next to Riley and put a tentative arm around her. "It's not your fault, Ri."

Riley leaned into Raven, buried her face in the curve of Raven's neck. Raven inhaled the lavender scent of Riley's shampoo, her thighs tensing with a wave of pure lust. She tightened her arms around Riley and tried to remind herself that this was only a friend seeking comfort. Riley's job meant everything to her. Taking care of people was what she did, what she lived for. Like that little girl in the hallway.

When Riley finally got herself under control, there was an awkward moment where they separated. Riley grabbed more tissues and wiped her face while Raven ran her hands down her jeans and then stood, going back to her chair, picking up her coffee and twirling it between her palms.

Riley stood. "I'm sorry. I shouldn't have come here and laid this on you. It's just … I just … can you tell me what's going on? The hospital won't tell me anything."

"The hospital's lawyer told you not to talk to me."

"Fuck the lawyer. He's trying to pin the whole thing on me to save the doctor and the hospital." She fisted her jacket at her chest and dropped to the couch again. "They've suspended me, Rave." Tears welled in her eyes again, but she brushed them away with her fists.

Raven fought the urge to get up and wrap Riley in her arms again. Her chest ached. She wanted to fix this so Riley wouldn't be hurting anymore. "It's early yet. I've put in a request to have Ena's body exhumed for an autopsy. There's reasonable grounds for that based on what we know so far and the hospital lawyer's reaction. She didn't have cancer, Ri. We believe she was poisoned. Did anyone come into the hospital with Ena?"

Riley shook her head. "No, the paramedics brought her in."

"Did she request that you call anyone?"

"She was unconscious when she came in. She never regained consciousness." Riley wiped her eyes again then fisted the soggy tissues in her lap. The tissues vibrated, the only sign Raven could see that Riley was shaking. "Her next of kin was listed as Kiran Hayes. He didn't answer any of the calls we placed. We left voice mails, but he didn't return our calls."

Kiran Hayes? Raven had never heard the name before, but she thought of all of the cards in Ena's drawer signed with a K. "Did you follow protocol for a patient coming in with Ena's symptoms?"

Riley hesitated then answered, "No. See that's the problem. We would have ordered tests. No one did. And no one questioned it. We would have. If a doctor hadn't ordered tests in that situation, we would have questioned it."

"This is going to sound crazy, but I think the reason no tests were ordered is due to some hocus pocus."

"Witchcraft? I thought you didn't believe in that stuff."

She believed in it, she just didn't practice it. "How would you explain it?"

Riley shook her head. "I can't. It doesn't make sense." The tears began again. "I don't know what to do, Rave. I'm not just going to lose my job. I'm going to lose my license."

"The first thing you do is you don't talk about it to anyone, especially the police. Your union pays for your legal fees. Get a lawyer. A good one. One that can file suit against the hospital for wrongful dismissal if this doesn't get resolved."

"I don't want some fricking wrongful dismissal suit. I want my job."

"Just do it. Get the lawyer. Don't talk to the hospital or to anyone else."

Riley nodded and stood again. She started for the door and Raven followed, not knowing if she felt any better or if there was anything she could do to help. At the door, Riley turned.

"You don't think I killed your mother, do you?"

"No, Ri. I don't." Raven shoved her hands in her pockets because she was desperate to reach out and touch Riley's blotchy face.

Riley closed her eyes and nodded again. "Okay. Okay." She opened the door and fled to her car.

Raven stood in the doorway until the taillights of Riley's little red SUV disappeared over the hill, her heart breaking a little more. She didn't think that was possible which had her wondering just how much more she could hurt.

Raven retrieved a bag of supplies she'd left on the kitchen island and grabbed a paring knife from a drawer. She took them into the living room, moved her coffee table over to the window and sat down on the floor in front of it, facing the lake view. She removed a fat white candle from the bag and used the paring knife to carve the three moons into it - the waxing moon, the full moon, and the waning moon. Setting it on the table, she lit it and turned out the lights. A soft glow filtered in from the stove light in the kitchen and the flickering light of the candle danced over the living room walls. She took a stick of sage out of the bag, lit it, and went around the room, spreading the smoke with a cupped hand to cleanse the space of negative energy.

Then she sat on the floor facing the candle and drew her feet up to her thighs in the lotus position. She laid the backs of her hands on her knees and touched her middle fingers to her thumbs. She hadn't meditated for years. She needed something to calm the constant ache in her chest since she'd lost Riley and she was hoping this would help. Closing her eyes, she could see the glow from the candle's flame. She focused on that and her deep breathing, but her mind kept wandering to images of Riley.

There was a connection between them from the first moment they looked at each other. Raven had brought a teenaged boy into the ER after he'd been beaten by his father. Riley walked out of the triage area and they stood there staring at each other. Riley had her hair back in a tight twist and her green eyes were glowing, vibrant against her pale skin. The freckles across her nose were the sexiest thing Raven had ever seen. She couldn't take her eyes off Riley until the boy cleared his throat, startling her out of a daze. To this day she didn't know how long they stood there ogling each other. As soon as the boy was settled into a treatment room, Raven asked Riley out to dinner. That had been nearly four years ago and they'd been together ever since. At least, until Riley broke up with her nearly a month ago.

"Focus," Raven whispered and let the thoughts of Riley

drift away, bringing her attention back to the flame and her breaths. The first time they'd made love was right where Raven was sitting, with the moon shining in the window, giving Riley's skin an ethereal glow. Raven hadn't been a virgin, by a long shot, but she was sure that it was the first time she'd ever made love. One light touch with the tip of Riley's finger could set her aflame. Sex with Riley was more intense, more pleasurable, more satisfying than anything Raven had experienced.

The air gusted out of Raven's lungs and she dropped back onto the carpet, disgusted with herself. Trying not to think about Riley made her unable to think of anything but. Now she was missing her and so aroused she thought she might explode.

Maybe keeping busy is a better option.

"How am I supposed to sleep if I can't stop thinking about her?"

Wear yourself out. Go for a run or go down to your gym.

"Does it get any easier?"

No, not really. Not when you love someone with your entire being. I ended up having to take sleeping pills.

Well, that explained why Ena never woke up in the middle of the night.

Why? What was happening in the middle of the night?

Raven surged to her feet, blew out the candle, and fled to her room. She stripped off her clothes and threw on a pair of track pants, a sweatshirt, and her running shoes and was out the door. She didn't even bother to stretch. She set off at a full out run and let out a long, deep primal scream.

Chapter 5

Raven let herself into Adara's back door at seven-thirty the next morning, just in time to catch Adara removing a tray of muffins from her oven. A long dark braid flecked with grey hung down Adara's back, reaching her tailbone. She had a quiet beauty, a plump face with kind brown eyes. She limped to the kitchen island, deposited the tray of muffins on a cooling rack and then pulled the oven mitts off her hands.

When Raven reached for a muffin, Adara reached across the island and slapped her hand away. "Honest to goodness, child. Doesn't anyone feed you?"

Raven laughed and then came around the island, deposited a kiss on Adara's cheek and grinned. "Just you."

Adara picked up the tea towel and whipped it at Raven's butt. "Sit down. I've got a plate warming for you." She limped back to her oven, pulled out a plate of bacon, eggs, and hash browns and set it in front of Raven.

The ketchup bottle gave a wet fart as it dumped a large blob of ketchup next to the home fries. Raven set the bottle down and picked up the knife and fork as Adara set a cup of coffee in front of her. "Ah, thank you. You are a goddess."

Adara's laugh filled the room, loud and robust. She cocked a hip, placed her fist on it. "You only say that when I heap food in front of you."

"You know I love you, Adara." Raven threw her a wink and dug in. "So, what are all the treats for?" She motioned to the muffins and assorted baked goods sitting on the island.

"Full moon on Sunday." Adara brought a plastic tub over and began to stack various baked goods inside, each layer separated by a sheet of wax paper.

"Ah, gathering of the coven. What happens with Ena gone?"

Adara shrugged. "Looks like the coven members want to put it to a vote. Of course, you can only vote for those qualified to serve as High Priestess. You must be a third-degree and adept." Adept referred to someone who had mastered the discipline of self-development.

"So, how many are qualified?"

"Oh, only a handful, I guess." Adara placed the now full container on the kitchen counter, brought over an empty one, and continued with her meticulous layering. "Myself included." She did a quick curtsey, making Raven laugh.

"Would you want that?"

Adara stopped stacking and stood a little straighter. "I don't know, honey. It will be impossible to replace Ena. I don't think anyone could fill those shoes." She waved her hand in front of her wet eyes. "Oh, dear. Where did that come from?" She limped off down the hall to the washroom waving her hand in front of her face the entire way.

Adara and Ena had been best friends since they were in kindergarten. Their relationship splintered a bit when Adara took Raven in, but it didn't stop Adara from being in the coven and Raven supposed they got along all these years despite her. She hadn't wanted to take Adara's best friend away from her, but she'd needed a roof over her head and Adara offered.

When Adara came back in, she was smiling, no sign of tears. "So, tell me what's bothering you, sweetie."

"Nothing's bothering me." Raven finished her breakfast and used a napkin to wipe her face.

You can't tell her, Rave.

"You can't fool me, honey. I know you too well, remember. You haven't been sleeping. Is it a case? I saw on the news about the body of that girl being found just on the outskirts of town."

"Yeah, I caught that one."

"Dear Goddess, sweetheart. I don't know how you do it. There must be a career out there that's not so morbid."

Laughing, Raven picked up her plate and came around the island. "I'm sure there is, but I've got the one I want." She placed her dishes neatly in the dishwasher then turned back to Adara. "You saw Ena over the last few weeks of her life. What happened? I know she was sick, but it came on rather fast, didn't it?"

Raven Sage Bowen!

Adara placed her hands on the counter, just in front of the sink, and stared out the window. "I suppose it did. She didn't really complain, she just looked very pale and tired."

"Did she see a doctor? Go to a walk-in clinic?"

Adara huffed out a short laugh. "You know your mother. Stubborn as a mule. I tried to get her to go see Simone. She said it was just a bit of the stomach flu."

A silent tear glided slowly down Adara's cheek as she continued to stare blankly out the window, her knuckles white where she gripped the counter.

"Do you know who called the ambulance for her?"

Adara sniffed, swiped a hand across her cheek then shook her head. "I don't know, honey."

Stepping in beside Adara, Raven wrapped her arms around her. "I'm sorry. I didn't mean to upset you."

"Oh, don't be sorry, sweetie. I understand you want to know what happened to your mother." She leaned her head against Raven's upper arm. "Cancer's a horrible disease." Then Adara straightened and drew in a deep breath. "Enough of this crying now," she said and plastered a smile on her face.

"Yeah, I've got to get to work." Raven gave Adara's cheek a peck then turned and swiped a steaming muffin from the island. "Thanks for brekky."

Adara grabbed the tea towel and snapped it at Raven's ass, missing by mere millimetres. "Land sakes, child. Cops aren't suppose to steal."

Raven laughed all the way down the driveway. She got in her car, took a big bite of oatmeal walnut muffin and closed her eyes, savouring the warmth and taste. "Yum."

You have to be careful, Rave. I know you like to confide in Adara, but you can't this time.

Good mood spoiled. How did she know she confided in Adara? Not that it was much of a stretch to figure out. The woman had raised her from the age of fifteen on.

Would it surprise you to know Adara took you in because I asked her to?

Raven's nostrils flared, heat rose up her neck and flared over her face. "You what?"

You were so angry at me and I didn't know why. I followed you to the park that night and then I called Adara and asked her to go get you. She was supposed to figure out why you were so angry and then bring you home again.

The warm muffin was squished into a ball in Raven's fist. She got a napkin from the glove box, lost the muffin, and wiped her hand off. She didn't have time for Ena's crap. She had to get to work. She put the car in reverse and backed out of Adara's driveway then headed towards downtown. What Ena said explained how Adara just happened to wander by and find her sitting on the carousel in the park that night. The two of them planned it. She trusted Adara all these years and it was all a lie.

Can I ask you a question?

"Do I have a choice?" Raven growled. A dull headache spread from the back of her neck up to her temples. She tried to relax her shoulders and crack her neck. It just made it worse.

Did Gregor make a pass at you when you were twelve?

Raven slammed on the brakes and pulled to the shoulder, throwing the car in park before getting out and slamming the door behind her. Her vision kept greying, like she was going to pass out. She placed her hands on the hood of the car and bent her head forward.

He did. Didn't he? I was seeing him when you were twelve and the night you stormed out of the house he was there. Is that why you were so angry?

She didn't care who was watching. Raven screamed, "Get out of my head!" Her fists were clenched tightly, the veins in her neck pulsing madly. She literally felt all of the colour draining from her face. Oh, God. She was going to pass out right here on the side of the road.

She heard tires on gravel and looked up to see a car coming to a stop just behind her vehicle.

Mick hopped out, rushing towards her, eyes wide like a spooked horse. She whipped open the driver's door of Raven's Charger, grabbed Raven's hand, and steered her towards it. Then she pushed her back until her calves hit the door frame and she dropped onto the seat. Mick placed her hand on the back of Raven's neck and pushed until her head was between her legs.

"Okay, just try to breathe now."

Now she had to add embarrassment to the mix. "I'm okay." She swatted Mick's hand away, but she wasn't quite ready to lift her head from between her legs.

"Have you gotten any sleep yet?"

"Yes." She'd tossed and turned again even after a two hour run. But she managed a good four hours when she finally did drop off.

"You want to tell me what's going on, DC?"

Raven could see Mick's boots directly in front of her own. If she threw up, she was pretty sure she could pull her own boots out of the way and decorate Mick's. "Get in line." At least Ena had gone quiet again.

"With who?"

"What?"

"Get in line with who, DC?"

Oh, yeah. Jesus, she was losing it. She fisted her hands in her hair. Ena said she'd get out of her head when she found her killer. So, priority one – find the sorry son of a bitch who killed her mom. She lifted her head, slowly. Everything would stop spinning any minute now.

"Maybe a trip to the emergency room wouldn't be a bad idea?"

Raven frowned up at Mick. "Do I look that bad?"

Mick winced. "Honestly?" Then nodding, "Yeah."

"It's nothing. I was just feeling a little nauseous. I'm fine."

Mick stared down at her, eyes narrowed. "Can I ask you a question?"

"Why do people ask that when they're going to ask you anyway? It's like a warning – I'm going to ask you something bad."

"Not bad." Mick grinned. "Just personal. Are you pregnant?"

Raven choked. On what she had no idea because there was nothing in her mouth to choke on. She coughed and sputtered until Mick placed a hand on her head and shoved it between her legs again. "What the hell is wrong with you?"

"Well…the lack of sleep, the nausea … I just wondered if, you know?"

"What? You thought maybe Riley knocked me up?"

Mick sputtered out a short laugh before turning serious. "No, not Riley. Jax."

"What the frig do you know about Jax?"

Mick sighed and crouched down so she was at eye level with Raven. "I should have probably told you this the other day, but I'm a little bit psychic."

"What the hell is a little bit psychic? Either you are or you're not."

Mick's little nose wrinkled. "I pick up little bits and pieces from people."

Oh, this was friggin' perfect. "So how much of my personal business do you know?"

Nose still pinched, she held up her thumb and forefinger half an inch apart. "Little bits and pieces."

"Do you know about my mom?"

"What about your mom?" Mick screwed up her nose. "Exactly?"

"Oh, Jesus." Raven dropped her head again.

* * *

Raven and Mick sat staring at each other over jumbo coffees at a table for two in the Solstice Café.

"Everything. Every little bit you know about me." Raven didn't care how bad it was at this point, she just wanted all of it out on the table. When Mick remained silent, she growled, "All of it."

"Okay, okay." Mick glanced around at the empty tables then turned her gaze back to Raven. "I know your mom's talking to you."

Raven shoulders relaxed infinitesimally. At least now she had someone she could confide in about Ena being in her head. "Okay. What else?"

"Does all this really matter, DC? I mean, will it help anything?"

"All of it. And considering you know all this crap about me, I think you better start calling me Raven."

"Okay, Raven." Mick took a slow sip of her coffee then set it down and stared at it.

"You're stalling." Raven's fists clenched on the table and a thick vein in her neck pulsed.

"I know what you're trying to hide from your mom."

Her coffee went flying with the table when Raven shot to her feet, but Mick's somehow ended up in her hand. She sat there holding it up, staring wide-eyed up at Raven. The staff behind the counter stopped what they were doing and stared over at them.

A woman wearing the deep purple café uniform rushed over. "Oh, did you spill hot coffee on yourself? Are you okay?"

"We're fine." Raven stormed past the woman and out the door. No one … no one knew what she was hiding from Ena, except Raven and Gregor. That bastard. Jesus. She paced back and forth near the dumpster, away from the windows and the peering eyes of the café's staff.

"You do realize that at some point you've got to let it out. It's eating you alive, Raven."

"Sure, now you call me Raven." She hadn't even heard Mick come out. She just *poofed* out of nowhere and stood leaning against the brick wall, sipping her coffee that hadn't spilled all over the floor.

"All of these panic attacks aren't healthy."

Raven stopped her pacing to glare at Mick. "I don't have panic attacks."

"Oh, okay." She took another sip of coffee while Raven went back to pacing. "You did ask me to tell you all of it."

True. She just didn't know how to handle anyone else knowing. "Listen. We can't talk about this. I can't think about it, do you understand?"

"Yeah, you don't want your mom to see it."

"Yeah, yeah. That's right."

"I think you might be a smidge," her voice jumped an octave and she pinched her thumb and forefinger together. "Too late."

"Ah, fuck." Raven dropped her ass to the curb, lowered her head between her legs, and shoved her hands in her hair.

Mick took a seat next to her on the curb. "It's not healthy keeping all of that inside."

"Really? Where do you propose I put it?"

"Raven. I'm saying that you can talk to me about it."

Whoa. Yeah, not helping. Her fists squeezed tighter. What she wouldn't give for a couple of Advil right now. She pushed to her feet, thinking about the bottle of Advil sitting in her desk drawer. "We need to get to work. We're late."

She fought off the dizziness and made it to her car, slamming the door as Mick approached. She ignored her and pulled out. The kid was going to pressure her to talk until Raven blew. God help Mick when the lid came off her temper. Mick was only trying to help, but Jesus. She didn't realize she was playing with fire.

Raven walked into the detachment, made a beeline for the Advil in her desk drawer, and downed four of them with the coffee she picked up from the drive-thru before leaving the café. She'd barely opened her email when DS LaCroix shouted across the room at her. "Rave?"

"DS?" She shouted back then cringed at the pain that shot through her head.

"You need to head over to the courthouse. Your case is going before the judge in twenty minutes."

This just as she opened the email informing her of such. She picked up her coffee as she got to her feet and headed to the locker room. She wasn't exactly dressed for court, but she had a suit in her locker just in case of situations like this. She slammed the door open and found Mick sitting on the bench in front of her locker with her head in her hands. At least it was until Raven slammed the door open. Her head shot up and she jumped to her feet. She hadn't been crying, but she looked pretty wrecked.

"What?"

"Nothing." Mick dusted off her spotless uniform. "I was just pulling myself together."

"Why?" It was Raven who needed to pull herself together, wasn't it? What did Mick have to pull together?

"It just … takes a lot out of me."

"What does?" She wasn't making any sense and Raven didn't have time to drag it out of her. She pulled her locker open and stripped off her shirt and pants, pulling a white dress shirt out of her locker. She shrugged into it and began working at the buttons. "What takes a lot out of you?"

Raven looked up to find Mick staring at her then she turned her head away quickly and blushed.

"Wow. You do have a girl crush on me." Mick turned a brighter shade of red and Raven laughed.

"No, I don't." Her eyes danced around the room, everywhere but in Raven's direction. "I'm not gay, Raven."

"Oh, okay," Raven said in her best Mick impression.

"I'm not. I'm just really jealous of your body. How much time do I have to spend in a gym to get that ripped?"

Raven laughed again. "I think you better just move in."

"I'm not that fat." Mick's arms met across her chest, several inches below her scowl.

"I didn't mean you were. I have a home gym." She pulled on a pair of black pants then fished a pair of black boots from the bottom of her locker and sat on the bench to put them on. "I try to go for a run and workout every morning."

"Yeah, so … I should just move into a place with a gym or get a home gym. Got it."

"I still think you have a girl crush though." She stuck her arms into a grey tweed blazer. "Come on. We're going to court."

* * *

Raven didn't give another thought to what had upset Mick. She met quickly with a crown attorney before going before Judge Cromwell. It took less than five minutes to convince him to order the exhumation of Ena's body for autopsy. Then they went right back to Emily McMurtrie's case. Raven explained her theory about the Dating Pool to Mick on the way back to the detachment. She changed back into her jeans, everyday boots, and pale blue sweater then spent the better part of an hour tracking down an e-tech at Headquarters and explaining to him what she wanted, which was basically to find common admirers on each of the victim's profiles on the Dating Pool's website.

"You know we could probably do this ourselves," Mick said.

"Yeah, but it would take us ten times as long." Raven checked her watch. By now, Ena's body would probably be on its way down to Orillia for autopsy. They could have an answer on cause of death by the end of shift.

You already know the answer.

Raven dropped her head to her desk with a thump then lifted it a bit to thump it down again.

"Headache back?" Mick asked.

"Yes," Raven answered, a little too forcefully.

"Oh, that headache."

Why on the Goddess's green earth did you think that you couldn't talk to me about Gregor, Rave? No wonder you hate me. Do you think I would have kept him around if I'd known?

Raven lifted her heavy head and looked at Mick with her saddest, puppy dog eyes. "Please shoot me. Just pull your Sig from its holster, point it at my head, and shoot."

"Sorry. This is a conversation that's about fifteen years late." Mick stood and smiled. "I'm just going to grab something from the squad room."

"Oh, no you don't. Get back here. We're working."

"We're waiting," Mick called over her shoulder and continued out of the room.

She's right, you know? We should have had this conversation a very long time ago.

"I'm not having a conversation with you," Raven whispered, glancing around the room.

You can just think what you want to say. I'll hear it.

"Oh, no you don't. Get the hell out of my head." Damn it, damn it, damn it. How the hell do you get away from someone who's in your head? She pushed to her feet and walked out of the bullpen and right out the front door. And kept walking. A good paced walk might ease some of the tension.

Rave?

"Stop it. Your body is on its way for autopsy. You have my word that I'll find whoever killed you. Now, get the hell out of my head." She walked three blocks before she sighed with relief that Ena had disappeared again. Then she thought she heard someone weeping. She looked all around before she realized it was in her head. "Oh, my God. Are you crying?"

There was no response other than her mother sobbing in her head. Not just sobbing, but howling. Her headache was coming back full force. She couldn't hear herself think. All she could hear was the bawling. "Stop it. If you're going to cry like that, take it somewhere else."

Raven was so distracted she stepped into the intersection without looking. The screech of tires drowned out the howling and Raven dove. Pain, sharp and shockingly severe, shot through her hip right down to her toes. She was spinning, spinning, spinning and the world went black.

Chapter 6

Raven thought her head was pounding before. Now it felt like someone was jack-hammering it. She tried to pull herself out of a nasty dream where she'd been hit by a car, but she just couldn't wake herself up. Her whole body hurt. If she could just shift her position, she could snuggle back in and sleep comfortably. She tried to roll to her side and couldn't. It was like something was holding her in place.

"I think she's waking up."

That sounded oddly like Jax's voice. She tried to open her eyes to see, but they were too heavy. What would Jax be doing in her bedroom anyway?

"Are you sure the pain meds are working. She looks like she's hurting."

Definitely Jax.

"We only dole out the good stuff around here. Especially for our VIP patients."

Now she knew she was dreaming. Riley and Jax wouldn't both be in her bedroom having a friendly conversation. And why the hell did everything hurt so damn much?

"Ooh. She does look like she's hurting. She's grimacing."

Mick?

"Well, that's definitely not a smile."

Adara? What the …? She struggled to open her eyes and

75

five sets stared back down at her. Was that LaCroix? Dreaming. "Can you shut off the pain?" If that was her own voice, it sure as hell didn't sound like it, unless she'd been in the dessert for a month. Without water.

"I thought you said you gave her the good stuff," Jax said.

"We did. It's not going to take away all of the pain," Riley shot back.

That was more like it. Snipping at each other sounded normal.

"I thought we agreed on getting along," Adara's soft voice said. "Rave doesn't need more stress."

Raven struggled to open her eyes again. "You," she glared at Adara. Her right eye felt weird, but she glared anyway. "You only took me in because mom told you to."

Raven, stop. You can't tell her.

"You need to shut up."

Rave.

"Must be the drugs," Mick laughed. "She's not herself." She leaned over the bed rail. "You're in the hospital, Raven. Do you remember?"

"I remember everything hurts." Raven attempted to lick her dry lips, but her tongue was just as dry.

"Yeah. You're pretty banged up and your head took a good knock. But, other than that, you're great," Mick reported.

"Great?" Was she serious? "Can I have water?"

"I'm going to sit you up a bit, Rave."

She heard Riley's voice just as the bed began to move, pushing her up into a sitting position. Her stomach roiled. "Oh. Don't do that." She started going back down again, then stopped in a semi-sitting position. At least she didn't feel like she was going to lose her breakfast. She opened her eyes again, with less difficulty this time. The same five faces stared at her. "What? Do I look that bad?" They nodded in unison.

"Hey," Riley smiled down at her. "How are you feeling?"

"I feel like I got hit by a friggin' truck." But, it was worth it to see Riley smiling at her like that. "Water?"

"Oh, yeah." Riley brought a cup to her lips and gave her a tiny sip. Then another, until she had her fill.

"When can I go home?"

"The doc wants you to stay the night because you hit your noggin pretty good. Do you remember coming in?" Riley asked. "You were awake when you got here."

"I was?" She had a few flashes – a bright light in her eyes, people scrambling around her.

"Do you remember what happened?" Mick asked.

"Yeah." Raven scanned the faces still gawking at her. With LaCroix there, she was careful what she said. "I needed to go for a walk, clear my head. I wasn't really paying attention. It was totally my fault." Totally Ena's fault. "I stepped out into the intersection without thinking. It wasn't the driver's fault."

"The driver was Jaxon," Adara said.

"Oh, God. I'm sorry, Jax. It was totally my fault." The look on Jaxon's face - brows drawn in, his mouth a grimace - made Raven feel sick. It didn't matter that it wasn't his fault, he blamed himself anyway. Raven reached for his hand and found bandages wrapped around her own. She gave his hand a little squeeze in reassurance and then lifted her hand again to look at the bandages.

"Road rash," Riley explained. "Your face, too."

Riley grazed her fingers over the scrapes on her jaw and then over her swollen right eye.

"I'll get you an ice pack for that," Riley said and left the room.

Raven turned to Mick. "You'll follow up on the Dating Pool thing?"

"Don't worry. I've got it covered."

"Yeah, I know, Miss Efficient." She really didn't have time to lay in bed until morning. That reminded her of something else. "The autopsy results?"

"Not in yet. But, I've got that covered, too. You don't need to worry about a thing until you get out of here."

Riley came back in with another nurse in tow, Lori Metcalfe, a woman in her forties who wore her hair in a short dark bob. Riley handed her an ice pack which Raven placed gently over her right eye. She watched out of her left as Lori shot something into the IV line going into her left arm. Whatever she shot in there, it sent a cold sensation up her arm and then a wonderful warmth spread through her entire body, dulling the pain as it went. Her eyelids became heavy again.

"That should help with the pain and nausea," Riley said.

It was the last thing Raven heard.

* * *

Raven was asleep in her nauseatingly pink room when something woke her. She laid in the dark listening. The floorboard in the hall creaked and a sense of dread filled her. She knew what that creak in the middle of the night meant. Another creak sounded and Raven silently got out of bed, terror rushing through her veins. She frantically searched her room for a weapon and found nothing. Her breaths came short and fast, her stomach pitching and rolling.

Gregor's hand closed over her mouth, reeking of cigarette smoke and Raven gagged.

"Not a word. Not a sound. Or I kill your mom. Remember?"

Raven squeezed her eyes shut, praying for some kind of miracle to stop this insanity. Please, God. Please, Goddess. Please, someone.

"Remember?"

The hoarse whisper in her ear brought with it the scent of whisky and scraped the nerve endings from her nape to her tailbone. She nodded. She remembered. She remembered too well.

Gregor threw her on the bed and climbed on top of her, ripping her PJ bottoms off with one violent pull. Raven tried to scramble off the bed, but he just hauled her back.

His hand clamped down over her mouth again and despite knowing what he would do to her mom, Raven tried her best to scream. She kicked her legs, punched, tried to wiggle out from underneath him, but his strength was too much for her to overcome. Pain, burning hot, shot through her.

"Raven? Wake up, now. You're dreaming. Wake up, Raven."

Raven's eyes flew open at the sound of someone yelling her name. She tried to sit up, but strong arms pushed on her shoulders. She screamed, her dry, cracking voice turning it into a silent cry.

"Raven, you're okay. You're in the hospital and you're safe." Lori Metcalfe's eyes, a deep blue, were kind and smiling down at Raven. "You're safe."

Her erratic breaths began to slow. "Safe," she whispered. She began to relax her stiff muscles, slowly becoming aware that she was slick with sweat. "Just a dream." The room was dark, save the light streaming in from the hallway. She relaxed back into her pillow, but her neck and face burned.

"Sorry." She hadn't had a dream like that for years. Damn you, Ena. You see what you've done? Her eyes burned, but not a single tear fell.

"There you go," Lori said, her voice a soft caress. "I'm going to get you something to help you relax."

"No, it's fine. I'm fine." She just wanted Lori to go away now so she could wallow in solitude. Lori looked down at her with pursed lips and sad eyes and she hated the way it made her feel. She turned her head to stare at the wall and there was Jax, sitting on the edge of a chair, his face white, his beautiful blue eyes wide. She turned her head in the other direction.

Lori left the room and she sensed Jax move to the side of the bed. "Tell me who he is and I swear to God I'll kill the bastard."

"Who?" What the hell was he talking about?

"Look at me, Rave." He grabbed her chin and gently applied pressure until she turned and her eyes met his. "Who raped you? Tell me his name?"

Jesus. What had she said during that nightmare? His stare was so intense she tried to look away, but he only pulled her chin back again and waited for her gaze to meet his. "Tell me who he is. Who raped you, Raven?"

"Jax. Just stop, okay? It was a long time ago. A very long time ago."

"When you were a kid?" His big, strong hand combed through his hair and rubbed his scalp. "Jesus, Rave. You were just a kid?"

"Will you shut up? I don't know what you saw or heard, but you need to forget it, Jax. Just forget the whole thing." She rolled onto her side and buried her face in the pillow. "Go home," her pillow muffled voice mumbled. "Get the hell out of my room and go home."

"Rave?"

She could do rejection, too. "Get out."

Lori came back in the room and whispered with Jax. Raven couldn't make out what they were saying. Then one of them went out and she hoped to hell it was Jaxon. She felt a cool sensation in her arm again and flipped over to glare at Lori. "What did you just give me?"

"Just something to help you sleep peacefully."

Peacefully? Did that mean she wouldn't have another nightmare? She didn't have time to think about it. She glided off to sleep on a magic carpet of warmth.

* * *

Raven lifted the lid covering the plate that was supposed to be breakfast then slammed it back down and pushed the tray away. She attributed the nausea roiling in her belly to the meds she'd been given during the night.

"Hey," Riley said as she came through the door with a small black duffel bag over her shoulder. "How're you feeling?"

"Lovely," Raven grunted. "Do you think you could take this tray out of here?" She couldn't stand the smell of it.

Riley set the duffel bag on the end of the bed and lifted the lid on Raven's breakfast. "Not hungry?"

"No, it's making me nauseous."

Riley raised an eyebrow, but replaced the lid and carried the tray out to the hallway. When she came back in, she rested a hip on the edge of the bed. "So, other than nauseous, how're you feeling? Headache?"

Nurse Riley was in the building. "I'm okay. Aches and pains."

"You gave us a scare."

Riley dropped her eyes and Raven desperately wanted to take her hand and reassure her she was okay. It was all she could do not to reach for her.

"It's not like you to walk into traffic, Rave. I … I'm worried about you. You could have died."

Raven did reach for her then. Her fingers brushed over the back of Riley's hand and Riley pulled away. Her retreat was like a knife slicing into Raven's heart. "Maybe it would have been best if I did," she murmured, not expecting Riley to hear her.

"Rave?" Riley gaped at her with wide eyes. "How could you even think that?"

What she was thinking about was death and Ena and what happens after you pass. "Do you ever wonder what the afterlife is like?"

"No, not really." Riley cocked her head, her green eyes studying Raven's.

Raven closed her eyes and tilted her head back against the pillow. "I bet it's like feeling the warmth of the sun on your skin after a long winter; the peacefulness of waves lapping the shore and leaves rustling in the breeze. I bet it feels a lot like I feel right after we make love - sated and content with you in my arms, your scent engulfing me." She breathed out a long sigh and opened her eyes to find Riley glaring at her.

"When are you going to get it through that exceptionally thick head of yours that we're done? Over. The one thing I cannot tolerate or forgive is infidelity. Especially since you refuse to explain it to me."

Ouch. That hurt. That thread of hope that Riley would one day forgive her just frayed, unraveled, and snapped. Raven turned her head to stare at the wall and hide the devastation she was sure was written all over her face. "Sorry. Must be the drugs."

A few moments of awkward silence passed. Raven couldn't even sense Riley moving. Then Riley sighed. "Let's get you dressed and I'll drive you home."

"That's alright. Mick's coming to help me." At least she would be once Raven gave her a call.

"Oh."

There was hurt wrapped up in that small word and Raven wanted to wrap Riley in her arms and soothe it away. Instead, she closed her eyes, willing Riley to leave before the pain of not being able to touch her became unbearable.

* * *

By the time Mick arrived to pick her up, Raven was dressed in the jogging suit Riley brought in for her and pacing the halls. As soon as she spotted Mick, she headed for the parking lot with Mick jogging to keep up. When they got to the Charger, Raven extended her hand for the keys.

"Oh, gee. Don't you think I should drive? I mean, you just got out of the hospital."

"Gee? Really?" Raven stood waiting with her hand extended, eyes narrowed at Mick, until Mick dropped the keys into her palm. "Good choice."

She drove out to her cottage, left Mick in the living room, and took a long, hot shower. When she got out, she examined the damage in the mirror. She was bruised from head to toe. The worst of the road rash was on her jaw and down the side of her left hand and wrist, but she also had some on her left hip and down her left leg. The outside of her right thigh was completely black where the truck hit her and her right eye was black and purple. The swelling had gone down a bit though.

She started to put on a pair of jeans, but they were too tight for comfort with all of the bruising. She ended up in a loose pair of black dress pants and a light blue button down shirt. She added a belt and secured her weapon on her right hip, her handcuffs at the small of her back. It was uncomfortable, but she could bear it. When she came out of her bedroom, the aroma of bacon and eggs filled the air and she found Mick in the kitchen making a full breakfast. The coffee pot was full, so Raven grabbed a mug and sat at the breakfast bar.

"I hope you're making that for yourself because I'm not hungry."

"Did you eat at the hospital?"

"No. I'm just not hungry." The last thing she'd eaten was breakfast at Adara's the morning before, but she still didn't want anything to eat.

Mick fixed herself a plate and sat next to Raven at the breakfast bar. "This is a nice place you've got. I love the view."

"Yeah. It wasn't so great when I bought it. I've done a lot of work to fix it up."

"You do it yourself?" Mick shovelled a fork full of bacon and egg into her mouth.

"Yeah." Her next project was to build a huge deck and screen it in so she could sit outside and enjoy watching the sun set over the lake without being eaten alive by mosquitos. "Are you almost finished? I want to get going."

"Where?"

"What do you mean, where? Work." She gave Mick a playful slap up the side of the head and tried not to wince when the movement sent a flash of pain over her ribs.

"Um … You know you're supposed to take a few days off, right?"

Raven snorted. "As if."

With a sigh, Mick got up, cleared her plate off, set it in the dishwasher, and began to fill the sink to wash the pan she'd used to cook the bacon and eggs.

"Just let it soak." Raven tapped her fingers on the counter as she waited.

"What the heck is your hurry?" Mick asked. She dried her hands and then threw her jacket on. Raven was halfway to the car by the time Mick made it to the front door. "Should I lock it?"

"It's locked. Just pull it closed."

"Alrighty then." Mick pulled the door closed and jogged to the car, muttering, "I'm going to lose about ten pounds just chasing her around."

At the office, Raven went straight for her email and printed out the report from the coroner in Orillia. She scanned through it quickly, ignoring the words she couldn't pronounce or didn't understand. The bottom line was Ena did not have cancer. Ena's hair revealed she'd been ingesting arsenic for approximately a month before her death. Was it possible the chalice was laced with arsenic?

Yes. That's why it's missing.

"Oh, great. You're back."

I'm so sorry about yesterday, Rave.

Not talking to her. If I don't respond, maybe she'll get the hell out of my head and stay out. She placed a call to

Headquarters and arranged for a forensics team to scour her mom's place for the source of the arsenic and any evidence pertaining to her death. In the meantime, she sent a constable over to secure the house as a crime scene.

"Raven?"

Raven glanced up to see Mick charging across the room waving a file folder. She plopped herself down in the seat next to Raven's desk and threw the file folder in front of her, grinning ear to ear.

"What's this?"

"This is the common denominator in our red heads' Dating Pool profiles." Mick grinned again and squealed.

Raven flipped open the file and stared at the picture, then she slammed the folder closed and shot to her feet, the veins in her neck pulsing, her nostrils flaring in and out like a bull ready to charge. "Is this some kind of joke to you?"

Mick's smile disappeared, replaced by an open mouth and wide eyes. "No, of course not."

Picking up the folder, Raven slapped it against the desk. "This guy was linked to each of the vic's profiles?"

"Yes. He's the only one associated with all three. Why? What's wrong?"

It wasn't that hard to believe when she thought about it. The guy was a sexual predator who lived in the area. Raven knew exactly where he lived. It had been easy to do a property search and find his residence when she became a cop. She just expected him to prey on children. "Gregor Paigo?"

Mick took the folder from Raven and opened it on her lap. The photo depicted a man who appeared older than his 55 years. He looked like a gypsy with dark curly hair and a thick five o'clock shadow. He'd been a very good looking man in his day, but he looked haggard now. His dark eyes bore sagging circles and his skin was weathered. Mick's eyes travelled from the picture up to Raven.

"This is the guy who hurt you?"

Raven dropped back down into her chair before her knees gave out on her and winced. She'd forgotten how bruised up she was, but her body sure hadn't.

"Raven? Are you going to be able to handle this?"

She didn't deny or confirm Gregor had been the man who molested her for two years when he was seeing her mother. Mick knew. Could she handle investigating and arresting Gregor? Bet your ass, she could.

"We need more. Checking them out on a dating site isn't enough." Thinking of Riley, she logged onto the internet and navigated to the Dating Pool. She brought up Riley's profile page, but wasn't able to determine who viewed her profile or tagged her. "Get hold of the guy who did the initial search. I want to know what other red heads Gregor Paigo has been cyber-stalking."

Mick's colour drained from her face as she looked at Raven's screen. "You think he might try for Riley?"

"She fits the profile." A little too well for Raven's liking.

"We could use that."

She'd thought of it herself, but there was no way in hell she was going to put Riley in that position. "No, we'll find another way. We need evidence that Paigo was in Orillia at the time Emily McMurtrie went missing; Barrie when Sandra Kelway went missing; Gravenhurst when Charlene Brock went missing. We need solid evidence or a hell of a lot more circumstantial."

Mick's shoulders slumped forward. "I thought we had him. Crap."

"We will. We just have to build our case." She picked up the phone and called Dr. Mitchell. "Have you got anything back from the lab on DNA evidence in Emily McMurtrie's case?" She picked up a pen and grabbed a piece of paper out of her printer. "Yeah. Go ahead." She scribbled a number on the paper and pressed the release button on her phone. Then she dialed the new number. "Lab," she explained to Mick.

It took nearly ten minutes to get through to the tech who was processing the DNA evidence collected from Emily during the autopsy. Raven had to chock one up to cold Canadian winters, because the cold temperatures preserved evidence and they had a DNA profile. There was no match in the databanks, but if they could get a DNA sample from Gregor, they may have their case.

"Let's go for a drive."

Chapter 7

Gregor Paigo lived in a small, run down cabin on Gilleach Lake, south of Huntsville. Raven signed out a Suburban because the terrain to get to Gregor's cabin was treacherous and extremely muddy at this time of year. She wasn't going to risk getting the Charger stuck in the mud.

Mick had her hands spread out on the dashboard as they bumped over the hills and turns in the drizzling rain. Raven pulled the Suburban over to the side of the road and parked it. "We're going to walk the rest of the way. I want to get a look at the place without him seeing us or hearing the vehicle."

Raven opened her door and stared down at the muddy road for a moment then glanced down at her clean black boots. She'd known the road would be muddy, but she hadn't thought to bring waterproof footwear. She spotted a dry patch and made the leap only to double over, bend her right knee, and lift her leg. She hopped on her left foot for a moment and then eased her right leg down again. "Damn it."

Mick stood on the other side of the vehicle laughing. "Told ya you should have taken a couple of days off."

You have the power to heal yourself, Rave. Why don't you use it?

"Shut up." Raven limped to the side of the road where it was less muddy. They walked a couple of hundred yards down the road, their boots mushing through wet leaves, then turned south into the trees. The leaves weren't as soggy here and crunched under their feet. If Gregor was outside, he may be able to hear them, but no matter how quiet Raven tried to walk, the damn leaves and dry twigs crunched away. She pushed aside thin denuded branches reaching out from every direction. There was something haunting about being in the woods when the trees were bare. Once their leaves returned, it became a magical place to Raven. Especially when the sun speared through the canopy, falling in beams of light. She always felt like she could step into one of the beams and be transported somewhere else.

The cabin came into view, a dark shack with the lake behind it a dull grey under thick dark clouds. Raven breathed in the fresh lake air as a cool breeze gently swept over her face, soothing the raw skin and bruises. This was too beautiful a place for someone like Gregor. He didn't deserve the peace and quiet solitude of this serene setting.

A beat up old car with it's hood up, missing it's engine and wheels, sat at the side of the cabin, rust slowly eating it away. Car parts and other assorted bits of junk were scattered all around the property. The shingles on the roof peeled up at the corners and moss grew up the side of the north wall. The middle step of the three leading up to the front porch was missing and the deck appeared ready to collapse. The wood was grey, peeling in some places and green with moss in others.

One of the windows to the left of the front door, sported grey duct tape in an upside down Y shape repairing a crack. The screening on the screen door hung down from the top left corner and the old wooden door tilted precariously on its hinges.

Raven walked a little further down toward the water, getting a look at the back of the cabin. A sliding glass door led out to a sloping deck and, on the far side, a bay window jutted out from the dilapidated boards. The soft breeze now brought with it the distinct odour of sewage.

"Somebody actually lives here?" Mick wrinkled her nose and Raven snorted.

"It suits him." It may even be too good for the bastard.

"Jesus. Is that what I think it is?" Mick pointed to a small wooden building, about three feet by three feet and six feet tall. The door hung on an angle and featured a half moon cut into the top.

"An outhouse? Yeah."

"Eeew. Is that what smells?" Mick asked, pinching her nose.

"His truck's not here." Raven glanced at her watch. It was nearly noon. Gregor didn't work. He was on some sort of disability. She knew where Gregor would probably be. She'd seen his truck parked outside of The Muskokan, a local pub, nearly every day of the week from noon until he ran out of money or got too drunk. Or got kicked out. She wanted a look inside his house, but knew that, without a warrant, anything she found would be inadmissible. A damn cigarette butt would seal the deal, but she had no cause to go on his property and take it. "Let's take a drive and see if we can find him."

"What? You're just going to drive and hope you see his truck?"

"Nope. I'm going to drive by his favourite watering hole."

Mick trailed along after Raven, back through the dreary woods and down the muddy trail to the Suburban. They both wiped the mud off their boots with wet leaves.

"It's like he's living in 1920 or something." Mick climbed into the passenger seat with a scowl on her face. "It's nasty."

"Yeah, poor bugger. I'd much rather see him living out the rest of his pathetic life in a three by six cell with his toilet right next to his bed." Raven executed a three point turn and added, "And a big brute that calls him Sue sharing his cell." Mick laughed, but Raven was serious. "You have no idea how much better I'd sleep at night knowing he was locked up and being used as someone's little bitch every night."

"Raven?"

Raven's chest tightened, squeezing her lungs and making it hard to get enough air. She pulled to the side of the road, put the vehicle in park and jumped out. The pain that shot down her leg was almost welcome. It forced her mind off of Gregor and their past history. The mud made a sucking sound as she lifted her foot, but she just kept walking, making her way to the side of the road. She placed her hands on her hips and bent forward, wheezing.

Mick bent over next to her and placed a hand on her back, rubbing in a circular pattern. "Breathe in through your nose and out through your mouth." She demonstrated, taking a slow breath in and releasing it. Raven's breaths began to slow as she matched Mick's rhythm. "You know, you could have had him locked up any time by reporting what he did to you."

She knew it. Gregor Paigo was probably the reason she became a cop. She had this need deep inside her to see justice done for those who couldn't speak for themselves or defend themselves. But to report Gregor, to get justice for herself, she'd have had to risk Ena's life.

Swinging her arm around, Raven brushed Mick's hand from her back. "Alright, I'm good." She placed her hands on her knees, taking a few more breaths. "I'm good." The nightmares coming back and these little panic attacks or whatever they were had to stop. Between Ena and Gregor, all of the crap from back then was bubbling to the surface and she didn't know how the heck to push it all down again.

Mick took a step back and hooked her thumbs in her belt.

"Yeah, you're good alright."

"What the hell is that supposed to mean?"

"You know exactly what I mean. Raven, you need to talk about it."

You can talk to me, honey. I wish you'd told me when it happened.

Raven straightened and screamed at the sky. "Get the fuck out of my head. How many times do I have to say it?"

"Raven."

Mick placed her hand gently on Raven's arm and Raven pulled away forcefully. Her head was pounding again and her entire body throbbed. She pushed her hands into her hair and used her palms to massage her temples. "I'm sorry. I don't know what's gotten into me."

"Hmm." Mick cocked a hip, her head dipping to the side. "Lack of sleep and past trauma being triggered sound familiar?"

"Smart ass. Drive me somewhere I can buy a boatload of Advil, then we're going to the Muskokan."

"Whoohoo. Liquid lunch." Mick did a tip-toe dance trying to avoid the worst of the mud as she made her way to the driver's door.

"You're not drinking. You're going to see if you can swipe his glass or one of his cigarette butts." In her weakened state, mentally and physically, she didn't think she was ready for a face to face with Gregor. Especially when she had a Sig Sauer strapped to her waist.

"I am?"

"You are." Raven put her seat back and reclined. She thought it would feel glorious to lay back, but it only made the headache worse. She remained reclined, afraid if she lifted her head it would explode.

"Advil first," Mick said.

Raven opened one eye and looked up at Mick. She was

staring down at her with a frown and worry lines between her brow.

"Just drive. Please."

Mick sighed and put the car in gear. Raven was jostled around as Mick navigated the bumps and pot holes. She curled onto her left side and tried to ignore the burning pain from the road rash, her throbbing right thigh, the blinding pain in her head, and the incessant urge to throw up.

* * *

A short nap in the truck and a few Advil revived Raven enough she could hold her head up without feeling like someone slugged her with a baseball bat. Mick had changed into jeans and an oversized hoody to hide her weapon.

Gregor's white Dodge Ram truck was parked right in front of the Muskokan.

"So, I just mosey up to the bar, sit down next to him and order ... what?"

"I don't know. Coke, pepsi? What do you like to drink?"

Mick rolled her eyes. "A beer would be nice. He's really going to believe I dropped into a bar for an apple juice?"

Raven narrowed her eyes at Mick, but the kid was right. "One beer." She watched as Mick jumped out of the car and bounced across the parking lot to the bar. Raven stayed in the Charger, parked in the plaza next door. Although it was unmarked, it was pretty obvious it was a cop car. From where she was sitting, she had a great view of the patio at the back of the Muskokan where patrons went out for a smoke.

It was only about ten minutes later that Raven watched Gregor step out onto the back patio, light his cigarette, and take a long drag. He kept it between his lips as he hiked up his pants then took another long drag and blew it out. He looked like a harmless old man, but she knew better.

She was waiting for Mick to come out the back door and join him, so when Mick opened the driver's door, she nearly jumped out of her seat.

"Eeeeee." Mick held up a baggie with a beer mug sealed inside and squealed again.

"Shut up, will you?" She ducked down in the seat as Gregor looked over his shoulder at them. She didn't think he'd seen the mug, but he had seen Mick getting in the car. "Idiot."

"Sorry," Mick whispered.

"It's a little too late to whisper. The whole damn town heard you squeal like a pig."

"Well," Mick grinned. "I *am* a pig."

Raven shook her head as Mick laughed. She supposed the kid's adrenaline was pumping, so she couldn't blame her overzealousness.

When they got back to the detachment, Raven sent one of the constables on a run down to Orillia to deliver the mug to the lab. She typed up a quick report then grabbed Mick from the squad room and headed back out to the car.

"Haven't you had enough for the day?" Mick asked.

"Nope." What she wouldn't give to go home and crash. But, they had more than one investigation on the go. "I want to stop by my mom's and see how the forensics team is making out."

She tossed the car keys to Mick and Mick caught them one handed, but she just stood there.

"Look, I can go and check on the search and give you an update. Why don't I just drop you at home?"

Raven narrowed cold eyes at her and that got her butt moving toward the car. The drive over was quiet. Mick didn't say a word to Raven's relief. She didn't need Mick butting her nose into her business. She suspected the 'bits and pieces' Mick claimed to know about her was more than the pinch she indicated. She wanted to bury everything again, but she couldn't do that if Mick kept shoving it in her face.

The forensics mobile unit was on the street in front of Ena's house. A squad car sat in the driveway and another on the street. Mick pulled up behind the mobile unit and then looked over at Raven with those worry lines creasing her forehead and her lips pursed together.

"Are you sure you want to do this?"

"What is with you not wanting me to come here?" Having a psychic worrying over you going somewhere was unsettling to say the least. "What are you sensing?"

"Nothing. I – I'm just concerned about your health. You just got out of the hospital and you shouldn't be getting too stressed out."

"You didn't freak out about us going to Gregor's, but you're worried about me being stressed out here? Spill it, Warren. What's up?"

Mick raised her hands then dropped them to the steering wheel. "Nothing." Opening her door, she said, "Fine. Let's go."

It took Raven a minute to get herself out of the car and moving again. She was stiffening up and a hot bath was sounding better all the time. She tried to stretch her body, but it just made her hurt more. She approached a uniformed officer standing in the driveway. When he turned and she saw it was Constable Tate, she cringed. He was tall and lean with a shaved head to mask his baldness. He acted like he was God's gift, but Raven found him repulsive. "Constable Tate."

"Hey, DC." He screwed his face up. "Who won? The truck or the road?" He made a hacking sound like he was clearing phlegm from the back of his throat and Raven suppressed a gag.

"Ha. Funny." She didn't laugh. "How are things going here?"

"Smooth. Except for your dad over there. He's not too

happy about us being here."

"Excuse me?" Had she heard him right?

"Your dad. He's pissed."

"My dad?"

"Yeah. You know, the guy who lives here."

"What are you talking about? My mother was the only one living here, Tate."

"Oh. Well, isn't this interesting." He stuck his thumbs inside his duty belt, grinned from ear to ear then made the phlegmy sound, turned and spat on the lawn. "Why don't I introduce you to the tenant?" He nodded towards the house then followed Raven and Mick.

"Oh, boy," Mick said.

Raven stopped and turned to her then shot Tate the evil eye. "Is there something the two of you would like to share with me?"

"It's about bloody time. Are you the officer in charge of this fiasco?"

The voice coming from behind her had a thick Scottish accent. Raven turned and examined the tall, broad shouldered man walking towards her. He had raven black hair, ice blue eyes, and a face that was chiselled, strong, and downright beautiful. They studied each other, taking in the similarities, the differences. It was like looking at the male version of herself, although he was probably close to double her age. What little colour was in his face, drained. Even his lips turned white.

"You're Ena's daughter?" he asked.

"Who the fuck are you?"

He combed his fingers through his thick black hair at the same time as Raven then they both fisted their hands at their sides.

"Oh, this is good," Tate said with a snicker.

"Shut up." Raven and the beautiful man said together.

Oh, dear. Raven, honey, this is Kiran Hayes. My husband. Your father.

Raven's hand slid through her hair again and fisted there. "What the …?" Mick was at her side as she dropped to her knees then the man kneeled in front of her.

"I knew Ena had a daughter, love, but I swear to the Goddess I never knew you were mine. Why the bloody hell didn't she tell me?" He reached for Raven's hands and she pulled them away.

"You're Wiccan? You're a witch?" Raven asked in a hoarse whisper.

"Aye, love."

"Don't call me love."

"I'm sorry. I'm in a bit of shock as well, aye?"

Raven looked up at him, studying his face again. God, she was his spit. Except for the five o'clock shadow. Her hand brushed over her cheek then slid down over her throat as if to be sure she didn't have his stubble or Adam's apple.

"Why don't we go inside?" Mick said.

Raven looked around and it wasn't just Tate watching the show now. Three constables stood there gaping at them. "Aren't you people supposed to be doing something?"

"Not really," Tate answered. "We're securing the scene. It's looking pretty secure at the moment."

Mick helped Raven to her feet. Her face was on fire and it wasn't from the road rash. She let Mick help her inside, her eyes on the man in front of her. He kept looking over his shoulder, offering a thin lipped smile and then turning to look where he was going again. The forensics team was working in the kitchen, so they went to the living room, or the front parlour as Ena called it.

"I take it from your reaction Ena didn't tell you about me either, love." He stabbed his fingers through his hair then lowered himself into a black leather armchair. It fit him, like he belonged in that chair next to the fireplace.

"When did you marry my mother? Why didn't I know about it?"

"Well, lass, you weren't exactly on the best terms with your mum now, were you?"

"You weren't at her funeral."

"Ach, no. I couldn't get back on time, could I? We were at sea in the Med."

"Who's we?"

"Sorry, pet, I should introduce myself. Chief Petty Officer Kiran Hayes, Her Majesty's Royal Navy. And you? What's your name then?"

Did he just call her *pet*? "You're married to my mom and you don't know my name?" His hand slid through his ebony locks again and Raven found it oddly endearing. She had an idea now why people found her dark lashes and ice blue eyes so attractive. She couldn't take her eyes off his.

"God, I can't believe this is happening. Why didn't she say anything? Not a word? I knew she had a daughter, but she told me you didn't talk, didn't see each other. I'm afraid I don't know anything about you, love."

"Will you stop calling me love?" How could Ena do this? Her father was right here and Ena never thought to tell them about each other? Who does that? "I'm Detective Constable Raven Sage Bowen, Ontario Provincial Police."

"Well, that's fitting, isn't it? Serving your country like your father." His eyes sparkled as he grinned at her. "Aye, you're mine through and through. Are you always so banged up, love?" He swiped his hand through his hair and laughed. "Sorry, I can't help calling you love, for that's what I'm feeling, yeah? God, you're a bonnie sight, even if you look like you've been struck by a lorry."

"She was," Mick said.

Kiran's eyes widened. "You were struck by a lorry? Are

you alright then?"

"Fine." Raven's headache was back with a vengeance. She had so many questions she didn't know where to start. It was all too overwhelming. "You left before my mom learned she was pregnant with me. Why? Why did you leave?" If he'd stayed, Ena never would have ended up with that creep Gregor. How different things would have been if he hadn't bailed.

"I was twenty-five and madly in love with your mum. It was too much. I still had so much I wanted to do, aye? I went home to Scotland and then down to Portsmouth where I joined the Navy. I didn't stay in touch, so I suppose it's my fault. I was just so scared. Do you understand? For a young man to feel that much for a woman … well, I ran scared, didn't I?"

"Oh, Raven." Mick lowered herself to the arm of Raven's chair. "You can't think of it like that. You can't turn back the clock and change anything now."

"Would you shut up?" Raven growled through gritted teeth. "Go and get an update from the forensics team or something."

Mick pursed her lips and rose to her feet. "I was just trying to help."

Raven narrowed her eyes at her, her jaw muscles working back and forth. "You can help by getting an update on the search."

"How about I see if I can find something for your headache while I'm at it?" As she left the room, she muttered, "And something for your rotten mood."

"I heard that."

Kiran was on his feet and took a step closer to Raven. "I could mix you up a headache remedy, but they've banned me from the kitchen. Is it very bad?"

Raven had a weird sensation in her belly. It rose up her

chest to the back of her throat and her eyes burned. It must be from the concussion. She just wasn't feeling herself. She dropped her head into her hands and breathed. When she felt a little steadier, she rose to her feet.

"When she comes back in, tell her to send the update to my cell." She turned to leave, knowing she was running. But, hey, apparently it ran in the family. She fled out the door with the image of Kiran standing there with his mouth open and his beautiful eyes bulging.

She had one of the uniforms drive her home because Mick had her car keys. It wasn't until she got to her door and the uniform was driving away that she realized her house key was also on the ring Mick had.

* * *

Mick found Raven curled up on a Muskoka chair on her deck.

"That should teach you not to abandon your partner at a crime scene," she said as she helped Raven to her feet.

The cold must have seized her muscles up even more than they already were because Raven felt like a ninety year old, hunched over as Mick helped her to the front door. She was too tired and sore to be embarrassed though. Mick unlocked the door and Raven sighed as she stepped into the warmth. "Just take the car and pick me up in the morning."

"Don't you want the update from forensics?" Mick stepped inside and closed the door behind her.

"In the morning." Mick was a big girl. She could see herself out. Raven headed straight for her bathroom and ran a nice, hot, lavender scented bath. She sat on the edge of the tub for a moment while the room filled with steam and let it warm her. It wasn't that cold out, but she was chilled to the bone.

She waited until the tub was filled before she stood and stripped down. Then she scowled at herself in the steamy mirror. Ignoring the bruises and scrapes, she focused on the features she shared with Kiran Hayes. "Hmmph." There was no mistaking the jet black hair and blue eyes as pale as icebergs. But the shape of her eyes were also his, and the triangular jaw, minus the road rash. Her height was probably from him as well. Ena had been around five foot six, but Raven stood five feet ten. Kiran was well over six foot with wide shoulders and a narrow waist. He shared her love of working out by the looks of it. She wondered if he ran, too, then thought there probably wasn't a lot of room on a navy ship for running.

Ena hadn't told her much about her father. Only that he left before she knew she was pregnant and she never heard from him again. She must have loved him if she married him. She never expressed an interest in marrying any of her other lovers.

Remember I told you I had only ever felt love the way you love Riley once?

Raven eased herself into the steaming hot bath. "You really don't want to be around me right now. You think I was angry when I ran away from home? Why the hell wouldn't you have told me he was here and that you married him?"

Why didn't you tell me about Gregor?

"That's not even close to the same thing." Raven pulled her legs into her chest and let her head fall to her knees. "Go away."

I made a lot of mistakes and I've caused you a lot of pain, Rave. I'm sorry.

"Go away," Raven repeated. She tried to clear her foggy mind. There was too much stuff jumbled up inside of her head. She didn't need Ena in there adding to the mix.

I'm sorry, darling angel.

Ena hadn't called her that since she was a little girl. That weird feeling swirled around in her belly again, climbing up through her chest and catching in her throat. Her breath caught and she had to take some slow, deep breaths to steady her breathing again. She fisted her hands in her hair and let out a wild, primal scream. One of the advantages to living where she did was not having to worry about the neighbours hearing. Not that she screamed on a regular basis, but sometimes you needed to let off some steam before you blew. And she was close to blowing.

"Rave?"

Raven jolted at the sound of Riley's voice, surprised to see her standing in the bathroom doorway. For her not to notice someone come into her house, never mind into her bathroom, she had to be extremely distracted with everything buzzing around in her head. "What are you doing here?"

"Mick called me."

Raven narrowed her eyes. "Why?"

"Don't get your panties in a twist. She was worried about you and for good reason by the looks of it." Riley grabbed a white, fluffy towel from the rack. "Here. Let's get you out of there."

"I can get myself out of the damn tub." She batted away Riley's arm and grabbed on to the sides of the tub to push herself up. She made it about six inches before her elbows gave out and she dropped with a splash. She batted Riley's arm away again and managed to turn herself around and get to her knees.

"You really don't need to stand there and babysit me. It's humiliating enough without you staring at me." That sick feeling swirled through her stomach again, soaring up her chest and then sticking at the back of her throat. Her eyes burned and her breath caught. She wrapped her arms around her belly, leaned forward and groaned.

"Did they take x-rays of your ribs, Rave?"

"How the hell should I know? I was unconscious for most of it." She didn't think her ribs were broken anyway. It wasn't that kind of pain.

Riley sat down on the edge of the tub despite it being soaking wet. "It's alright to cry, Rave."

Bracing a hand on the edge of the tub, Raven turned to glare at Riley. "Why the hell would I cry?" She pushed herself up from her knees to her feet and grabbed the towel from Riley's lap. Her breaths were still ragged like she had no control over the sudden gasping.

"You're fighting it. You're right on the edge of a good, sobbing cry and you're fighting it." Riley took Raven's hand as she stepped over the edge of the tub.

She didn't cry. Not since she was a scared little girl. But, now she knew what that weird feeling in her belly, chest, and throat was. Raven dried herself off and grabbed her robe from a hook on the back of the door. She was about to shrug into it when Riley stopped her. "Let me take a look at your injuries first."

Raven hugged the towel to her body. "I'm fine, Ri. They released me from the hospital and they wouldn't do that if I wasn't okay."

"They released you with orders to take it easy for a few days."

"Why are you here? We're not together anymore. You have no obligation to take care of me. Just go." Oh, crap. That sensation was spreading through her again, making her eyes burn.

"You need to learn to accept help even if you won't ask for it. You don't have to go through all of this alone, Rave. Yeah, we're not together anymore, but that doesn't mean I don't still care about you."

Raven held her hand up, palm out. "Don't come here and say stuff like that when you're seeing someone else."

"Rave?"

"Seriously, Ri. Just go. I don't need your help." She limped into the bedroom, dropped the towel and slipped under her duvet. She laid on her stomach because it seemed to be the least painful position and turned her head away from the bathroom. She could sense Riley still standing there, but she was too tired and sore to deal with her. Riley needed to take care of someone. She was a born nurturer, so being off work she probably figured she would nurse Raven back to health. She didn't need a damn nurse.

She heard someone come in the front door and walk across the living room. Then Mick's voice called out, "I filled the prescription." The rustling of a paper bag came from the doorway of the bedroom. "Ri? You still here?"

"Yeah," Riley whispered. "Raven? Mick filled your prescription for pain meds. I'm just going to leave it on your nightstand and we're leaving."

"Fine. Bye." She listened as Riley laid the bag on the bedside table and then walked out to the living room with Mick. Mick must have found the prescription on the kitchen counter and gone out to fill it. She wasn't planning on getting it filled. Would they stop her from feeling like she was going to cry? She'd take them for that. She listened for the front door to open and close, but dozed off before she heard it.

* * *

It was still dark when Raven woke, although the sky had begun to lighten. Surprisingly, she'd slept quite well for a change. No nightmares, no tossing and turning, no waking up from pain. She felt like the tin man from the Wizard of Oz, though. A can of oil might help to loosen the stiffness in her muscles and joints. Sitting on the edge of her bed, she eyed the prescription bottle sitting on the bedside table. Did she take the risk of the pain medication making her loopy or persevere through the pain? She settled on a hot shower. By the time she dressed, she was moving a little easier.

Heading to the kitchen, she found Riley passed out on her

104

couch. She just shook her head and continued on. With a coffee in hand, she eased into her armchair and watched the day bloom over Fairy Lake, which seemed to match her mood – grey and dreary. She couldn't comprehend why Ena hadn't told her about Kiran. Even worse, Adara must have known about him and she hadn't said a word either. That, somehow, hurt more than her mother keeping it from her. She hadn't spoken to her mother in years, but she spoke to Adara every day.

Raven finished her coffee, put on a warm jacket and started searching for her keys. She searched all the usual places before she remembered Mick still had them. She peeked out at the driveway to be sure. Riley's car sat in her driveway, but the Charger was gone.

She called for a taxi and left a note for Riley.

Raven let herself in the back door and found Adara in the kitchen baking bread. She stood just inside the door for a moment inhaling the aroma and her stomach grumbled.

"Oh, good morning, honey. How are you feeling?"

Adara started across the kitchen and then stopped in her tracks as she studied Raven's face. Her smile faded away and she wrung her hands in front of her. "What is it, hon?"

"How long have Ena and Kiran been married?" Adara was the one person she trusted, the one person she thought had her back all this time. And she hadn't.

"Oh, dear. Well, I guess it must be coming up on ten years or so."

Heat shot up Raven's neck and exploded onto her face. "My father has been here all these years and you never thought to tell me?"

"Aah, but …" Her hands began to redden as she twisted them repeatedly. "He wasn't here very often, was he? He was at sea more than he was home."

"Why didn't you say anything? It's not like it's not obvious

I was his. I can understand why Ena didn't say anything, but you? I trusted you, Adara."

Adara's eyes lowered and she spoke softly. "It wasn't my place to tell you, now was it?"

Raven swiped her hand through her hair then massaged the back of her neck. "Were you reporting back to Ena about me all these years?" Raven didn't need to wait for a response, she saw her answer in Adara's reaction. She winced a teeny bit. It was barely detectable, but she caught it. She spun around, opened the door, and was through it faster than she thought her battered body could move. She hadn't realized how hard she pulled the door closed until she heard it slam behind her.

Her heart pounded in her chest as if it was desperate to escape. She felt a little dizzy, but pushed through it. It wouldn't do to pass out in the middle of the street. She'd let the taxi go, so she ploughed ahead, her adrenaline shrouding the pain.

It took her about thirty minutes to walk to the detachment and pull herself together. The bullpen was quiet. Dayshift officers hadn't arrived and the night shift had yet to come in from patrol for shift change. That gave her time to catch up on the reports from the autopsy and the search of Ena's house. The report from the lab on whether Gregor's DNA was a match for the evidence collected from Emily McMurtrie, Charlene Brock, and Sandra Kelway should be coming in soon as well.

She turned on her computer and went in search of caffeine while it booted up. A pot of coffee sat on the burner in the squad room that appeared to be more solid than fluid and smelled worse than it looked. She dumped it in the sink and got a fresh pot brewing. Leaning against the counter, she thought about Adara. She was the sweetest, most caring person Raven knew. But, now she was asking herself if she knew her at all. Adara had only taken her in at Ena's request and that was so Ena could keep tabs on her. Why? She hadn't cared what was happening to her under her own damn roof, but she wanted Adara to tell her everything going on in her life?

Of course I cared what was happening to you. Why didn't you say something?

"Damn you. Not here. Not now."

You said I didn't see you. Is that why you thought that? Because I didn't see what happened? I'll never forgive myself for that, for failing you, sweet angel.

Raven fisted her hand in her hair and pulled. She was either going to scream bloody murder or lose control of the tears that were fighting to get out again. With her jaw clenched, she said, "If you really gave a shit, why didn't you come for me?"

I did. I followed you, but you wouldn't have talked to me, Rave. Not in the state you were in. I figured you would talk to Adara and then we could work it out and you would come home. But, you didn't talk to her. You didn't talk to anyone, did you? Why, sweet angel? Why didn't you say something?

Raven started to push back against the memory that Ena's questions evoked then stopped herself. If Ena wanted to know, she would let her see it, let her experience it. She closed her eyes tight and remembered Gregor's stinking hand pressing over her mouth, his whiskey soaked breath filling her nose and curdling in her belly. His rusty voice whispering in her ear, *'Make a noise and I'll kill your mom. Wake her up and she's dead.'*

She let the whole sordid rape play out in her head and then his breath, warm and sticky against her ear, *'Tell anyone and she's dead. It will be your fault, Raven. You will have killed her.'*

"Rave? You okay?"

Raven opened her eyes to see silver haired Constable Gayle

Trewellyn staring at her. "Yeah." Her voice came out gravelly so she cleared her throat. "Yeah, just thinking through a case."

Gayle had been her training officer when she was a rookie. They rode together quite a bit on patrol, too. She'd put on a few pounds over the past few years after sustaining a back injury in a vehicular accident. She walked with a limp and Raven was always able to identify her by her gait whenever she was near, but she hadn't even heard her approach.

Gayle pulled two mugs down from the cupboard and filled them from the full pot of coffee. "Would that be the one involving your mom?"

"That would be one of them." Raven accepted the mug Gayle handed her and blew on it before taking a sip.

"Do you think that's wise? Investigating your own mother's death?"

"You know we weren't close."

"Doesn't matter. She was still your mom, Rave."

Raven took another cautious sip from her mug. She'd made a promise to Ena and she intended to see it through. She thought she might run into some interference from rank, but she hadn't expected to get it from Gayle.

"Remember the first lesson I taught you?"

It wasn't one she'd ever forget. Gayle hammered it into her frequently. "Never get emotionally involved in a case. I know." She still wasn't going to pass the case on to someone else.

Gayle blew out an exasperated breath. "You're not going to take my advice, are you?"

"If your advice is for me to walk away from this one, no, I'm not."

"You always were a stubborn little shit." Gayle pursed her lips then the edges of her mouth rose ever so slightly. "Well, I suppose you better give us a shout if you need backup."

Raven nodded and started to walk away. At the door, Gayle called after her and she turned to look over her shoulder.

"Put some ice on that face, would ya? It hurts to look at you."

Raven laughed. "Yeah, I'll get right on that."

Back at her desk, she opened her email and scanned through the inbox until she found the email from Dr. Maxwell. She read through Ena's autopsy report again and then Googled arsenic poisoning. Ena's hands and feet had the same weird rash listed as a side effect of arsenic poisoning. Why hadn't the ER doctor noticed the rash? She pulled a notepad out of her drawer and wrote down the questions she had. Was it possible to lace the chalice with arsenic so that Ena was ingesting a bit every day or did someone add the arsenic to whatever Ena drank out of it? What did she drink out of a chalice anyway? Eye of newt? Okay, eww. It was probably wine instead of some weird potion and it was more likely that someone put arsenic in the wine, not on the chalice.

Then why would the chalice and the card go missing?

Why was Ena so calm after what she'd let her see? The other day she'd sobbed like a child. Raven expected her to royally freak out.

I didn't cry the other day, Rave. And I never sob like a child.

"Uh, yes, you did. That's why I got hit by a damn truck. All I could hear was your wailing. I couldn't think and I charged out into the intersection without looking." Raven waited for a response, but was met by silence. Frowning, she went back to her email. There was nothing from the lab on Gregor's DNA and nothing from the forensics team on the search of Ena's house. She should have had them by now. She picked up the phone and put in a call to the forensics lab in Orillia.

The reports were sent to Constable McHaela Warren.

Raven's face burned when she got off the phone. She massaged her throbbing temples then opened her desk drawer for her bottle of Advil. The contents of the drawer were meticulously organized – pens lined up ruler straight with the caps all facing the same direction, notepads stacked neatly, paperclips in a small dispenser, stapler on the right side next to the staple remover. The bottle of Advil should have been sitting next to the paperclip dispenser. There was a small, one inch by one inch empty space instead. She slammed the drawer closed then had to open it again to put everything she just scattered back in its rightful place.

She forgot about the Advil when her computer pinged the arrival of a new email and she read over the reports she'd requested. The first report explained there was no trace of arsenic found in Ena's house save for the hair collected from her hairbrush. "Did you have a bottle of wine around that you drank from the chalice?"

Silence.

"A jar of eye of newt?"

Crickets chirped.

Great. When I actually need you, you're unavailable. Where did she go when she wasn't in Raven's head annoying her? "Hmmph." Raven looked around the bullpen, as if she might find her mother hanging around there. "Did a bottle of wine come with the flowers and chalice? Did someone take that, too?"

Raven turned back around at the sound of boots making their way down the hall and Mick popped her head around the corner.

"Oh, hey Raven. You're in early."

An ice blue glare froze Mick. "Care to explain to me why my reports were sent to you?"

"Oh … um." Mick's eyes travelled around the room and then came back to settle on Raven's. "DS LaCroix thought you should take it easy for a few days. So, you know … I, um, told him I could handle the cases."

"And why, exactly, did DS LaCroix think I needed a few days off?" Heat spread over Raven's cheeks again. She could almost feel the steam shooting out of her ears.

Mick took a step into the room with her shoulders slumped. "I, um, might have told him you weren't quite yourself."

"Oh, you're a doctor now? You've diagnosed me as unfit for duty?" Where the hell did Mick get off thinking she had the right to tell anyone she wasn't herself? Mick didn't even know her enough to know who she was.

Mick bravely walked the rest of the distance to Raven's desk and plopped herself down in the chair next to it.

"I'm sorry, Raven. You can't blame me after yesterday. I can't imagine the amount of stress you're under, not to mention your past being stirred up and brought to the surface."

Raven shot to her feet and lasered Mick with a death stare. "You have no right to get involved in my business. Do you understand, Constable?"

Mick flinched and shrunk into the chair. "Yes, Detective Constable. I understand." She pushed herself out of the chair and sulked out of the room.

Raven sank back into her chair and dropped her head into her hands. "Damn it." She couldn't deny she was holding onto her composure by a thin wire, ready to snap. And it wasn't Mick's fault. The kid was worried about her.

While she tried to decide if she should go after Mick or not, she opened the email with the results on Gregor's DNA from the beer mug Mick had procured. Raven read through the report twice because she couldn't believe it. There was no DNA found on the mug and the only fingerprints belonged to the bartender. It didn't make sense. She printed off a copy of the report and went in search of Mick.

She found her sitting in the squad room sipping a cup of coffee and looking like a kicked puppy. Raven took the seat across from her. "I suppose I owe you an apology."

Mick looked up at her and shook her head. "No, you're right. I stuck my nose in your business and I shouldn't have said anything to LaCroix. It wasn't my place."

"You shouldn't have called Riley last night either. She's not my girlfriend anymore."

Mick's eyebrows drew together and she narrowed her eyes. "I couldn't just leave you alone, Raven. Who else could I have called? Jaxon? Adara?"

Raven's hand dragged through her hair, leaving it sticking up. "No, you shouldn't have called anyone. I'm a big girl. I can take care of myself."

"Okay, next time I'll leave you to it." Frowning, Mick stared down at her coffee.

"I suppose you got a copy of the results from the DNA test on the beer mug?" Raven placed the printed report on the table and spun it around with the tips of her fingers so that it was right side up for Mick.

Mick's face reddened. "Yeah."

"Any idea why there was no DNA on the mug?"

Mick shifted in her seat, glanced up at Raven then dropped her head again. "The bartender had just poured him a new pitcher. She must have replaced his mug, too." She glanced up at Raven again. "I was watching Gregor. I didn't notice her switch the mugs out."

Shit. Now she'd have to figure out another way to get his DNA. She pushed to her feet as her cell phone began ringing and fished it out of her pocket.

"Bowen."

"Hey, Detective. This is Eric Theissen, the eTech at HQ. I've been fishing in the Dating Pool."

"Haha."

"Sorry. Couldn't help it. Anyway, I found three other red heads that Paigo has been monitoring. One in Penatang, another one in Orillia, and one in Solstice."

Shit. "Give me the name of the one in Solstice."

"I've just got a screen name. Care4U. I can get a full name, but it will take me a little longer."

"Get me the names on the other two and send them to my email. I've got a name for Care4U." She ended the call and dropped back into the chair. "He's monitoring Riley's Dating Pool profile."

"Oh, no." The blush drained out of Mick's face and her eyes widened. "What do we do now?"

"Saddle up. She's not going to want to hear this from me." Riley would think Raven wanted her to take her profile down from the dating website out of jealousy. She went back to her desk, shut down her computer, and grabbed her coat. Mick paced back and forth beside the car as Raven approached.

"I'm really sorry. I should have kept my eyes on the mug. I didn't even think. I just assumed it was the mug he'd been drinking out of. God, I'm such an idiot. I just got so excited that I got his DNA and got out of there."

"Mick? Shut up."

Mick came to a stop and looked up at Raven, her eyes drawn together.

Raven rested her forearms on the roof of the car. "It's done. Get over it. We'll figure out another way to get his DNA."

"If he hurts Riley, it's all my fault."

Oh, Jesus. If she could have reached over the car, she'd slap Mick up the side of her head to knock the stupid out of her. "Do you really think I'd let him get to Riley?"

"N-no, but…"

"No, stop that. Give your head a shake and snap out of your 'it's all my fault' pity party. We had an opportunity and it didn't pan out, so we move on. We're not going to stand here for half an hour and beat ourselves up over it. Got it?"

Mick nodded her head and slipped into the passenger seat. She kept her head down the entire drive to Riley's apartment building. Was she still kicking herself for not getting Gregor's DNA or was something else bothering her? Raven stared at her, trying to get a read, but she just wasn't sure what was up with her. "Are you going to sulk all day?"

"No." Mick popped her head up and frowned. "We're here. Sorry, I was … never mind." She clicked out of her seat belt and exited the car.

Raven scanned the parking lot and spotted Riley's car sitting in its usual spot. So, she'd wakened up and headed home. She used her key to let them in instead of buzzing up.

"Should you still have that?"

From sulking to interfering again. Great. This was going to be a long friggin' day.

"Have you ever heard of something called boundaries?" Raven asked.

Mick scowled, but it shut her up. Raven took the stairs two at a time despite the pain shooting down her right leg. She knew it was petty, but she smiled a bit as she listened to Mick's boots slapping on every step and her huffing and puffing as she tried to keep up. She waited for her at the top, raising her eyebrows. "A little out of shape, Mick?"

"Shut up," she panted. She bent at the waist, braced her hands on her knees and slowed her breathing. "You did that on purpose."

"What?" Raven raised her eyebrows again. "Did I force you to try to keep up?" She pulled the door open and breezed through it, letting it start to close behind her.

Mick's mild expletive sang out as she grabbed for the door.

Raven gave Riley's door a few good wraps with her knuckles and waited while Mick propped herself against the wall, still wheezing a bit, her cheeks flushed. Raven knocked again, a little harder and longer.

"Riley? Open up."

"Maybe she's not home yet."

"Her car's in the lot."

"Oh." Mick pushed off the wall, pulled her flashlight from her belt and banged on the door with it. They were met with silence.

Raven and Mick's eyes met, silently conveying they were both thinking the same thing. Raven took a step back, let her adrenalin power her kick which landed just north of the door knob. It splintered and she gave it another good kick to blow it wide open. As if Raven and Mick had practiced the routine for years, Mick went in low and to the left, Raven high and to the right, weapons drawn. They cleared the kitchen and living room and made their way to the hallway. As they rounded the corner, the gushing sound of the shower met their ears.

Raven pushed the bathroom door open, tip-toed in, and drew the shower curtain open a few inches. Riley let out a scream worthy of a Hitchcock film and clutched her hands over her heart. "Jesus, Rave. What the hell? You scared the shit out of me."

Raven pulled the curtain closed and leaned back against the wall, her heart pounding like a tribal drum. "You scared the holy bejeezus out of me, too."

Chapter 8

Raven stood at Riley's living room window, looking out over their little town. She could see Ena's house from here, standing proud on its hill above Fairy Lake. It made her think of Kiran Hayes wandering its rooms, stepping out into the huge yard to stand like a sentry looking out over the town or down on the lake. It suited him, that place of power. It would be his now, she supposed.

I told you the house is yours now, Rave. It's your place now.

Great. She's back. Raven turned to see Mick sunk in Riley's comfy leather couch. The creamy colour stood out against the dark rusts and browns of the area rug. She looked uncomfortable, sitting at attention as the couch tried to swallow her in its depths. Raven turned back to look out the window, gazing up at Ena's house. Why? Why give the house to her when it was Kiran's home?

It has been passed down through generations of Bowen women. It was passed to me by my mother with a promise it would be passed to my daughter. As you will pass it to your daughter.

Assuming I have one, Raven thought.

Oh, you will, my darling angel. You will have one, indeed. Just as you came to me as an unexpected gift, so too will yours.

Riley chose that moment to make her entrance. Her flaming red hair hung down her back in wild curls, still damp. Her pale green eyes hurled daggers at Raven, such a contrast to those cute little freckles speckling her nose. She wore a hunter green sweater, jeans, and bare feet that Raven found irresistibly sexy.

Riley cocked a hip, arms akimbo. "So, what's so damn urgent that you two found it necessary to break down my door?"

"You," Raven answered. "You're what's urgent and important." She nodded to the couch. "Have a seat and we'll tell you all about it." She waited until Riley perched herself on the edge of the couch and folded her arms across her chest.

"You've heard about the body of a young girl who was found outside of town a few days ago?"

"Yes." Riley's arms unfolded and she began to wring her hands in her lap. "What's that got to do with me?"

"She had red hair, green eyes."

"Do you know how many people have red hair and green eyes?" Riley asked.

Raven took a seat on the coffee table, facing Riley. "All of the victims who we believe are tied to the same offender have profiles on the Dating Pool."

Riley's eyes widened as the colour drained from her face. "You think that's where he's finding his victims?"

"Yeah." Raven nodded. Riley was getting it now.

"And you broke down my door when I didn't answer, thinking he had me in here?"

Mick tried to push herself up from the grips of the couch. Her feet went up in the air then came back down in a flash as her hips shot up and she hurled her body forward. It was like watching someone do that worm dance move on the floor. Both Riley and Raven broke out laughing.

"You could have just asked for a hand," Raven said.

With her face flushed bright red, Mick glared at Raven then

turned to Riley. "Before Raven asks you to take your profile down, would you consider being bait?"

"Mick? She's not going to be bait." Raven bent her head and took a deep breath. "We're not going to put her at risk."

"That would be my decision to make, wouldn't it? How many women has this guy hurt?"

Raven threw her head up and glared at Riley. "No, it's not your decision to make. I'm not letting this bastard get anywhere near you. Do you understand?"

Riley pursed her lips, narrowed her eyes. "No, I don't. If standing as bait helps to get this guy off the streets, to stop him from hurting anyone else, I'm all in. Do *you* understand, Detective?"

Raven shot to her feet and went back to the window, her fists clenched tightly. She stared out over her town, unseeing, images of Gregor doing to Riley what he'd done to her flashing through her brain.

"Just stop that. Stop that, right now." Mick charged to Raven and grabbed her upper arms. "That's not going to happen to Riley. We won't let that happen to her."

"Let what happen to me?" Riley asked as she joined them at the window. "What did you see, Mick? What was Raven thinking?"

Raven pulled her arms from Mick's grasp, her eyes moving back and forth between the two women. "Just how well do you two know each other?" She watched as if in slow motion Mick and Riley shared a quick glance then averted their eyes. "You're seeing each other?"

"It's not like that," Riley responded, but she still wouldn't look at Raven. "We're just friends."

"Then why do you both look so damn guilty?"

Riley slowly raised her head, meeting Raven's stare. "Because our friendship blossomed from talking about you." She shrunk back at Raven's glare. "Don't take it the wrong way. It's because we both care about you, Rave. We're both worried about you."

So, what? They'd been getting together behind her back and discussing all of her issues and –. Raven whirled around and gave Mick an icy death stare. "You didn't tell her –?" Oh, Jesus. Mick's eyes widened as that bright pink tinge returned to her cheeks.

"I wouldn't discuss that with anyone. Do you trust me so little?"

Raven sucked in a deep, audible breath through flared nostrils. "Trust you? You reached into my memories without my permission and stole something that didn't belong to you."

Mick's hands came up, palms out as she took a step back. "I can't help what pops into my head."

Raven pressed her fingers to her temples and told herself to breathe. She can't help what pops into her head? She knew what it was like to live like that. Walking around taking in everyone's crap, knowing what they were thinking about you. Was that why she suppressed her own *gift*?

Rave? Maybe it is time for you to let it out. Maybe that's why it popped into her head. You've been carrying it around with you for so long, bearing that burden all alone. It breaks my heart, darling angel. It breaks my heart.

Oh, damn. Raven swallowed, trying to rid herself of that urge to let go that was crawling up her throat again, flooding her burning eyes. "Shut up." She pressed the heels of her palms to her eyes. "Just shut the hell up."

Riley took a cautious step back, her eyes wide before they narrowed to slits. "It's not her fault, Rave. You don't have to yell at her like that."

Mick reached out a hand and gently grasped Riley's forearm. "It's okay. It's not me she's yelling at."

Dropping her hands from her face, Raven's eyes softened

on Riley. "I don't want that bastard anywhere near you. Because I know what he'd do to you. Because he raped me repeatedly from the time I was twelve until I was fourteen." She put a hand on the windowsill to steady herself and dropped her eyes to the floor. "I know what he'd do to you."

Repeatedly? Oh, dear Goddess, Rave. I thought it was only once. No wonder you hate me so much. No wonder you thought I didn't see you.

"I need to sit down." Ignoring Ena's words, Raven strolled stiffly to the armchair and collapsed into it, covering her face with her hands.

Why did everyone say talking about it made you feel better? She didn't feel better at all. Her stomach pitched and swirled, her eyes burned, and she wanted to scream or, even better, punch someone.

"You wonder why we're worried about you, Rave," Riley said. She sat on the arm of the chair and rubbed her hand up and down Raven's back. "You're working two cases – one involving your mother and the other involving your abuser. Rave? You can't keep this up."

Her breaths fired out in short gasps. She just needed to relax her tensed muscles and get her breathing slowed down and she'd be fine. Why had she told Riley? Stupid.

Riley slid off the arm of the chair and went to her knees in front of Raven. "Rave? It's okay to let it out, to cry. You're safe here. You know you are. Just let it out, babe."

No. Raven shook her head. She wasn't about to cry. She wasn't about to let Gregor Paigo make her weak and pathetic again. She wasn't going to give him that. She scrubbed her hands over her face then pushed to her feet. Riley leaned back on her heels as Raven stepped around her and went back to the window, bracing her hands on the sill. Looking up at Ena's house again, she thought it would never be hers. She could never live in that house with all of its horrible memories.

She shook her head again, trying to clear those memories from her thoughts. She needed to focus on the job. Riley was wrong there. She didn't need to pull back from the investigations. She needed them to keep her stable.

"I need you to delete your profile from the Dating Pool. Don't post anything on social media saying where you are or what you're doing." She turned from the window to face Riley. "If there is somewhere else you could stay for the time being, do it."

She turned her attention to Mick, who perched on the edge of the couch. "We figure out another way to get his DNA and go from there. I'll arrange for surveillance on Riley and the two other potentials."

Mick nodded silently and Raven wondered just how much of her thought process had 'popped' into her head. Turning back to Riley, she asked, "Is there somewhere you can stay?"

The left side of Riley's mouth turned up as she squeezed her eyes shut. "No, not that I can think of. Anyway, once my door's fixed, I'll be fine. I won't open the door unless it's someone I know."

Considering how easily she got through the door, Raven wasn't secure in Riley being safe here. Why she hadn't thought to use her key instead of kicking down the door, she had no idea. She supposed she panicked, too desperate to get through the door to think about using her key. "Would you consider staying at my place until we have him in custody?" At least she had a security system and Gregor wouldn't know she was there.

Riley blew a breath out from between her lips, making a raspberry sound. When her eyes met Raven, her brows were drawn in. "If I agree to stay, you have to understand that it doesn't mean we're getting back together."

"Understood." And she did understand, even if it tore her

heart a little more.

While she waited for Riley to pack, she checked her email and found her e-geek had sent her the names of the other two potential victims – Sabrina O'Connor from Penatang and Rachel Weiss from Orillia. She placed a call to DS LaCroix to arrange surveillance on Riley and the other two women and was ordered back to the detachment.

She got Riley settled at her place first. She didn't let her bring her car because she wanted it left in her parking spot. It made it look like she was home and Raven would do the surveillance on the building herself, if necessary.

* * *

LaCroix was in his office when Raven arrived and took a seat across from him.

"Why aren't you at home resting, Bowen?"

"You know I can't sit these ones out, DS. I'm a little sore, but there's nothing broken or seriously injured. I'm okay for full duties."

He leaned back in his chair, tented his fingers in front of his chest and studied her for a moment, as if he could determine her mental and physical states that way. Maybe he could. Raven sat stone faced, meeting his gaze.

"I'm going to recommend you see a therapist."

Raven shot to her feet. "What? I don't need a goddamned therapist."

LaCroix's eyebrows rose, but otherwise he didn't move. With an audible exhale, Raven slumped back into her seat.

"I don't need a therapist, Grayson."

LaCroix leaned forward. "You're investigating your mother's murder, Bowen. I don't care how sound you are mentally or how removed you are from your mom emotionally, that's enough to shake you. If for no other reason, see the therapist to ease my concern."

Damn, he really knew how to play her. One visit and she

could convince the therapist she was fine. "Okay."

He leaned back in his chair again and smiled. "I'll set it up and let you know where and when."

Shit. "Thanks, DS." She went to her desk and ran a search on the two names that Eric Theissen, the e-geek, had sent her.

Rachel Weiss was a twenty-eight year old living in Orillia. Raven searched for her on Facebook and learned she was a hotel manager at the Stone Gate Inn, a high end hotel in Orillia. She lived within walking distance of her workplace, which, to Raven, meant she'd be an easy target especially if she worked shifts. She scanned through her posts and noted that they were all 'public' since she could view them without being Rachel's 'friend'.

She moved on to Sabrina O'Connor from Penatanguishene and got a hit from their local OPP Detachment. Sabrina O'Connor had been reported missing that morning.

"Shit." She shot up and charged back into LaCroix's office. "Sixteen year old Sabrina O'Connor didn't make it home from work last night in Penatang. She was reported missing by her parents this morning. I need a warrant, DS. I need to get into that bastard's cabin."

LaCroix pressed his lips together then nodded. "Let's see if we can get it based on him being the common denominator on the Dating Pool site."

Raven nodded and rushed back to her desk to get the paperwork going. As soon as she finished, she had a uniformed officer deliver the request directly to the courthouse. Then she picked up the phone and called the constable who filed the missing persons report in Penatanguishene. Constable Craig Allen told her Sabrina's parents reported her missing that morning. She was supposed to walk the two blocks home after she finished work at Subway at ten o'clock last night. She called her parents to say she was on her way at five past ten, but she never made it home. They'd called her cell phone repeatedly and contacted all of her friends. The father, Declan O'Connor, went out looking for her at ten-thirty and found no trace of her. Constable Allen followed her route home in the daylight that morning and found no sign of a struggle, no sign of what might have happened to Sabrina.

Raven gave him a bit of the background on her investigation and informed him they were trying to get a warrant to search a suspect's residence. She told him she'd keep him updated. And now, all she could do was wait. Instead of waiting around and driving herself crazy, she switched over to Ena's case.

She rounded up Mick, gave her an update, and headed out to see if they could catch Ena's physician, Dr. Simone Wagnar, in her office.

Raven approached Dr. Wagnar's secretary and presented her badge. "I need to speak with Dr. Wagnar. Is she in the office?"

The secretary's smile disappeared, replaced by a frown. "Ah, it's going to be a while, I'm afraid. There are a lot of patients waiting. Dr. Wagnar is a bit behind."

"She's going to be even more behind, because you're going to fit me in as soon as she's free."

"What is this about, Raven?"

"Ena didn't have cancer. Dr. Wagnar is going to want to see me." Raven pushed her badge back into her pocket, keeping her eyes locked on the receptionist's.

The receptionist got to her feet, keeping her hand on the back of her chair until she steadied herself and then she walked over to catch Dr. Wagner before she went into the next exam room.

"Dr. Wagnar? Raven is requesting to see you about Ena."

Simone Wagner was tall and curvy, an imposing presence in any situation, including wearing a white lab coat over a figure-hugging electric blue dress and torturous black heels. Her long, dark hair hung loose, shimmering down her back. Large, smoky grey eyes found Raven and she smiled. "Raven? How are you, sweetheart? What on earth happened to your face?"

Raven took a step back as Wagnar approached. The woman had damn near asphyxiated her with a bone breaking hug at Ena's funeral. "I'm fine. I need to ask you a few questions, Simone."

"Questions?" Wagnar asked, her smile fading.

Raven glanced over her shoulder at the people in the waiting room. More than half of them were staring up at her. "Is there somewhere private we can talk?"

Wagnar led them through to her office. Once the door was closed, Raven asked, "When was the last time you saw Ena?"

Wagnar lowered herself into her desk chair, crossed her long, shapely legs at the ankle, and sighed. "It breaks my heart she passed before you two mended your differences. She loved you so much, Rave and you never got the chance to see that, to experience how much she cared for you."

So much that she didn't even mention my name to my father, her husband? Yeah, she loved me alright, Raven thought. "When was the last time you saw her, Simone?"

Simone closed her eyes. "About a month before she passed. We were at a fundraiser for the hospital."

"Did she look well? Did she complain she wasn't feeling well?"

A deep line formed between Simone's perfectly shaped brows. "She seemed fine, looked fine. I literally don't remember Ena ever complaining about not feeling well." She picked up a pen from her desk and twirled it between her fingers.

"She made an appointment to come in and see you recently." She was grabbing at straws now. Simone hadn't seen her since before she began to get sick.

Simone pursed her lips and closed her eyes again. "Sadly, yes. She tried to get in to see me the week before she passed, but I was away at a conference. She had an appointment for last Thursday, two days after she passed."

Convenient. Raven couldn't help narrowing her eyes at Simone. "You're still a member of the coven, aren't you?"

Simone smiled. "Yes, of course." Her held tilted as she examined Raven. "When are you going to join us again, Rave? You know it's where you belong. It's your home, your family."

Yeah, right. "What do you know about Kiran Hayes?"

"Your father? Well, now. Aside from being absolutely delicious, he's our HP. He was, and has always been, Ena's partner. The ying to her yang, so to speak." She waved a hand in dismissal. "Oh, I know he disappeared for a few years, but he was always in Ena's heart. Always." She smiled, just a slight raising of the corners of her mouth. "I don't know what he's going to do without her."

Was she the only one who hadn't known her own father? Why would Ena do that to her? To both her and Kiran? Would he remain the High Priest without Ena being High Priestess of their coven? She had no idea how that worked. Ena had been the HPS since her own mother passed away, before Raven was born. How the opening would be filled was beyond her. Adara said that the coven wanted to put it to a vote. "How does the coven choose a new High Priestess?"

"I'm not exactly sure. It's not something we planned on having to do in the near future. The coven *was* Ena. Do you understand? I don't know that it can survive her loss. I'm sure we will try, but she was such a presence that it just won't be the same. Unless maybe …" She studied Raven again and her red painted lips curled up. "Unless you were to step into your mother's shoes. Your personality is certainly big enough to resurrect what Ena has built over the years."

"I don't plan on returning to the coven." Raven shoved her hands into her pockets and leaned back against the wall. She supposed it was a compliment Simone thought she could step into the HPS role. But, it wasn't something she would consider doing. She rebelled against Ena's coven and witchcraft because of the shame that bullies and idiots at school made her feel. She had the bloody hell beat out of her because she was 'different' and she didn't plan on becoming something that would cause people to whisper behind her back, give her accusing stares, ostracize her from the small community.

Simone gave her a sultry smile. "Well, that *is* a shame."

Heat spread up Raven's neck and flared through her cheeks. Did Simone know she was ashamed of Ena's religion? Thinking that made her feel small. Everyone, including her mother, had a right to their own religious beliefs. Why was she so judgemental after all these years?

"Tell me why you're asking all these questions about Ena?"

Simone's question brought Raven out of her thoughts and she wondered if she did it on purpose. "The emergency room handled Ena as if she had fourth stage cancer. They made her as comfortable as possible and let her die. But, she didn't have cancer. She was poisoned with arsenic over the last month of her life."

Simone's right hand covered her heart, her eyes wide and unfocused. "Oh, dear Goddess. Where did the diagnosis of cancer come from then? The report I received from the hospital listed her cause of death as fourth stage stomach cancer."

"They don't know and they didn't perform any tests to confirm that diagnosis." Raven watched Simone closely, but her shock and dismay seemed genuine. "Does that seem plausible to you?"

"No. No, it doesn't make any sense." She looked up at Raven with her grey eyes glistening with moisture. "It doesn't make any sense."

"Is it possible someone hexed the doctor and nurses?"

The hand splayed over Simone's heart fisted until the knuckles turned white and her face paled to nearly the same colour. "You think a member of the coven killed Ena?"

"I'm asking you if that's possible."

Simone closed her eyes again, forcing a single tear to slide down her cheek. "Yes, I suppose it is. But, it goes against everything we believe in. Eight words the Wiccan Rede fulfill – An it harm none, do what ye will."

* * *

"She really wants you back in the coven," Mick said as she settled into the passenger seat.

"Not going to happen." Raven made no effort to start the car. She sat there staring out the windshield at nothing. How the hell did she prove someone hexed the emergency room staff? Who would believe her? She'd just make a fool out of herself. What she could prove was someone putting arsenic in whatever Ena drank out of that Chalice. Adara would know. But there was someone else she could ask. Kiran Hayes. So, which one did she want to see less? She lowered her forehead to the steering wheel.

"I vote for Kiran."

Raven turned to glare at Mick who smiled at her and shrugged.

"I thought you said you only picked up little bits?"

Mick shrugged again, the innocent smile still spread across her face. "You need to speak to him at some point."

"Why?"

The smile was replaced by a blank look. "Um, he's your father."

"So? I've gone twenty-seven years without one." Was she

supposed to just welcome this stranger into her life because he looked like her? What if he was a creep? What if he was like Gregor? God knew her mother had horrible taste in lovers. And speaking of her mother, why had she gone silent again?

"He's not like Gregor." Mick's eyes were drawn together in that puppy dog sad way.

Pity. That's what she read in Mick's face, in her eyes. Raven turned to stare out the driver's side window. Just make a damn decision and get it over with. Adara or Kiran? Since they both lived relatively close, Raven started the car and drove in the direction of their homes. It wasn't until she dove past Adara's quaint little house that she realized she made her decision before she even got in the car. She glanced over at Mick and caught her smiling.

"It's only because I want another look at the crime scene."

"Oh. Okay."

Damn Mick and her psychic abilities. Raven turned into Ena's driveway and the first thing she noticed was Ena's black Mercedes SUV wasn't there. Even better. She'd get a look around without having Kiran Hayes as a distraction.

"You still need to talk to him."

"Oh, for Christ's sake. Between you and Ena I have no friggin' privacy. Get the hell out of my head." Raven got out of the car and slammed the door then kicked the tire for good measure. Damn it. She hopped around on one foot until the pain subsided. Now she could add a sore toe to her list of aches and pains.

Mick stared at her over the hood of the car then dropped her eyes when Raven glared at her. "I'm sorry. You're absolutely right. It's an invasion of your privacy and I'll try my best to block it."

"You can turn it off?" Raven narrowed her eyes to slits.

"I can try. I think I've just kind of tuned into you. I can try to tune out or block it."

"What the hell does that mean? You can try?"

"Okay." Mick's hands came up, palms out, and she took a step back. "I'll tune out. Okay?" Her eyes met Raven's then she dropped her head and stuck her hands in her coat pockets.

"All this time you could have just tuned out? Is that what you're saying?" Jesus. Total invasion of her privacy. Why the hell had she taken this kid on? The quick glance and hurt she saw in Mick's eyes told her she hadn't quite tuned out yet. "Get out of my head."

"I'm sorry. I can't help it. I really can't."

Raven remembered being able to tune into people's thoughts. Why anyone would want that particular power, she had no idea. She started blocking it all out when she was very young. She wasn't even sure when. Before Gregor? Possibly. She'd definitely blocked it by the time he moved in with Ena. That's what her mother had meant when she said, *"You have great powers, Rave. You've only to open yourself to them."* She didn't want to open herself to it. She didn't want to hear what people were thinking. They'd looked at her like she was some kind of freak and she supposed she was. The little witch. The daughter of the whore witch who lived on the hill. Yeah. She didn't want to know what people thought of her or her mother. She'd just wanted to be a normal kid that fit in. That's all. Was that too much to ask?

"Raven?"

"Yeah?"

Mick nodded toward the house. "Are we going in?"

"Yeah." How long had she been stuck in her head, lost in memories long forgotten? Blocked out? Suppressed? Why had she done all that? Because of what the community thought of them? She combed her fingers through her short, black hair leaving it spiked up and unruly and looked up at the house picturing that bubble gum pink bedroom. God, it made her sick just picturing it. Why the hell hadn't Ena changed that miserable room?

She walked up to the kitchen door and paused there with her key in the lock. She'd escaped Gregor one night by sneaking down and spending the night on this porch. The next time she tried it though, he found her and dragged her back up to that horrid bedroom.

She had a flash of that last night, of the nasty fight she had with Ena, the things she yelled at her. She'd regurgitated all of the horrible things that people thought about her mother. And she was ashamed of herself as she thought about it. She lashed out and hurt Ena as much as she could just because she was hurting and couldn't tell Ena why. She hiccupped when her emotions caught in her throat and struggled to tamp it all back down. Not here. Not now. She steeled herself and turned the damn key, flung the door open and stepped inside.

The forensics team had left black finger print dust on just about every surface. Raven's first instinct was to clean it, but that was for Kiran now.

Raven turned in a circle, taking in all of the dried plants hanging down from the ceiling, the huge kitchen with all of its rustic pine, and the massive island where Ena spent much of her time.

"I love this kitchen, the feel of it," Mick said in a quiet voice.

There were more happy memories in this room than bad ones. Raven tried to see it from Mick's perspective. Taking it all in as if she'd never seen it before. She was drawn to Ena's Book of Shadows. What did the forensics team think of that? The massive leather-bound book contained all of Ena's spells and potions in her own fancy hand writing. It contained everything she'd learned from her own mother, spells and what-not that had been in the family for generations and passed down from mother to daughter time and time again. Raven ran her hand over the worn leather. She used to have her own Book of Shadows where she wrote the spells and recipes for potions her mother was teaching her. Every witch had their own, written in their own hand. It was an old tradition brought into being to protect witches during the times they drowned them, hung them, or burned them at the stake. If a witch was caught, her Book of Shadows couldn't incriminate other witches as it was written only in her own hand.

Still to this day, witches fiercely protected their own. It was a hard lesson learned during desperate times. Most of those who were put to death for the crime of practicing witchcraft were not even witches. Such was the paranoia of the times. Odd, that she still remembered much of what Ena taught her and that her Book of Shadows could draw out those memories of times spent together while Ena entertained her with simple spells and silly potions. "Hmm." Raven smiled and drew her hand away from the book.

Mick leaned against the counter with her thumbs stuck in her duty belt watching Raven with a smile.

"It must have been pretty cool growing up with Ena for a mother."

You would think so, Raven supposed. And she guessed it had been up until she began to feel the wrath of those who didn't approve of who they were. She'd been stupid, really. When she looked back on it now, she had been a fool to let what other people thought of them rule her. "I guess," she answered.

Raven studied the surface of the island counter. Beside the Book of Shadows were the tools Ena used on a daily basis. Her athame with the three moons at the hilt of the black handle and the pentagram at the end of it. The blade was curvy and sharp on both sides. At the top of the workspace sat a white marble mortar and pestle, a fat white candle and, beside it, an incense burner with several sticks of patchouli scented incense scattered at its side. A large platter sat in the middle of the workspace with hand drawn symbols in ink and a pentagram carved into it. Next to the platter sat a scourge made of soft leather with eight trails, each having five knots. A white hilted knife sat next to that. Bottles and jars of Lord only knew what were scattered about the space.

Resting on the platter was Ena's weathered wand made of old willow. Raven traced the pad of her finger down its smooth length and Ena's power sizzled up her arm. She drew her hand away, puffed out her cheeks and blew out a breath. Wow. Tingles shot down her spine.

The only things missing from the space were a bottle of wine and the elusive chalice. Just as she was bending to open the cupboard below the island, her cell phone rang.

"Bowen."

"It's LaCroix. We didn't get the warrant, Rave. I'm sorry. There just wasn't enough for reasonable grounds."

"Goddamnit." She whirled around, barely surpassing the urge to throw her phone across the damn room. "He's friggin' well got Sabrina, Grayson."

"Get me more and I'll get you the warrant." He ended the call.

She didn't have to tell Mick what LaCroix told her. Mick looked as pissed as she was.

"Are we just supposed to stand by while he rapes and kills that poor girl?"

"Let's pay Gregor Paigo a little visit." Raven was just angry enough to go face to face with the bastard.

Chapter 9

Raven winced every time the Charger hit a pothole or bump in the dirt road leading to Paigo's cabin. It had the upgraded suspension of the police package, but she still hated taking it over this God forsaken road. Her last ride had been a heap of junk with over 400,000 kilometres on it. She didn't want to trash this one and risk getting another junker.

She pulled over at the same spot they'd left the Suburban on their first trip out here and they made their way through the woods. They were still a good fifty metres from the cabin when the sound of anguished screams echoed all around them.

"That's probable friggin' grounds," Raven growled. She picked up her pace and pulled out her cell phone. When LaCroix answered she asked, "Is a woman screaming bloody murder enough? We can hear her from a good fifty metres out from Paigo's cabin."

"Jesus, Rave. Stand down and wait for backup."

"Get a damn ambulance rolling, too." She shoved her phone back in her pocket and drew her weapon. She wasn't waiting another half hour for back up to arrive. He'd had Sabrina for a good sixteen hours now and God only knew what condition they'd find her in. She came to a stop just inside the tree line and listened. Branches cracked in the breeze, water sloshed against the shore, Mick's breaths staggered, and her own heart pounded in her ears. Gregor's truck wasn't in the driveway. "He's not here."

"What do we do?"

Raven turned to Mick who had that deer in the headlights look. "Take a few deep breaths, will you?"

Mick nodded and sucked air in through her nose.

"We're going to get her out. Okay?"

Mick nodded again.

"Draw your weapon out of your holster, Warren."

"Oh. Yeah. Got it." She fumbled for her Sig, pulled it out and pointed it in front of her which just happened to be at Raven's belly.

Raven grabbed the barrel and pushed it to the side. "Have you ever drawn your weapon in the line, Mick?"

"Oh, um. No." She shook her head furiously and shifted her weight from foot to foot.. "No, I haven't."

Oh, man. She was in trouble. "Why don't you stay here while I go in? If Gregor pulls up, call my cell."

"If he comes back, he'll see our car on the road."

Placing a hand on Mick's shoulder, Raven met her eye to eye. "I'm not leaving her in there. If he comes back, you call me and we deal with it. Okay?"

Mick nodded. "Have you done something like this before?"

"I've been in dangerous situations." Enough with the questions already. They were wasting time. "I'm going in."

"Oh, geez. This isn't good."

Of course it wasn't friggin' good. Raven made her way to the back door, keeping her ears peeled for the sound of a vehicle approaching. She pulled herself up on the dilapidated deck that looked like carpenter ants had finished with it years ago and sidled up to the sliding glass door just as another ear piercing scream burst out from inside. It faded to nothing then began again, scratched and weary. Raven pushed on the door handle and the door slid open about six or eight inches then caught on something. She was thin, but she wasn't sure if she could fit through the narrow opening. She went in with her gun hand first, levelling it around the room until she was sure she was clear. The road rash on her jaw tore open as she tried to squeeze her head through and all she could think about was how many germs from the filthy door were crawling into the wounds.

"Eew, eeeww, eeewww." She should be wearing a freaking hazmat suit.

The kitchen sink and counters were piled with dirty dishes, take out containers, and empty beer bottles with bugs and flies circling. Raven's delicate nose screwed up at the phenomenal stench of rot. The floor looked like it was made of dirt.

Another round of screams began as she rounded the corner into the living room. It didn't look much better than the kitchen. She could tell there was carpeting under her feet, but the colour was anyone's guess.

Metal springs creaked as the screams drew weaker and Raven followed the sound down the short hallway. There were two doors. A door on the left led to a bathroom that hadn't seen a bottle of Lysol in it's entire existence. The door on the right was closed.

"Sabrina? I'm a police officer. I'm coming in to get you out of here."

"Wait," a gravelly voice yelled. "He rigged something up to the door. You have to come in from the window."

Crap. "Tell me what you see on the door?"

"There's a string tied to the handle and it runs over a hook then there's a thing. It looks like a grenade or something."

Double crap. "I'm going to try the window. Okay? I'm not leaving you here."

"Okay. Okay. Thank you. Thank God."

As Raven made her way down the hall Sabrina's sobs echoed behind her. She went to the front door, checking in all directions before she came out and rushed down the porch steps. The window leading to the bedroom was a good six feet off the ground. Raven holstered her weapon and dragged a couple of old tires over to the window. Using the wall to keep her balance, she bashed the window with her elbow and did little more than give her funny bone a good jolt. "Goddamnit."

Scanning the yard, she eyed a rusty tail pipe about three feet long. She jumped down from the tires and retrieved it then climbed back up. With one good whack the glass shattered and she used the pipe to clear the remaining shards. Sabrina was still crying inside. Raven grabbed onto the window sill, realizing too late she'd missed a shard of glass, and hefted herself up and into the room.

"Oh, thank God. Thank God," Sabrina cried.

Raven pushed to her feet, took one look at Sabrina and stumbled back as the room began to spin. Sabrina's wrists were bound with grey duct tape to the spindles of the headboard. Her ankles were similarly bound, her legs spread wide open. Raven pulled a pocket knife out of her front pocket and hacked away at the tape around Sabrina's wrists, which were covered in blood, fresh and old. She hoped to hell Sabrina didn't have blood born diseases because she had an open wound on her hand from the glass shard in the damn window.

"Okay. You're okay." She tried to keep her voice soothing despite the blood racing through her veins and her heart beating a tattoo. One hand freed, she moved to the other side of the bed then freed each of Sabrina's feet.

Sabrina sprung herself up from the bed and into Raven's arms.

"Okay. I've got you," Raven whispered. "We're going to get you out of here, okay?"

Sabrina clung to her and sobbed. Raven scanned the room for clothes or shoes, but found nothing except the sheet on the bed. She grabbed it while Sabrina clung to her, drawing the sheet around her as best she could then carrying her over to the door. She studied the string from the grenade back to the door then shook her head. The string was looped over the door handle with enough slack that she could just pull it off. She could have just eased the door open and removed the string from the handle. She supposed that was exactly how Gregor would have gotten back in the room.

When Sabrina loosened her grip, Raven placed her hands on Sabrina's shoulders and pulled back. "Do you think you can walk?"

Sabrina nodded. She swiped her arm over her face and sniffed. They just stepped out into the hallway when Raven's cell phone rang. She pulled it out of her pocket at the same time she heard the sound of a diesel truck roaring up the road.

"Oh, shit." She ducked down, put her shoulder into Sabrina's waist and pushed back up to her feet with Sabrina folded over her shoulder. She doubled stepped through the living room and kitchen to the sliding door. With the toe of her boot, she knocked the stick blocking the sliding door out of the way, threw open the door, and then closed it behind them.

Her phone had stopped ringing, so she dialed Mick and waited, pressed up against the back of the cabin. When Mick answered, she whispered, "Where is he?"

"Shit. Shit. Just going in the front door. Get the hell out of there."

"We're coming to you." She ran down the steps, thanking the Goddess when they didn't give out and she didn't trip, then she charged for the tree line with Sabrina weeping against her back, Raven's right leg screaming where Jaxon's truck had hit it. She made it to the tree line just as a shotgun blasted somewhere behind her.

"Go, go, go," Mick shouted.

She stepped in behind Raven and Raven was sure she was pushing on Sabrina's back. She stumbled then got her footing again and pushed on with the leaves crunching under their feet. Denuded branches and twigs grabbed at them and tore into exposed flesh. Sweat trickled down Raven's back. Or was it Sabrina's blood? She gagged and ran on, her boots thundering over the ground. When she caught sight of the Charger, she felt that odd sensation in the back of her throat again. Oh, dear God. She was not going to cry.

"Keys." Raven stopped and turned to Mick, poking her hip out so Mick could grab the keys from her pocket. Mick pulled them out and unlocked the car just as she heard the rumble of the diesel truck starting up. She pulled open the back door and Mick helped her get Sabrina onto the back seat before she pulled open the front passenger door and drew her weapon.

Gregor's white truck accelerated up the lane. She aimed for the right front tire as the truck came barrelling towards them. Her shoulder jerked as the loud crack of her Sig repeated through the trees, the pungent odour of gun powder burning Raven's nostrils.

The tire blew and the truck veered to the right, away from them, and slammed into a tree releasing a great bang and the crunching and twisting of metal. A hiss sounded and then the driver's door creaked open.

With her heart bashing against her chest, Raven yelled, "Put your hands up where I can see them." She didn't see his hands, but the barrel of a shotgun as Gregor slid out of the truck. "Put the gun down or I'll shoot." God, she didn't want to shoot him. She wanted him to spend the rest of his rotten life in a prison where everyone knew he was a child molester.

Everything slowed. The barrel of the shotgun rose up, aimed right at her. She shouted one more time for him to put the gun down, watched as he pumped the forearm and then she fired, milliseconds before she saw the flash from the shotgun. She ducked down behind the door waiting for the shot to rain down on the Charger, but it blew into the bush to her right.

Mick popped up from behind the back door looking like her eyes were about to explode out of their sockets. "Oh, shit. Are you shot?"

"No." Raven had to hold back a laugh. She finally found out what it took to get a curse word out of Mick. She peeked out from behind the door. Gregor was on the ground, his bloody hands clasped to his chest. The shotgun lay on the ground a few feet in front of him. Raven kept her gun trained on him as she closed the distance between them. As she got closer, she realized it wasn't his chest that was bleeding. She'd shot him in the right hand. The wooden stock of the shotgun was splintered. Her shot was probably the reason his blast missed its target.

Raven placed her boot on Gregor's shoulder and shoved him onto his belly as he squealed like a pig as she holstered her weapon then pulled his arms behind his back and cuffed him.

"My hand. What the fuck's wrong with you? I'm shot for Christ's sake."

"Sorry, Gregor." She smiled when he looked into her face and recognition lit his eyes. "I'm not feeling a hell of a lot of sympathy for you."

* * *

The bright lights of video cameras and camera flashes accosted Raven as she stepped out of the emergency room doors. Her left hand was bandaged with stitches spanning her palm where the glass shard in the window had cut into her. The needles she'd had to freeze her hand for the stitches had made her sick to her stomach and she was glad that Riley hadn't been there to see it, or anyone else she knew for that matter.

Reporters shouted out questions from every direction. It all jumbled together so that she couldn't understand what anyone was asking. How they'd gotten her name or knew who she was baffled her. She was relieved when LaCroix stepped in beside her although she had no idea where he came from.

"One question at a time please," he shouted to be heard over the din.

"Harrison MacNamara, CTV News. How did you track down the man who abducted Sabrina O'Connor and was he the same man responsible for the deaths of Emily McMurtrie, Sandra Kelway, and Charlene Brock?"

"Detective Constable Bowen and Constable Warren have been working this case since the discovery of Emily McMurtrie's body several days ago. I can't give you any details as this is an ongoing case, but their investigation led them to the perpetrator in time to save Sabrina O'Connor who was abducted after leaving her workplace in Penatanguishene last night."

Raven watched LaCroix as he answered several questions. He handled the media like he did it everyday. When he had to think about his answer, he rubbed the scruff on his face with his chin between his thumb and forefinger.

LaCroix told the reporters he'd take one more question and pointed to a woman with her light brown hair pulled back into a ponytail who elbowed her way to the front.

"Kelsey St. Germaine, National News. I have a question for Detective Constable Bowen."

LaCroix turned his head to look at Raven and she nodded

her assent.

"Gregor Paigo was a member of your mother's Wiccan coven and lived with your mother for over two years just over a decade ago. Did you know back then that he was a sex offender? Did he molest you, Detective Constable Bowen? Is that the reason you left home at the age of fifteen?"

Raven literally felt the blood drain from her head. Her face tingled and the edges of her vision darkened.

"That's enough." Kiran Hayes pushed his way through the horde of reporters, took hold of Raven's elbow, and steered her away from the mob, back into the hospital. LaCroix followed them as reporters shouted out questions in a frenzy.

Raven's chest tightened up, making it impossible to draw in a breath. As Kiran rushed her through the halls, she pulled at the neck of her sweater as if that would help her to breathe. They burst through the doors at the side of the hospital just as Riley pulled to the curb in Ena's SUV. Kiran opened the back door and Raven folded herself into the car. Instead of getting in the front, Kiran rounded the car and got in the back beside Raven. Once they were in, LaCroix gave the roof of the car two quick slaps with his palm.

"Go," Kiran shouted as soon as he closed the door.

Riley burned rubber as she pulled away from the curb and kept glancing back at Raven who was bent over, clutching her chest and sucking short, wheezing breaths in through her mouth.

"Can't breathe."

"Slow breaths, now," Kiran said. "Breathe in through your nose. That's it, love."

Raven didn't have the energy to tell him not to call her that. If she could catch her damn breath, she'd tell him to shut the hell up. Let him try sucking air in through his damn nose when his lungs refused to expand. Yet, she did what he was telling her. Her head spun and little bright spots danced in front of her eyes. Oh, damn. She was going to pass out. She glanced up at Riley while the darkness crept in from her peripheral vision. "Can't breathe." She barely heard her words as the darkness took her under.

When she came to, her head was in Kiran's lap and his hand circled her back. Mortified, she pushed herself up then pressed her hands to her throbbing temples.

"Welcome back, love."

At least she was breathing normally now. She glanced over at Kiran and he smiled. Raven groaned and massaged her temples.

"Headache?"

Duh. What was his first clue? "Yeah. I need a couple of Advil, a hot shower, pizza, and a beer."

Kiran laughed and it sounded as beautiful as his thick Scottish accent, low and rumbling, almost musical in its cadence. "In that order?"

"Yeah, pretty much." She just wanted to be home and disinfect herself after being in Gregor's filthy cabin. Thinking of Gregor brought back the memory of the reporter's question and she groaned. It was probably already being broadcast on the National News Network and they'd keep replaying it until the whole country was sick of it or the next hot news item broke. How the hell did they dig up that information so fast?

Riley pulled into Raven's driveway and as soon as the locks clicked open, Raven opened her door and jumped out of the car before Kiran tried to help her. She got to the front door and patted her pockets for her keys before she realized Mick had them again. She should have been waiting for her with the Charger in the hospital parking lot. She took out her phone to call Mick and had to wait for it to power on as she'd turned it off when she was in the ER. Twenty-three missed calls, mostly from Adara, but a few from Mick and Jaxon, waited for her. One from LaCroix after they left the hospital. She put the phone on silence so she could ignore any incoming calls and texts then called Mick.

"Hey, Raven. Are you okay?"

"Yeah." How often was she going to hear that question over the next few days? "Riley and Kiran drove me home."

"Yeah, Riley let me know. I'm just at the detachment finishing up the reports then I'll change and bring your car over."

"You didn't have to do the reports. I could have done them from home."

There was silence for a moment. Riley used her key to open the door and Raven walked in, closely followed by both Riley and Kiran. "Mick? Are you still there?"

"Yeah, sorry. Ummm. When I bring your car over, do you think we could talk? There's, um, something I need to say to you."

"Is everything okay?"

"Yeah. Yeah. It's just … well, I'd rather talk to you face to face."

The kid sounded so serious and nervous and Raven couldn't figure out what the heck she would want to discuss. Now it was going to bug her until Mick came over and said what she needed to say. "I guess I'll see you in a bit then."

"Yeah. Okay. See you in a bit."

When she got off the phone, Riley and Kiran were sitting on the couch in the living room. Kiran had the TV remote in his hand and he pointed it at the TV, turned it on, and tuned it to the National News Network.

"Must you?" Watching that crap was the last thing Raven needed.

Kiran clicked off the TV and set the remote on the coffee table. "Sorry, love. I thought it might be wise to do some damage control."

"Damage control?"

"Aye. See what they're saying so we can figure out what to do about it."

Raven crossed her arms over her chest and scowled. "*We* are not going to do anything about it. They'll move on to something else soon enough."

"That's your strategy then? Ignore it and hope it all goes away?"

Who the hell did he think he was? She just met him yesterday and he thought he could come to her rescue then decide what she was to do about something that was none of his damn business?

"We're just trying to help, Rave," Riley said. "I don't understand why you didn't file charges against that bastard a long time ago."

Because he would have gotten out on bail while he waited for his trial and he would have used that time to kill Ena and maybe her as well. Raven had no doubt he would have done it. She got up and went to the window to look out at the moon's shimmering reflection on the lake, but it was overcast and there was no glow, no light. Just pitch black beyond the light shining out from her living room. Another two days and it would be a full moon. And the coven gathering. With Gregor in custody, she could focus on Ena's murder.

"You look a fright, darling," Kiran said.

"Gee, thanks." Raven looked down at the blood stains on her shirt and pants, the scrapes on her right hand, and her bandaged left hand. She couldn't really argue with him and that was not even taking into consideration what her face must look like. She knew she had fresh scrapes from the branches and twigs grabbing and whipping at them when they were running through the woods and the scrapes on her jaw had been ripped open. They'd disinfected the wounds at the hospital, but she still felt filthy and gross.

"I'm going to take a shower and change."

"I'll order that pizza."

Well, look at that. Her father was proving to be useful. As soon as that thought passed through her mind, Raven berated herself. It wasn't his fault. He hadn't even known she existed. Why the hell hadn't Ena told them about each other? And why had she gone silent?

Raven went into her bedroom, closed the door and stripped down, placing her clothes into a plastic bag so she could throw them out. Or burn them. That would be satisfying. She cranked on the shower as hot as she could stand it and scrubbed her skin where it wasn't scraped or cut then thoroughly soaped the areas that were, ignoring the sting.

She fluffed her hair and patted herself dry with a towel. Her jaw was still bleeding, so she dabbed it with a tissue and then spread a good coating of Polysporin over it. She'd tried to keep her throbbing hand dry, but the gauze wrapped around it was soaked. Riley would fix that for her. She dressed in a warm sweat suit, retrieved the first aid kit from the bathroom cabinet and walked out to the living room. As soon as she did, Kiran and Riley's conversation stopped and they stared at her.

"What?"

"Nothing," Riley said. "Feel better?"

"A bit." She passed the first aid kit to Riley. "Could you re-dress my hand?"

Riley patted the couch next to her and opened the first aid kit on the coffee table. She took Raven's hand in hers so gently Raven was shocked by the jolt that ran up her arm and soared straight down to her core. She inhaled sharply and Riley's eyes shot up from her hand to meet Raven's. Raven held her breath. Oh, this was a bad idea.

"Does it hurt?"

"Ha. Yep." If Riley thought her reaction was pain, she'd let her think it instead of embarrassing herself. Damn Ena for passing down her voracious sexual appetite. She wanted to scoop Riley up in her arms, carry her into the bedroom, and –. Her eyes met Kiran's and her arousal vanished, replaced by a burning heat searing up her throat and spreading over her face.

Kiran smiled. "Alright, pet?"

"I'm not a damn pet."

"Och, sorry, love. It's a term of endearment at home. Doesn't have the same meaning here, I suppose?"

Riley cut through the gauze and peeled it off of Raven's hand. "Oh, Rave. You should probably ice this."

She'd known it was swollen, but it appeared more so now and felt tight and uncomfortable. The colour of the skin surrounding the cut was an angry red. It had been red when she got the stitches, but not that red. "Do you think it's infected?" God knew what filth was on that window. "Ew, eew, eeewww." She shuddered, a full body, grossed out kind of shudder. "Maybe they didn't clean it out well enough in the ER."

"I'm sure it's fine. It's too early for an infection to have set in. A little ice and some antiseptic ointment and I'll re-wrap it for you."

Riley massaged Raven's hand around the cut, barely putting any pressure on it. It sent tingles up Raven's arm. She glanced over at Kiran and he was smirking at her. *Smirking!* Was he psychic, too? Raven pushed to her feet. Despite the hot shower, her whole body ached. "I'll get the ice."

She got a handful of ice from the freezer and put it in a Ziploc baggie then wrapped a tea towel around it and placed it in her left palm. The heat and throbbing calmed instantly. She was heading back into the living room when the doorbell rang and she changed directions.

"I'll get it." Kiran rose and Raven watched his long strides carry him down the hall, graceful yet strong. He returned moments later carrying two large pizzas.

Raven wasn't going to snub her nose at the amount of pizza, but did they really need that much? "Who are you planning on feeding?"

"Oh, well. You can never have enough pizza. What doesn't get eaten can go in your fridge for tomorrow, yeah?" He set the boxes down on the counter and helped Raven gather plates, napkins, and three bottles of beer.

Kiran carried everything out to the living room, serving Riley and Raven before placing three slices on his own plate. Once settled in his chair, he picked up the bottle of Coors Lite and examined the label. "Well, it's not Guinness, but it will wet the throat, aye?"

"Aye. It will do that." Raven held a slice of pizza in her right hand while her left hand was fisted loosely around the ice filled tea towel. Like an expert, she folded it a tiny bit to keep it from buckling when she took a big bite out of the tip. Oh, yeah. She needed that. She couldn't quite remember the last time she ate.

"I came over to see you this afternoon," Kiran said. He took a bite of pizza, chewed, and swallowed before continuing. "Ena's lawyer is expecting us in her office at ten tomorrow morning."

"Ena's lawyer?"

"Aye. She'll be reading her will, I suppose."

The house. She left her that damn house. "I don't want the house, Kiran. It's your home, you keep it."

"Oh, no. She's always been very clear on that point. That house gets passed down from daughter to daughter in the Bowen line."

Raven dropped her slice of pizza on top of the other one on her plate then tossed the plate onto the coffee table. Way to ruin her appetite. "Being in that house makes me sick, *aye*? I don't want her damn house."

Kiran's eyes flared, his jaw muscles rippled and then his expression relaxed for a second before he pursed his lips. It was like she could see his whole thought process on his face. He was pissed that she mocked his accent and then it dawned on him why she didn't want to be in that house. All of her nightmares lived within those walls. The three times she'd been in it over the past few days had brought back both good and bad memories, but the thought of living there, of passing that bedroom every day, just made her skin crawl.

"Och, I'm sorry, Raven." He set his slice of pizza on his plate and left it sitting in his lap while he wiped his hands on a napkin. "I'm not good at this, d'ye ken? I don't know how to be a father or deal with the trauma you've suffered. But, I look at you and there's no mistaking you're mine." He placed his right hand over his heart. "The moment I saw you, my heart grew in size. I went from the despairs of grief to the joy of knowing you're my daughter. No matter what the lawyer says tomorrow, Ena's already left me the greatest gift I could have dreamed of. Why the bloody hell she didn't tell me about you, I can't imagine."

He was right about there being no mistake she was his, but Raven had no idea how to respond to the rest of what he said.

"I want to help, love. I can't stand to see you carrying around so much pain."

"You don't know me. You don't know what I'm carrying around." Was he some sort of psychologist with ESP? Or… she turned her head to study Riley. Riley averted her eyes and stared down at the floor as Kiran stabbed his fingers through his hair. "Did you two sit around all afternoon talking about me?"

Riley rolled her eyes. "Why do you have to get pissed off when people are just expressing their concern for you? We care about you, Rave. We're worried about you. Don't condemn us for that."

"Where were all of you when I actually needed the help?" Raven shot to her feet, her fists in tight balls at her sides. The ice pack in her hand sprung a leak and the water seeped through the tea towel. "When I was a little girl trying to fight off a man twice my size who told me if I woke my mother up, if she found out what he was doing, he would kill her. Where were you then?" A sob tore free from her throat and she fled to her room, slamming the door behind her. She knew she was being irrational, but the fact that Riley told Kiran infuriated her. How could she? Now she had an inkling of what Riley had felt at her betrayal.

She leaned back on the door and clutched her right fist to her heart. Holding her breath, she fought against the emotions that strained to break free. She drew her sleeve across her eyes then released her breath and sucked in more air through her nose. Held it in. Her entire body trembled, but she wasn't sure if it was anger or something else. For fifteen years she'd held it together, pushed all the pain, the fear deep down where she didn't have to deal with it. Now it was coming at her from every direction. First Mick, then Ena, Riley … and now the entire friggin' country thanks to that reporter from NNN.

They were right, too. She was falling apart. She was on the brink of losing it. She was going to have to deal with it all somehow and she didn't damn well want to.

"Rave?" Riley said softly as she tapped on the door.

Raven pressed her back harder into the door when she heard the handle twisting. Why couldn't they just go away and leave her the hell alone?

"Mick's here. She said she needed to speak with you."

Raven threw her head back and it hit the door with a thud. Shit, damn, bugger, hell. She drew in a deep breath then let it out slowly, trying to relax her tense muscles as she exhaled.

"Send her in here."

Stepping away from the door, Raven flicked on the overhead light and made her way to the sitting area in front of the sliding glass doors leading out to a small deck. She stood at the window staring out at the darkness. Just knowing the lake was out there calmed her. She closed her eyes for a moment and pictured the light dancing over its rippling surface. It cleared her anger and anxiety better than anything else could.

Mick stepped into the room wearing jeans and an untucked button down shirt. She had her jacket in her hands and was wringing it like a wet rag. That reminded Raven of the wet tea towel in her own hand and she tossed it onto a side table. "Have a seat," she said, nodding to the chairs beside her.

Mick crossed the room and dropped onto the edge of one of the chairs, placing her elbows on her thighs. "I wanted to apologize for this afternoon."

"You've got nothing to apologize for."

Mick's head flew up. "I froze. I freaked. I was no help to you whatsoever."

"Is that how you see it? Because what I saw was someone who I gave an order to who carried out that order. I asked you to stay back and call me if you heard a vehicle approaching. You did that. You let me know his location, so we could make a run for it. You didn't freeze."

Mick stared up at her with her mouth agape and Raven lowered herself into the chair next to her.

"Look, until you're in that type of situation, you have no idea how you will react. But, I guarantee that you will dissect every moment of this afternoon and critique your own behaviour until you can't stand it any more. Then, the next time you're in an intense situation, you'll respond differently.

You'll be less fearful. You'll have already played out in your head how you want to react."

"Really?"

"Yeah. The first time I was in a dangerous situation, I nearly peed my pants."

Mick laughed. "I don't believe that for a minute."

"It's true." Raven stood and went to the window again, staring out. "If you're hungry, there's tons of pizza in the living room."

"I could go for pizza."

Mick crossed the room, her steps a little more confident than when she'd come in. She turned at the door and said, "Thanks, DC."

When she closed the door behind her, Raven went back to staring out at the black night.

* * *

Just when Raven was beginning to think Riley, Kiran, and Mick were never going to leave her living room, there was a knock at her bedroom door and Riley stepped in, closing the door behind her.

Raven shifted her body, giving Riley her back, and continued to stare out the window. She couldn't handle looking at Riley. Not in this room, where they'd fallen asleep wrapped up in each other night after night. Images of hot sex and tender caresses flooded her mind.

"You haven't eaten," Riley said.

"Not hungry."

"Rave?"

Raven heard Riley's exasperated sigh from across the room.

"Go home, Riley," Raven said quietly. She was calm after spending more than an hour at her window and she wanted to stay that way. She was hoping for a good night's sleep, if her uninvited guests ever left.

"I thought you wanted me to stay tonight."

"There's no reason to. Paigo is behind bars." She knew why Riley wanted to stay. She needed someone to take care of and she thought Raven needed her care. She didn't.

"I really am concerned about you, Rave. I'm worried that dealing with losing your mom, pursuing a case against your abuser, and the media finding out about your past is too much. I'm worried you can't handle everything that is happening right now."

Raven wanted to laugh, but she was worried it would trigger the tears she'd been fighting for days. "I can handle losing my mom. I can handle Gregor Paigo. I can handle the damn media. Do you know what I can't handle, Ri? I can't handle losing you. So, unless you're ready to take me back, it's probably easier all around if you just leave."

There was a long silence followed by two soft clicks of the door being carefully opened then closed.

A gust of air released from Raven's lungs and her body deflated against the window. For a moment there she thought maybe, just maybe, Riley was going to take her back. How many times over the past couple of days had Riley said she cares about her? She really couldn't take much more of this. Every time Riley rejected her was like losing her all over again. The ache in her chest seemed to increase every time they parted. She wanted her lover back. Her loving, compassionate, nurturing, sweet, sexy lover.

I'm so sorry, darling angel.

And … she's back.

You don't have to suffer alone, Rave. I'm here for you. I've been in your shoes. I know what it's like to lose the one person who holds your heart.

"And we all know how you got through your lonely nights, pining for your lover." Ena sighed and Raven figured she'd get some peace and quiet now.

Will you tell me why you cheated on Riley?

Raven snorted. "I've been asking myself that question for weeks."

You're not usually attracted to men. Have you asked yourself why, all of a sudden, you were attracted to Jax?

"Raging hormones?"

People don't normally change their sexual orientation just because they're horny.

The short hairs on the back of Raven's neck stood up. "What are you trying to say?"

Maybe I'm suspicious because of what happened to me, but it doesn't make any sense, Rave.

"So you think someone put a spell on me so that I'd sleep with Jax? What possible reason would anyone have to do that?"

Hey, you're the detective. I'm just an old witch.

Raven laughed and it felt good. It felt good to finally have a short conversation with her mother without getting defensive and angry.

Chapter 10

For the first time in her life, Raven called in sick. She figured she could still work Ena's case and by not going to the office, she could avoid LaCroix's interrogation about the allegations flying around that Gregor Paigo molested her. She'd taken the chicken way out, too. Instead of calling LaCroix directly, she left a message with the night sergeant.

It was a mild morning, so she pulled on a sweater and curled up in a Muskoka chair on her deck, sipping her coffee. Birds chirped madly in the woods surrounding her cottage and the light breeze pushed waves into the shore with a slow whoosh, whoosh. Raven took a deep breath of fresh, clean air and smiled. It had been a long, cold winter and she missed mornings like this where she could just sit and unwind.

She allowed herself a good half hour to bask in the morning sunshine then hit the shower and got herself ready for the day. She opted for a pair of loose jeans and a royal blue button down shirt.

There were only a handful of cars in the parking lot at the lawyer's office. She pulled the Charger in next to Ena's Mercedes. She supposed that Kiran's navy training would ensure he didn't turn up late for appointments. He was sitting in the waiting room in a fitted charcoal suit and a royal blue shirt. Raven nearly laughed. At least she wasn't wearing a tie and a suit. His tie was a few shades lighter than his suit and had a gold tie clip in the shape of an anchor. Very navy.

"Nice shirt."

Kiran smiled. "Good morning, Raven. How are you today, then?"

"Good. You?"

"Fine. Fine."

"Isn't Adara coming?"

"No." Kiran shook his head. "She only asked for the two of us."

That's odd. She fully expected Adara to be there. She hadn't returned Adara's phone calls, but she was going to at some point. Maybe she'd take a run over there after she told the lawyer she didn't want Ena's house.

The reception desk was a long, arcing counter of dark wood matching the heavy double doors which Raven suspected led to the offices. The firm name was displayed in brass letters across a wall painted deep blue.

"Pfeiffer, Pfeiffer, and Coles," Raven read the firm name aloud then lowered herself into one of the plush black leather chairs and brushed her boot over the thick pile of the dark blue carpet. "I guess they do alright."

"It would appear so."

Okay, so he was pissed at her for what she regurgitated out last night, but what was she supposed to do when they'd been ganging up on her, talking behind her back. Lord knew what they were saying.

"Mr. Hayes, Ms. Bowen. Would you follow me, please?" The receptionist, a tall blonde wearing black stilts and a tight fitting mini dress the same tone as the navy blue carpet, stood in front of the desk. Raven felt completely under dressed. Why hadn't she worn a pair of dress pants at least?

She followed Kiran and the blonde through the double doors, down a hallway passing offices on both sides with glass walls and doors facing the aisle. The inside row, on the left, had no windows, but the offices on the right featured views of Lake of Bays with the sun glistening off its surface. How did anyone get any work done? Raven would be staring out at the lake all day.

They were led into a conference room with a long table, stained dark with layers of lacquer giving it a smooth as glass finish. Black leather chairs circled the table. Kiran and Raven pulled out a chair and sat side by side. Across the room, a large flat screen TV faced them. The receptionist picked up a remote from the counter behind them and turned the TV on. "Kiara will be with you in a few minutes." She stepped out of the room, closing the door behind her.

Raven looked at Kiran. "Does this feel a little weird to you?"

He shrugged then they both jumped when Ena's voice filled the room.

"Hello, Kiran. Raven." Their heads whipped around at the same time to find Ena smiling at them from the TV.

"Jesus." Raven slapped her hand over her heart to keep it from leaping out of her chest.

"By now you've probably figured out you are father and daughter." Ena stopped speaking and her gentle blue eyes glistened. Her long, mahogany hair was pulled away from her face with clips and flowed down her back. She'd always been slim, but her face appeared almost skeletal, her eyes shadowed with dark circles.

It was the first time Raven had been face to face with her mom in twelve years. Sure, she'd heard her voice for the past few days, but it wasn't the same as seeing her face. She caught her bottom lip between her teeth to keep it from quivering.

"You're both probably angry with me for not telling you about each other. I'm not going to try to explain myself right now. I've made each of you a video you can watch in private." Ena swiped a tear from her cheek with a bony, trembling hand. "God, how I wish I was sitting in that room with both of you. I wish I could be there when you first meet and recognize each other. You're both so much alike. Everyone who knew you before you left, Kiran, knew Rave was yours. And everyone who's met you since you came back, those who knew Rave, knew you were each other's. I kept waiting for the two of you to run into each other in town or for someone to say something, but it never happened." She swiped a hand over her cheeks again. "Anyway, that's for another time.

"Rave, my darling angel." Ena looked straight into the camera with her eyes glistening like the lake on a sunny day, crow's feet crinkling at the corners. "I've waited for so long, but Adara kept telling me you weren't ready, that you wouldn't talk about why you hated me so much. I should have come to you years ago." She sniffed and someone slid a box of tissues in front of her. She pulled two out and dabbed her eyes. "You're not supposed to come to the end of your life and have so many regrets. I've made so many mistakes. God, I've missed you every day for twelve years, two months, and sixteen days." She dropped her head into her hands and her shoulders shook.

The screen went black and then the image of Ena reappeared. She was no longer crying, but she looked just as miserable.

"Kiran, I know I've explained this to you, but Rave has never heard it, so please, bear with me, my darling. The house and the land have been in the Bowen family for over a hundred and fifty years. It's your legacy, Rave, passed down from mother to daughter as I hope that you will one day pass it to your daughter." She waved a hand in dismissal and said, "You'll do a much better job of it than I did. You have Kiran's sensibility there.

"Along with the house and the land comes the Bowen money. I'm sure you won't mind that I'm giving Kiran five million of it. It's only a drop in the bucket, after all. Your trust fund will continue to be deposited into your account on a monthly basis, Rave."

"What trust fund?" Five million is a drop in the bucket? What?

"I've also left five million to Adara in my will. I've instructed Kiara that she's only to get that money if Raven can clear her as a suspect in my murder. You see, someone in the coven has been poisoning me. We've discovered someone has been giving me arsenic for nearly a month now. But, we've discovered it too late. I won't survive the next few days.

"Kiara has the lab results and the name of the doctor who has been treating me. She'll give you that information today, Rave. Please, find out who did this. I couldn't go to Simone or trust anyone in the coven." She blew out a stuttered breath and waved her hand in front of her face. Someone off screen said something and Ena shook her head. "No, let's just keep going, please.

"Kiran?" Tears glistened on her cheeks and she gave them a quick swipe with a tissue. "I love you with all of my heart. You know that. I know the sea is the love of your life, but I hope you will take some time to get to know Rave. You'll be so proud of her and the beautiful young woman she's become. She's so like you, my love. The protector. Yet she has my stubbornness and, Goddess help her, my fiery passion."

Kiran glanced at Raven and raised his eyebrows then the corner of his mouth turned up and he turned back to the screen.

"Take care of our baby, love." Ena hiccupped and covered her mouth and nose with her hand as tears flowed freely down her cheeks. "I know you'll understand why it was necessary to keep Raven's paternity as quiet as possible. She'll need your protection now."

A box of tissues slid in front of Raven. She looked up to see a woman with black rimmed glasses perched on the end of her nose and dark brown hair done up in a fancy twist with a pencil sticking out of it. She smiled at Raven and nodded to the box.

Raven touched the pads of her fingers to her face and pulled them away to study them. They were wet. She pulled three or four tissues from the box and covered her face with them. How had that happened?

"I love you both. See you on the other side." The picture of Ena with her shoulders vibrating faded to black.

"I'll give you a moment." The woman in the black glasses turned the TV off and slipped out of the room.

Raven turned to Kiran. "Do you know what she was talking about? The thing with the trust fund?"

Kiran frowned at her. "I believe Adara would have taken care of the particulars for you."

"I've never heard anything about it." Had Adara been putting it away in a bank account for her? Why wouldn't she have said something? Yeah, she was definitely going to have to pay Adara a visit.

"What was she talking about with the paternity thing? Why would I need your protection?" She could damn well look after herself.

"Ah." Kiran's face flushed and the vein in his neck pulsed. "You come from a line of pure witch blood, which is very rare in the present day."

"I know that. The Bowen line is one of the last remaining pure bloodlines."

"Aye, and the Hayes bloodline is one of the few others in existence."

Raven stared into Kiran's ice blue eyes. If both her parents were of pure bloodlines, that meant …

Kiran nodded as if he was reading her mind. "Aye. That would make you the most powerful witch in North America."

"Not really. I haven't practiced magick since I was twelve." *Remember.*

That one word from Ena was a whisper, as if it had blown through Raven's mind on a breeze. Remember what?

The woman came back in the room with an accordion file and placed it on the table before taking a seat across from Kiran and Raven.

"Kiran, we've met, but I haven't had the pleasure of meeting you, Raven. I'm Kiara Pfeiffer. Looking at the two of you is like having double vision. I can't believe how similar you look."

She pulled two thick manila envelopes out of her folder and slid one over to Kiran and then one to Raven. "There's a private video for each of you in there as well as the documents you need to sign. It will be a while before the money and the estate are transferred. Once Ena's taxes are paid, that will move forward. But, you have your trust fund, Raven. That should be enough to keep up the maintenance on the land and the house."

"Hold on a moment. I've never heard about a trust fund until today."

Kiara stared at Raven wide-eyed. "I don't understand. Adara Kirby set that up for you on your eighteenth birthday. She brought us your account information and we've been making the deposits to your account every month."

"I think I'm going to need you to give me this account information because I've never seen a dime. If I had been told about a trust fund when I was eighteen, I would have told Ena to keep her friggin' money. And while we're at it. I don't want her house either. You can give that to Kiran."

"No, I'm sorry, I can't. It has been decreed down the generations that the house, the land, and the money be passed from mother to daughter. It's yours, Raven. Until you pass it on to your daughter."

As if she was going to have a daughter. If she had her way, she'd be spending the rest of her life with Riley, so she didn't think either one of them would be getting knocked up any time soon.

Oh, sweetheart. You already are.

Jesus. What the hell was she talking about now?

You were with Jaxon, Rave.

Raven shot to her feet, knocking her chair backwards. She quickly picked it up and pushed it back into the table. "I-I need to go." She fumbled with the heavy door and bumped into the door jamb as she tried to pass through. Her chest burned as she cleared the reception area and made it out to the fresh air. She bent over, tried to breathe, and slid her hand under her shirt, over her belly. When was it she slept with Jaxon? Four or five weeks ago? When was her last time of the month? Oh, shit. She sat on the sidewalk and bent over with her head between her knees.

"Raven?" Kiran called out as he rushed to her side. "What it is, love? Is it the trust fund?"

"No. Christ, no. I don't give a shit about the damn trust fund." If she was pregnant, that would explain all of these emotions she was struggling with, wouldn't it? She wasn't losing it. She was just pregnant. Just pregnant? Holy, shit. "I need to go t-to the drug store."

Kiran refused to let Raven drive, so they walked the two blocks to the pharmacy. He refused to wait outside, too. Much to Raven's horror, he followed her down the aisles as she tried to find the pregnancy tests.

"Will you tell me what's going on, love? You're as white as

chalk."

How did she explain everything? She turned to him and raked her hand through her hair. "It's Ena. This is going to sound crazy, but she's been talking to me since she passed." She expected him to look at her like she was a complete idiot, but his face lit up. He flashed a brilliant white smile and his eyes, icy blue flames framed in dark lashes, sparkled.

"You can communicate with her? Oh, blessed be. Can you tell her I love her? I miss her so much." His smile faded and he pressed his thumb and forefinger to his eyes. "Oh, dear God. I'm sorry."

Tell Kiran I'm here. I'm right here.

"She said to tell you she's right here." Okay, this was just too weird. She wasn't going to act as some sort of liaison between her parents. God only knew what they'd want to say to each other. Ick.

"Oh, babe. I'm sorry I wasted so much of our time being away at sea. I thought we had a lifetime still ahead of us. I thought I would retire in a few years and we would spend the rest of our days together. I'm so sorry, darling."

"Can I just remind you that we're standing in the middle of a store." So not doing this. Why did they have to wait for this moment to confess their love for each other for God's sake?

Kiran ran his hand through his hair and looked at Raven with a pained expression. "She wasn't the only one who made mistakes, who has regrets, aye? I'm sorry, love. I didn't mean to embarrass you."

She was about to get a lot more embarrassed. The pregnancy tests were sitting on the shelf right behind him. "She's not there all the time. She just pops in and out. Anyway, while we were at the lawyer's, she said something. That's what upset me."

"What did she say, love?"

She thought about telling him not to call her that. Again.

But, it was becoming kind of endearing. It made her feel all warm inside. Her hand went to her belly, rested there for a moment, and she pointed to the shelf behind him.

"I need one of those."

Kiran turned around and looked at the shelf then took a big step back. "Oh. Alright then. Do you mean to tell me I'm going to be a grandfather?" He looked at Raven with his eyes wide, his face a little pale.

"That's what I need the test for."

"But, I thought …" He blew out a short laugh. "I'm sorry, love. I thought you were gay. Yesterday … Riley. Well, she said you just broke up."

"Yeah. We did." This was not a conversation she wanted to have with Kiran.

"So, you're bi-sexual?"

"Can we just buy the damn test and get out of here." She grabbed at the first one in her reach and stomped off to the cashier.

Kiran chased her down the aisle. "I'm sorry, love. This isn't the time or the place for that conversation. I'm just a little … well, I'm not very good at being a father yet, am I?"

Raven whirled on him, stopping him in his tracks with her icy glare. "I'm twenty-seven freaking years old. I've lived my entire life without a father. What the hell makes you think I need one now?" She regretted her words the moment they were out of her mouth. He looked at her as if she'd just sucker punched him.

"Oh, aye. I understand."

He walked to the exit and pushed the door so hard it bounced back and nearly took him out.

Shouldn't have done that. She pushed Ena out of her life and now she was doing it with him. She looked down at the box in her hand and wondered if she'd do it with her kid, too. Would she suck at being a mother? The last thing she wanted was to have a kid and make her feel like she didn't matter.

She made her way to the cashier, relieved when she didn't know the woman at the till and there was no line up. She placed the box on the counter and fished a twenty dollar bill out of her front pocket. The woman smiled at the box then up at Raven.

"Your first?"

Raven nodded. Her first what? Pregnancy test? Because if she knew if she was having a baby, she wouldn't need the damn test. She thanked her lucky stars when the woman rang her up without another word. Raven took her change, swiped the bag off the counter, and high tailed it out of there. She half expected to find Kiran sitting in Ena's car in the lawyer's parking lot, but he'd gone. She was just about to get in her car when she heard her name and turned to see Kiara running toward her in her spiked heels.

"You left without your documents," she said as she handed Raven the manila envelope.

Raven stared at it, but made no attempt to take it from Kiara.

"I've included the banking information for your trust fund."

Raven continued to stare at the envelope. Accepting it didn't mean she was accepting the house and the money. She needed to find out where the trust fund money had been going, but she could do that and not bother with the rest of the contents of the envelope. She reached out and took it from Kiara's hand. "Thanks."

Kiara didn't let go of the envelope. "Take some time to read through it, Raven. Do that for yourself if not for her." She released her hold when Raven nodded.

Raven got in the car and started it up. She was already backing up as she fumbled with her seat belt. She'd go home, pee on the stupid stick and then go to the bank to find out what happened to the mysterious trust money. Once she knew what the deal was there, she could go and visit Adara and get to the bottom of everything.

She was pulling onto her road before she knew it and it struck her that she couldn't remember most of the drive home because she'd been so involved in her thoughts. If she was pregnant, did she stand a chance with Riley? Jaxon would probably go ballistic and want to marry her. Jesus. This mess would destroy Jaxon and make Riley alienate her even more than she already was.

Half way down her road, she spotted a satellite truck, then another. Slowing to a stop, she stared out in disbelief. Cars and vans with the logos of every TV and radio news station in the Province lined the road. Her cottage was surrounded by reporters, videographers, and photographers. She reversed down the road until she found a spot where she could turn around then sped off in the opposite direction. Who the heck would have given them her address?

She drove back towards town wondering where she could go to pee on the stick. Riley's was out. Jaxon's was even less appealing than Riley's. She didn't want to go to Adara's until she found out what the bank had to say. If Ena, who'd been Adara's best friend, considered Adara a suspect, then Raven had to do so also, even if it went against everything she knew about Adara.

Raven pulled into the Solstice Café's parking lot and parked the car then took out her cell phone. She still had it on silent mode. On the bottom left corner of her screen, the phone icon showed a red number in the top right corner displaying 112 missed calls plus voicemail. Her voicemail would only hold three messages, so anyone else trying to leave a message would get a recording telling them the mailbox was full. For that reason, she didn't check the messages. She scrolled through the list of phone numbers.

Most were numbers she didn't recognize. She figured the media not only discovered her home address, but her cell phone number as well. But, how?

The numbers she did recognize were calls from Adara, Jaxon, Grayson, and Mick. None from Riley. That figured, didn't it? The one person you do want to call, doesn't. She called Mick and when she picked up, she didn't give Mick the opportunity to speak.

"Where are you?"

"Um…at work."

"Can you go home? I mean …" Crap. "Can I meet you at your place? I just need a few minutes."

"Raven? What's going on?"

Raven closed her eyes, drew in a deep breath and released it, trying to calm her fluttering heart. "My place is surrounded by reporters. I need to borrow your washroom for a few minutes."

"The media has kind of descended upon Solstice. There's a mob of them at the detachment, too. When I leave here, they're liable to follow me, Raven. They know we worked on the Paigo case together."

"Okay. Never mind." She disconnected the call and stuffed her phone back in her pocket. Then she sat there staring at the building through her windshield. Was she really considering doing a pregnancy test in the café washroom? Yes, damn it. She was dying for a pee. She scanned the parking lot for a vehicle with a news station logo on it. Nothing. Stuffing the pharmacy bag inside her jacket, she dashed to the ladies room and locked herself into one of the two stalls.

Reading the directions on the box took seconds. Raven ripped the box open and followed the directions word for word. And then she waited. She didn't want to look at the stick, so she set an alarm on her phone to time the five minutes it was supposed to take the stick to register a result with either a plus sign or a minus sign. It was, without a doubt, the longest five minutes of her life. What the hell was she going to do if it turned out positive? She wasn't ready to be a mother, especially not a single mother. How was she supposed to raise a baby with her career? She could get called out at any time of the day or night.

Then there was the issue of carrying a kid around in her belly for nine months, getting bigger and bigger until she couldn't move and her ankles swelled up beyond recognition. Was she allowed to work out if she was preggers? Run? Could she drink coffee? "Oh, damn. Please be negative."

The alarm sounded on her phone and as she turned it off she wished it hadn't sounded so soon. She wasn't ready to look at the damn stick. Her heart beat a battle of tribal drums against her chest. She placed her hands on either side of the stall and lowered her forehead to the door, the cool metal soothing her burning skin. Breathe. She should have gone to Riley's. If she passed out, she'd land on the dirty washroom floor. Not that it looked filthy or anything, but who wanted to lie on the floor of a public washroom? Worse yet, what if she landed on the toilet. Ew.

She knew she was stalling, being a weak idiot. Time to put on her big girl pants and get it over with. What's the worst that could happen? Oh, yeah. She could be pregnant and alone. She forced herself to turn and look at the stick sitting on the box on top of the toilet paper dispenser. The little window displayed a clear, blue plus sign.

It could be wrong, couldn't it? Maybe she should get another test to make sure. Or … shit. She'd known it in her gut, haha, before she even took the test. As soon as Ena said it, she knew there was a little life inside her. That's why she'd panicked.

What the hell was she going to do?

One step at a time, darling angel. The first thing you need to do

*is find Jaxon and tell him. I robbed you of the chance to know your
father and I robbed Kiran of the joy of seeing you growing up. Don't
do that to your child.*

As much as she didn't want Ena's advice at the moment,
she was right. It was Jaxon's child, too and he had the right to
know. She put the stick in the bag, stuffed the box into the
garbage and washed her hands, careful not to get the
bandage on her left hand wet. It wasn't an easy task. Neither
was trying to rub her right hand and her left fingers dry
under the blower.

She went to the counter to buy a coffee then couldn't
decide what to order. She couldn't have caffeine, could she?
She stared up at the drink menu. If she ordered a decaf, the
staff would get suspicious. They knew exactly what she
ordered every time she came in or went through the drive
thru – large, double double. Raven stepped up to the counter
and Irene had already rung her coffee into the till.

"Can I get a chocolate milk instead? I feel like something
cold." There. That wasn't suspicious. She had a perfectly
good reason for ordering a chocolate milk.

"Oh, sure." Irene deleted the coffee and rang in a chocolate
milk. "I think this is the first time in the five years I've
worked here that you haven't ordered a large, double double,
Raven."

Raven stabbed her fingers through her hair, leaving a large
tuft sticking up and leaning to the left. "I've already had my
quota for the day. I'm on a new fitness regime." She handed
Irene a five, accepted the change and stuffed it in the front
pocket of her jeans.

"Looks like it's one hell of a regime. You're pretty banged
up." She pointed to Raven's face. "I heard you've had a rough
week. We saw you on the news last night, honey."

Great. "Yeah, it's been a rough one." She picked up her
chocolate milk and fled.

In her car, she locked the doors and pulled out her phone. She had double as many text messages as she had missed calls. Jaxon had sent her nearly twenty text messages since the previous afternoon. Most of them said, "Answer your damn phone" or "Call me". With her stomach churning, she sent him a text. 'Are you at work? We need to talk.' Then she waited, staring at her phone.

Her body jolted when the phone began buzzing in her hand. The display showed an incoming call from Jaxon. She answered, "Hey."

"Finally. I've been trying to get hold of you since yesterday. Are you okay?"

Those emotions she was having a terrible time avoiding soared up through her chest, clogged in her throat and made her eyes water. "Yeah, but I really need to speak with you. In person."

"Rave? You don't sound so good, babe."

Her entire body began to shake. She pursed her lips and squeezed her eyes shut, pushing everything down.

"Rave?"

"I'm here." She told herself to breathe, but she was afraid if she let her breath go, everything she was trying to hold back would tumble out.

"Where's here? I'm coming to get you."

"No, not here. Can I meet you at your house?"

"You're scaring me, Rave. What's going on?"

"I'll meet you at your place." She hung up, lowered her head to the steering wheel and released her breath with a great whoosh.

Chapter 11

Jaxon was already parked in his driveway when Raven pulled in behind him. She slid into the passenger side of his truck, the pharmacy bag crinkling in her trembling hand.

He examined the abrasions and bruises on her face with lips pursed to a fine white line. "You okay?"

"Yeah." She didn't like the sound of her own voice. It was more of an exhale than a word that rushed out of her lungs. Then she shook her head and said, "No. No, I'm not." She handed him the bag, the plastic shaking furiously as her stomach did cartwheels and a few back hand springs.

Jaxon took the bag from her, pursed lips turning into a frown. "You're scaring me, Rave. What's this?"

He opened the bag and stared into it for a few moments. She knew exactly when it clicked what he was looking at. His eyes went from narrowed to bulging and his mouth dropped open. Raven dropped her head into her hand.

"You can't mean your pregnant?"

Raven spared him a quick glance. His eyes were still bulged out, but there was something else there. Anger? His face had become flushed and there was a thick, ropey vein bulging in his neck.

"That's what the stick says."

Jaxon closed the bag and dropped it in her lap. "So, why

are you showing it to me? We used protection, Rave."

Her mouth dropped open. Was he saying it couldn't have been him; insinuating she'd slept with another man? She snatched up the bag, opened the door, and slid down to the driveway.

"Fuck you," she said before she slammed the door. She would figure this out on her own. She didn't need a damn man to accuse her of being a slut.

Jaxon shot out of the truck and rounded the back before she had a chance to get in her car. Grabbing her by the shoulders, he glared into her eyes.

"Don't you dare drop this on me and take off. You don't get to do this to me."

Raven brought her hands up in front of her, shot her forearms out to the side and then down to dislodge his hands from her shoulders. Her blood was running hot through her veins, her heart beating too fast, pounding in her ears. She darted around him and threw herself into her car, locking the doors as soon as she slammed it shut. She wanted to punch him, claw him bloody. The last thing she expected was for him to suggest it wasn't his baby. She didn't know what reaction she had expected from him, but it certainly wasn't that.

She threw the car in reverse and shot out of the driveway with the tires squealing. Jaxon chased her out of the driveway, yelling at her to stop. When she shoved it into drive and slammed her foot down on the accelerator she saw him out of the corner of her eye darting back to his truck. She had a few seconds head start to try to lose him which wasn't an easy task in their small town. She weaved back and forth through some of the side streets and when she was sure he wasn't right on her tail, she shot up an alley and parked behind a big delivery truck.

She dropped her head to her forearms crossed over the

steering wheel. This couldn't be happening. She loved her job, but she didn't see how she could manage to put in the hours she did with a baby to look after, especially if she was going to have to do it on her own. And she would be on her own. Riley would never take her back now. Her pregnancy and then her child would be a constant reminder of her betrayal.

Then there was Jaxon. Even if his reaction to the news of her pregnancy had been positive, the simple fact was she didn't want him. Eventually, he would grow to resent her. She stabbed her fingers into her hair again, fisted her hands in it and barely contained the urge to let loose a rip-roaring primal scream.

He'll come around, darling angel. He just needs some time to let the news sink in.

Ena's voice reminded Raven she had a case to solve. She needed to put all thoughts of the tiny little life growing inside of her aside and focus on finding Ena's killer. But first, she needed to head to the bank to find out what was happening to the trust fund money. Ignoring Ena's words, she picked up the envelope sitting on the passenger seat and rifled through the papers for the banking information. It wasn't even her bank that the account was set up in, but it was in her name. The address was Adara's, but that could be because it was Raven's address when the account was opened just prior to her eighteenth birthday. But, why would Adara go all the way into Huntsville to open the account when she could have done it in Solstice and why hadn't she told Raven about it?

It was then Raven caught sight of the amount of the monthly deposits. She rubbed her eyes and then looked at the figure again, sure she had mistaken the amount. The figure on the page didn't change. Fifteen thousand dollars was deposited on the twenty-first of every month. *Fifteen thousand?* All she could think about was nearly starving to death while she was going through the police college and then the sacrifices she made to scrape up enough money for a deposit on her cottage. Fifteen thousand a month worked out to one hundred and eighty thousand a year for nearly nine years. That would bring the total up to around one point five million dollars. This didn't make any sense. Adara wouldn't have let her suffer through college and saving for her house if she knew about this money. Not only that, but Adara was on a fixed disability income and Raven had never known her to spend beyond her means.

On the drive to Huntsville, Raven's thoughts bounced back and forth between the money and the pregnancy test. Those pregnancy tests weren't a hundred percent accurate, were they? It could be a false positive. There was no reason to get all freaked out until she could confirm without a doubt that she was pregnant. The only way to know for sure was to make an appointment to see a doctor and for some reason she wanted that doctor to be Dr. Simone Wagnar. She hadn't seen Simone in that capacity for years, but she didn't have a regular physician and she didn't want to go to the walk-in clinic and have a stranger examine her, especially if she ended up with a male doctor.

As soon as she pulled into a parking spot in front of the bank, she called Simone's office to make an appointment. She was hoping to get an appointment next week or the week after, but the receptionist said Simone was in urgent care the next morning and would fit her in. That meant she had less than twenty-four hours before she had to face the reality of her condition. Twenty-four hours to pray that there wasn't a tiny life growing inside her. Until Simone told her she was preggers, she was going to go about her life as if she wasn't.

Raven gathered the legal documents pertaining to the disbursement of the trust fund and made her way into the bank. Instead of lining up for a teller, she went to the customer service desk and asked to speak to someone about her account. She was asked to take a seat and settled herself into a hard, straight-backed chair against a wall. She hoped to hell they didn't make her wait too long because she didn't want to sit there alone with her thoughts. As much as she tried to put it out of her mind, she couldn't stop thinking about what she would do with a baby, besides the obvious. She couldn't picture herself with a big, pregnant belly or, good Lord, delivering a Jaxon sized baby. That thought had her squeezing her thighs together and wincing. What the hell had possessed her to have sex with a man? Damn you, Jaxon Lang.

"Miss Bowen?"

Raven's eyes focused on the young man standing in front of her. He didn't look like the banker type. He looked like a high school jock with his wide shoulders and thick neck. His dark hair was styled to perfection in the latest shaved sides style. "Yes?"

"Are you okay? Would you like a glass of water or something?"

Did she look that bad? She knew the colour had drained from her face because she felt it, like gravity forced all of the blood in her body to drain to her legs. She wasn't too sure if she could get to her feet without passing out. Her hand went to the hollow of her throat. "No, I'm fine. Thank you."

He nodded then waved his hand in the direction of a row of glass walled offices. "Right this way, please."

Raven followed him to his office and took a seat across the desk from him.

He folded his hands on the desk and said, "What can we do for you today, Miss Bowen?"

"It's Detective Constable Bowen, actually." She didn't know why she said that. She didn't like being called Miss Bowen. For some reason it felt like an insult.

"Of course, I'm sorry. I'm Brian."

Raven slid the papers across the desk to Brian and explained that she wanted information on the account named in the document.

"Sure. Have you got your debit card with you?"

"No, sorry. I haven't got one."

Brian smiled. "How about a photo ID?"

Raven slid forward and reached into her back pocket for the black leather wallet she kept there. She opened her badge and O.P.P. ID and slid it across the desk to join the papers.

"Wow," Brian grinned. "I've never actually seen a police badge. It's nice. Shiny."

Really? Shiny? This guy got his vocabulary from the same place Mick did. Raven pasted on a smile then returned the wallet to her pocket.

"Okay, let's bring up your account then." He tapped away on his keyboard and then turned his monitor so Raven could see it. "Looks like your balance is just under two million dollars."

That was a lot more than she expected. She frowned as she looked at the screen. "Can you bring up the account activity for say…the past year?"

Brian tapped at his keyboard again. The $15,000 monthly deposits plus interest were the only activity.

"Is it possible to get a printout of the account activity dating back to the time it was opened?"

"That shouldn't be a problem."

It took a while because Brian had to bring the lists up year by year for the past nine years, but Raven walked out with the printouts dating back to whehn the account was first opened and a *shiny* new bank card. The only activity during that whole time were the deposits and the interest accrued. So, Adara had opened the account in Raven's name and then just left it alone.

Raven's next stop was Adara's place. The whole way there she tried to keep her mind off of what might be happening in her belly and focused on Adara and the stuff she'd been keeping from her all these years. She tapped her knuckles against the kitchen door before letting herself in.

Adara sat at her kitchen island with her Book of Shadows open in front of her. She smiled at Raven, closed the massive book and slid off her stool. "I've been trying to call you. Are you okay?"

Adara wasn't her usual bright self this afternoon. She stood there nervously wringing her hands, her eyes wide open and sad. Guilty perhaps?

"Yeah, I'm fine. I've silenced my phone."

"Ah, yes. The media have been calling here looking for you as well. I've had to turn my ringer off. If you're trying to get hold of me, let it go to voice mail and let me know it's you. I'll pick up."

Raven nodded and shoved her hands in her jeans pockets leaving her thumbs hooked out over the edge as she rolled back on her heels. "Can we talk, Adara?"

"Yes, of course. Would you like a coffee?"

Would she ever. But she couldn't have caffeine until she knew for certain if she was pregnant or not. "Uh, no thanks."

Adara's eyebrows shot up. It wasn't like Raven to turn down a coffee. Instead of leaving Adara suspicious, Raven said, "I just had one."

"Well, why don't we go into the parlour then."

Raven followed Adara to the front room and waited for Adara to settle in her favourite chair by the fire. It was a comfortable room with a large screen TV hanging over the fireplace, thick carpeting in a faded blue. The sunlight speared through thick slatted blinds in a bay style window. The couch and the chair were thickly cushioned in a cream colour, the walls decorated in a pale yellow that added to the room's warmth. Raven had spent so much time in this room over the years it still felt like home. She took her usual spot on the couch, but instead of sinking into its comfortable depths, she perched on the edge and ran her hands down her jeans. Where to start?

"I know you're upset with me," Adara said. "And you have every right to be. I did take you in at Ena's request, but I would have done it anyway, Raven. You're as much a daughter to me as you are to Ena. I love you as my own."

Raven let out a long sigh. She felt like an idiot for doubting Adara, the one person who'd always been there for her, the one person who provided a safe home for her. Adara never had strange men coming and going like there was a revolving door at the entrance. It had just been Adara and Raven. Adara *saw* her, whereas Ena rarely did. "I know. I love you, too."

Adara's hand covered her heart as her eyes pooled. "I was so worried. I don't want you to hate me, Rave. All I've ever done is try to look out for you."

"Can you tell me about the trust fund?"

Adara's eyes widened again. "Trust fund? Oh, yes. My goodness, I forgot all about that."

"You opened an account in my name for the payments to be deposited into."

"Yes. I opened the account and then forgot about it. Although they do send a statement every month. I have them all in my files, if you want them."

"Why didn't you tell me about it?"

"You were still so angry at your mom, I knew you wouldn't want anything to do with it. So I just did what I was told and let it be."

"You were reporting back to mom about me the whole time, weren't you?"

Adara broke eye contact and stared out the window. Raven waited for an answer. She wasn't about to let Adara off the hook, but she gave her a few moments before she prompted her again. "You were, weren't you?"

With a heavy sigh, Adara returned her gaze to meet Raven's. "She was my best friend, honey. Always. She loved you with all of her heart, so of course she wanted to know how you were doing."

"But, you never encouraged either of us to try to resolve our differences."

Adara pursed her lips and looked away again. When she turned back, her eyes were glistening and a fat tear rolled down her cheek. "I didn't want to give you back, Rave." She sniffed. "I couldn't stand to lose you." Adara dropped her face into her hands and wept.

"Is that why you didn't tell me about Kiran? You were afraid to lose me to him, too?" If that were the case, would Adara go so far as to put a spell on her to sleep with Jax to break her and Riley up? Was she jealous that she was spending too much time with Riley and not stopping by as much as she used to?

"Oh, dear Goddess." Adara let out a long wail as if she were in great pain. "It wasn't my place, Rave. I'm so sorry for what I've put you through. I couldn't stand the thought of losing you and I felt it was Ena's place to tell you. Do you understand?" She pulled a tissue out of her sleeve and blew her nose then continued to weep into her hands.

Raven took a deep breath then huffed it out. Adara had no family of her own aside from Ena, Raven, and the coven, so Raven could hardly blame her for wanting to keep her as her own child. She moved to the arm of Adara's chair, wrapped her arms around her and placed a kiss on the top of her head. "It's okay. I didn't want to lose you either."

* * *

Raven left Adara's berating herself for doubting the only person she'd been able to count on. Why Ena was suspicious of her best friend and the sweetest person Raven knew was beyond her.

She was the only person with access to my house and she was in my house every morning for the last month of my life. She could very well have put poison in the Chalice.

Raven got into her car and slammed the door, fisting her hands tightly around the steering wheel and growled through gritted teeth, "She was your best friend, loyal to you for your entire lives. She took in your daughter and kept her safe, which is more than I can say for you."

You really know how to hurt someone, Rave. I know I failed you. It's my biggest regret in life. I tried so hard to get you to talk to me back then. If only you'd told me at the very start, I could have protected you, sweetheart.

"He would have killed you."

No. I would have killed him. *Had I known what he did to you, I would have killed him.*

Raven's chest tightened in that uncomfortable way that was beginning to feel familiar. The ferocity in Ena's voice, the raw emotion as she spoke had Raven wondering if she had prolonged her own suffering by not opening up to her mother. All she wanted back then was for Ena to wrap her in love and stop the abuse, but she hadn't been able to risk Gregor killing Ena.

You didn't hate me after all. You loved me too much to risk him hurting me.

The ferocity was gone and in it's place was the soft, loving coo of a mother. Raven fisted her hand over her heart trying to absorb the pain. "I've never hated you. I resented you for not protecting me, for not seeing what I couldn't tell you."

I'm so sorry, my sweet angel. I'm so sorry.

Ena's voice shook as she spoke then there was only silence. Raven dropped her head and rested her forehead against the steering wheel, admitting to herself for the first time that what Gregor did to her wasn't entirely Ena's fault. Her resentment caused her to blame Ena and judge her for her beliefs. Ena was entitled to practice witchcraft and dedicate herself to the Wiccan religion. Raven had no right to judge and condemn her for that.

A tap on the window jolted her out of her reverie. Her head shot up to see Adara staring in at her, concern drawing her eyebrows together.

"Raven? Are you okay, sweetie?"

Raven stuck her key in the ignition and turned it enough to allow her to roll down her window. "It's okay, Adara. I was just thinking." How long had Adara been watching her? Had she witnessed her talking to Ena? Had she been close enough to hear?

"Are you sure? You look upset."

Forcing a smile, Raven said, "Yeah, I was just thinking about a case I'm working." She didn't know why she was lying. She never lied to Adara.

"The Emily McMurtrie case? I thought that was solved."

"Yeah. Just tying up loose ends." She reached out and took Adara's hand. "Everything is okay. Really."

Adara smiled and squeezed Raven's hand before releasing it. "You'd tell me if something was wrong, wouldn't you?"

"Of course. You've always been the one person I could talk to. That's why I came here, Adara. I couldn't stand for there to be any animosity between us."

Adara's eyes lit up and she smiled brilliantly. "I love you, sweetie."

"Love you, too."

Raven started the car as she watched Adara walk back into the house. What Ena said about Adara being the only one who had access to the house swirled around in her mind. Was that why she found it necessary to lie? She was letting Ena cause her to doubt Adara again. Was Ena manipulating her?

Was she jealous of Raven's relationship with Adara?

Of course I'm jealous of your relationship with Adara. I have been since the day you left home, sweet Angel. But, that's not why I want you to be wary of her.

Raven reversed out of Adara's driveway and began to drive towards town with no particular destination in mind. She just didn't want Adara to catch her talking to Ena again. "Who delivered the chalice and the flowers?" She needed to track down the delivery to prove the chalice had been there and was missing.

I don't know. They were left on the back porch one morning. It was Adara who found them there and brought them in.

"They were left outside the kitchen door?" That was odd. Any deliveries would have been left at the front door unless whoever made the delivery knew Ena. "Were they cold? Could you tell if they'd been sitting out there for long?"

The chalice was in a gift bag. I opened it right away and I don't remember it feeling cold.

Raven pulled the car to the side of the road. "What did you do with the gift bag?"

It should be in the cupboard in my office. I keep all of my wrapping paper and gift bags in a bin on the shelf in there.

Raven waited for a break in traffic then pulled a U-turn and headed for Ena's house. "Don't disappear on me. I need you to identify the bag."

Oh, this is exciting. I'm beginning to see why you enjoy police work.

Raven rolled her eyes. She studied the house as she approached Ena's and confirmed that anyone delivering a package would have left it at the front door instead of going around to the side entrance to the kitchen which was hidden from view when you pulled into the driveway. She parked behind Ena's car, a little disappointed that Kiran was home. She retrieved her evidence kit from the trunk and approached the side door.

Normally, she would have let herself in, but it felt like a stranger's house now that she knew Kiran was living there. She knocked on the kitchen door and waited. She was about to knock again when the door flew open and Kiran stood there in faded blue jeans and a white t-shirt. His hands were covered in pale yellow paint and there was a slash of paint across his handsome face. For a man in his early fifties, he was in great shape. Through his white t-shirt, Raven could see the square slabs of his pecs and the ripples of washboard abs.

"Raven? Hello. I wasn't expecting you." He opened the door wider and took a step back. "Come in. You don't need to knock. It's your house, love."

Raven frowned at his comment. He knew she didn't want the damn house and he knew she didn't want him to call her love. Stubborn old fart. "I need to find something in Ena's office. Is that okay?"

"Aye. Help yourself." He motioned to the stairs. "I'll be upstairs. If you need anything, just give me a shout."

Raven nodded, wondering why he was painting if he thought she was going to get the house. She watched him as he jogged up the creaking stairs and listened to his footsteps going down the hall. If she wasn't mistaken, he had gone into her old room. Curious, she made her way up the stairs.

Bright light shone into the dark hallway from her childhood bedroom along with a tune she couldn't identify playing softly. She made her way quietly down the hall and peeked around the door frame. All of the furniture had been removed and the floor was covered by drop cloths. The sickening bubblegum pink walls had been covered with the pale yellow she'd seen on Kiran's hands and face.

Kiran's back was to her as he rollered a second coat of paint on the far wall, his movements in rhythm to the tune emanating from the small boom box sitting on the floor. He turned, moving towards the paint tray sitting on the floor in the middle of the room and froze when he saw Raven in the doorway. His hand dropped to his side and he straightened to his full height.

"Raven?" He swiped his free hand through his hair, leaving a stripe of paint in it, looking like a little boy who'd been caught with his hand in the cookie jar. "I'm sorry, love. I thought maybe you'd be more comfortable with the house if I got rid of your old room, made it new. Or different. I guess I'm trying to paint away your bad memories, darling."

Raven stood there staring at him with her mouth open. He was doing this for her after the way she treated him?

"Please, say something." His eyes pleaded with her.

"Why?" It was all she could think of to say in that moment.

His short laugh portrayed his nervousness. "Because I knew the room held bad memories for you." He placed the roller in the paint tray, rubbed his hands down his thighs, leaving yellow streaks on his jeans, and turned sad eyes on Raven. "I don't know what to do for you, love. I know you're hurting, but I don't know how to fix it. Moving furniture and painting I can handle. Being a father? Well, that's new territory for me."

Raven could only stare at him. She swallowed the knot in her throat, turning away from him so he couldn't see the emotions she was sure were written all over her face. "Thank you." Her lower lip trembled as she spoke, so she bit into it. Had anyone ever done something like that for her before? She didn't think so. It seemed this man felt something for her even though they just met and despite how rude she'd been to him.

"You're welcome, love. Would you do something for me?"

She knew she should turn around and face him, but she turned her head to the side instead, seeing him in her peripheral vision. "What do you need?"

"Would you give me a chance to be your father? I can't promise I won't make mistakes, Raven. But, I promise I'll try my best."

Her chest tightened and her eyes pooled despite trying desperately to push it all back. She dropped to a crouching position and covered her head with her arms. This was too much. She'd been on her own for years. Even with Adara, she felt alone in the world. Hell, she was alone when she was with Ena. Could she let this man in and risk getting hurt?

She felt Kiran next to her then his arms wrapped around her, cocooning her in his warmth. Raven did something she hadn't allowed herself to do since she was a little girl – she let go. Leaning into him, she buried her face in his chest and wept. Kiran's big hand cradled her head, holding her to his chest as he rocked her in his arms.

Raven cried until she was sure she had no tears left. When her ragged breaths returned to normal, she pushed away from Kiran, embarrassed by her loss of control. "Sorry," she whispered as she dried her cheeks with her hands.

"Don't be sorry, love. I have a feeling that was a long time coming."

Kiran stayed at her side, but made no attempt to touch her or pull her back in. He gave her the space she needed to regain control. She had to give him points for that. "I…" She pointed towards the hallway and pushed up to her feet. "I need to go."

"Alright then, love," Kiran whispered.

* * *

Raven stood in the middle of Ena's office with her evidence kit in her hand, still shaking from her emotional outbreak. It took a minute for her to remember what she was looking for. Oh, yeah. Gift bag. She slid open the closet door, pulled a large bin from the shelf and set it down on the floor. Inside was a massive collection of gift bags and wrapping paper.

"What does it look like?" She waited for Ena's response and was met with silence. "Damn it, Ena. Where the hell are you?"

Raven slapped the lid back on the bin and clicked it into place by slamming her fist in the middle of it. She was going to have to take the whole bin until she could get Ena to identify the bag. She carried it out to the kitchen and placed it on the counter near the door then went back for her evidence kit. As she came out of the office, Kiran was coming down the stairs carrying a large cardboard box.

"Have you got a minute, love?"

Raven placed her kit by the door then turned to him. She was hoping to get out before she ran into him again. "Yeah, what's up?"

"I came across this box in your mother's closet." He set it on the kitchen island. "It's got your name on it."

Raven closed in on the box as if she was approaching an explosive device. She peered at the elegant scroll written in black marker across the top – *For Raven*. Had Ena done this before or after she knew she was dying?

"I'll carry it out to your car for you, aye?"

Raven's eyes met Kiran's over the box. He was looking at her like he was trying to figure out if she was still fragile and emotional. She just wanted to get out of there, away from the man who was making it very hard not to love him and let him be the father he wanted to be. It made her feel like she was going to lose control and the last thing she wanted was to blubber on his shoulder again. She nodded. "Yeah. That would be great. Thanks."

She swore Kiran's ice blue eyes twinkled when he smiled. He hefted the box off the island counter and they took everything out, loading it into her trunk. Her eyes met Kiran's for a second before she dropped her gaze. "So…

thanks." God, this was awkward.

"Will you come for dinner tomorrow? Six o'clock?"

Her gaze flew up to meet his again. That was the last thing she was expecting. She wanted to say no, but she couldn't think of an excuse. "Yeah, sure." His eyes lit up again and Raven felt her heart swell. Maybe it wouldn't be so bad to get to know him a bit. She motioned toward her car door then dropped her hand to her side, her palm slapping against her thigh. "I need to go."

He stepped into her, wrapped her in his warm, strong arms, and squeezed.

"Alright, then. I'll see you tomorrow." When he stepped back, he placed a sweet, chaste kiss against her cheek then walked around the car and stood at the edge of the driveway. Raven's chest and eyes were on fire. She'd stiffened and didn't hug him back, but she wanted to. She was stopped by the urge to collapse into those strong arms and let go again. She'd already made a fool of herself once. She wasn't about to do it again.

Raven got in the car and began reversing out to the road. He watched her the whole time then waved when she shifted into drive. Raven waved back and then sped off, not exactly sure where she was going. She couldn't go home because of the media camped out around her little cottage. She didn't want to go to Adara's. Riley's and Jaxon's were out and she didn't want to call Mick again.

So, she drove aimlessly, thinking about Ena and Kiran and how different her life could have been if Kiran hadn't left all those years ago. Or, if he'd come back before Ena got involved with Gregor. She was so lost in her thoughts she neglected to check her surroundings, not noticing the car that pulled in behind her until it's red and blue lights began to flash all around her and it's siren squealed. She flashed her eyes to her rear-view mirror and recognized the SUV belonging to DS LaCroix.

"Damn it." She didn't want to deal with him yet. But, she pulled to the side of the road and sat there with her hands white knuckled around her steering wheel. She waited until he was beside her door before rolling the window down.

"Is your phone broken, Bowen?"

"No, sir." Raven continued to stare straight ahead as LaCroix sighed loudly. He was pissed at her and she couldn't blame him.

"Here's what your going to do. You're going to drive to the detachment and pull your vehicle into the garage so you're not hounded by the media. Then you go straight to my office and wait for me. Got it?"

Her hands were still white knuckled on the steering wheel despite the gash in her palm. She needed more time before she dealt with this, but she wasn't going to get it. Time to face the music, damn it.

"Yes, sir."

LaCroix tapped the roof of her car twice before walking away.

Chapter 12

Raven felt like she was doing the walk of shame as she made her way through the detachment to LaCroix's office. No one said a word, but she could feel everyone's eyes on her. She met Mick's gaze for an instant before Mick dropped her eyes. When she stepped into LaCroix's office, she slammed the door behind her and dropped into one of the chairs facing his desk wondering how long he'd make her sit here and wait. She could still feel everyone's eyes boring into the back of her head.

Every second that ticked by felt like an eternity. The second hand on the clock above LaCroix's desk appeared lethargic, every tick and tock amplified. Raven began tapping her fingers against her thigh then bouncing her legs on the balls of her feet. What the heck was taking him so long? He had no right to make her sit here and wait when she was supposed to be off sick. Okay, so she wasn't sick, but he didn't need to know that.

She nearly jumped right out of her seat when the door flung open. She turned her head to see LaCroix carrying two large coffees. He set one down on the desk in front of Raven and took his to his chair. Raven stared at the cup wondering how the hell she was going to drink it? Would it hurt the baby to have one coffee? God, she really wanted it.

She picked up the cup, opened the lid and took a long sip. God, it was good. Until she opened her eyes and found LaCroix staring at her with a scowl on his face, she hadn't realized she'd closed them.

"What?"

"You missed your appointment with the psychologist this afternoon, Raven."

"I didn't know I had an appointment."

LaCroix exploded out of his chair, banging his fist on the desk on his way up. "Damn it, Raven. I've been trying to call you all day." His palms landed on the desk and he leaned over it, an imposing figure making her feel small in her chair. "I must have sent you fifty text messages. Why the hell aren't you answering your phone?"

Now he was pissing her off. She didn't deserve to have him yelling at her and trying to intimidate her. She pulled her cell phone out of her pocket and threw it on the desk between LaCroix's hands.

"Someone gave my cell number to the media, so it's been ringing non-stop. Oh, and my home address as well. I went to the lawyer's this morning about my mother's estate and when I tried to go home, it was surrounded by satellite trucks and reporters."

A frown line appeared between his brows. "No one should be able to access your number or your address." He picked up her phone and scrolled through her call log and text messages. "Who would do that? Riley?"

"No, she's not vindictive." Raven put the coffee cup back on LaCroix's desk, dropped her elbows to her knees and rested her head in her palms.

"Jaxon?"

Jesus. Did everyone know her business? "He wouldn't hurt me either." Except he had, but he wouldn't have sicced the media on her.

"The same person who killed your mother?"

Raven's head shot up to meet his gaze. "What?"

"If they know your investigating her case, they may be trying to sidetrack you. Why? Who do you think would do something like that?"

"I was thinking Tate. I totally didn't go there with Ena's killer." She swiped her hand through her hair as a chill ran down her spine. "That would mean Ena's killer knows my cell phone number and address."

LaCroix lowered himself back into his chair and tented his fingertips together then tapped his forefingers against his lower lip. "I don't like this, Rave. I don't like it one bit." He sat forward and grabbed a notepad, turning it around and sliding it over to Raven before slapping a pen on top of it. "Write down every member of the coven who knows your phone number and address."

Raven stared hard at the notepad. She could only think of three people that fit that criteria and she didn't want to write down any of their names. She glanced up at LaCroix and the expression on his face told her he wasn't messing around. Her fingers passed through her hair again before she snapped up the pen and scribbled three names across the paper – Adara Kirby, Kiran Hayes, and Dr. Simone Wagnar. She slapped the pen onto the desk and shoved the notepad back to LaCroix then slumped back into her chair and crossed her arms over her chest.

LaCroix spun the pad around and read the names. "What's your gut telling you, Rave?"

"I need to check with the Royal Navy in the UK, but I think Kiran Hayes was on a ship in the Mediterranean when Ena was being poisoned. Simone was supposed to be away at a conference for the last week of Ena's life. Again, I've yet to confirm that."

"That leaves Adara."

"She was Ena's best friend, Grayson. She's been like a mother to me since I left home. She couldn't have done this."

Don't forget who could have gotten into your head to distract you before Jaxon hit you with his truck.

Now she shows up? What the hell did she mean by that? It was Ena who was balling in her head when she walked out into traffic.

No, darling angel. It wasn't. Have you ever known me to cry like that?

"Rave?"

"Sorry, what?" Had he been talking to her?

"I asked if you'd found any evidence yet?"

She couldn't answer his question because she hadn't checked her emails yet today. Surely Mick would have picked up any reports that came in from the lab or the Medical Examiner. "I need to check my emails."

"What the hell have you been doing all day?"

Raven frowned at him. "I called in sick."

"Bullshit. You're never sick. What the hell have you been up to all day, Rave?"

Damn him. "I needed a personal day to deal with personal crap. Okay?"

"Like your father suddenly turning up?"

Her blood began to boil and she felt the heat flare up over her face. "It's called personal crap because it's no one else's business, including yours."

"It's my business if it effects how you do your job. You were supposed to be in the psychologist's office over an hour ago and since that was a condition to you continuing to work this case, you're officially off of it."

Raven shot her feet, leaning over LaCroix's desk. "You can't do that. I had a perfectly good reason why I didn't get your messages."

"God, you frustrate the hell out of me, Rave," he said as he scrubbed his hands over his face.

"Please don't take me off this case."

He pursed his lips into a fine line. "Don't make me regret this. I'm going to reschedule you to see the psychologist and I want you to get a new cell phone number by the end of the day and text me so that I have it. Got it?"

"Yes, sir." She lowered herself onto the edge of the chair.

"Good. Now we need to discuss Gregor Paigo."

Shit. She knew it was coming and still it hit her like a brick between the eyes. "What about him?"

"Did he molest you when you were a child? Is he the reason you left home, Rave?"

He asked the question so gently, it was a complete contrast to what the words evoked. Raven dropped her head into her hands again, sliced her fingers into her hair and fisted them, hoping that would stop them from trembling. But, it didn't. The trembling seemed to start deep inside, spreading out in waves.

"Rave? There's no statute of limitations on child molestation."

So not ready for this. She raised her head despite the pounding at her temples. "If I did what you're asking, it would be played out in the media. They're all over Solstice trying to get a piece of me. What do you think would happen if we charged him?" In a roundabout way, she just answered his question. She just hoped he wouldn't press her any further.

LaCroix dropped back into his chair with a pained expression on his face. "Jesus, Rave. How did you get through testing and the academy with all of that locked up inside you?"

Raven narrowed her eyes at him. Had Mick told him all about her history with Gregor? Did he know more than she just admitted to? "How much do you know, Grayson?"

"I know Gregor Paigo lived with your mother for a period of two years beginning fifteen years ago. He'd been gone for a year when you left home twelve years ago. Did he come back? Is that why you fled?"

Raven's bottom lip began to quiver, so she lowered her head into her palms to try to hide it and get control of herself. Her belly roiled with that sick feeling you get when something goes horribly wrong.

"I don't expect you to talk to me about it, Rave. But, I do expect you to talk about it with the therapist."

She took that as an excuse to escape, left the coffee on his desk and moved to the door. Just as she pulled it open, he added, "Oh, and you are joined at the hip with Mick until this is all sorted out."

She turned back, shoving the door closed again. "Excuse me?"

"You heard me. You don't go anywhere without her. I don't want you on your own until we know who and what we're dealing with."

"By *what* do you mean hocus pocus?"

He tried, and failed, to suppress a smile. "Is that what you call it?"

Raven rolled her eyes then pulled the door open again and crossed to her desk. She didn't want to be anywhere near Mick because she knew Mick would pick up on her pregnancy, if she hadn't already. Was that why she'd asked her if she was pregnant the other day? Had Mick sensed it? No, she couldn't think about it until she saw Simone, who had just become a murder suspect. Damn it. She picked up her phone and called Simone's office. The receptionist picked up on the third ring.

"Hi, it's Detective Constable Bowen."

"Oh, hello Raven. Did you want to change your appointment?"

Raven pulled the receiver from her ear and stared into it for a moment. Had she not just introduced herself as Detective Constable Bowen?

"No, no. Could you tell me the name of the conference Dr. Wagnar attended last week and also the name of the hotel she stayed at?"

"Oh. This is about your mother's passing. You need to check her alibi. Um, hang on a minute." Raven could hear papers rustling around before the receptionist's voice sounded again. "It was the Boston Medical Conference and she stayed at the Marriott in downtown Boston."

Raven scribbled out the information onto a piece of scrap paper. "Great. Thank you." She hung up and then made the call she'd been dreading. She dialed Ena's house number. Kiran picked up almost immediately.

"Hey, it's Raven."

"Hello, love. Is everything alright?"

"Yeah, I … um, I need a contact number so I can verify your whereabouts for the last month of Ena's life." She was met with silence and the longer it went on, the more she wondered if he'd been lying about where he was.

"I'm sorry. Are you asking me for an alibi?"

Shit. "Yes, I'm afraid so."

"Do you have a pen handy?"

When Raven said she did, he rhymed off a long number.

"That will put you in touch with my superior, aye? Or you can call the Navy directly, just keep in mind they're five hours ahead of us. Alright?"

"Yeah, thank you." And she meant it, for him not making it weird.

"I loved your mother, Raven. If I'd known our time together was going to be cut short like this … Well, I would have done things differently, aye?"

"Yeah, I know."

"I'll see you tomorrow then, yeah?"

"Yeah." Raven set the receiver gently into the cradle. She had no doubt Kiran loved Ena and she could see why Ena loved him. She wished things could have been different too and that she'd had the chance to know her parents together.

She spent nearly an hour on the phone, but she didn't feel any better when both Simone's and Kiran's alibis check out. That left Adara and Raven just couldn't wrap her head around Adara poisoning anyone, never mind her best friend. What possible motive could she have had? Jealousy over Ena's role as High Priestess? Money? Did she know Ena was going to leave her five million?

Yes to both, darling angel. She was jealous and she knew about the money.

Raven's elbows hit the desk with a thud and she dropped her head into her hands She couldn't believe what she was about to do. She pushed up to her feet and walked the twenty feet to LaCroix's office feeling like her boots weighed a hundred pounds each.

"DS?" She waited for his head to pop up. "I need a warrant to access Adara Kirby's financial records."

"The other two's alibis panned out?"

Raven nodded,.

LaCroix turned his chair so he was facing Raven. "Are you sure you want to continue to investigate this case?"

She closed her eyes for half a second to push all of the pain down deep. It felt so wrong to be delving into Adara's affairs. "Yes, sir. I need to finish it."

He pursed his lips, but nodded. "Very well. Get your warrant."

It took another fifteen minutes to type up the warrant request and send it off. When she checked the time, she remembered she needed a new cell phone number. Oh, crap. She had half an hour to get to the mobile carrier's store.

Raven grabbed her coat off the back of her chair and headed for the garage where she parked her car.

In the hallway, she was stopped by Mick's voice calling after her. "Where are you going?"

Damn. She forgot she was supposed to be glued to Mick. She turned to find Mick by the squad room door dressed in jeans and a sweatshirt. "I have an errand to run."

"Alright. Give me a sec to grab my coat. I'm coming with."

* * *

They left the safety of the garage with Mick driving and Raven laying down in the back seat, hoping the reporters wouldn't follow Mick and, to Raven's surprise, it worked.

Raven texted her new number to LaCroix, dispatch, Mick, and Riley. She called Kiran and when he didn't pick up she left her new number on Ena's voice mail, finding it a little creepy Ena's voice was still on there, inviting the caller to leave a message at the tone. She purposely didn't give Adara her new number, hoping it was Constable Tate who gave out her information and he would get the new number from dispatch and do the same thing. She still couldn't put that on Adara. She knew Adara, inside and out. She couldn't have done all of this.

Now she had the issue of where she was going to stay tonight. She couldn't go home because of the media surrounding her cottage unless she wanted to make a dash through the throngs of reporters and that just might be worth it.

"You're not going to be able to hide from them forever. Why not go home, tell them you have no comment, and hopefully that will be the end of it?"

Raven glanced over at Mick. She'd been sitting quietly in the passenger seat for the past few minutes while Raven was busy on her phone. Mick shrugged her shoulders.

"Do you really think they'll leave if I do that?"

"Maybe," Mick answered.

"What if they keep throwing those questions at me? I don't know how to respond to that." God, was she really considering talking to them?

"You just keep telling them you have no comment and then just go into your house."

"Where are you going? Home?"

"No, I put my bag in the trunk. I'll be staying wherever you are."

Raven's nostrils flared. Damn LaCroix. How was she supposed to go see Simone in the morning with Mick in tow? "You'd have to sleep on the couch. Why don't you just come back in the morning?"

Mick let out a quick laugh. "Are you kidding? LaCroix would murder me."

"I'm not some weak kid who can't protect herself. *And*, I have a weapon."

"Is it really so hard to let people who care about you take care of you, Rave? I know I freaked out when we were at Paigo's, but if anyone tried to hurt you, I wouldn't freeze like I did then. I wouldn't hesitate to use my weapon."

Raven's chest tightened, her eyes burned, and she had to look away. Her hormones must really be out of whack. At that thought, she had to remind herself not to think about being preggers and that only made her not be able to stop thinking about it. "You better damn well stay out of my head if you're going to stay with me."

"I already told you I would try my best."

"Yeah, but you were in my head when you said I wouldn't be able to avoid the reporters."

"Oh, was I? Sorry, I hadn't realized."

Raven scowled at her. "Do you have any control whatsoever over your ..." She was about to call it her gift, but she hated that word. It wasn't a gift, it was a curse. "Your psychic ability?"

Mick's eyebrows drew together and her eyes narrowed.

"Yes, of course, I do. Mostly. Do you have any control over yours?"

Answering that question would be admitting she had that ability and she didn't want to admit it. She blocked it out completely years ago. She wasn't sure you could get something like that back after blocking it for so long. Then she remembered the words she heard in her head just before Ena's time of death. *You have great powers, Rave. You've only to open yourself to them.*

It's true, Angel. But, I understand now why you wanted to block them. And suppressing them helped to keep you safe.

Raven ignored the fact that Mick was sitting right beside her. Mick knew her mother was talking to her anyway, so why hide it? "Why did you send me that message on your death bed? Of all the things you could have said to me, why that?"

Because the Goddess blessed you with great powers. You shouldn't deny the gifts you've been blessed with, darling Rave. Mick could help you to tune yourself back into your psychic ability. There's a reason for everything, Rave. I believe Mick came into your life at this time for a purpose. Let her help you and then go to the gathering of the coven and find my killer.

Raven slouched forward, wrapped her hands tightly around the steering wheel and rested her forehead on it. "Seriously? You want me to find your killer using psychic powers I've been blocking for fifteen years?"

I'm saying it will help you. It will help you to stay safe, as well. Someone was able to hex the staff at the hospital and they were able to get into your head before you were hit by a truck. You need to use your powers to be able to protect yourself, my darling.

She could find the killer using the powers of investigation and she could protect herself without psychic powers just fine, thank you very much.

It's not just yourself you have to think about now, Rave. You have to think about the safety of your daughter, too. She could have been killed when Jaxon's truck hit you. Please, my darling angel, use your powers so that you can protect yourself and my granddaughter … Kiran's granddaughter. You're the most powerful witch I've ever known. Not only do you have the powers of the Bowen line, but you have the powers of your father's people. That's where your psychic powers originated.

Raven turned to glare at Mick. Was she listening in? Mick glanced over at her, offered a thin lipped smile, shrugged and then went back to staring out the window. Raven dropped her forehead back onto the steering wheel, banged it softly several times and then sat up straight.

"If I'm so powerful, why do I need protection?"

There will be many who covet your powers. The kind of power you have is rare. You were already at risk being a Bowen. Being a Bowen-Hayes doubles that. The time is here for you to remember what I taught you.

"What does that mean?"

Remember your dreams.

Remember what dreams? "I don't understand."

Silence. Damn it. Why did Ena have to disappear when she needed her? It seemed not much had changed in twelve years.

Time to put her big girl pants on and stop hiding from everything, starting with going home. She wasn't going to let the damn media keep her from her own home. She reversed out of the parking spot, but she had one stop to make before heading home.

She drove to Solstice General Hospital, told Mick to wait in the car, and headed in to make a deal with the hospital administration. They must have known who she was because the head nurse came out to meet her, accompanied by the hospital's lawyer, Robert Stanson. Good, he was just the person Raven wanted to see.

"Mr. Stanson. I'm glad you're here. As you've probably heard, my mother, Ena Bowen, did not die from fourth stage stomach cancer. She died from arsenic poisoning." There was nothing the hospital staff would have been able to do to save Ena when she came into emergency, but Raven wasn't about to tell Stanson that. "I won't sue the hospital for negligence on one condition."

Stanson managed to look down his nose at Raven even though she was taller than him. "And what is your condition, Constable Bowen?"

"That's *Detective* Constable Bowen. My condition is that you reinstate Riley Gallagher with full pay for her lost time."

"And if Ms. Gallagher is not reinstated?"

Raven flashed him a sweet smile. "Not only will I sue the ass off the hospital, I'll make sure Riley Gallagher has the best damn wrongful dismissal lawyer money can buy." She didn't wait for an answer. She turned and walked out, leaving Robert Stanson sneering after her.

She got back in her car with a smile on her face.

"Where to now?" Mick asked.

"Home. Let's face the frickin' press."

Mick smiled and said, "Yes. That's my girl. Don't let them force you into staying away from your own place."

"What are you? My cheerleader?"

"If that's what you need, sure."

Raven just shook her head. The courage she felt moments ago faded with every kilometre. The closer she got to home, the more her stomach knotted. By the time she pulled onto her road, her palms were sweaty, and her mouth was dry. As she neared her driveway, people began to exit their vehicles and move onto the road. She had to drive at a snail's pace so she didn't run anyone over and the whole time people were flashing their cameras and shouting out questions, mostly about Gregor Paigo molesting her as a child.

"It's okay," Mick said in a soft voice. "They can't hurt you. They're only questions and you don't have to answer them."

Tell that to her heart, which was bouncing around in her chest like a super ball on steroids. She suspected if she looked down she'd see it throbbing through her skin. When she finally made it to the driveway, she was relieved all of the reporters stayed out on the street. No one tried to trespass onto her property. Raven ran her sweaty palms down her thighs then looked over at Mick.

"I don't know if I can do this."

Mick reached out and took Raven's hand in hers. "I'll be right there with you. All you have to do is tell them you have no comment now or at any time in the future."

It was as if Mick was downloading calmness from her hand to Raven's. It spread up her arm and then through her entire body bringing a sense of serenity.

Raven yanked her hand from Mick's with the sudden thought that Mick had the ability to get into her head before the accident and to mess with the minds of the hospital staff. Mick's mother was a member of the coven and for all Raven knew, Mick could be, too. Mick also could have given out her cell phone number and home address. Ena seemed to trust her, but could she take Ena's word for it. Damn it, she didn't know who to trust.

"Shall we do this?" Mick's hand was on the door handle as she smiled at Raven.

Raven placed the heel of her hand over her heart and tried to massage it into slowing down before she opened her door. The crowd at the end of the driveway began to shout before she could even get out of the car.

As they approached the end of the driveway, Mick grabbed onto her hand again and the sense of calmness began to flood through her. She pulled her hand away and glared at Mick.

"Shouldn't you ask someone's permission before you do something like that?"

"Like what? Taking your hand? Sorry. I just thought you might like a little support."

Did Mick really not know the effect her touch was having on her? Raven didn't believe that for a second, but why would she lie about it? And if she was lying about that, what else was she lying about?

They stopped at the left side of the end of the driveway so the camera angles wouldn't include footage of her cottage and Raven waited until all of the shouting died down. "I have no comments to make in regards to Gregor Paigo and the ongoing investigation, nor will I have any comments in the future."

While she was talking, Raven spotted the reporter who first broached the question about whether Gregor Paigo molested her while he was living with her mother. They made eye contact and Raven motioned her over. If she remembered correctly, she'd identified herself as Kelsey St. Germaine from NNN. She still restrained her light brown locks in a tightly pulled back ponytail. Up close, she could see tiny laugh lines at the corners of Kelsey's brown eyes that put her in her forties, older than Raven first suspected.

Raven ignored the questions being shouted out again and walked back down the driveway until they were out of earshot from the other reporters. "I need to know where you got your information about Gregor Paigo living with my mother."

Kelsey frowned. "I'm afraid I can't tell you that."

"I realize you want to protect your source, but the person you are protecting may be a person of interest in my investigation. I need the information." Raven towered over Kelsey with her hands on her hips, a position of authority which was usually very intimidating, but it didn't seem to phase Kelsey.

"I'm not protecting a source. I really don't know who gave us the information. The call came into our station from a blocked number."

"Do you have a recording of the call?"

"No, I don't believe so. One of our operators took the call and wrote down the information that was given."

"Did that include my cell phone number and home address?"

"Yes."

"Do you realize that releasing that information to the public could put me in grave danger?"

"We didn't release it, Detective. Yes, we used it to try to contact you and to come here, but we didn't give out your number or your address to anyone, including other members of the media."

So, whoever called NNN also called other news media. "Thank you." Raven began to walk away and the woman grabbed her by the forearm.

"Wait. Would you give me a comment? Did Paigo molest you all those years ago?"

Raven turned her head to look over her shoulder and gave the reporter an icy glare.

"Take your hand off me before I arrest you for assaulting an officer." When the woman released her grip, Raven went to the car, grabbed the gift bag bin and the envelope from the lawyer and rushed into her cottage. She dropped everything on the kitchen counter and went to look out the living room window over Fairy Lake, letting the rippling surface calm her.

A few minutes passed before the front door opened and Mick's grunts echoed from the foyer. Raven turned to see Mick's face beetroot red as she carried the big box Kiran had placed in her trunk. The strap of her black duffel bag began to slide down from her shoulder and she wobbled with the box.

"Help," she squeaked.

Raven crossed the room and took the box from her. "Why the hell did you bring this in?" She placed it on the coffee table as Mick took several gulps of air then plopped herself onto the couch.

"It was in your trunk. I figured you might want it."

"So, now you're going to be on national TV lugging that big box into my house and the whole world will see my damn address."

Mick's eyes widened to the size of saucers. "Oh, crap. You don't think they would have actually filmed that, do you?"

Raven wanted to laugh. She knew it was petty to enjoy putting that little bit of fear into Mick, but damn it felt good.

"No, I doubt it. Your ass is not exactly breaking news."

"Not funny," Mick said with a pout.

At the sound of knocking on the door, Mick was on her feet with her hand on the weapon at her hip.

"Jesus, Mick. Chill. It's just someone knocking at the door." Raven moved to the door, but she had her hand resting on the butt of her gun, too. Peering through the peep hole, she saw Kelsey St. Germaine standing there and eased the door open about six inches.

"I called the station and talked to the operator who took the call. He said it was a woman and he could probably recognize her voice if he heard it again."

Was this some sort of trick to get Raven to talk to her? An idea struck and Raven told Kelsey to wait there. She closed the door and went into the kitchen for a pad of note paper and wrote down Adara's phone number. She opened the door just enough to pass the paper through to Kelsey. Tell him to call this number and see if he recognizes her voice." Since Adara was screening her calls, he'd probably get her voice mail and that should be a good enough sample for him to be able to identify her as the caller or rule her out. As she closed the door, Raven said a silent prayer it hadn't been Adara.

She went back into the living room, hefted the box off the coffee table and carried it through to the sitting area in her bedroom. Then she retrieved the bin and the envelope and set them on the top of the box before joining Mick in the living room again. Except Mick wasn't in the living room. Raven found her in the kitchen making dinner. Hell, she could get used to someone cooking for her. "What are you making?"

"Oh, I'm just throwing together a salad and I thought we could eat some of the leftover pizza."

Raven didn't have the makings for a salad in her fridge, so Mick had to have brought them with her. Instead of getting in the way, Raven headed back to her perch at the living room window. She was almost there when there was a knock at the door again. She changed directions and peeked out again to be sure it was Kelsey, then she opened the door a crack, not sure she wanted to hear what Kelsey had to say because she had a sinking feeling in her gut.

"Yeah?"

"He got an answering machine, but it was definitely the woman who called in the tip."

Shit. This couldn't be happening. Adara simply wasn't capable of doing any of this. Had someone impersonated Adara's voice? Someone who could get into her head and the heads of the people working at the hospital when Ena was brought in? That gave her another idea. She started to close the door.

"Wait." Kelsey's toe edged past the door. "Please. Just answer a few questions and then I won't bother you anymore."

"It's an ongoing investigation. I can't make any comments."

"Is he being charged with molesting you then?"

"No comment. Now or ever."

"If he molested you, Detective, there may be other young women out there he hurt, too."

She'd known that she probably wasn't the only one he'd hurt. She'd wondered for the past fifteen years if he was out there hurting another innocent child.

"Don't you think he should pay for his crimes?" Kelsey asked.

Ouch. That was below the belt. Of course, she did. She just hadn't been able to file a report while Ena was still alive and at risk. "You need to leave now."

Kelsey let out a long sigh then slid her foot back so Raven could close the door. As she did, Kelsey said, "Contact me if you change your mind. There's going to be more, Detective." Her card slid through the mail slot in the door.

* * *

Raven ate quickly then excused herself and escaped to her room. The large box sitting on the table called to her. She set the gift bag bin and the manila envelope from the lawyer aside and circled the box. What the heck could be in there? She wasn't sure she wanted to know. Instead of giving in to the temptation to open it, she picked up the manila envelope and pulled out the legal papers.

A DVD case dropped onto the floor at her feet. She stared down at it for a moment before bending over to pick it up. Ena's elegant scroll across its surface matched the one on the box. Exactly. It also read 'For Raven'. So, the box was probably put together around the same time Ena recorded the DVDs.

Which one did she start with – the papers, the box, or the DVD? She reached up and turned the reading light on and began to scan the papers. She couldn't muster any interest in reading through all of the legalese for a bunch of stuff and money she didn't want, so she tossed them aside and put the DVD on.

When Ena's image appeared on the screen, it was like she was sitting down with her, as if they were just having a normal conversation. Too weird.

Ena sat at her kitchen island. By the look of the sun shining in the windows, it was taped in the morning.

"Hello, darling angel. Please don't turn this off. Give me a chance to try to explain myself. I know I was a terrible mother and I'll never forgive myself for that. I love you with all my heart, Rave. I always have and I always will. I have so many great memories of the first fifteen years of your life, right up until that horrible night when you became so enraged with me." She spoke quietly, wheezing between words. "I've tried several times to record this video, angel. After all these years, I'm not sure how to talk to you anymore. It almost feels like you're a stranger to me. And I suppose that's my fault. I don't know how many times I watched you leaving school or coming out of the police station. I even followed you home several times, but I never got up the nerve to approach you. I suppose what stopped me was the memory of your words on the night you left home. I'm still not sure what, exactly, I did to make you hate me so much, but I'm so sorry, darling. I'm so sorry."

Ena's frail hand covered her mouth as she coughed. She reminded Raven of pictures she'd seen of holocaust victims, reduced to skin and bone. If Adara had done this, how could she have watched her wither away day after day? How could she endure watching her best friend suffer like that? It couldn't have been Adara. She just didn't have that in her.

Ena pulled a tissue from a box on the counter, but instead of using it, she balled it in her fist. Raven paused the video. Sitting on the island next to the box of tissues was a beautiful silver chalice.

"Bingo." She punched the air. "There's a big, fat piece of evidence right there." She tried to settle into watching the rest of the video, but her blood was racing through her veins. Ena had been right about someone stealing the chalice and she finally had evidence it existed.

"I have so many regrets, my angel. So many. I should have told you about your father from the very beginning. I should have done everything in my power to track Kiran down to tell him he was a father. He would have been an incredible daddy and you look just like him, Rave. I'm so sorry I robbed you of that chance to know him, but I need you to know I did it for your own safety. If the wrong people learn your parentage, you'll be in grave danger. For years I've been surrounding you with protection spells. Now that I won't be there to protect you, Rave, you must remember everything I taught you. It's all there in your dreams."

Ena held the tissue to her mouth as she coughed. It took the breath from her lungs and she wheezed while she recuperated. When she finally looked back up at the camera, her eyes had sunken deeper and her skin was a pasty grey.

"Kiran came back into my life about two years after you left home. He proposed to me that same night. I know I had a lot of lovers over the years and I think that may have something to do with our issues, but I've never loved a man the way I've always loved your father. I know you hated me bringing lovers home, but we're such sexual creatures, you and I. That's one thing you got from me and I swear to the Goddess that everything else about you is all Kiran." Although Ena seemed very weak a moment ago, she lit up when she talked of Kiran, lit up in a way Raven had never seen before.

"We left the next day, got married in Scotland, and then we spent two weeks in the south of France. When we returned to Solstice, I debated with myself whether to tell you about each other or not. I couldn't do it, angel. I'm so sorry, but your safety –" Ena's hand came up to cover her mouth again, her whole body convulsing as she coughed, wheezing with every intake of breath.

"Oh, dear. Deep breaths now, honey." Adara's voice boomed after Ena's soft words.

Raven turned the volume down and watched as Adara entered the frame and rubbed Ena's back while she tried to get her breath back.

"I've brought you something for the nausea." Adara set her purse on the island and took out a white and pink box of Gravol. She removed the small bottle from the box, opened the lid and removed the seal, all on camera, then she walked out of the frame and returned several moments later with a pitcher of water and poured it into the chalice.

Didn't prove anything, Raven thought as she watched Adara hold the chalice up to Ena's lips.

Ena began coughing again. "Easy now," Adara said.

When Ena had taken both pills, Adara put the chalice back on the island and walked out of the frame again with the water pitcher. A chill ran down Raven's spine as she pulled out her cell phone and dialed Ena's home number. When there was no answer, she didn't leave a message. She pushed play again, focusing in on the time and date stamp on the video. If it was correct, it was the day before Ena's death.

"There you go. Rest now, sweetie." Adara perched on a stool and took Ena's hand in both of hers.

Ena's voice sounded like a whisper on the wind and Raven wasn't sure what she said, so she hit rewind and turned up the volume.

"Raven?"

"I'm sorry," Adara said and patted Ena's hand. "I tried, Ena, but she just won't listen to reason, I'm afraid."

Ena responded by tilting her head back slightly and

squeezing her eyes shut, releasing fat tears that slid silently down the sharp angles of her cheeks. Then the screen went black. Raven hit rewind again and replayed the last bit. She was sure Adara was unaware of the camera and Ena didn't look like she was in any shape to turn the camera off, so what happened to the rest of the video? Who turned it off or edited whatever else had been on there out? Or had the camera battery simply died?

She grabbed the papers from the lawyer then pulled her phone from her pocket and dialed the number on the letterhead. As it began to ring, she checked the time on her watch. Six o'clock on a Friday. There wasn't much chance of anyone still being in the office. She was surprised when a cheery female voice answered and put her through to Kiara Pfeiffer.

"This is Detective Constable Bowen. I have some questions regarding the DVD Ena left for me."

Kiara made a noise that sounded like a frustrated sigh. "You haven't read the papers I gave you."

"What does that have to do with –"

"Read the papers."

Raven was about to respond, and not too kindly after being cut off, when she realized the call had ended. Did Kiara just hang up on her? Wow. This woman had a hell of a lot of nerve. Raven grabbed the papers again and sifted through them, scanning the documents until she came across a sheet that didn't appear to be part of the legal package. It was an email from Ena to Kiara, dated the day of Ena's death.

Kiara,

I have packed the evidence in a box for Raven and left it in the back of my bedroom closet. So, that's it. Everything is done and now it's just a matter of time. Thank you, again, for all you've done for me over these past few weeks.

Blessed be.
See you in the afterlife,
Ena

Raven set the papers on the desk, pulled the utility knife out of her pocket and sliced through the tape on the top of the box. Opening the flap, she peered into the box. Everything was wrapped in newsprint and before she could start to unwrap it, she needed gloves and her evidence kit.

Chapter 13

Raven came out of her room to find Mick sunk into her couch with her feet up on the coffee table and a big bowl of popcorn on her lap. She was watching some stupid reality show which, to Raven's mind, was a total waste of time.

Raven headed for the door, then detoured into the bathroom to look out the window. She breathed a sigh of relief when she saw all of the media vehicles had departed. Thank God. Hell, she'd even thank the Goddess for that one. As she headed for the front door again, Mick's voice called out like she had her mouth full of popcorn. "Where are you going?"

"Don't stress your pretty little ass. I'm just grabbing something from the car." She barely got the door open before Mick was at her side, wiping her greasy fingers on the thighs of her jeans. Raven stopped in her tracks, her fists landing on her hips.

"I think you're taking LaCroix's orders a little too literally."

"He said joined at the hip, we're joined at the hip. I couldn't forgive myself if anything happened to you and I was sitting on my pretty little ass watching TV."

"Fine." Raven hit the remote and the Charger's trunk popped open. Despite her anger at being babysat, her eyes continuously swept from the woods at her left, across the front of the house to the woods on the other side and then back again. Her ears were tuned into the wind and the soft waves hitting the shore behind her. She listened for the crack of a stick or the crunching of leaves that would tell her something was moving in the woods, but she heard none of those signs. Mick just had her paranoid, that's all. She grabbed her evidence kit, all of her senses still on alert, and breathed a sigh of relief when she shut the door behind her, locked it, and set the alarm.

Mick followed her through the living room.

"What do you need your kit for?"

"That box that you carried in?"

Mick nodded.

"Ena left it for me. Apparently, it contains evidence." She set the kit on the floor next to the table the box was sitting on, opened it, and grabbed a pair of purple nitrile gloves, snapping them on. "Grab some paper and a pen. You're going to document everything we pull out of this box."

Mick patted the front pockets of her jeans, as if she would find a pen and paper in them.

Raven nodded towards the bedside table. "Check the drawer." Crouching down, she pulled the tray up in her evidence kit to reveal the deeper compartment. She was running low on evidence bags. If she'd been on her game instead of the emotional roller coaster ride with all of her personal crap, she'd have restocked it. She unfolded a large piece of paper and laid it out over the table.

Paper and pen in hand, Mick pulled one of the chairs closer to the box and made herself comfortable. Raven instructed her to write the date and time and a brief description of how they came into possession of the box. Then she used a digital SLR camera to photograph the box. With that done, Raven pulled out the first object her hand found and carefully removed the newsprint over the paper on the table.

"Bingo," she said when the chalice was revealed. Why the hell would Ena tell her it was missing if she knew where it was this whole time? It looked like a wine glass except it was silver and had the three moons engraved on the outside of the cup. The stem had a band at the top which was intricately carved with a Celtic design. Below it, the stem curved then met the base, carved to match the band. Raven set it on the paper and photographed it before sealing it into an evidence bag.

The next item Raven pulled out of the box required two hands. She knew what it was before she attempted to lift it out. She circled her hands around the heavy base and lifted the large object, placing it gently onto the paper on the table. The paper wrapped around the top of the object fell away, revealing a flower arrangement that had definitely seen better days. Raven wasn't good with flowers, but she recognized the gerbera daisies and carnations. She wasn't sure what the others were, but the lab would figure it out. There was a stick protruding from the faded flowers that still held the card. "Why did you lie about this stuff?" She whispered.

"Pardon me?" Mick asked.

"Nothing." Raven carefully removed the rest of the paper, revealing a fine china vase decorated with soft pink flowers and olive green vines. She leaned over to read the handwritten card –

Even with a sun so bright,
  Shadows are cast,
  And some never see the light.
  The time has come at last,
  To step out of the dark,
  Let go of the past.

* * *

What the hell does that mean? Where the heck was Ena when she needed her? She turned the stick around, looking for the florist's name on the back of the card, but it was blank. Raven took her time photographing the flowers, vase, and card. She took a picture of the rhyme written on the card with her cell phone so she could study it later then placed the flowers, vase, and card into a brown paper evidence bag. She sealed the bag and wrote the date, time, and her initials over the seal.

When she looked back into the box, there was an envelope sitting on top of a piece of cardboard that lay flat about half way down. The envelope wasn't sealed and inside it she found several photographs of the chalice and the flowers. In one of the photos, a lavender gift bag sat right behind the chalice. Raven dropped the photos onto the table, opened the bin and found the gift bag, then placed it into an evidence bag as well.

Peering into the box again, she pulled the piece of cardboard out. Beneath it lay a neatly folded black cloth with deep purple and bright gold embroidery which Raven recognized immediately as Ena's robe, the one she wore to special Wicca ceremonies and rites. She ran her hand over the silky smooth material and memories from long ago flooded into her mind – hanging on to Ena's robe and hiding behind her at a gathering of the coven. She must have been three or four and the memory was just a quick snapshot in time. She remembered watching Ena, so regal in that robe, lifting her hands in the air and reciting a rhyme. She'd been mesmerized, watching her mother call forth the four elements – earth, air, water, and fire.

She caught herself smiling at the memory then pushed the robe to the side. Beneath the robe was the worn, brown leather cover of her old Book of Shadows, the one she'd been writing her own spells and potions in when her mother had been training her. She was eleven or twelve when she stopped having anything to do with witchcraft. Why would Ena have saved the stupid thing knowing she didn't want anything to do with it? It was like her bedroom. Ena kept it the exact same as when she still lived there. Was she not able to let go of the past? Is that what the card on the flowers was referring to?

Raven started to close the box up when the light caught something at the side of the box at the bottom. She pulled out the DVD cover and written on the outside in Ena's script writing were the words 'For Raven'. She glanced over at Mick while she tapped the DVD cover against her finger tips. Mick already knew just about everything about her, so why not just watch it in front of her. With her mind made up, she put the DVD in her DVD player and sat on the end of her bed to watch.

The first part of the video was the same as the video she watched earlier. At the point where the previous video ended, this one continued to play.

Tears streamed down Ena's face after Adara told her Raven wouldn't listen to reason. It pissed Raven off, because she hadn't even known Ena was sick. Adara never talked to her about Ena. Even though it angered her, it wasn't evidence Adara had anything to do with Ena's death.

"I'm sorry, dear," Adara said.

"It's fine. I need to go lie down, Adara. Would you mind?"

Adara looked a bit shocked. "Oh, yes, of course." She got up and gathered her bag from the counter. "You'll call me later?"

"Yes. I'll call you after I have a nap." Ena smiled, but it didn't reach her heavy eyes.

Adara nodded then turned and walked out of the frame. The back door clicked closed off screen and Ena pulled her cell phone from her pocket. Her hands shook as she tapped the screen then held the phone to her ear.

"She's gone. You can come now." She ended the call and slid the phone back into her pocket. Ena turned back to face the camera with a small smile, her frail hand pushing her long, mahogany hair from her face. "I don't remember where I was when Adara came in." She laughed at herself. "I want you to know I'm so proud of you, Rave. I was at your high school graduation and I was there when you graduated from the police academy. Did you know you're the only one in the Bowen line to become a police officer? From what I hear, you're very good at your job." Her smile lit up her gentle, blue eyes, the crows feet making them kinder somehow. "So proud of you, darling angel."

There was a knock at the door and Ena turned to face it. "Come in, Kiara." She pushed to her feet and had to hold onto the counter. Kiara rushed to her side and made her sit back down.

"I wish you wouldn't stay here by yourself, Ena. You're too frail."

Ena waved her hand. "I'm fine. Really."

Kiara frowned at her as she removed a mason jar from her purse. "Did you see her put anything into the water or the chalice?"

Ena shook her head. "No, but her back was to me when she was at the fridge and she took her time there."

Kiara put on thin, blue gloves then picked up the chalice and emptied its contents into the mason jar. She screwed the lid on and placed a strip of white tape over the lid, sealing it to the glass jar. She scribbled her initials over the seal and wrote the date and time beneath them. "I'll get this to the lab this morning. We should get the results back in a day or two."

Ena dropped her head as she nodded.

Kiara sighed and took a seat next to Ena. "You're sure it's Adara?"

Ena nodded again. "No one else has had access to that water jug. Adara has been here every morning for the past month. It has to be her."

Raven glanced over at Mick when she heard her gasp. Her eyes were wide and her hand covered her mouth. Raven turned back to the video, wondering if Adara could really be that cold. She'd told the media about Gregor's connection to her and Ena as well as given out her cell phone number and address and she would never have believed that of Adara. Could she also be so wrong about her being Ena's killer?

Kiara's hand covered Ena's on the counter. "I'm so sorry, Ena. I wish there was something we could do."

Ena smiled and her other hand came over Kiara's and patted it. "I know. I'm sorry, too." She nodded towards the camera. "Shall we finish this."

Kiara nodded and turned to the camera with her eyes pooling. "Hello, Raven. You've got one hell of a strong mother here."

Ena shook her head. "Not so strong, or I would have been able to resolve our differences a long time ago. I know you don't want to hear it, Rave, but I've missed you so much. I'll be dead within a few days and my only regret in life is not resolving our differences. I've missed out on so much of your life. I wish I could go back to that horrible day and change everything." She wiped her wet eyes with the heals of her hands then looked up at the camera again. "Since you're such a smart cop, I guess you've figured out that we suspect Adara has been the one poisoning me over the past month. We had the water from my jug in the fridge tested a few days ago and it came back positive for arsenic. The pitcher that was in the fridge contained clean water before Adara came in this morning. So, along with the water from the chalice, we'll send in the water from the pitcher to have it tested again. Kiara will get the results to you.

"I know this is going to be hard for you, Rave, because Adara has been like a mother to you when I failed miserably. I think she never wanted to give you back. I've asked her just about every day to talk to you and tell you how much I wanted to talk, but I'm not sure she ever did. I've asked her to tell you I'm dying, but I don't think she really did that either." She pursed her lips then shook her head and dropped it. "Maybe she did and you just really don't want anything to do with me. I don't know."

Kiara's hand slid over Ena's shoulders and she pulled her in for a hug. Then Kiara faced the camera. "We think Adara is fed up of being in Ena's shadow. She wants the coveted role of High Priestess in the coven and the only way to do that is to get rid of Ena."

Raven pursed her lips, her hands fisting in her duvet. What Kiara suggested was insane. Adara didn't care about being High Priestess. Ena was the one with the huge ego who needed to be in charge. Adara was happy to be in the shadows.

"Of course, I don't expect you to take my word for it, Rave," Ena said. "I know how close the two of you are. In a couple of weeks, there will be a full moon. Go to the gathering, Rave. If Adara truly is the one who's poisoning me, she'll make a play for HPS."

Ena began to cough again. Kiara got a tissue for her then held her as she hacked up her lungs. When the coughing fit was over, Kiara said, "Let's get you upstairs to bed, Ena. You need to rest, honey."

Ena got to her feet then looked into the camera again. "Goodbye, baby girl. I love you so much." Tears flooded her eyes then spilled out and the screen went black.

Raven sat staring at the blank screen with her hands still fisted tightly in the duvet. She heard a sniffle and looked over to see Mick's face in her hands and her shoulders shaking.

"Oh, for the love of God. Why the hell are you crying?"

Mick raised her head, eyes bloodshot and puffy. "Why aren't you? Have you no feelings at all?" She dropped her head again.

Raven clenched her teeth. She wanted to send her fists into something and Mick was looking a little too tempting. She closed her eyes, took a couple of deep breaths, relaxing her muscles as she breathed out. Maybe her feelings were numb when it came to Ena. Maybe when someone hurts you so much, your feelings numbed to stop the hurt. God, she didn't know. When it came to Ena, she was definitely blocking her emotions, but it was in self-preservation.

"I'm sorry," Mick mumbled. "That was uncalled for."

Raven shook it off and reached for the papers from the lawyer. Ena said Kiara would get the results of the water tests to her. She went through the papers more closely. The first several pages dealt with the house and the money Ena left. She found the lab results in the middle of the stack of pages. The water tested the day before Ena's death did contain arsenic. Then there was Ena's statement detailing how they discovered she was being poisoned and who she believed was poisoning her. She didn't just accuse Adara, she stated that everyone in the coven had reason to kill her if they coveted the High Priestess roll or perhaps they wanted Kiran.

There were questions rolling around in Raven's head she wanted answers to. Who called 911 on the morning Ena passed? Who knew she was going to emergency, so they could hex the staff into believing Ena had cancer? Raven separated the papers, leaving the ones pertaining to Ena's will on the table. She bunched the rest in her fist and darted out of the bedroom.

"We're going out," Raven shouted as she grabbed her coat from the back of the couch.

Mick met her in the foyer wiping her damp eyes. "Where

are we going?"

"The detachment." She'd fill her in on the drive over.

They were just getting in Raven's car when Jaxon's truck pulled in behind her.

"Shit." Raven got out of the car then leaned her head in the door. "Stay here." She slammed the door then walked to Jaxon's truck. She didn't want to be within Mick's hearing distance. "I can't talk, Jax. I'm working."

"Screw that, Rave. Either we talk or I'm just going to follow you until you do." His fists landed on his hips as he glared down at her. "Did you know that your phone is out of service?"

"Yep." Too bad it wasn't as easy to change her address as it was to change her phone number. She stood her ground, not letting Jaxon's assertive stance get to her. "I don't have anything to say to you."

"We need to talk about this, Rave. You can't just drop something like that on me and walk away."

"I can if you're going to call me a slut."

Jaxon spun around and rubbed his hand over his scalp. "Jesus, Rave. I didn't call you that."

"You insinuated it wasn't yours, that I slept with other guys." She hated being branded with the same iron as Ena. She hadn't taken countless lovers to her bed, as Ena had. She didn't deserve to be treated like the town slut just because her mother had been. Jaxon was the only man she ever slept with. She'd slept with a few women, but not many and she'd been in a relationship with them before she slept with them.

Jaxon rubbed his scalp then put his hands on his hips again and stared down at the ground. At least his hands weren't fisted now.

"I didn't react well. What the hell do you expect when you drop something like that on me, Rave?" He turned slightly and raised his head until they were looking into each other's eyes. "What am I supposed to do? I love you, Rave, but I know you'll never love me back. I don't know what I'm supposed to do here."

"Neither do I and I didn't ask you for anything. I don't want anything from you."

"Ouch." Jaxon dropped his head and turned away again.

"Don't guilt trip me, Jax. You hurt me this morning by insinuating the baby isn't yours. How the hell do you think I feel? I didn't plan this. I didn't want this. I'm not ready to be a mother."

"What are you going to do?"

"I haven't got that far yet. I don't know."

Jaxon turned back to Raven and she was surprised to see tears in his eyes. "I want to know my kid, Rave. I want to be a part of our kid's life."

Oh, damn. When the hell could she get off of this emotional roller coaster ride? She pursed her lips tightly together to stop her lower lip from quivering, but it didn't work. Jaxon reached for her and tried to pull her to him, but Raven placed her hands on his pecs and pushed back.

"I can't, Jax." Giving him the slightest hope they could be together wasn't fair to him and the last thing she wanted was for Riley to suddenly drive up and see them embracing or for Mick to tell Riley they'd been in each other's arms. "I need to go."

Jaxon took a step back. A gush of air escaped his lungs that sounded like a short laugh, but, by the look on his face, was anything but. His beautiful blue eyes reddened and glistened. He shook his head and pulled his truck door open.

"We're not done, Rave." He climbed in and slammed the door.

Raven stood there until Jaxon's truck disappeared down the road. He was right. They needed to talk. But, there was no sense in doing it until after she saw Simone. She got back in the car. Mick kept her head turned, staring out the passenger window. What the hell crawled up her ass? Raven left her to stare out the window. She wasn't in the mood to talk anyway.

The crowd of reporters had disappeared from the detachment. Who knew it would be so easy to get rid of them all? Obviously, Mick did. "You were right about talking to the reporters. Thank you."

Mick turned to Raven with a tight smile. "You're welcome," she said and turned her head back to the window.

"Are we okay? Did I do something to piss you off?" Raven asked.

Mick shook her head. "No. That video just really affected me. Seeing your mom like that; knowing she was dying and not being able to make amends with you."

Raven's back straightened, her lips pursed tightly together. She manoeuvred the car into a parking spot then slammed it into park. "I didn't know she wanted to see me. Adara never told me she was sick and wanted to talk to me. I didn't know."

"Would you have gone to see her if you had?"

It was a question Raven couldn't answer. Deep down she had always hoped Ena would seek her out and make things right. She wanted Ena to come after her the night she ran away, wanted Ena to choose her over Gregor, but she hadn't known Ena did follow her that night and called Adara to go get her from the park.

"Do you think someone hexed you and Ena so you didn't resolve your issues? Could someone have blocked your feelings for each other so you didn't pursue a resolution to your problems?" Mick asked.

Raven's head snapped up and she met Mick's stare. "Why would anyone do that? How could you even think that?"

"Someone who was lonely and had no family of her own, wouldn't have wanted to let you go. Honestly, Raven, you should have had an emotional reaction to that video despite your issues with your mom."

"That's just crazy. Adara is the sweetest, most selfless person I know. She didn't want to lose me, but she wouldn't have hexed me or her best friend."

"Are you maybe wearing blinders where Adara is concerned because you're so close?"

Raven dropped her head into her hands then combed her fingers through her hair, over her scalp down to the nape of the neck. She left her hands there, massaging the tense muscles in her neck and shoulders. She was getting a headache from all the crap floating around in her brain. Between the investigation into Ena's death, all of the Gregor Paigo crap, her possible pregnancy, losing Riley, and the possibility Adara killed her mother, there was too much. Her head was going to explode if she didn't get a grip on all of it.

"It's because I know Adara so well that I know she couldn't have done this."

"How do you know she hasn't been screwing with your head all along?" Mick asked with an exasperated sigh. "It sounds like Ena desperately wanted to fix things between you for the past twelve years. Something prevented that from happening."

"Do you remember what Simone said about the Wiccan Rede? Eight words the Wiccan Rede fulfill – An it harm none, do what ye will. What you're accusing Adara of goes against everything the Wiccan religion stands for."

"Well, someone has violated that rede, haven't they?"

"Ugh," Raven groaned, massaging her temples in slow circles. "I've got too much scattered in my head. I need to lay it all out where I can see everything or I'm never going to be able to keep everything straight." She got out of the car, retrieved her evidence kit from the trunk and headed for the back door of the detachment with Mick on her heels.

"Like a murder board?"

"Yeah. One for Ena's case and one for Gregor Paigo's."

"I thought we were done with Paigo."

"I wish," Raven murmured. She'd do Ena's board first, mainly because she wasn't quite ready to put her own face up on Paigo's board as one of his victims, but she knew she had to do it if she was going to try to find out if he molested any other children before or after her.

She dropped her evidence kit off at her desk and made her way into LaCroix's office. "I've got some more evidence in Ena Bowen's case. She left evidence with her lawyer that the water in her water pitcher contained arsenic."

"Any ideas how it was getting there?" he asked.

Raven sighed and dropped into one of the chairs facing LaCroix's desk. "Ena suspected Adara, but she also said anyone in the coven had reason to kill her if they wanted the High Priestess role."

Frown lines appeared between LaCroix's eye brows. He leaned back in his chair, rubbing his jaw.

He didn't have to say anything for her to know what he was thinking. "I can handle this case, Grayson. Don't pull me off because you think I'm too close to Adara."

"Can you be objective where she's concerned?"

"Yes." There was no hesitation in her answer. If there had been, she had no doubts he would have pulled her.

LaCroix looked up at Mick, who stood in the doorway. "Can I rely on you to kick Raven's ass if she isn't being one hundred percent objective when it comes to Adara Kirby, Kiran Hayes, or anyone else in the coven?"

"Yes, sir."

He went back to rubbing his jaw with his eyes on Raven's and let out a long sigh. "This goes against my better judgement, but I'm going to leave you on it for now. Constable Warren is to inform me if there are any issues developing. Understood?" His eyes went from Raven to Mick and back again.

They both answered in the affirmative.

* * *

Raven pulled a massive white board on rollers out of a storage room and dragged it into the bull pen next to her desk. She printed Ena's drivers license photo and taped it to the top of the white board, centred in the middle. Next to it, she wrote the particulars – Ena's name, date and time of death, and cause of death. Then she took a step back and stared at the board. She needed to know who the members of the coven were. She'd been out of it for too long.

"Mick?" Raven turned to find Mick reading the papers from the lawyer she'd brought with her. It made her smile. Not everyone would take the initiative to learn all of the details like Mick did. In fact, in Raven's experience, it was quite rare. "I need to identify the members of the coven. Do you think your mom would do that for us without notifying the coven members?" She couldn't ask Adara for the simple fact that she was on top of the suspect list.

Mick winced. "They're a pretty tight and loyal group."

"Yeah, but one amongst them murdered their leader."

"True that." Mick sighed and sank back into her chair as if she was deflating. "I think I can remember everyone's first name, but I don't know all of the last names."

It suddenly dawned on Raven she had another source she could tap for a list of the coven members since he'd been ruled out as a suspect. She pulled out her cell phone and dialed Ena's home number. Kiran answered on the second ring.

"Hello, love."

The endearment caught Raven off guard. "Uh, yeah, hi. Um, I was wondering if you could give me the names of all of the coven members."

"Ah..."

The silence seemed to stretch out for eons. Raven was about to ask if he was still there when he spoke again.

"You do realize we're a secretive bunch? Many of the members don't want it known they're members, aye?"

"I realize that and I'll protect those who are innocent, but one among you is a murderer."

"Aye. You're right, of course." Kiran huffed into the phone. "Can I email you the list?"

"Yeah, sure." Raven gave him her email address. "Oh, and about dinner tomorrow."

"You can still make it, can't you?"

"Yeah, but my boss has my partner glued to me until we arrest Ena's killer. Is it okay if I bring Mick with me?"

There was a long silence again. Raven pulled the phone from her ear to check that the call hadn't ended, but it was still active. She put it back to her ear again. "Are you still there?"

"Aye." That little word that he used so often sounded different almost every time he used it. Sometimes it was a question, other times it took the place of yes. Sometimes it was said lovingly. This one sounded angry, like he was barely holding on to his rage. "Has your life been threatened, Raven? Are you in danger?"

"No." Geez. "No, it's just a precaution."

"I'm not so sure I like the idea of my daughter being a cop. I just found you, love. I don't want to lose you."

"Don't worry. I'm not going anywhere. That's why Mick is shadowing me. We're not taking any chances. Okay?"

He exhaled a loud breath. "Alright, love. Bring Mick to dinner. And ... be safe, Raven."

"I will. I am." She ended the call and shoved the phone back into her pocket. It was weird having someone care about her that much and he'd only just met her. What would it have been like growing up with him around?

She looked up at the board which still only had Ena's picture and the barest facts next to it. She stepped up to the board and on the far left wrote 'Suspects' and beneath that she wrote 'Coven Members'. She wouldn't put any names up there to protect their anonymity. In the middle, below Ena's photo, she wrote 'Facts' and on the far right, she wrote 'Motive'.

According to the documents from the lab included in the papers Raven received from Ena's lawyer, a sample of water from the water pitcher was taken before Adara arrived at Ena's the morning prior to her death. They took another sample from the water jug after Adara left. The first sample was clean. The second sample contained arsenic.

Under the 'Facts' column, Raven wrote 'Arsenic in Brita water pitcher ==> Adara Kirby?' Under 'Motive', she wrote 'High Priestess position?'

"It's really not looking good for Adara," Mick said.

"I just can't wrap my head around Adara killing her best friend so she could become High Priestess. She was content playing second fiddle for thirty years and all of a sudden she's willing to kill for it? It doesn't make any sense."

"Insanity rarely does."

Raven turned to Mick. "You think she's insane?"

"I don't know." Mick shrugged. "How would you explain it?"

"There has to be another explanation. A scorned lover from Ena's past?"

"How would he have poisoned her water every day?"

Raven scratched the back of her head then crossed her arms over her chest. Mick had a point. If it wasn't Adara, who would have been able to access that water jug?

"If it looks like dog shit, and it tastes like dog shit –"

"It's probably dog shit," Raven finished. "I know, but …"

"I get it," Mick started when Raven didn't finish her thought. "She raised you and you feel for her, but from where I'm standing, it had to be Adara."

What they had was circumstantial at best. And a lot of hocus pocus, which wouldn't exactly be easy to prove. Raven approached the white board and under *Facts*, she wrote, 'Hair sample taken from Ena Bowen at 1035 hours on Monday, March 28 tested positive for arsenic. Water sample taken from Ena's water pitcher at 0900 hours on Tuesday, March 29 tested negative for arsenic. Sample taken forty-five minutes later, after Adara Kirby's visit, tested positive for arsenic. People who had access to the water pitcher during said time period – Adara Kirby, Ena Bowen, and Kiara Pfeiffer.

Mick's eyebrows shot up. "What possible motive could Ena's lawyer have to kill her?" As far as Raven knew, Kiara wasn't a member of the coven. But, she knew something about Ena that Raven hadn't even known. She turned to Mick. "Money. Ena was worth billions." The hole in that theory was Kiara only had access to Ena's water pitcher on that one day, not the entire month prior to her death. Nor would she have had the power to hex the hospital staff when Ena went into emergency. Which were exactly the points Mick voiced once she was able to pick her jaw up off the floor at the news of Ena's worth.

Raven stared at the board and told herself she was an idiot to ignore the overwhelming evidence piling up against Adara. If she hadn't known Adara as well as she did, there would be no doubt in her mind she was guilty. But, the motive just didn't add up for her. It had to be something more than becoming the coven's HPS. It had to be the money. She picked up a red dry erase marker and put a big dollar sign in the motive column then tossed the marker on her desk. Without turning to face Mick, she said, "Do me a favour. Get started on a board for Paigo on the other side of this one. I'm going to go and listen to the 911 call that brought the paramedics to Ena's house on the morning of her death."

Chapter 14

Raven returned to the bull pen seeped in frustration. It felt as if this day had lasted for eons and she didn't think she was any further ahead than she'd been yesterday as far as the investigation into Ena's death was concerned. Sure, they had more evidence, but the direction the evidence was pointing in just didn't feel right to her. She slumped into her chair, threw her feet up on her desk and leaned her head back.

"No luck on the 911 tape?" Mick's voice floated from across the bull pen.

Raven opened her eyes without moving another muscle and watched Mick swaying towards her with two steaming mugs in her hand. She had a pen sticking out of her wavy blonde hair where it was tied in the back. From Raven's angle, it looked like someone stabbed it into her head.

"No. No voices. It sounds like the phone dropped to the floor and then nothing. I listened to the stupid thing five times."

"So, Ena made the call herself?"

"It would appear so." Raven had listened for footsteps or a door closing, anything to indicate someone other than Ena made the call, but it just wasn't there. "The call was made from her home phone, so they had her address and responded. I talked to one of the paramedics who responded and he couldn't tell me where he got the diagnosis of stomach cancer."

Mick set a mug in front of Raven and took the chair next to her desk, blowing in her own mug before taking a tentative sip. "So, what's next then?"

Raven was about to call it a night when she looked up at the board Mick had been working on. Gregor Paigo's face stared down at her and it made her stomach roil. Pictures of his four recent victims ran down the left side of the board. The similarities they shared with Riley were like a slap in the face. Did Paigo target fair skinned red heads because he knew about Raven's relationship with Riley or was she reading too much into it? She might never know. Thank God he was locked up and Riley was safe.

Dropping her feet to the floor, Raven reached for her keyboard. She opened her web browser then pulled up her Facebook page. She found a picture in her photos from grade seven, taken days after she'd cut her long hair, days after the first time Gregor Paigo came to her in the night. She printed the picture then walked to the board and stuck it up on the right side. Beneath it, she began writing dates and times.

"Jesus," Mick squealed. "You remember every date? Every time?"

Raven ignored her question and continued to write.

Mick's hand reached out and rested on Raven's forearm. "Are you sure you want to open this can of worms, Rave?"

No, she wasn't sure at all. Raven pulled her arm away and stared at the board. "Who interviewed Paigo? Did he confess?" If she'd been on her game and not so distracted, she would have read through the interview report.

"Um…" Mick said. Her wide eyes met Raven's and she swallowed. When Raven glared at her, Mick winced. "He refused to talk to anyone but you."

That took the wind out of Raven's sails. She dropped back

into her chair as all of the air shot out of her lungs. "Fuck me." Of course he did, the sick bastard. "Why the hell didn't you tell me that?"

Mick glanced over at LaCroix's office. "He's not about to let you interview Paigo, Rave."

Raven pushed to her feet, ignoring the throbbing in her right thigh as she marched over to LaCroix's door. He was tapping away at his keyboard with two fingers.

"Is Paigo still in lockup?"

LaCroix looked up at Raven and then over her shoulder at Mick. His mouth thinned to a fine line. "Forget it, Bowen. You're not interviewing him. We've got enough evidence against him to put him away."

"I can get him to talk." Even as she said it, the thought of interviewing Paigo made her stomach pitch. "If you're so damn worried, come in with me."

He studied Raven for a moment before he sighed. "Why the hell would you want to put yourself through that?"

It was an easy question to answer. "Charlene Brock, Sandra Kelway, Emily McMurtrie, and Sabrina O'Connor."

An hour later, Raven sat at a scarred table facing Gregor Paigo. She'd spent most of that hour going over the reports submitted by the forensics team who scoured Paigo's house and truck. He'd kept souvenirs from each of the victims and he'd been stupid enough to have taken pictures with his cell phone of the victims in the same bedroom Raven found Sabrina O'Connor. LaCroix was right about having enough evidence to put him away. They didn't need his confession, but Raven couldn't back down from the challenge. There were a couple of questions she wanted answers to.

She had to keep thinking about his victims to keep herself from bolting out the door. Her hands were fisted under the table so Paigo couldn't see them shaking.

"You wanted me, you've got me. Talk."

It gave Raven great pleasure to see Paigo's hands trembling in handcuffs attached to a D ring on the table even though she knew it was probably due to alcohol withdrawal. His right hand was wrapped in thick bandages that already looked filthy. The last fifteen years had taken a toll on him. He was no longer the good looking, fit man he used to be. He'd lost a lot of weight, looked weathered and beaten, and reeked of stale tobacco.

He smiled at Raven, a grotesque curling of his lips. "Have you missed me, Rave?"

LaCroix shot out of his seat, slapped his hands down on the table, and yelled, "You sick bastard."

Paigo leaned back in his chair, the smile replaced by a grimace. Raven couldn't help the laugh that escaped her throat at seeing Paigo shrink away in fear. LaCroix was an imposing figure, tall and broad shouldered. And he was angry enough to throttle Paigo. Raven placed her hand on LaCroix's bulging bicep until he eased back a bit.

"If that's all you've got to say, we're out of here," Raven said, surprised at how calm she sounded. "You've left us enough evidence that we don't need to talk to you, Gregor. You're going to be spending the rest of your miserable life behind bars."

"Then why are you here?" Paigo asked as LaCroix eased back down into his chair.

"You tell me," Raven said. "You asked for me."

Gregor leaned toward Raven, rattling his handcuffs against the table. "I want a deal."

Raven and LaCroix looked at each other and laughed.

"You won't be laughing when I tell you Ena didn't die of cancer," Paigo growled.

The laughter stopped abruptly and Raven turned hard eyes on Paigo. "Tell me something I don't know." Raven saw the surprise register in Paigo's eyes before they narrowed. He stared at her as if he was trying to determine how much she knew.

"Give me a deal and I'll talk."

Raven pushed her chair back, the legs scraping against the tile floor. "Not a chance in hell," she said as she rose. She nodded to LaCroix and they both left the interview room.

Mick came out of the observation room, which they referred to as the box, and joined them in the hallway.

LaCroix placed his hands on his hips. "He knows who killed your mother, Rave."

Swiping her hand through her hair, Raven paced the hall. "It's more than that. He's involved in it, Grayson. He's fucking involved in it." She turned to Mick. "Did you pick anything up?"

"No, but I got the same vibe you did. He's in it."

* * *

The drive back to Raven's was quiet. Mick stared out her window and Raven couldn't figure out why she was so melancholy tonight. Was it really seeing Ena on that video, or was something else disturbing her? She wasn't up to broaching the subject with her. She had her own woes this evening.

Driving up her road, she caught sight of two vehicles in her driveway and muttered an oath. Her headlights lit up Riley and Jaxon, deep in conversation on the porch. Would this day ever end? Raven turned the car off and just sat there, not wanting to get out.

"Everything okay?" Mick asked.

"No, not really." She blew out a long, slow breath then pushed her door open. The sooner she got this over with, the sooner she could go to bed and forget this day ever happened.

Jaxon and Riley both stood as Raven approached. Riley rubbed her palms down her jeans, which wasn't a good sign.

She was nervous. Had Jaxon told her about the baby?

"What's up?" Raven asked as she climbed the steps. She barely got to the top step when Riley lunged forward and landed in her arms. Raven felt like she'd just won the lottery. She closed her eyes to savour the feel of her, not knowing how long it would last. She pressed her nose into Riley's hair and breathed in the essence of spring – wild flowers and fresh rain. When she opened her eyes, Jaxon stared down at his feet with his hands fisted at his sides.

"I got my job back," Riley whispered in Raven's ear, sending shivers down her spine. "No lost pay." She stepped back then brushed a soft kiss to Raven's cheek. "I brought some beer. Thought maybe we could celebrate." Her smile could have lit up the whole town. Getting her job back was like getting her life back and Raven couldn't deny her a little celebration.

"Yeah, sure." Jaxon glared at her then, as if she would get drunk while she was carrying their child. "Why don't you and Mick head in. I need to talk to Jaxon for a moment."

Still grinning, Riley hefted up her case of beer while Mick unlocked the door and the two of them disappeared inside. Raven stared at Jaxon and waited. His face was red and a thick, ropey vein in his neck pulsed.

"You're going to have to tell her at some point, you know?"

"I haven't even been to the doctor yet, Jax. Until she confirms I'm pregnant, I'm not doing anything."

He took a step towards her and she took one step back. "So what? You're going to go in there and party because you haven't confirmed it with your doctor? Seriously, Rave?"

"I didn't say I was going to party." Damn him. He didn't have the right to judge her or to preach to her.

Jaxon scrubbed his head with his palms. "You're tearing me up inside, Rave." His voice cracked and his palms slid down to cover his eyes. "God, I love you so much and knowing you'll never feel the same is tearing me apart. I want our baby. I want us to raise it together. I want …"

She knew what he wanted – a life together; to be a family. "I'm sorry, Jax. I don't know what to say." She never should have slept with him that night. She'd screwed up both their lives.

No, you haven't. It was fate, my darling. You were meant to have his daughter.

Raven had never planned on being a mother. She didn't know the first thing about raising a child and, God help her, she didn't want to be responsible for messing up the kid the way she had been.

You'll be a much better mother than I ever was. I made so many mistakes, have so many regrets. If I could turn back time, Rave … If I could just turn back time.

While Raven was preoccupied with her mother's voice in her head, she didn't notice Jaxon stepping up to her. His hands cupped her cheeks and he tilted her head up until her pale blue eyes met his.

"There's no hope is there? You wouldn't marry me for the sake of our baby?"

"God, Jax." Tears welled in her eyes and her entire body tensed as she tried to force them back. "We'd just end up resenting each other, hating each other. How would that help our child?"

"Your child?"

Both Raven's and Jaxon's heads whipped around to find Riley standing in the doorway, a look of utter shock on her face. Jaxon dropped his hands to his sides and stepped back from Raven. She felt like he was abandoning her to face a firing squad on her own.

"Riley," Raven breathed.

"You're pregnant?" Riley stepped out and closed the door behind her. Her light green eyes wide and her pale skin nearly translucent. "You're having Jaxon's baby?"

The tension in Raven's body racked up another notch. "I haven't been to the doctor yet."

Riley looked back and forth between Raven and Jaxon until Jaxon finally spoke with his head hung low. "She took a home pregnancy test. It was positive."

Raven could only stare at Riley and watch the emotions play across her beautiful face. Her eyes glistened and a fat tear spilled out and rolled down her cheek. Then she walked towards the porch steps. Raven reached out to her, but Riley pulled her arm away.

"Don't. Just … don't." Riley raced down the steps and got into her car. Gravel spit out behind her vehicle as she tore off down the road.

Raven watched until Riley's taillights disappeared over a hill. She had to force herself to breathe when her heart and lungs wanted nothing more than to surrender. She figured she knew how Jaxon felt.

"Go home, Jax." The lack of emotion in her voice surprised her, although it shouldn't have. It matched the way she felt – dead, devoid of life.

Jaxon walked down the steps to his truck as if his body weighed a ton. He didn't say a word or lift his head. He just got in his truck and drove away.

"How could you say I will be a good mother when I hurt everyone around me?" She asked, but she got no response from Ena. Typical, she thought. Never there when she actually needed her.

I'm here, darling angel. I know you would never let harm come to your daughter. You would never make the mistakes I did. I'm ashamed of what I let happen to you. You would never do that to your daughter.

For the first time in a very long time, Raven wished her mother was there to wrap her arms around her and tell her everything would turn out okay. She couldn't stop the flood of tears from ripping out of her. She dropped to the ground, brought her knees in tight to her chest, lowered her head, and sobbed. When arms wrapped around her and drew her in to a warm body, she was surprised that it was Mick and not her mother.

"It will all work out," Mick whispered, rocking Raven back and forth. Raven turned her head into the curve of Mick's neck and let it all out, tears wrenching from her very soul. Of course, Mick knew everything. Damn her.

* * *

Raven paced the exam room as she waited for Dr. Wagnar to come back with the results from her urine sample. Stupid to be anxious when she already knew what the answer would be. The first thing she'd done when she woke up that morning was race to the bathroom and toss her cookies. She stopped pacing and slid her palm across her lower belly. "What am I going to do about you?" she whispered.

Love her.

Ha. She already did. Crazy. It was probably the size of a pea, if that.

The door to the exam room opened and Raven dropped her hand to her side as Simone closed the door behind her. She sat at the small desk in front of a computer and waved to the seat beside the desk.

"Have a seat, Raven."

Raven took a deep breath and dropped into the chair.

Simone smiled, her deep brown eyes sparkling. "You are indeed pregnant, Raven. Congratulations."

Raven dropped her face into her hands. Now she couldn't ignore it, couldn't pretend it wasn't true.

"You're not happy about your pregnancy?" Simone asked.

With her face still buried in her hands, Raven admitted, "I cheated on my girlfriend with a man. I ruined my relationship, hurt a man who loves me. Is this the Goddess's way of punishing me?"

"Do you want to keep the baby, Raven?" Simone asked in a soft voice.

There was no way she could even consider an abortion. She thought about it as she laid in bed last night, but only for a second before she decided that wasn't an option. Could she give it up for adoption? No, she already loved it too much.

"Yes, I want to keep her." She couldn't do anything but.

"I'm referring you for an ultrasound. The hospital will call you with an appointment."

Raven popped her head up. "The hospital? Is there somewhere else I can go?"

"I suppose. If you want to go down to Orillia, we could arrange that. Are you worried Riley will find out?"

She should have known Simone knew about her relationship with Riley. It wasn't exactly a secret in their small town.

"She already knows. I just don't want to hurt her any more than I already have."

"You probably wouldn't even see her. The imaging department is on the other side of the hospital from the ER." Simone took Raven's hand and gave it a little squeeze. "It's much more convenient than driving an hour down to Orillia every time you need an ultrasound."

The way her luck was going, Riley would happen to be in the imaging department at the exact time Raven came in. But, it wasn't like Riley wasn't going to see her around town with a big, fat belly.

"Fine. I'll go to the hospital here."

On the way to the car, Mick shuffled along beside Raven trying to keep up to her long strides.

"Are you up for stopping by Adara's place?" Raven asked. "I'd like to see if you can pick anything up from her?"

Mick's eyes widened. "Oh. You mean you want me to read her?"

"Yeah," Raven nodded. "Can you do it?"

Mick screwed up her nose. "I can try, I guess."

You can do it yourself, Rave. You've been blocking it for years. Just open yourself up to your gift and you'll be able to read Adara yourself.

Raven had no idea how to remove the block. She didn't even know how she blocked her psychic ability all those years ago.

As soon as they sat in the car, Raven's cell phone rang.

"Bowen."

"Hey, Rave," LaCroix said. "Adara Kirby's financial records are in. She owns her house outright and has for over twenty years. No mortgage and she's got a small amount in her savings account. She's on a disability, but as far as I can tell that's the only income going into her account every month. She doesn't use it all since she doesn't have to worry about a mortgage payment. She puts nearly a quarter of it into her savings every month. It looks like she's very careful with her money."

"Well, so much for that theory," Raven said. "The only motive I can figure is the HPS angle. It's not enough for her to commit murder over."

"I don't know, Rave. Maybe we're missing something. If Gregor Paigo is somehow involved, maybe it's a revenge thing."

"Yeah, maybe. I'll keep looking." If Paigo was involved, was he in cahoots with Adara? Had he convinced Adara to seek revenge for what she perceived as years of being second fiddle to Ena?

When she ended the call, Mick said, "When you think about what was written on the card that came with the flowers Ena received, it kind of fits. I mean, if Adara felt like she was living in Ena's shadow all these years, getting rid of her means she can come out into the light."

Raven pulled up the picture of the card on her cell phone and read the rhyme again.

Even with a sun so bright,
Shadows are cast,
And some never see the light.
The time has come at last,
To step out of the dark,
Let go of the past.

Mick was right. It fit.

"When we get to Adara's, see if you can pick anything up. Has she been jealous of Ena all these years and finally lost it?"

"I'm thinking yes," Mick answered. "I imagine thirty years in someone's shadow is enough to put you over the top. Ena had everything – money, a hot husband, a lead role in the coven. What did Adara have except chronic pain?"

"Me. She had me, damn it. But, by the sounds of it, Ena was nagging her daily to try to get me back. Adara didn't want to lose me and it sure looks like she sabotaged any chance Ena and I had at a reconciliation."

"Maybe that's part of the motive," Mick said. "Maybe she was worried Ena figured out what she'd done over the years to keep the two of you apart."

"Maybe," Raven said, but she was distracted now, thinking about her psychic ability. As she drove, she tried to reach out to Mick in her mind and got nothing. How had she done it as a child? As far as she could remember, it had just come to her. She drew in a deep breath then exhaled slowly, trying to relax, to rid herself of the tension in her neck and shoulders. After several deep breaths, she felt calmer, more grounded.

She tried to reach out to Mick again and felt her shock.

Then Mick started laughing. Slowly at first and then a full out belly laugh.

"What?" Raven asked, slightly offended. She watched Mick, doubled over laughing, and couldn't help the giggle that sprung from her own throat. Eyes back on the road, she worked hard at suppressing her own laughter. "What?" she snorted. "What's so funny?" Then Raven was laughing so hard she had to pull over to the side of the road. She had no idea why she was laughing except Mick was laughing so hard it made it impossible for her not to. "What the hell is so damn funny?" Raven shouted and Mick finally began to ratchet back her laughter and started to cry.

"Oh, Jesus. Now what?"

"Sorry." Mick sniffled. "You caught me off guard. Maybe you should warn me before you try something like that."

"What?" Raven shouted. "What the hell did I do?"

Mick swiped her hand over her cheeks and turned to stare out the window. "You got into my head. No one's ever done that before."

It was more than that, Raven thought. Her reaction was too extreme.

"It's not like I got anything, except your surprise and shock at me doing it." She wondered if Mick's reaction had anything to do with why she appeared so sad over the past day or so. Was she hiding something? Something to do with Ena's case?

Mick turned her head and met Raven's eyes and she looked like she was going to start crying again. "No, nothing to do with the case."

"Really? You can get into my head so easily and you get all weird when I do it to you?"

"I don't consciously try to get into your head, like you just did to me. I just hear your thoughts sometimes. They're so damn loud it's hard not to hear them."

So, was she doing it wrong? Should she just be trying to listen instead of breaking into someone's mind? Raven took a deep breath and closed her eyes, listening. What she heard was Mick chanting, *Don't read my thoughts, don't read my thoughts.*

Raven narrowed her eyes at Mick. "What are you hiding?"

A big, fat tear dribbled down Mick's cheek and she quickly swiped it away. "Nothing. It's private. It's personal."

"Okay. Fair enough." She didn't want to invade Mick's personal business. If it had to do with the case, she'd probe, but not if it was Mick's personal stuff. She eased the car back onto the road and headed for Adara's. At least she was a little more confident in trying to listen to Adara's thoughts.

"If you want to get your gift back, Rave, go back to your roots. You probably had more Wicca and witchcraft training by the time you were seven than most Wiccans get in their lifetime."

True that, Raven thought. But, she'd also been blocking all of that for the past fifteen years or more. She knew where to start though – meditation and grounding. Back to the basics.

When Raven pulled into Adara's driveway, Mick asked, "What's the game plan?"

It was a bright, sunny Saturday morning. Raven could think of better things to be doing, like sitting on her deck and enjoying the sun reflecting off Fairy Lake. "I don't know. Let's just make it a friendly visit and see if we can pick anything up."

They went around to the kitchen door and Raven tapped lightly on the door before she opened it. Adara was at the kitchen island with her massive Book of Shadows open in front of her. She closed it and pushed it aside as she looked up.

"Rave, I've been trying to call you. Your phone is out of service."

"Yeah, sorry about that. I had to get a new number." She'd forgotten all about the new cell number and not giving it to Adara. "I'll give it to you before I leave."

Adara came around the island, wringing her hands. "Are you okay? I know you've been through a lot and I was worried when I couldn't contact you. I came over to your cottage this morning, but you weren't there."

"Yeah, yeah, I'm fine. Have you met Mick? PC McHaela Warren? She's been working the Paigo case with me."

Mick stepped forward and extended her hand to Adara. Adara took it in both of hers and held it there.

"Yes, we know each other, Rave. McHaela's mother is a member of the coven."

Mick smiled. "How are you Ms. Kirby?"

"Oh, fine, fine. But, please, call me Adara. I feel old enough without being addressed as Ms. Kirby." She patted Mick's hands and released them then turned to Raven. "Where's my hug, sweetie?"

Raven bent over to hug Adara and the whole time she was wondering if this sweet woman who had cared for her and loved her was really capable of murdering her mother. When she straightened, Adara took her hands.

"You seem tense, Rave. Is everything okay?"

"Yeah. We just thought we'd stop by and say hello."

"Are you working today then? Will you stay for lunch?"

"We're still working on the Paigo case." Raven took out her cell phone to check the time. "We probably have time for a bite though. What are you making?"

Adara beamed up at her. "Your favourite. How would that be?"

"Yeah, that sounds perfect." She'd felt so sick when she got up that she hadn't had any breakfast. Now, she was starving and there was no sign of the nausea now.

"Grilled cheese and tomato soup it is then. Is that okay

with you, McHaela?"

"Mick, please. Yes, that sounds great." She whispered to Raven, "Was that your favourite when you were twelve?"

"Still is my favourite. What's wrong with grilled cheese and tomato soup?" Raven arched a brow at Mick and Mick laughed.

They took a seat at the kitchen island and Adara rushed over, scooped up her Book of Shadows. "Let me just get this out of your way." She shuffled down the hall into her office.

Adara never had a problem leaving her Book of Shadows open on the kitchen island, but when Raven thought back over the past few weeks she realized every time she came into Adara's kitchen she would close the book. And now she was rushing off with it. Raven wanted a look inside that book. She closed her eyes, focused on her breathing and tried to listen, but got nothing. Adara closed the door on the office when she emerged into the hallway, shuffled back into the kitchen, and began preparing their lunch.

"So, tell me, why are you still working on the Paigo case? I thought that was all wrapped up."

Raven had never spoken to Adara about what Gregor Paigo had done to her. Did she know? She had to have heard the allegations on the news about when Gregor lived with Ena, but had she known before that?

"We're investigating whether or not there were more young girls he sexually assaulted." She watched Adara closely for her response. She turned from buttering bread to look at Raven, her eyes watery.

"There's more children out there he's harmed?"

Raven still didn't have a clue if Adara knew or not. "It's possible. We need to investigate further."

Adara nodded then turned back to buttering the bread. Weird, Raven thought. She wondered if maybe Adara wasn't able to broach the subject of Gregor molesting her. Maybe she just couldn't deal with it. Raven couldn't blame her. She couldn't deal with it herself. Since she was worried Adara might be thinking about Gregor, she didn't want to even attempt to tune into her thoughts and hoped Mick would be able to get a read on her.

"So, are you ready for the gathering tomorrow night?" Raven asked Adara, hoping a change in subject would help to settle them both.

Adara placed an assembled grilled cheese into the frying pan. "The gathering?" Keeping her back to Raven, she picked up a spatula and poked at the sandwich. "Yes, why do you ask?"

Another weird response. "You were busy baking. I just wondered if you had everything ready."

"Yes. Everything's ready."

"What will happen at the gathering? Will there be a memorial or something?"

"I suppose, in a way. The coven will need to process their grief."

"And there will be a vote to choose a new High Priestess?" Raven remembered Ena saying that, if Adara was involved in poisoning her, she'd make a play for the HPS role.

Adara looked over her shoulder. "Are you interested in the coven all of a sudden, Rave?"

Raven didn't like the look Adara was giving her, like she was pissed Raven was asking questions about the coven. It just made Raven want to push the envelope.

"Simone thinks I'd make a good replacement for Ena as High Priestess."

The spatula landed on the stove top and Adara whipped around, throwing daggers at Raven with her eyes. "You haven't had anything to do with the coven for years. You can't just expect to waltz in and take over. You have no right." Adara's nostrils flared as she drew in a sharp breath.

Raven was worried about Adara's blood pressure. Her face turned deep red and she was vibrating, her fists white knuckled at her sides.

"I never said I was interested in taking over the coven, Adara. I said Simone thought I would suit the role." She slid off her stool and walked over to the stove, picked up the spatula to flip over the grilled cheese then gave the soup a quick stir. "There's no reason to get so upset."

Adara took the spatula from her and nudged her away from the stove.

"I'm sorry. I don't know what came over me. I've just been so worried about you and I don't know what's going to happen to the coven without Ena. She was the coven. Always has been." Tears pooled in her eyes.

It had to have been hard on Adara losing her best friend. Ena was the only person besides Raven Adara had been close to. If she hadn't murdered her, she was probably going through a lot of stress and grief. Raven leaned back against the counter and crossed her arms over her chest.

"Would it really piss you off if I came back to the coven?"

Adara's soft brown eyes met Raven's and then she turned back to preparing the next grilled cheese.

"You would need to be re-initiated. It's been years, honey. You have a lot to learn and practice before you would be ready. But, Simone is right. You have the charisma to lead the coven. You're just not ready for it yet." She cut the sandwich that was ready, poured a bowl of soup and placed them in front of Mick. "Here you go, dear."

"Tell me about Kiran Hayes. What's his role in the coven?" Raven asked.

"Kiran?" Adara's hand spread over her heart and her face flushed. "He's High Priest. He has been since he and Ena came back from their honeymoon."

Whoa. Did Adara have the hots for Kiran? Did she think

she would step into the HPS role and win Kiran Hayes's heart?

Adara set a plate and bowl on the island and motioned for Raven to take a seat then went back to preparing her own sandwich. Raven couldn't make eye contact with her. Adara kept her eyes on the food she was preparing and her back to Raven as much as possible. Raven huffed then grabbed a bottle of ketchup from the fridge and went back to her stool. She squirted a huge blob of ketchup onto her plate and dipped her grilled cheese into it.

Mick waved her spoon at Raven's plate. "With all that ketchup, why bother with the soup?"

Adara laughed. "Rave considers ketchup a vegetable." She took the stool next to Raven and dipped her grilled cheese in her soup.

"You haven't told me about Kiran," Raven said.

"What do you want me to say, sweetie? He is what he is. He's dedicated to the British Navy. The sea has always been his first love. Don't get me wrong, he loved Ena, but he couldn't give up the Navy."

Raven watched Adara closely as she spoke. The flush returned to her face and she kept her eyes down.

"What was he like in the coven?"

"He's a talented witch, if that's what you mean. Powerful. He's loyal, kind." Adara stared blindly at the window as she spoke in a dreamy voice. Her blush deepened and her voice hardened. "He'd have made a damn good father if he'd been given the chance."

"You're angry at Ena for keeping us apart?" Raven asked.

Adara finally made eye contact with Raven. "Aren't you?"

She wanted to say Ena made a lot of mistakes, but she thought she truly wanted to make amends and repair their relationship and she suspected Adara kept them apart in the same way Ena kept her from her father. "I think there's a lot I don't know yet, so maybe I should reserve judgment until I have the whole picture."

Adara stared hard at Raven. She tried to blank out her thoughts because she felt like Adara was trying to read her, felt like she was invading her thoughts. She'd never quite felt anything like that before.

"Well, maybe you should spend some time with Kiran then," Adara said as she turned back to her meal. "He'd have more answers for you than I would."

Raven wasn't so sure about that. She glanced over at Mick, wondering if she picked anything up from Adara. Her brows were drawn together, a somber expression on her heart shaped face. She couldn't tell if Mick had read Adara or not, so, while she ate, she quieted her mind and tried to *listen*. What she got shocked her – not from Adara, but from Mick. Adara was thinking about Kiran, Mick was thinking about *Jaxon*.

Raven sucked in a sharp breath, dropping her sandwich on her plate. She pushed her stool back and got up to pace around the kitchen, glaring at Mick. Mick was in love with Jax. Mick glared right back at her, but her face was flushed.

"What's wrong, Rave?" Adara asked, watching her pace.

Raven shook her head. "I've just remembered something about the case we're working on. We have to go." She turned to Mick. "Now." Mick's dour mood of the last couple of days finally made sense. She was feeling probably the same way Riley was. The people they were in love with were having someone else's baby. Were Mick and Jax seeing each other? God, what a mess she'd created.

They were out of the house in less than a minute with Mick jogging down the driveway trying to keep up with Raven's long strides. Raven waited until they were in the car and backing out onto the road before she let loose.

"Are you seeing Jax or just admiring him from afar?"

"This really isn't any of your business," Mick answered, sitting stiffly in her seat, back ramrod straight.

"Really?" Raven yelled. "You've been prying into my mind since I met you and you're telling me this is none of my business? He's the father of my baby, Mick. The man is head over heels in love with me."

Mick winced and sank back into her seat. "He wouldn't be if you let him go. You don't love him."

"If I let him go?" She had, hadn't she? She told Jax that she would never love him the way that he loves her. She was being an idiot getting mad at Mick for loving him. If Jax could love Mick back, it would be better for all of them.

Mick must have been reading her thoughts because her voice softened. "We've been dating for a while. Nothing too hot and heavy."

"You're sleeping with him?"

Mick's face flushed again. "That's really none of your business."

Raven rolled her eyes. "Right. It's okay for you to rape my mind, but what's in yours is private."

Mick's head whipped around, her eyes wide. The flush disappeared, her face pale and maybe a little green around the gills.

"Is that how you feel? Like I raped your mind?"

"I didn't invite you in," Raven said. "In fact, I've told you plenty of times to stay out of my head." Mick turned away, staring out the passenger window. Fine, Raven thought. Let her brood about Jax.

"Did you pick anything up from Adara?"

Mick kept her gaze focused out her window. "She's definitely hiding something. She was blocking me."

"What do you mean she was blocking you?" Raven asked, her fingers tapping against the steering wheel.

"Just that. She's good, too. I couldn't get anything."

"How do you block a psychic from getting into your head?" If Adara could keep Mick out of her head, Raven wanted to know how to do it, too.

"Practice," Mick answered. "It takes some skill and a lot of practice."

All this time, Raven had thought Adara's psychic skills were weak. But she was beginning to see that wasn't the case. Could she have been so wrong about the woman who'd taken her in? Had Adara been hexing Raven and Ena, keeping them apart? Had she tried to kill Raven by sending her into the path of Jaxon's truck?

Chpater 15

Raven parked in Ena's driveway with the grilled cheese sandwich she'd eaten feeling like a brick in her stomach. She drew in a deep breath and released it slowly, concentrating on easing the tension in her shoulders and neck as she blew out.

"I know this has all been hard on you," Mick said. "I just want you to know that I'm here for you."

Despite all of her intrusions into Raven's mind, she knew Mick meant well. "I know," she said in a quiet voice.

Mick smiled weakly. "And I'm really sorry for raping your mind."

Great. Now she felt like a total ingrate for saying that.

"I've never really thought of it that way," Mick continued. "But, you're right. I've totally invaded your privacy."

Well, damn. Raven stared blindly out the windshield and took another deep breath. "What's done is done. We can't change it now."

Mick's smile widened. "You're alright, Raven."

"Yeah, I know," Raven smiled. Then she thought about Riley. Did she still think Raven was alright? Did she still love her or was it too late? God, she hoped not. The heel of her palm connected with her chest just above her heart and she rubbed there unconsciously. Mick opened her door and got out of the car while Raven took another deep breath.

When she stepped out, she stood staring at the house that had been in the Bowen family for generations. Generations of witches. What would her life have been like if she'd embraced that side of her instead of rebelling against it? What if she hadn't blocked her psychic abilities? Would she have been able to warn Ena and prevent Gregor's attacks?

I should have seen it. I should have protected you.

Hot tears filled Raven's eyes. "I should have told you," she whispered, knowing Mick was standing on the other side of the car. "The first time it happened, I should have told you."

You were a child and scared he would carry out his threats. But, yes, you should have told me, baby. I would have made damn sure he never hurt you again.

Raven closed her eyes, forcing two fat tears to slide down her cheeks. She brushed them away with her sleeve and sniffed.

"Raven?" Kiran called out from the side porch, his hand in the air, waving.

"Are you okay? Do you need some time?" Mick asked.

Raven looked at Mick over the roof of the car, standing with her hands tucked in the pockets of her jeans. "Would you mind? I'd like to take a walk on the cliffs."

"Yeah, sure." Without another word, Mick strode up the driveway to meet Kiran.

Raven didn't wait around. She headed towards the cliff at the back of the house overlooking Fairy Lake.

"Would you hang around for a bit and talk?" she asked Ena.

Of course, darling.

She walked to the edge of the cliff with the breeze teasing her hair and took several deep breaths of clean, fresh air.

"Why didn't you tell me you had the chalice and the results of the water tests all along?"

I didn't want you to solve my murder too quickly. I needed time.

I suspected someone influenced Adara to do what she did. I don't think she would have come up with this scheme on her own because it goes against her sweet nature. Someone put her up to it.

"Why Gregor? Was it because of me?"

I had him expelled from the coven. He must have been holding a grudge against me all this time.

"Why did you have him expelled?"

Simone came to see me one day. She told me Gregor came on to her and when she rebuffed his advances he got violent. He tried to force her, but she managed to knee him in the groin and get away. The night we had that horrible fight, I asked him to come to the house so I could tell him he was no longer welcome in the coven and if he ever came near any of the members again, Simone and I would go to the police.

"Did Adara know about this?"

No. It never went further than Simone, Gregor, and I.

Raven closed her eyes and stood there a moment just feeling the breeze and the sun on her face. What a mess she made of things that night. Ena hadn't been renewing her relationship with Gregor, she was ousting him from the coven. If only she hadn't freaked out and taken it out on Ena.

You gave some advice to Mick earlier. You said what's done is done. We can't undo the past, sweetheart. We can only heal from it.

"That's why you hung around, getting into my head. Not to solve your murder, but to resolve our issues."

Yes, darling angel.

A sob ripped through Raven's chest and then something miraculous happened. Her mother's arms wrapped around her, cocooning her in a loving warmth she hadn't experienced for fifteen years.

"Mom," she rasped.

I'm here, baby girl. I'm right here.

"I'm sorry. I'm sorry I was so horrible to you that night."

Shhh.

Ena's fingers threaded through Raven's hair as she cradled her head. She wanted to stay there in Ena's embrace forever. She didn't notice the wind picking up until it was stealing her breath away. The ground beneath her rumbled and the edge of the cliff began to break away. Raven began to slide towards the edge where the cliff dropped off and jagged rocks waited thirty feet below. The force of the ground quaking knocked her off her feet and she clawed at the rock, tearing her nails as she desperately tried to grip onto something. She kicked her legs, now dangling over the edge, as if trying to swim up the cliff. Her lungs seized making it impossible to draw in a breath.

It's Adara. She's doing this. Rave! Use your powers.

Raven saw Kiran and Mick charge out the kitchen door and race towards her, but she was slipping steadily closer to the edge and they were too far away. All she could think about was her baby. She'd never even have a chance to live. She watched Kiran sprinting, his face pure white, his eyes bulging. She'd never get a chance to know her father.

"I love you, mom," she croaked. She hadn't realized she was weeping until she heard her own voice crack.

Hang on, angel. Use your powers. You are a powerful witch, Raven Sage Bowen. Use your powers. Remember what I taught you. Remember your dreams.

She was slipping further, her legs now dangling over the edge as she kicked and clawed. Kiran came to an abrupt stop and thrust his arms up in the air. She couldn't hear what he was saying over the hammering wind until Ena's voiced sounded in her head, matching the motion of Kiran's lips. Their combined power like an electrical current crackling in the air.

I call upon Earth, the power to make.
I call upon Air, the power to take.

I call upon Fire, the power to grow.
I call upon Water, the power to flow.
Stop this spell meant to harm,
Heed our power; undo this evil charm.
Still the earth, calm the wind,
Evil forces rescind!
As we will, so mote it be.

The wind ebbed just as Mick reached Raven and grabbed onto her arms, dragging her away from the edge of the cliff. Raven wasn't sure if the ground was still trembling or if it was just her. She thought she was dead, was certain she was going to end up impaled on the rocks below. She curled in on herself, on the baby growing in her belly while Mick rocked her. Kiran reached them and scooped Raven out of Mick's grasp and into his arms. He carried her back to the house, murmuring she was okay over and over again, while Raven remained curled in a tight, trembling ball.

* * *

The rich, mahogany table was set with Ena's best china and crystal goblets, glinting in the flickering flames of long, white taper candles. Kiran had gone all out with roast beef, Yorkshire pudding, roast potatoes, and glazed carrots and green beans. Raven would have devoured it if she didn't feel so sick. Her chest felt tightly restricted. Every breath was a hard fought battle. Her fingers were raw and she'd lost the nail from her right middle finger. The cut she sustained on her palm the day before throbbed like a bitch. She was sure it was expanding and contracting like you'd see in a cartoon. Kicking against the rock ledge had slashed and bruised her shins. Despite how much her entire body hurt, she was alive. But, damn, it had been close.

The clatter of cutlery against china brought her back from the edge of the cliff.

"You're not eating," Kiran said.

Raven focused on her plate where she'd been pushing the food around and then carefully laid the fork down. "I'm sorry. I know you went to a lot of trouble cooking, but I'm just not hungry." She used her knuckle to push the button on her iPhone sitting on the table next to her, to check the time once again. LaCroix was working on a warrant for Adara's house. Even though it was Saturday, she was hopeful he would get it pushed through.

Just the thought that it was Adara who tried to kill her grated on her nerves. She trusted Adara, loved her. Did she really just try to kill her?

Yes, she did. I'm so sorry, Rave.

Raven was surprised Ena was still in her head. They made peace with each other. She thought Ena would have passed over to the other side.

"How can you be so sure?"

Both Mick and Kiran looked at Raven, but neither one of them raised an eyebrow at Raven's question or at who she was asking it to.

Everyone has their own unique energy. I'd recognize Adara's anywhere, although her power was much stronger than I've ever known it to be.

"You helped Kiran stop her. Would she have felt your energy?"

Yes.

Raven dropped her head and began to run her fingers into her hair. Even that stung like hell and she winced as she pulled her fingers out, waving her hand to ease the pain.

Twelve years. She let Adara be her mother figure for twelve years when she should have been with Ena. God, she was such a fool.

You were a child, Rave. If anyone is to blame for the time we lost together, it's me.

"If we're going to blame someone, let's put it on the shoulders of the woman who kept us apart all these years." The evidence was on the videotape. Adara had clearly lied to Ena about trying to get Raven to come and see her. At this point, Raven had no doubts Adara had been doing her best to keep them apart for the past twelve years. "She'll come after Kiran now, too." After the show they put on out on the cliff, Adara would know they were on to her.

No, sweet angel. I won't allow her to harm another soul.

Well, that explained why Ena was hanging around instead of crossing over. The shrill ringing of her cell phone had Raven nearly falling out of her chair. She fumbled with the phone trying to pick it up then, giving up, she used her knuckle to answer the call and hit the speaker button. "Grayson? You got the warrant?"

A loud sigh of frustration seeped out of the speaker. "No. Judge Cromwell is away for the weekend and they haven't been able to get hold of him. Apparently, he's at his hunt camp. I've sent Tate to him, but it's a good six hours away."

And knowing Tate, he'd take his sweet time getting there. By that time, Adara could have destroyed her Book of Shadows. Hell, she could have done it already. Raven pushed to her feet and began stalking back and forth like a caged tiger. "I'm going over there."

"No," Grayson said. "You have no way of protecting yourself if she uses this hocus pocus crap against you, Rave. She damn near killed you this afternoon."

"Aye," Kiran agreed, his eyes like frozen lasers blasting Raven. "You'll not be going near her."

"I'm not planning on going over there and riling her up. I want to make her think we have no idea it was her. If she thinks we're clueless, she's less likely to get rid of evidence. Think about it, Grayson. It's going to be hard enough to prove what she's done. If she gets rid of the physical evidence, we've got nothing."

"Oh, I don't know about that," Kiran said. His icy glare melted away and the edge of his mouth curled up ever so slightly. "I think there's a way to get a confession out of her and protect Raven from any further harm."

Raven stopped pacing, staring into Kiran's eyes. "How?"

"You said she lost her cool when you mentioned becoming the coven's HPS."

"Yeah." It was the only time Raven had ever seen Adara get angry.

The Cheshire cat had nothing on Kiran's grin. "I propose you come to the gathering tomorrow … in Ena's robes."

Raven's mouth dropped open. He wanted her to walk into the gathering wearing the robes of the High Priestess and shock Adara into a reaction. She began pacing again. "I haven't been to a gathering since I was twelve. I wouldn't know what the hell to do anymore."

"Then we've a lot of work to do tonight," Kiran said.

"How will you keep Raven safe?" LaCroix's voice drifted through the phone.

"Ena and I were able to stop Adara this afternoon. With the power of the entire coven, Adara's hands will be tied."

"I still can't believe Ena is helping you from beyond the grave," LaCroix said. "How the hell am I going to explain all of this to the brass?" He huffed and muttered a few colourful oaths. "I take it you're still at your mother's house?"

"Yeah," Raven answered

"Stay there. I'm on my way over."

The line went dead.

The last thing Raven wanted was for LaCroix to see her in her current state. Aside from the new injuries, she was pretty sure she was still shocky. When Kiran brought her into the house, it took her a while to smooth herself out. She hid in the bathroom for a while, calming her anxiety and grounding herself by naming the objects and colours she saw around her. Kiran had wanted her to go to the hospital to get checked out, but she insisted she was fine. Even now, he was keeping a close eye on her, looking for signs she was about to lose it. She couldn't blame him. She'd been moments away from a panic attack since Mick pulled her off of the edge of the cliff. Nearly dying rocked her to the deepest part of her soul, but she refused to let Kiran or Mick know it.

Kiran rose and began clearing the table and Raven picked up her plate using her palms at the edges, drawing a scowl from Mick.

"Don't you dare." Mick jumped up and took the plate from her. "Just go sit down or something. Let us clean up."

"Aye," Kiran said over his shoulder. "I still wish you'd get those fingers and your legs looked at."

Raven spread her hands out in front of her and examined her fingers. She'd cleaned them up in the bathroom, but they still looked a mess. Still, there wasn't much they would be able to do with them at the hospital. She didn't need stitches or anything. It was just going to be awkward for a while.

She resigned herself to letting Mick and Kiran deal with the dishes and settled into a chair by the fire in the living room. She still felt chilled to the bone, shivering slightly even with the heat of the fire. As soon as she got comfortable, her eyelids grew heavy. She thought she would just close them for a minute.

She woke to the lovely sound of Riley's voice saying her name and a warm hand gently rubbing her knee. She wondered if she was dreaming before forcing her eyes open and staring into Riley's.

Riley smiled. "Hey."

Raven blinked a couple of times to make sure she wasn't seeing things then said, "Hey. What are you doing here?" She sat up, stretching her neck to get the kinks out from sleeping in an awkward, upright position. Riley's eyes flashed over Raven's shoulder and Raven looked back to see LaCroix standing behind her with a dark haired woman. She wondered for a moment if LaCroix had a new girlfriend. She was about his age and just his type – tall, lean, and drop dead gorgeous.

"Sarge." Raven got to her feet and turned to him.

"Detective Constable Raven Bowen, this is Dr. Kirsten Shoal," LaCroix said.

Raven raised an eyebrow. "Doctor?"

LaCroix cleared his throat. "She's the psychologist I was telling you about."

Raven took a step back and bumped into Riley. Turning, she said, "Sorry." Then her attention was back on Dr. Shoal. "You came here to see me?" Damn him. She wasn't ready for this. Not now. Not when she was feeling so vulnerable already.

"Riley's going to have a look at your wounds then I'd like you to sit down and talk with Dr. Shoal," LaCroix said.

Whipping her head around, Raven stared dumb-founded at Riley. She cheated on her, got knocked up, nearly lost her job for her and still Riley came out to tend to her wounds? Did Riley still love her? Or was she just being her kind, nurturing self? She couldn't tell because Riley dropped her head, her hands stuffed in the front pockets of her low-riding, faded jeans. Damn, she looked … sexy. A wave of arousal spread through Raven's body. It was the first time she felt warm since the cliff incident. And because she desperately wanted to lean in and devour Riley's mouth, she turned back to LaCroix. "This isn't necessary, DS."

"Oh, yeah, it is," LaCroix said. "Shall I get a mirror so you can see what I'm seeing, Rave."

I'll be with you when you talk to her, if you want. This is long overdue, my sweet angel.

Kiran and Mick stepped between LaCroix and Riley, so Raven had a semi-circle of people staring at her like she was in the middle of an intervention. She supposed she was. In fact, as she looked at each of the faces in that semi-circle, she realized this was exactly what that was – an intervention.

"I've had a rough day already. Can't this wait?"

Dr. Shoal took a tentative step forward in black slacks with a razor sharp edge down the front and an ivory silk blouse. "Raven? May I call you Raven?"

Raven stepped back, berating herself for being such a coward. She nodded her head. "Yeah, sure."

"Thank you. I'm not here to force you to do anything you're not comfortable with, Raven. I just came to have a conversation and see how you're coping with all of the stress you've been under lately. Your sergeant just wants to be reassured you're capable of doing your job without distractions."

Well, didn't that make her feel like a spoiled five year old? Having a conversation didn't sound so bad. "Okay."

"Why don't you let me take a look at your hands and your legs first?" Riley picked up the first aid kit sitting next to the chair Raven had been sleeping in and motioned to the couch. "Take a seat."

Raven glared at Mick. Someone obviously filled Riley in on her injuries. Neither Kiran nor Mick knew how bad her shins were. Kiran had given Raven a pair of Ena's jeans to change into because hers had been torn to shreds and bloody, but they hadn't seen just how badly cut and banged up her legs were. She really didn't want to do this with an audience.

"Can we go into Ena's office?" Raven didn't wait for an answer.

* * *

Raven plunked herself down in the big, comfy chair in the corner of Ena's office where Ena used to curl up with a book.

Riley grabbed the chair from the computer desk and rolled it over in front of Raven.

"Why are you doing this?" Raven asked as Riley took her right hand and examined the tips of her fingers and the missing nail.

Riley sighed and their eyes met. "Grayson asked me to come over since you wouldn't go to the ER."

"So, you're doing this for Grayson?"

"No," Riley said with a frown. "I'm doing it for you, Rave." She tucked her hair behind her ear then placed a small basin on her lap under Raven's finger tips. "Always for you."

Hope soared in her belly leaving her feeling like she was on a rollercoaster ride. "So, you still love me?" Her normally raspy voice came out all breathy.

Riley's frown deepened as she poured some sort of antiseptic over Raven's fingertips. She may as well have poured acid on her. Raven hissed, her eyes watering at the stinging sensation.

"Holy hell, that hurts."

"Did you even bother to clean these wounds?"

"Yes, of course I did." She ran her hands under cold water to ease the pain. That qualified as cleaning them, didn't it?

"Tell me what happened."

Raven sighed, knowing Riley wanted to get her talking as a distraction technique. Talking, but not about their relationship. Grayson or Mick had probably already told her what happened. Riley took her left hand and began to unravel the bandage covering the cut in her palm. She examined it closely then made a tsking sound.

"You've pulled a couple of the stitches. You really should go into the ER and get this looked at."

"Not going to happen. At least, not tonight. I've got too much work to do." The sting gradually lessened on her right hand and she braced herself for the antiseptic on the fingers of her left hand.

When Riley had her left hand poised over the basin, she repeated, "Tell me what happened."

"Someone tried to kill me." Riley poured and Raven let out a scream worthy of a Hitchcock film. "Damn it, Riley. Isn't there something a little gentler you can use?" Raven took short, gasping breaths through the worst of the pain. It wasn't until it eased a bit she noticed Riley staring at her with wide eyes and a slack mouth. "What?"

"Who's trying to kill you?"

Raven lifted both her hands and waved them like she was trying to dry nail polish. "I can't talk about it. It's an active investigation."

"Jesus, Rave." Riley's eyes glossed over with unshed tears.

The way Riley was looking at her confirmed she still loved her. Raven wanted to pull her into her lap and hold on to her for the next year or so.

"I love you, Ri."

"Raven … don't. Please." Riley set the basin aside, picked up a roll of gauze, and began wrapping Raven's fingers.

"I'm sorry I hurt you, Ri. I've never regretting anything more in my life. When I was out there hanging on the edge of that cliff, knowing I was going to die … that my baby was going to die without ever having a chance at life …" Raven's eyes burned and her nose began to run. She sniffed and swiped her sleeve over her eyes.

Riley stopped wrapping the gauze and stared at Raven with her brow drawn in and her lips pursed. The hair she tucked behind her ear had fallen forward, framing her angelic face in flames, the freckles dotting her nose belying the seriousness of her expression.

"It wasn't my life that flashed before my eyes. It was you. All the great moments we spent together – sitting on my deck watching the sun set, holding hands, laughing so hard it felt like we'd done a thousand crunches, making love in the morning, in the shower, in the lake..."

"Rave." Riley sighed, closed her eyes and when she opened them they were a glistening, mossy green. "You have to stop doing this."

Raven looked away, biting down on her bottom lip to keep it from trembling. She closed her burning eyes and concentrated on breathing. The elastic bands tightened around her lungs again and all she could think was maybe she would have been better off if she had gone over the cliff.

Don't ever think that, darling. You have everything to live for.

Everything? In the span of a few weeks she'd lost the woman she loved, her mother, and the woman she thought loved her like a daughter.

And you've gained a father and a daughter.

A daughter she was going to have to raise on her own.

Well, it's not like you can't afford a nanny.

A half laugh, half sob escaped Raven's throat. She bit her cheek and squeezed her eyes shut to keep from breaking down in tears. She wouldn't cry in front of Riley. Not after her rejection.

"Okay," Riley said softly, pressing the last piece of tape in place. "Let's have a look at your legs."

Raven spread her hands out in front of her and stared at her white capped fingers. "Jesus. I look like Mickey Mouse."

Her jeans were too narrow to pull up enough to expose her shins, so if Riley wanted to take a look at them, she was going to have to remove her jeans. How the hell was she supposed to undo the button and zipper to get her pants off?

"My shins are fine," Raven said, pushing to her feet. "I took care of them already."

Riley crossed her arms over her chest and shook her head. "Uh-uh. Sit your ass down and I'll pull up the legs of your jeans." Raven watched her as she studied her pant legs and knew the exact moment it dawned on Riley that the pants would have to come off. Her face flushed a lovely shade of rose. As far as awkward moments went, this one was stellar.

"Oh. Well. You'll have to take them off." Her spine straightened and she reached for Raven's waist. Raven lifted her shirt a little more than was necessary to expose the button on the jeans. Her belly was one of her erogenous zones. Riley fumbled with the button and zipper. Those green eyes kept flicking up to take in Raven's ripped abs.

"Can you handle it from here?" Riley asked.

Disappointment sliced through Raven, but she knew it was for the best. She wanted Riley. Then and there, even with her father and the others just down the hall. She carefully slipped two fingers into the waistband at either side of her hips and shimmied them down, over black lace boy shorts, to her mid thigh. Then she sat back down again to gently pull them over her battered shins. She'd wrapped them in gauze to keep Ena's jeans from getting bloody, but even through the gauze it was apparent her lower legs had swollen. Blood seeped through in several spots and she dreaded Riley pouring that antiseptic on them.

Riley used scissors to cut through the gauze then gently peeled it away from the wounds. She gasped as the gashes and bruises were revealed. "Oh, Rave."

"It's not as bad as it looks," Raven admitted. She hadn't even felt it when she'd been on the edge of the cliff. It wasn't until the shock and adrenaline began to wear off that her legs and fingers began to throb. The angry bruise on her hip and the road rash down her left side from being hit by Jaxon's truck made her look even worse.

"Some of these need stitches, Rave. Like it or not, you're going to the hospital." Riley cleaned out the wounds. "I'll go see if Kiran has a pair of sweats you can wear so you can at least get in and out of them yourself."

Well, damn. Raven was looking forward to Riley helping her back into the jeans. Now all she had to look forward to was hours sitting in the emergency room, needles to freeze the cuts that needed stitches, and someone stabbing her with a needle to sew her up.

You have the power to heal yourself, Rave. Why don't you use your healing powers?

"I haven't done that for years."

It's not something you forget, darling angel. You were doing it before you were a year old. I'll never forget the first time you conjured energy in your hands. I put you in your playpen while I worked on some potions. All of a sudden the room was washed with a golden light and you were giggling. I looked over and you had a beautiful ball of golden light hovering above your palms. No one taught you how to do that, Rave. It's something inside you. It's part of who you are.

She hadn't forgotten drawing energy into her hands. She used to love the sensation of that warm, pulsing orb. It was just that she hadn't done it since she was twelve years old. She cupped her hands in front of her and, slowly, a golden ball of energy emerged out of nowhere, hovering over her palms. She could use it to heal her wounds and save herself a trip to the hospital, but how would she explain it to everyone?

"Holy, mother of God. What the hell is that?" Riley stood in the doorway with a pair of track pants over her arm. Her eyes bulged and her mouth was wide open. The room was filled with golden light and a warm, loving energy.

Cat's out of the bag now, Raven thought. She increased the size of the ball until it encased her entire body in glowing light. She watched in awe as the wounds covering her shins closed and sealed and the bruises faded. Then she drew the energy back in, the ball becoming smaller and smaller until it faded away.

"What was that? Is that magic? What did you do?" Riley's words came out rapid-fire. She rushed across the room and lowered to her knees to examine Raven's shins.

Raven held out her hands. "Could you unwrap these for me?" She couldn't do it herself and she wanted rid of the Mickey Mouse look.

"Oh, my God. I've never seen anything like this. You just healed your wounds, Rave. How did you do that?"

"It's just one of the benefits of being a Bowen." She continued to hold her hands out, but Riley just stared up at her.

It's not just the power of the Bowen line that you have, angel mine. You have the power of your father's people, making you the most powerful witch I've ever known.

Except she didn't want that power; hadn't wanted it for a long time. She shook her hands in front of Riley. "Take it off. Please."

Riley rose to her feet and gestured towards the chair in the corner. Once Raven was seated, Riley took her right hand in hers, settling it on her lap. "Is that something you can teach someone?"

Raven raised an eyebrow. "I don't know. It's just something I've always been able to do."

"Because you come from a long line of witches?"

"I suppose. Hereditary witches can inherit the powers of their ancestors. The Bowens are a powerful line, but so is the Hayes line apparently."

"So you have powers from both your mother and your father?"

"And their ancestors, yes."

Riley gasped as she removed the gauze from Raven's right index finger. The scrapes and cuts were gone, as if they'd never been there. "Why haven't you used your powers all these years? You have a very special gift. How can you waste it?"

Raven rolled her eyes. "What do you think people would do if they knew what I could do?" Raven already knew the answer. She lived through the stares, the judgement, the suspicion. She'd been bullied, ostracized, excluded. All because she was 'different'. "People fear what they can't explain or understand." She wondered how she was going to explain her sudden healing to Grayson and the therapist.

"I'd like to learn more about your heritage and your religion."

Raven stared at Riley as she continued to unwrap her fingers. "Why?"

"It interests me. Wicca sounds like a beautiful religion, seeped in nature and mysterious Goddesses."

"I guess. But, why would you want to know about my heritage if you don't want me?"

Riley stopped unwrapping the gauze and stared into Raven's eyes. "Just because we're not together doesn't mean we can't be friends."

Raven flexed the freed fingers of her right hand and stood up. "I can take it from here," she said, beginning to unwrap the fingers of her left hand. She didn't want to be friends. She didn't think she could handle seeing Riley all the time. At least, for now. It was too hard. "Do you think you could tell Grayson I need to go to the hospital for stitches? I don't know how to explain to him or that doctor how my wounds have suddenly healed." She didn't look at Riley as she spoke.

"Yeah, sure."

Raven gathered up the gauze and put it in the trash bin under Ena's desk then she went to the window, giving Riley her back, and stared out at the darkness. She was hyperaware of Riley, still sitting in the chair a few feet behind her. She wasn't making any moves to leave, so Raven resigned herself to saying what was on her mind.

"Every time I see you and you make it clear you won't take me back, it's like ripping open the wound again. It hurts, Ri. I can't keep doing this. It's killing me."

"Rave, you *cheated* on me. How could I ever trust you again?"

Raven slowly turned to face Riley. She was sure the pain was evident in her expression, but she couldn't help it. Nor could she help the tears threatening to spill from her eyes.

"Why would you want someone you don't trust as a friend?"

Riley's mouth dropped open. "You know what they say. Once a cheater, always a cheater."

Raven laughed, although she didn't find it funny. "Not in this case."

"Why's that?"

"Because I know what it cost me and the price was way too high."

"Then why did you sleep with him, Rave?"

Raven turned back to the window and squeezed her eyes shut, remembering Riley telling her she was too closed off. She desperately wanted to open up to Riley.

"I wish I had the answer to that. Jax has been my best friend since we were toddlers. I've never been interested in him that way. I'm still not interested in him that way. I don't know what the hell happened, what possessed me to sleep with him. I can't figure it out." Hell, she wasn't even interested in men. She'd been over it in her head hundreds of times over the past few weeks and still couldn't make any sense of it. It went against her very nature.

You have to wonder if you were under a spell.

"Why the hell would anyone do that to me?"

"What?" Riley asked.

To keep you close. Listen to me, Rave. Adara's powers have increased tremendously. If you were spending all of your time with

Riley, she wouldn't be able to access your powers.

Raven's mouth dropped open. As much as she didn't want to believe it, it was the first explanation for her behaving out of character that made sense. Was that why Adara took her in and made sure she didn't reconcile with Ena? To steal her powers? Oh, dear Goddess. *Adara raped me,* Raven thought. *She raped both Jax and I.*

Oh, sweet angel. Please don't think about it like that. Think of the precious child you've been blessed with.

"Rave?" Riley's hand touched Raven's shoulder.

Raven jerked away from her touch. "I'm sorry," she whispered. "I need you to go."

* * *

Raven stayed at the window until she heard Riley, Grayson, and Dr. Shoal leave. When she wandered into the living room, Kiran and Mick's conversation ended abruptly. She was getting tired of people talking about her.

"If you have something to say about me, say it to my face, not behind my back."

"Sorry, love," Kiran smiled and raised his eyebrows. "Your hands look healed."

"Yeah, a little magick healing session."

Kiran got to his feet, walked to Raven and took her hands in his, examining them. "Your work?"

"Yeah."

His eyes met hers and he grinned. "You've got your granny's healing powers, love. She'll be thrilled."

"My granny?"

"Aye. Ruari Persephone Hayes. High Priestess of the Highlands Dragonfly Coven in Inverness, Scotland. She's also a very powerful and renowned psychic."

Well, that explained where her psychic powers came from. Ena had skills, but nowhere near as powerful as Raven's had been and when she needed help to control her psychic abilities, Ena hadn't been much help.

"Will you show me how you heal?" Kiran asked.

Raven shrugged. She couldn't see any reason not to. She cupped one hand out in front of her, palm up. A golden glow appeared first, like a mist becoming thicker. It formed into a ball, bathing every corner of the room in soft, golden light.

"Brilliant," Kiran breathed. "May I touch it."

With another shrug, Raven gave a little push with her hand and the ball floated towards Kiran. He held out his hand and the glowing orb hovered just above his palm. "Oh, aye. You've a beautiful energy, love. It's like being held in a warm embrace."

Mick dropped her butt onto the couch. "Wow. I've never seen anything like that."

Raven drew the orb back to her and let it dissolve.

Kiran grinned and clapped his hands together. "Shall we get started then? We've a lot to do."

"Yeah," Raven answered. Anything to get her mind off what Adara may have done.

"The first thing we need is a protection spell. I don't want to take any chances of Adara harming you again." He reached into his pocket and pulled out several items. He handed a small white sack tied with a white cord to Raven. "This is a simple, but powerful, protection spell."

Raven took the sachet from him and tucked it into her front pocket. She didn't have to ask what was in it. She was very familiar with protection spells. Ena had made her practice them regularly. Besides, she could smell the cinnamon, cloves, anise, and peppercorns.

Kiran stepped towards Raven and lifted a silver chain around her neck. Hanging from it was a silver circle with a pentacle in the middle. The words humus, spiritus, aura, caminus, and aqua were printed around the circle. "The pentacle is a powerful symbol of protection. Wear this and keep the herbs with you at all times. Aye?"

Raven nodded and placed her hand over the pentacle. She could feel its power and energy and felt protected, safe. "Thank you."

With a nod and a smile, Kiran said, "It's yours, love. It belonged to my granny, Saffron Eaglesham Hayes. I think she would have wanted you to have it."

Raven felt her eyes pool. It was weird having a whole new family she didn't know and a father who seemed to love her despite just meeting her. Unconditional love. That's what she was feeling from him. "What about you? Shouldn't you have protection?"

Kiran reached into his pocket and pulled out another white sachet. "Aye, I have one, too." His eyes all but twinkled. "As does Mick. You can use your wee ball of golden energy to protect you as well. Use it as a shield."

Raven blew out a breath. "I feel like I'm preparing for battle."

"That we are, love. That we are." Kiran picked up a duffel bag and nodded to the door. "Off we go, then."

They walked from the house to a clearing in the woods where the coven gathered for ceremonies and celebrations. Kiran set up the altar on a granite rock at the front of the clearing with supplies he brought in the duffel bag. Then he cast the circle, using his athame. Raven was surprised when he followed this by sprinkling salt around the perimeter of the circle.

"Do you really think we need that?" The salt was another source of protection.

"We'll take no chances, aye?"

Raven nodded and watched as he evoked the elements at the four quarters of the circle - earth to the north, air to the east, fire to the south, and water to the west. She wasn't sure why he was bothering to cast the circle in the first place. They weren't here to perform a ritual. But, she remained quiet and let him do his thing.

When he finished, he walked up to the altar and turned to face Raven. "I'll need to initiate you as a coven member."

Raven's eyes popped. "Why?"

"Because I'll be bringing you into our circle tomorrow evening and presenting you as my choice for our new High Priestess. You need to be a coven member for me to do that."

"You do realize I have no desire to return to the coven?"

"If you choose to leave the coven after we oust Adara, so be it. What level did you reach before you left the coven?"

"I was second-degree."

Both Mick and Kiran looked surprised.

"At twelve years of age?" Kiran asked, his voice a bit higher than usual.

Raven nodded.

"Do you feel confident in being re-initiated at that level?"

What did it matter? She wasn't going to stay in the coven. "I guess."

"Alright, then." He pulled several ropes from his duffel bag and turned to face Raven again.

She'd been through enough initiations, and seen many more, to know the drill. She removed her clothes, set them aside in a pile, and stood before Kiran to allow him to bind her. Then she knelt in front of the altar.

"Care to join her, Mick?" Kiran asked with a smirk.

Mick laughed. "I'll be joining at some point, but not quite yet."

Chapter 16

Raven laid on her back staring up at her bedroom ceiling afraid to move a muscle. She was barely keeping the nausea at bay. If she didn't make it into the bathroom soon, she was going to have a hell of a mess to clean up. The knock at her bedroom door had her about to growl at Mick when she heard Riley's voice.

"Rave? Can I come in?"

A wave of nausea kept her from answering. She rolled to her side, dropped her legs over the edge of the bed, and nearly tossed her cookies right there and then. She hobbled into the bathroom and fell to her knees just in time to hurl into the toilet. Riley was right behind her, grabbing a clean wash cloth and running it under the tap. Raven was too involved in losing the contents of her stomach to pay her any mind. Then the cool damp cloth at her nape felt too good for her to shoo Riley off. She hurled until she was sure her stomach had turned inside out. This whole pregnancy thing was a bitch.

With a groan, Raven leaned back against the cool glass wall of the shower. Riley came at her with a freshly doused wash cloth and Raven held up her hand to stop her. "What are you doing here, Ri?" She asked in a scratchy, raw voice.

Riley cocked her head to the side. "I thought about what

you said last night and I'm calling bullshit. There's no reason we can't be friends."

Had Riley not heard how painful seeing her all the time was? Hurting Riley again was the last thing Raven wanted to do, so she took a moment to try to figure out the gentlest way to say what she needed to say.

"You keep telling me I have to stop trying to get you to take me back, but you keep coming over here, giving me mixed signals. I can't get over you, Ri, if you're around all the time." She felt like a complete shit when Riley's face dropped.

"Oh, I see." Riley folded the wash cloth into a neat square and placed it on the counter. "I'll just …" She waved her hand towards the bathroom door. "Go, then." She was out the door in two steps and then came to a halt. Turning slowly, she met Raven's eyes. "Could I just ask you a question?"

"Yeah, sure."

"The rumour at the hospital is that you came in and threatened to hire the most expensive lawyer you could find to sue them for wrongful dismissal if they didn't take me back. Is that true?"

"You didn't deserve to be suspended. You didn't do anything wrong."

Riley's eyes drifted up to the ceiling. She nodded a couple of times before turning and leaving. Tears flooded Raven's eyes and she fought to keep them at bay. Leaning her head back against the glass, she wondered why the hell she should bother getting up off the floor.

Within minutes, Mick was standing in the doorway. "Geez, look at the state of you."

"Shut up," Raven croaked.

Raven swallowed her pride and let Mick help her up. They'd spent half the night with Kiran preparing for the gathering of the coven and still Raven felt completely unprepared. It wasn't like she was really going to become the coven's HPS, but it had her nerves frazzled just the same.

The warrant to search Adara's house came through at eight in the morning, but Raven was holding off on serving it until Adara left for the gathering. She didn't want her tipped off until they could play out their operation and hopefully get Adara to confess.

Kiran and LaCroix arrived at Raven's after breakfast. Unfortunately, LaCroix had Dr. Shoal in tow. Raven sat down with her in her bedroom and stared blankly out at the lake. She knew she had to do this or LaCroix wouldn't let her participate in the days events, so she resigned herself to opening up as much as she could.

"How long will this take?"

Dr. Shoal looked at Raven with warm eyes and a slight smile. She was dressed casually today in skinny jeans and a flowy white blouse. "That depends on you." She pulled a notebook and pencil out of the messenger bag she'd deposited beside her chair and set them on her lap.

"I wasn't close to my mother." Raven figured that would ease Shoal's concern at least a bit.

"Do you regret that now that she's gone?"

Damn. She wasn't expecting that question. Thinking about the twelve years she lost with her mother was painful now that she was convinced Adara kept them apart. She should have done more herself to repair her relationship with Ena.

"Yeah, I do."

When Dr. Shoal just sat quietly waiting, Raven took a deep breath then told her the story starting from the fight she and Ena had on the night she left home right up to what Raven had seen on the video of Adara saying she talked to Raven, but she refused to see Ena.

"Really, you've lost both of the mother figures in your life in a short period of time."

"Yeah, pretty much," Raven said, but she didn't want Dr.

Shoal to think she lost her entire family. Thinking of Ena's words, Raven said, "But, I gained a father." And a daughter. With that thought, a warmth spread through her body, centring around her heart.

"Can you tell me why you left home at such a young age? What drove you and your mother apart? What did you argue about the night you left?"

Raven figured Dr. Shoal already knew the answer. If LaCroix hadn't told her his suspicions, surely she'd seen it on the news. She stared out at Fairy Lake. The sky was clear today, the lake a sparkling, deep blue. The sun reflecting off of the lake's ripples gave the appearance of tiny stars dancing across its surface.

"Turns out it was all a misunderstanding." That was true. She thought Ena was getting back together with Gregor when she was actually kicking him out of the coven.

"What was the misunderstanding?"

Crap. She'd be damned if she was going to open up about Gregor Paigo. "Look, I had a lot of resentments towards my mother back then for an assortment of reasons. People looked down on us because of what we were and I was bullied in school for it. I hated being different than everyone else."

"Hm. Those don't sound like misunderstandings."

Raven clenched her fists then consciously relaxed her muscles. "I thought she was getting back together with an old boyfriend I couldn't stand and I lost it. Turns out she was never planning to get back together with him. That was the misunderstanding."

"And that kept you apart for twelve years?"

Raven exhaled forcefully. She was pretty sure she saw steam coming out of her nose.

It's okay, Rave. You can trust Dr. Shoal. She'll understand.

She'll understand? Did that mean Dr. Shoal had been through something similar? Raven slowed her breathing while looking out at the lake. Then she *listened*. What she heard was not that Dr. Shoal would use what happened to Raven against her, but she would respect her more for talking about it. That took strength. Keeping it buried didn't. Raven turned and met Shoal's eyes for the first time since they sat down. It wasn't pity she saw in Shoal's kind eyes, it was compassion.

"I've never talked about it before. With anyone."

"I know," Shoal said quietly.

Raven bobbed her head in short, rapid nods and turned back to the lake. She took several deep breaths trying to get up the courage to get the first sentence out. After that it had to get easier. She crossed her arms, hugging herself in an attempt to get warm.

"One of my mother's boyfriends started coming into my bedroom in the middle of the night when I was twelve years old." She spoke so fast it probably sounded like one long word to Dr. Shoal.

I'm so proud of you, sweet angel.

Her mother's words brought tears to Raven's eyes.

"The same boyfriend you thought she was getting back together with on the night you left home?" Shoal asked.

Raven nodded.

"When you look out at the lake, what do you feel?"

Raven's head whipped around to face Shoal. What the hell kind of question was that? Hadn't she heard what Raven just said?

The edge of Shoal's mouth curled up in a half smile. "What do you feel?"

Light twinkled over the surface of the lake and Raven could hear the soft whooshing of the waves caressing the rocky shore through the open window. She breathed in the fresh scented air on the light breeze flowing into the room.

"Calm."

Shoal nodded now. "You're using it to ground yourself, aren't you?"

With a shrug, Raven answered, "I guess, yeah." To her surprise, Dr. Shoal closed her notepad, tucked it into her messenger bag, and got to her feet.

"That's it?" Raven asked.

Shoal smiled warmly. "The concern was you may be having a difficult time coping with everything, but from what I've seen, you are doing as well as can be expected. I would like to keep seeing you to help you in processing your past trauma, if you're comfortable with me."

The first session hadn't been nearly as bad as Raven expected and it had the added benefit of getting LaCroix off her back, but she wasn't sure she wanted to subject herself to this on a regular basis.

At Raven's hesitation, Dr. Shoal placed a business card on the table. "Why don't you think about it and call my office for an appointment."

Raven liked the fact Dr. Shoal didn't try to pressure her into talking or to committing to future appointments. Maybe seeing her wouldn't be so bad.

"Yeah, okay. Thanks."

When Dr. Shoal left, Raven stayed where she was, staring out at the lake, playing the plan for the gathering through her mind. Kiran was convinced it would set Adara off and she would reveal herself as Ena's killer, but Raven wasn't so sure. She was also nervous about Adara's reaction after what she experienced yesterday. Adara was more powerful than anyone had guessed and the Goddess only knew what she had up her sleeve. She pushed to her feet and went over to the box sitting in the corner. Opening the lid, she reached in and pulled out the black silk robe that had been Ena's and slipped it on over her clothes. She was taller than Ena, but it fit perfectly. Ena's power seemed to be woven into every fibre.

You will have my power in addition to your own tonight, angel mine. And you will have my protection.

"You weren't able to protect yourself." It was out of Raven's mouth before she even thought about what she was saying. "Oh, shit, I'm sorry."

No, you're right. I trusted Adara. It didn't occur to me that I was being poisoned until it was too late.

"I wish I'd been there for you. Maybe if –"

What's done is done, remember. No regrets, darling.

Tears welled in Raven's eyes. "I love you, mom."

Oh, Rave. I love you, too. More than you'll ever know.

Raven reached into the box and pulled out the last remaining item. It was a lot heavier than she remembered. She was sure there weren't this many pages the last time she'd seen her Book of Shadows. She placed the leather bound book on her bed and flipped it open to the last entry. Her brows drew together. It was dated less than six weeks ago and written in her own handwriting, but how could that be?

Remember your dreams.

Ena's voice whispered through her mind as she flipped through the vellum pages. There were four or five entries a week going back years.

When you decided you didn't want anything to do with magick, I didn't argue. I thought it would be safer if the world didn't learn of your powers. But, I had to continue your training for your own protection.

"How? When?"

I came to you in your dreams, darling angel.

Memories came flooding back - practicing her art with Ena long into the night, studying witchcraft and personal development, honing her psychic abilities. Not just Ena. Raven gasped, her hand flying to her heart. Simone stood by

Ena at the altar in the woods as Raven knelt before them, sky-clad and bound with the colours of a third-degree priestess.

I needed a witness and I trusted Simone more than anyone. Well, except for Kiran, of course, but he was at sea. You, my darling angel, are a third-degree priestess of the Solstice coven and very much qualified to take over as High Priestess. It's your place, Raven Sage Bowen. Your birthright.

Raven was still reeling at the plethora of memories flooding her brain. But, Ena was right. All of the knowledge and skills she would need to lead the coven were there. Ena had been grooming her for the role for years. But, did she want it?

* * *

"You don't still need the list of coven members, do you?" Kiran asked. He sat with his feet up on the recliner in Raven's living room. It was Raven's favourite chair, but she found she didn't mind her father sitting there.

"No, I guess not." Raven eased herself down onto the couch and reached for the mug Mick placed on the coffee table for her.

"This is coffee. I can't drink this." She looked over at Mick with a frown. That was just plain mean.

"Don't worry," Mick grinned. "It's decaf. Kiran brought it over."

Damn these pregnancy hormones, Raven thought. Tears welled in her eyes again. "You brought me decaf?" How had he even thought to do that?

"I know you love your coffee," he grinned. "Like father, like daughter, aye? I couldn't imagine giving it up."

Raven stared down at the mug cupped between her palms. Her father was the sweetest man alive. She took a tentative sip, expecting it to taste less like the coffee she loved, but it didn't. It tasted great. "Oh, it's good." She closed her eyes and breathed in the aroma.

"You sound surprised, love. It's the Solstice Café's brand. That's your favourite, isn't it?"

Goddess love him, he really was the sweetest man alive. "You're really starting to grow on me, Pops."

Kiran cringed. "If you're going to call me something other than Kiran, can we make it Da or Dad?"

Emotions clogged Raven's throat and she swore her heart swelled in her chest. Dad. She never thought she'd have someone to call that name. She took another sip of her coffee and cleared her throat. "Thanks for getting the coffee, Dad."

She watched as Kiran's eyes filled and his white teeth flashed with a wide grin. "You're welcome, daughter."

A knock sounded at the door and Mick jumped to her feet, sniffing and wiping tears from her eyes. "I'll get it." She was back less than a minute later with a frown and sad eyes. "Raven, Jaxon is at the door. He'd like to speak to you."

Raven got up and walked to the front door, stepped out and closed the door behind her.

"Hey."

Jax's face was red and that thick, ropey vein in his neck throbbed, his hair standing up in all directions.

"First, are you okay?" Jax asked.

"Yeah, of course."

"Second, is the baby okay?"

"Yeah, she's fine. Why – oh." Someone told Jax about the cliff incident. "We're both fine, Jax."

"Damn it, Rave. You should have called me. When Maxine told me you nearly fell off a cliff, I was scared to death. What the hell happened?"

"It's a long story and I'm sorry, I never even thought about calling. I've had a lot going on."

His nostrils flared as he sucked in a breath. "That's no excuse. You're carrying my baby."

Like she didn't know that. "Will you calm down. I said I'm

sorry. This is new to me, too, you know. I'm not used to having to report in."

That seemed to calm him down. His wild eyes softened and his eyes locked onto hers. "You're really okay?"

"I'm fine. Really." Thinking of the baby inside her and that Jaxon had a right to her too was really going to take some getting used to. "We're going to have to sit down and figure out how we're going to handle everything, but it's going to have to wait another day or two."

"Sometimes I hate your job, Rave. Knowing you'll be taking our baby to work with you scares the crap out of me."

"I know."

"Can I take you out to dinner on Tuesday?" He asked. "Not a date or anything. I just want to talk about how we're going to do this. I want to be part of our baby's life."

"Sure. Tuesday works."

Jax nodded and started down the porch steps.

"Hey, Jax? Can I ask you a question?"

He turned and stared up at her. "Sure."

"Are you dating Mick Warren?"

He studied her face for a moment before he answered. "We've been out a few times."

"Do you like her?"

Jax breathed out a heavy sigh. "Why are you asking, Rave?"

"Because I know she really likes you and she's solid. You two would make a good couple."

A sheepish grin brightened Jax's face. "Are you trying to match-make so I forget about you?"

Raven laughed. "Maybe."

"Yeah, I really like her. She's different than the other women I've dated. In a good way."

"Would you like to come in for a coffee?"

Raven breathed a sigh of relief when Jax came back up the

steps. She left him in the living room with Mick and took Kiran into her bedroom to work on their preparations for the gathering some more. She needed to fill him in on her status as a third-degree member of the Solstice coven.

Chapter 17

"Target is in the driveway loading boxes into the side door of a silver Dodge Caravan."

"Ten-four," Raven responded into her police radio as she sat in her vehicle around the corner from Adara's house. They'd left Kiran at Ena's to prepare for the gathering which would take place in the clearing in the woods near the house. The first part of the gathering was the Full Moon Ritual, a sacred religious ceremony. Raven wasn't needed until after that part of the evening and she wanted to be at Adara's when they went in to see if she could get a look at Adara's Book of Shadows before making her way to the gathering.

"Target is leaving the location in the silver van."

"Ten-four," Raven responded.

Out of the blue, Mick said, "What you did this morning was very sweet – inviting Jax in for coffee then leaving us alone. You didn't have to do that."

Raven could feel Mick's eyes on her, but she continued to gaze out the passenger window. Had she done that for Mick or for more selfish reasons? "I want him to be happy."

Mick gasped. "And you think being with me will make him happy? You have no idea how much that means to me."

Raven turned then, her eyes locking on Mick's glassy ones and she smiled. She supposed she did believe Mick was the one Jax would be happy with.

"Target has arrived at the Bowen residence."

"That's our cue," Raven said, breaking the emotional moment between them. "Let's roll."

They didn't have to break Adara's door in because Raven had a key. She entered through the kitchen, expecting to find Adara's Book of Shadows sitting on the island, but it wasn't there. She went straight down the hall to the office where Adara took the book the day before and found the office door locked. That was strange. It hadn't had a lock when Raven lived there.

"Mick?"

Mick joined her in the hall and studied the door. "On three?"

Raven nodded and counted to three. They kicked the door, just above the lock at the same time and the door flew open.

Raven stepped inside with her mouth agape. What had been Adara's quaint little office had been transformed into some kind of dark magick altar. Raven's hand unconsciously covered the silver pentacle beneath her shirt. The once beautiful oak planked floor had been painted black and an inverted pentagram was carved into it. A black candle was positioned at each of the five points of the pentagram, flickering in the dim light of the room. A bowl of gold and silver sat in the exact centre of the pentagram.

Raven stepped closer, fearing what the dark liquid filling the bowl might be. An herbal scent mingled with melted wax. "Shit, that's a potion." Looking over her shoulder at Mick, she said, "This is set up for some sort of spell. She's planning to do dark magick tonight."

"If we blow out the candles and get rid of that stuff, will it stop her from doing whatever she's planning?"

"I don't know, but it's worth a try." They blew out the candles and Raven picked up the bowl. Sitting beneath it was a photograph of Kiran. "Oh, damn. What the hell is she going to do?"

Mick leaned over and studied the photo. "Do you really think she'd hurt Kiran?"

"I didn't think she'd hurt me," Raven said. She put the picture in her pocket and flushed the contents of the brass bowl down the toilet, leaving enough residual liquid in the bowl for forensics to test. Raven had one of the crime scene techs collect the evidence and take it out to their mobile unit.

She found Adara's Book of Shadows sitting on a small desk in the corner of the room and flipped it open to the back. It was all documented – the spell she used to keep the hospital staff from doing any tests on Ena, the spell she used to distract Raven so she walked into traffic, the spell she used to nearly knock Raven off of the cliff, plus many more Raven didn't have time to read through. She took a picture of the last few pages with her cell phone and went out front to turn Adara's house over to the Forensics Unit. The gathering was about to begin and she wanted to catch as much of it as she could. She looked around for Mick and found her in the Black Magick room.

"Time to go, Warren."

"Raven?" Mick said in a wounded voice.

"What?"

"You need to take a look at this."

Raven walked back to the book and quickly read through the spell holding Mick's interest.

"You need to tell Riley," Mick said.

Hot, burning rage raced through Raven's blood. Adara *had* cast a spell to make Raven sleep wwith Jaxon.

"It doesn't make a difference."

Mick gasped. "Of course it does. Riley can't blame you for sleeping with Jax if you were forced to do it against your will."

'It doesn't change anything," Raven growled. She wanted to get her hands around Adara's neck and squeeze the life out of her. "I still cheated on her."

* * *

Mick and Raven approached the clearing through the woods, the full moon lighting their way. It shone down on the clearing bright enough to make identifying the twenty or so gathered there fairly easy. Some were dressed in casual clothes and a few wore robes much like Ena's HPS robe. Kiran stood tall at the front of the circle wearing a robe that matched Ena's with intricate gold and purple embroidery on the black silk. At his side stood Simone Wagnar, who Kiran asked to step in as acting High Priestess for the Full Moon Ceremony which Wiccans referred to as an Esbat Ritual. He trusted her more than anyone else in the coven and that, along with Ena's vow of confidence, had been enough for Raven. She supposed that meant she trusted Kiran and that was saying a lot because the only other men she'd trusted in her life were Jaxon Lang and Grayson LaCroix.

They took up a position behind a thick copse of trees to watch the rest of the ceremony and Raven handed Mick her phone.

"Read through the pictures I took of Adara's Book of Shadows. See if you can figure out what Adara is planning." She wanted to keep her attention on the coven members, Adara in particular. While she scanned the crowd, Raven pulled on Ena's HPS robe.

Mick turned her back on the clearing to keep the light from Raven's phone from giving away their position and went to work reading the pages from Adara's book.

Raven located Adara near the front of the circle. She was wearing a black robe signifying her status as a third-degree priestess. She could have formed her own coven years ago. It was even encouraged that second and third-degree priests and priestesses break off and form their own covens, expanding and growing the Wicca community. Instead she killed her best friend in order to take over the Solstice coven. Raven couldn't come to terms with it. It had to be more than just the coveted High Priestess role that fuelled Adara's murderous actions.

Use your gift, angel. You will see what's inside of her.

The last time she tried that, she was sure Adara had known. Raven didn't want to spook her yet. She wanted Adara's surprise reaction to what they planned.

Kiran and Simone were just beginning to complete the Esbat Ritual. Raven figured she had less than five minutes before making her grand entrance.

"Oh, shit," Mick gasped. "Adara isn't going to hurt Kiran. She's going to bind him to her with a Black Magick love spell."

Raven shot Mick a look over her shoulder. "What? She's going to do what?"

"That concoction in her creepy black room? Kiran and Adara have to drink some of it on the full moon and Adara has to chant the spell thirteen times. She's also going to rig the vote for High Priestess. There's a spell here to make everyone vote for her."

"Jesus. She doesn't just want Ena's role in the coven. She wants Ena's life." Did Adara know the house would go to Raven and not Kiran? Did she think she would move into Ena's house with Kiran, have Ena's money, and live Ena's life? Raven found Adara at the front of the gathering. She didn't appear to be carrying anything. Then her eyes went to the tall figure looming over Adara's right shoulder dressed in jeans and a dark hoody with the hood pulled over his head. He leaned forward as if whispering something in her ear. Hanging over his shoulder was a messenger bag. Was he carrying the potion for her?

"Can you communicate telepathically?"

Mick handed Raven her phone. "No, why?"

"I need to warn Kiran."

Just as she said that, Kiran faced the coven members and announced it was time for coven business.

"The Elders have expressed their wish to select a new High Priestess by election," he began. "Those of you who have been nominated, please step forward."

That was Raven's cue. She pulled the hood of the robe over her head and continued to watch.

Adara took a step forward and Simone left the altar to stand at her side.

"As High Priest, it is my right to appoint a High Priestess and I have chosen to do so," Kiran said. There were gasps and whispers throughout the membership.

Adelle Warren, Mick's mother, opened a gate in the protective circle allowing Raven entrance and then closed it behind her. Raven walked to the altar and stood beside Kiran with her head bent low. Kiran stepped in front of her, lowered her hood, and grinned.

"Adara's going to try to put a love spell on you," Raven whispered. "Don't drink anything she gives you." She would have sworn Kiran's eyes twinkled in response to her warning.

"Oh, love. You needn't worry about that." He turned and addressed the membership. "I introduce to you the new High Priestess of the Solstice coven, my daughter, Raven Sage." With that he stepped back to Raven's side.

"No," Adara shouted. "She's not even a member of the coven. She hasn't practiced the craft for years. You must be a third-degree priestess to be eligible for High Priestess."

Kiran stared her down. "Ah, but she is a member of the coven. She has been initiated as a third-degree priestess. Simone?" He nodded in Simone's direction.

Simone took a short step forward then turned to the

gathering. "I can attest to witnessing Raven's initiation as a third-degree priestess."

Adara's face turned bright red. She glared at Kiran. "You can't do this. You must put it to a vote. You must heed the desires of the Elders and the membership."

Raven heard Kiran's sharp intake of breath over Adara's shouts. His jaw clenched tight, as did his fists at his sides.

"You dare to speak of the desires of the coven? You, who have made a mockery of everything we stand for?"

Raven closed her eyes and took three cleansing breaths then reached out with her mind, like a wave spreading out until it engulfed the entire gathering. Most of what she picked up was surprise and wonder at Raven entering their circle in Ena's robes. Raven honed in on Adara's energy. She could feel Adara's shock and anger, but she had a block in place preventing Raven from reading her thoughts.

The man at Adara's shoulder was a different story. He wasn't experienced in the ways of the coven and had no idea what was happening. He stood a few steps behind Adara, as if awaiting her command. He was nervous and confused. This wasn't what Adara told him would happen. He began looking over his shoulder, looking for a way to escape.

Adara shot her arms up in the air and began mumbling a spell over and over. Lightning formed and shot down from the sky, striking the altar just behind Raven and Kiran. Splinters of granite shot all around them as heat sizzled and the air emitted a distinct electrical odour.

Raven jolted, but Kiran didn't move. Slowly his arms rose from his sides until they were in the air, his palms facing the coven members. "Beloved coven, I give you Ena's murderer, her own best friend."

This wasn't going as they planned. Gasps and murmurs rose as Raven's eyes danced back and forth between Kiran and Adara.

"Eight words the Wiccan Rede fulfill – An it harm none, do what ye will," Kiran quoted the Wiccan Redes. "'Tis the Old Law that no one may do anything that may harm any of the Craft. You have broken our truest laws, Adara Kirby, and you must be ousted from the coven."

"You simple man. You understand nothing. She stood at the helm of this coven for over thirty years with the prestige of the Bowen name and the Bowen money. She had everything, including you. I worked just as hard. I put all of myself into this coven for just as long as she did. It's my time to reign." Adara shot her arms into the air again.

Kiran's arms shot out over Adara and Raven stepped between them. "Stop." The crackle of lightening sounded above her and without conscious thought, Raven placed a dome of protection around the entire coven. Lightning strikes surged towards the clearing, one after another, bouncing off the protective shell. "Stop," she screamed. The spell wouldn't withstand much more. She felt like everything was happening in slow motion as she watched Adara lower her arms until they were outstretched towards Raven. Adara's eyes narrowed, her nose scrunched up, and her mouth set in a twisted snarl.

How could this be the same sweet and loving woman who raised her? The woman before her was filled with hate and resentment. In her anger and loss of control, Adara dropped the protection she had placed on her mind. Raven felt the loathing and jealousy Adara had been harbouring for years, all the way back to when Ena and Adara were young girls. And now she was turning that loathing on Raven herself. Blue sparks arced between Adara's fingers. A bright blue bolt shot out of Adara's hands and Raven simply raised her right hand, palm facing Adara. The bolt came to a halt and then shot back at Adara, hitting her mid-abdomen. Adara screamed and sank to her knees.

"Sisters and Brothers," Ena's voice came calm and serene. It wasn't in Raven's head this time and she watched in shock as Ena appeared before her, faint at first and then becoming a solid form.

Kiran stepped forward, his voice cracking, "My love." Tears formed in his ice blue eyes as Ena faced him, her palms coming up to cup his cheeks. Her smile was bright and her hazel eyes sparkled. This wasn't the sick and hollowed form of her mother Raven had seen in the videos. She was healthy and vital.

"You're dead," Adara growled through clenched teeth, still doubled over, clutching her belly. "I killed you. You're dead."

"Sisters and Brothers," Ena began again. "You've heard Adara's confession. Her actions go against everything we believe in and so, I put to you that this woman is no longer Wiccan. She is no longer a member of this coven."

Adelle Warren stepped forward. "High Priestess, who would you have as head of our coven?"

Ena seemed to float to Adelle. She brushed her hand over Adelle's hair and placed a chaste kiss on her cheek before drifting back to Kiran. Her hand slipped through the crook of his arm and he looked down at her adoringly.

Seeing her parents like this made Raven wish she could have the last twelve years back. Had Adara not kept them apart, she would have had over a decade with them, surrounded by their love.

"That is for Kiran and the Elders to decide," Ena answered. Her arm encircled Raven's waist and pulled her into her side. "Of course, I would like my daughter to lead the coven, but it is her choice whether or not she wants to return to the Wicca way of life and step into her destiny as a daughter of the Bowen line." She looked up at Raven with a smile and tears in her eyes. "She has great power, as you've just seen, but she also has the kind and loving heart of a Wiccan. She would honour the coven in the HPS role."

As she spoke, Ena began to fade and Raven's heart sped up. "Can't you stay?" Raven whispered. "I don't want to lose you now we've found each other again."

Ena hugged Raven and kissed her cheek then just stood staring into her eyes. "I'll always be watching over you, my sweet angel. Always. I made many mistakes with you, Rave. Perhaps the biggest was in thinking I needed to protect you from your powers. I understand now how wrong I was. You, my darling angel, are our salvation. Not just for the life you carry and the Bowens to come, but for all of our kind. I'll see you in your dreams, for there we will meet many times throughout your life."

With a smile she turned to Kiran. "And you, my love. Don't mourn for me." She wiped tears from his face with a gentle caress. "Within a year, you'll find a new love. Just know that she's someone I approve of, someone who will make you happy. You'll never forget what we shared and that is all I can ask. I want you to be loved and happy, Kiran, and know that I will love you always."

Kiran lowered his forehead to Ena's. "You are my always and forever. I love you with all of my heart and soul. I don't know how to survive without you, love."

Oh, my God, Raven thought. They're going to kiss right here in front of everyone. She turned away just as their lips met and focused her attention on Adara, still doubled over. She signalled for Mick and Adelle opened the circle to allow her in. Mick bent over Adara, pulling handcuffs from a pouch on her belt, and began to recite the Miranda warning.

Raven scanned the crowd for the tall man with the hoodie and wasn't surprised to find him missing. Coward. But, that was okay. She caught a glimpse of his face when she was facing down Adara. She glanced over her shoulder expecting to see her parents still wrapped up in each other, but Ena's form was fading to nothing but a glowing golden light.

"Blessed be," Ena said and the light vanished as if it imploded in on itself.

"Blessed be," Ena's coven answered back in unison.

Raven bent over clutching her chest, feeling the loss so deeply she thought she might be having a heart attack. Strong arms wrapped around her and she was drawn in to Kiran's muscled chest, engulfed in his warmth. He rocked her back and forth, brushing a kiss over her temple.

"We'll get through this together, aye?"

The lump in her throat prevented her from responding, so she nodded against his chest.

Kiran lifted his head and addressed the coven with a gravelly voice, "Sisters and Brothers, please join us at the house for a celebration of Ena's life."

Raven smiled at that. Kiran hadn't been able to attend Ena's funeral and he deserved this celebration. It was a chance for her to have a do-over as well. She harboured so many resentments towards Ena during her funeral. This time she would pay her mother the proper respect.

* * *

Raven stood against the wall in Ena's great room, watching and listening as Ena's closest friends passed around champagne and shared stories of their experiences with Ena. She found herself doubled over laughing on occasion, but overall she felt a deep sadness at not having shared those kinds of moments with her mother. The last twelve years were now a huge, gaping hole in her soul.

Simone joined her, sipping on a glass of champagne. "That was quite a spectacular display of power, Raven."

Raven snorted. "It wasn't all me." In fact, she was sure that it was mostly Ena. She hadn't even thought about what she was doing, she just acted.

"Oh, no," Simone said with a sultry smile. "That was all

you, darling."

Raven's eyebrows drew together. "What makes you say that?"

"It was all your energy, Rave. Ena's energy didn't join in until she appeared before us, *after* you took Adara down."

"She did that on purpose, didn't she? She wants me to have confidence in my powers."

A slow smile graced Simone's face again. She took a small sip of champagne and said, "You're a Bowen-Hayes, Rave. If you don't have confidence in your powers, no one does."

Raven's hand covered her abdomen, thinking about the next generation of Bowen in her belly. God, she was going to have to teach her witchcraft because the poor kid would undoubtedly have powers she would have no idea how to control.

She watched as Kiran entered the room and was immediately engulfed in women. He smiled at them, but it didn't match the overwhelming sadness in his eyes.

"You looked good up there with him tonight," Raven said to Simone.

"Mmmm, it's hard not to look good next to him."

Raven laughed, studying the star struck expression on Simone's face. "Ena doesn't want him to be alone."

"What he needs right now is a friend. The man is grieving the loss of the love of his life."

"I know how he feels," Raven mumbled to herself. "I suppose you're right."

Simone's eyes left Kiran and roamed back to Raven. "The difference being, Riley is still alive and well. You can still get her back, Rave."

Raven shook her head. "No. She's done. She doesn't trust me and she needs to."

Simone put her arm around Raven's shoulder and squeezed. "Funny thing about trust, Rave, is that you can rebuild it." With that she walked away to join the assembly of women surrounding Kiran.

Raven followed her over to say her goodbyes. Adara was on hold at the detachment and she also had the matter of the tall guy in the hoodie to sort out.

* * *

LaCroix refused to allow Raven to question Adara, so she got comfortable in the the box while LaCroix and Mick took their seats across from Adara. She looked like a completely different woman than Raven had seen just hours before. She was back to being the meek and mild woman Raven had known.

"I'm not going to waste my time talking to you, Adara," LaCroix said after reading Adara the charges against her, which ranged from first-degree murder and two counts of attempted murder all the way down to illegal possession of a controlled substance for the arsenic they found in one of her bathroom cabinets. "We've got more than enough evidence to put you away for the rest of your miserable life."

As he spoke, Raven watched the ire rise in Adara's eyes. Her eyes narrowed, jaw clenched, and her face flushed red, slowly transforming back to the woman Raven faced in the clearing.

"Would you like to give a statement?" LaCroix asked.

Adara's face softened and she gave LaCroix an evil grin. "No comment."

LaCroix nodded to Mick, signalling her to take Adara back to lock up. Mick removed one of the handcuffs attached to a D ring on the table and secured Adara's hands before leading her out while LaCroix joined Raven in the observation room.

"She's up to something, Grayson, and I think I know what it is." When LaCroix told Adara they have enough evidence against her, Raven could almost see her racing thoughts and she knew the moment Adara had come up with a plan.

LaCroix raised his eyebrow at Raven. "Is that so?"

"Yeah," Raven grinned. "What time does Tate come on shift?"

Chapter 18

While they waited for Constable Darren Tate to arrive for the night shift, Raven applied for one more warrant. Then she went to work setting up additional surveillance devices in the lockup area and in the evidence room before settling down to type up her reports.

Mick blew out a breath and deflated into the chair next to Raven's desk.

"How about I run over to the café for a large double double decaf?"

Raven was half way through the second sentence on her report. She dropped her head back and closed her eyes. "Oh, God, yes."

Laughing, Mick said, "If I didn't know better, I'd swear you just had an orgasm."

She got a glare from Raven. "Really? Do you really have to go there?" She hadn't had sex in far too long. Just hearing the word orgasm brought images of Riley to her mind and she really didn't need that distraction at the moment.

"Sorry," Mick said, but she had a smirk on her face. "I'll be back in five."

Raven ignored her, tapping away at her keyboard again. By the time Mick returned, she was filing her completed reports.

Mick had a cup in each hand and offered one to Raven. She

accepted the decaf and peeled back the lid, breathing in the aroma before taking a sip. Damn, it was good.

"Bowen," LaCroix called out from across the room. "Your warrants are in."

Raven leaned back in her chair and smiled. "Ten-four, sir." Everything was falling into place.

*　*　*

Mick and Raven watched on the CCTV system as Constable Darren Tate entered the lockup area less than ten minutes after coming on duty.

"Bingo," Raven said.

"I can't believe Tate is involved in all of this," Mick whispered, as if Tate could hear them. "How deep do you think he's involved?"

"All the way," Raven answered. "I'm willing to bet he's linked to Paigo in some way."

They could see Adara at the bars of her cell now, talking animatedly with Tate. He nodded several times and then Adara waved her hand out to her side as if dismissing him. He turned and left lock up.

"Pretty obvious who's giving the orders," Mick said.

Raven switched monitors, bringing up the camera for the evidence room. "Yeah, it's like he's her little bitch."

They waited a good forty-five minutes before the evidence room's CCTV camera went black. There was a sudden dimming in the room that drew Raven's attention to it.

"He cut the camera feed." She moved to the monitor and brought up one of the cameras she installed earlier. The lights came on in the evidence room and Tate stood in the doorway. He glanced over his shoulder and closed the door behind him. Raven switched to another monitor, bringing up another camera, this one focused on the aisle where evidence boxes with Adara's name on them had been planted after they shipped the real evidence down to Orillia for safe keeping. It took Tate a few minutes to locate them and then he carried one box at a time, stacking them next to the door. Then he left the room, turning off the lights and leaving the boxes next to the door.

Raven followed him on a monitor displaying multiple cameras inside and outside of the station. He checked the hallways, squad room, and the bullpen before going out to the parking lot. He got in his vehicle and brought it around to the side door, close to where the evidence room was located. Raven waited until he was going back for the last box before she sent a text to LaCroix.

"Let's go," she said to Mick.

They walked out the front door and Mick turned to the left, Raven to the right. Raven jogged around the building and waited just around the corner. When she saw the lights from LaCroix's SUV, she stepped around the corner with her gun raised, facing the front of the car. Tate stood behind it, closing his trunk.

"Step away from the vehicle, Tate, and let me see your hands," she called out. The look on his face was priceless. His bulging eyes darted around looking for a way out.

"Hands," Raven yelled.

Tate's right hand reached for his weapon, but it wasn't in its holster. Mick was right behind him and had lifted it out. She pushed him onto the trunk, securing his hands behind his back before he realized what was happening. Raven's heart swelled in pride. "Yeah, she'll do," she murmured to herself.

Mick removed Tate's duty belt and LaCroix patted him down.

"What the hell?" Tate yelled. "I was just going out on patrol. What the hell is this?"

LaCroix pulled him off of the trunk and Mick popped it open. "Want to explain what you're doing with the evidence from the Adara Kirby case in your trunk, Constable?"

LaCroix asked.

"I-I was just … uh, I …"

"Yeah," Raven said as she approached. "You were just … uh … what?"

Tate jumped back into LaCroix, screaming, "Keep her away from me."

Raven nearly doubled over laughing. What the heck did he think she as going to do to him?

Mick and LaCroix escorted Tate into an interview room and Raven had two uniforms carry the boxes back inside. They were just filled with photocopy paper to weigh them down, but now they were evidence as well. Evidence with Tate's fingerprints all over them because he hadn't bothered to glove up. Idiot.

They left Tate sitting in the interview room while they executed the warrants. They began with his locker at the station and his patrol vehicle before moving on to his personal vehicle and his apartment. The first three gave them nothing except the evidence boxes.

Raven and Mick climbed the three flights of stairs to his apartment about an hour behind the forensics team. They donned paper booties and signed in with the uniformed officer at the door. The first thing Raven noticed when she opened the door was the smell of rot, like food had been left out too long. She scanned the room, taking in the empty beer bottles on nearly every flat surface and food containers scattered about. Clothes were scattered over various pieces of furniture and it looked like the guy didn't own a vacuum. One of the forensics guys met them just inside the door with a massive grin on his face. He pushed thick black framed glasses up his long nose.

"You're going to want to see the room down the hall. First door on the right."

"Bingo," Raven said. This is what she expected. Darren

Tate wasn't a member of the Solstice Coven, but she was damn sure he practiced magick. Black magick. Her long legs carried her quickly down the hall with Mick double stepping behind her. At the doorway, she stopped and looked in, expecting to see a similar room to Adara's redecorated office and she wasn't too far off. The floor was painted black with a large inverted pentagram carved into the centre of it. Unlit candles stood like sentinels at the five points. The altar along the far wall contained spell books and the various tools of the trade.

Cheryl Danby, one of the forensics techs, worked in white, hooded coveralls and glanced over her shoulder at them. "Oh," she said, and turned around to face them. "You're going to want to step in and take a look at the wall behind you."

Raven took two long steps forward and turned. Her jaw dropped as her eyes busily scanned the photograph laden wall. It was covered top to bottom and left to right with pictures of herself going back to her early teens. Tate hadn't lived here that long though. He was sent to Solstice after graduating from the Police College. Before that, she wasn't sure where he lived, but it wasn't around Solstice. So, who had taken all of these pictures?

"Paigo," Mick whispered, either figuring it out on her own or reading Raven's thoughts.

"Get Simone Wagnar on the phone," Raven ordered. "See if she knows if Gregor Paigo has a son."

While Mick was busy with that, Raven called LaCroix. "I need to know who Tate's father is. Can you look it up for me?"

"I can. Care to fill me in?"

Raven explained the photos and why Tate couldn't have been responsible for all of them.

"As far as I know, Tate was raised near Ottawa. I'll check

his birth records and see if his father is listed," LaCroix said.

"Thanks," Raven hung up and went into the master bedroom. The double bed was unmade, as if Tate had just gotten out of it after a night of tossing and turning. Clothes were scattered around the room and beer bottles littered the night stands. She found spare uniforms in the closet, which confirmed this was Tate's room. In the second bedroom, she stared at the neatly made up bed, the bare walls, and clean surfaces on the dresser and end tables. At first glance, it appeared this was an unused guest room. Raven checked the closet first and found a row of plaid shirts and jeans hanging in it. The drawers were filled with t-shirts, underwear, and socks – all neatly folded. It appeared that Gregor Paigo wasn't the filthy pig his property on the lake suggested. In fact, the bastard didn't live there. It had probably been sitting empty for years. Damn it. She should have picked up on that.

"Dr. Wagnar said that if he has any kids, she doesn't know about it," Mick reported as Raven stepped back out into the hallway.

"Oh, he has at least one," Raven said. She stuck her head back into the room with the black floor and inverted pentagram. "Cheryl? Could you have someone fingerprint the spare bedroom. Light switches, closet doors, door knobs. I want it thoroughly printed."

"On it," Cheryl said.

"Let's go back to the station and interview the weak link in this trio," Raven said to Mick.

"Which one is the weak link?"

"Tate." He was the one with the most to lose. He was the one they were going to be able to break. He may have even been an unwilling accomplice in all of this. He'd gone up to Judge Cromwell's hunt camp to get the warrant signed for Adara's house, yet he hadn't tipped her off.

As soon as they got back to the station, Raven went into

the CCTV room to review the footage of Tate at Adara's cell in lock up, zooming in on Adara.

"What are you looking for?" Mick asked, hovering over Raven's shoulder.

"Watch," Raven answered.

Unless you were zoomed in, you wouldn't have noticed Adara's lips moving, but they were and they were moving rapidly.

"She's saying a spell," Mick said.

"Yeah, she is."

"You think Tate took the evidence out of the evidence room without knowing he was doing it?"

"I don't know if he knew or not, but I don't think he had a choice."

They left the CCTV room and headed for LaCroix's office, but he wasn't there.

Mick followed Raven to the observation room. Tate paced back and forth along the back wall, stopping every now and then to scrub his hands over his face. He still wore his navy blue uniform pants and shirt, but his belts and Kevlar vest had been removed. He'd undone the top few buttons on the shirt and a white t-shirt was visible beneath it.

"Fuck, fuck, fuck," his voice grumbled through the intercom, but he didn't sound angry. He sounded scared shitless.

"Coffee?" LaCroix asked, entering observation with a tray holding three coffees. Raven stared at them longingly. He didn't know she was pregnant.

"I'm sure one won't hurt," Mick whispered. "It's after two in the morning and you've been up since about six yesterday morning."

So had Mick, but she didn't mention that. Maybe she thought it was harder on Raven because she was pregnant and she was probably right. Raven felt exhausted and every inch of her body ached. God, she wanted that coffee. LaCroix slipped one out of the tray and handed it to her. She couldn't not take it. He'd know something was up because Raven always drank coffee.

"Thanks, Sarge."

Raven filled him in on what they'd seen on the CCTV as they watched Tate pace nervously.

"You think Adara put some kind of spell on him?"

"Yeah." Raven took her first sip of coffee and closed her eyes to savour it. She couldn't say it tasted any different than the decaf, but for some reason it was a whole lot better.

"You okay," LaCroix asked.

"Oh, yeah. I just really needed this caffeine kick."

"So, how do you want to go at this?"

Raven watched Tate for a moment, mumbling to himself as he paced back and forth.

"Let's bring in the video from the evidence room. See what he has to say about that." She went back to her desk and grabbed her laptop then entered the interview room with Mick while LaCroix watched from the box. They took their seats while Tate continued to wear the thin carpet bare across from them. Raven set up her laptop and brought up the surveillance footage. She cued up the clip in lock up first. "Take a look at this," she said, swivelling the laptop around to face him. Tate placed his hands on the table and leaned over. While he watched the video play through, Raven watched his expressions.

"So what? I checked on a prisoner. There's nothing wrong with that."

"Okay," Raven said, spinning the laptop around to face her. She cued up the segment from the evidence room and spun it around again. "Tell me about this."

While he'd been attentive and curious watching the first video, he was anything but watching this one. His face turned red, his exhalations heavy. He clenched his hands into tight fists on the table. Raven pushed her chair back a few inches to be ready in case he turned violent.

"You already know I took the boxes out of the evidence room. I was transporting them down to Orillia."

"Really? There was no order for them to be transferred."

Tate swiped at the laptop, sending it sailing towards the end of the table and Mick caught it before it flew over the edge.

"This is bullshit. There was an order on the sergeants desk when I came in. You must have done something with it." He pointed his finger at Raven. "You're setting me up. You've always had it out for me."

Raven smiled up at him. "We've been to your apartment, Tate."

That shut him up pretty darn quick. He spun around as if he'd been punched. "Fuck."

Raven rose out of her chair. "You can either sit down and have a calm conversation with us or I'll walk you down to lock up and place the multitude of charges against you including accessory to murder and accessory to attempted murder."

He was definitely in panic mode, breathing like a bull facing a matador, his face resembling a red traffic light. He dropped his face into his hands and swore again. "It's not going to make any damn difference. You're not going to believe a word I say. You may as well just lock me the fuck up."

Raven pulled the laptop towards her and brought up the video from lock up again. She zoomed in on Adara's face and turned the laptop towards Tate again.

"She's chanting a spell, isn't she? She's compelling you to remove the evidence."

Tate turned, dropping his hands from his face and studied

the laptop screen. "That's how she's doing it? She's using a spell on me?"

"Sit down, Tate. Tell me what you know," Raven said. "And how Gregor Paigo is involved in all of this."

He looked at her with an expression of utter shock. "How do you know about Gregor?"

His birth records listed his father as unknown, but Raven was sure Gregor Paigo was Darren Tate's father. "You share an apartment and some of the photos of me in your black magick room date back to when you would have been ten years old, long before you came to Solstice."

"It's his room, not mine. I don't have anything to do with that stuff."

"Yet you were at the gathering of the coven tonight."

"She asks me to do stuff for her and I can't say no. It's like I have to do it. I have no choice."

"What else has she asked of you?"

"Nothing. This only started after you arrested Gregor. I swear to God I had nothing to do with what Gregor was doing or what Adara has been up to. The two of them have been working together, either in Gregor's creepy room or in hers. After he was locked up, she started calling me, telling me she needed help. All I did was carry a thermos for her to the gathering. She gave me some weird verse that I was supposed to chant thirteen times along with her. That was it."

"Did you know what you were doing when you removed the boxes from evidence?"

Tate dropped his head into his hands, elbows on the table. "Yeah, but I couldn't stop myself. I had to do it. Just take me down to lock up. You're not going to believe anything I say."

"I believe you," Raven said.

Tate's head popped up and he stared into Raven's ice blue eyes. "You do?"

"You went out to Judge Cromwell's hunt camp to get him

to sign the warrant for the search on Adara's house, but you didn't tip her off. That tells me you're on the up and up."

Tate sagged, as if all of the tension in his body suddenly released.

"Tell me what you know about the four women Paigo abducted."

"I don't know anything about that. Honestly, I don't."

"You must have seen my pictures on the wall of his ... whatever that room is."

"Yeah, but I thought he was just obsessed with you, you know? You're hot, Raven. I thought he just had a thing for you."

She didn't know whether to be flattered or repulsed. She needed to interview Paigo and find out why her pictures were plastered on that wall. Had he put some sort of dark magick spell on her?

"What about Adara? What do you know about what she was up to?"

"Nothing. You have to believe me. I don't know what she did to Ena Bowen. I know you charged her with Ena's murder, but I don't know anything about it."

Raven let out a frustrated sigh and signalled to LaCroix through the two way mirror. He entered the room and told Tate he was on suspension, but he was free to go. Raven, Mick, and LaCroix went back to his office where LaCroix made a call to let the officers assigned to tail Tate know he was leaving the building. Raven sank down into one of the chairs facing LaCroix's desk.

"I need to interview Paigo again."

"Let's call it a night," LaCroix said. "I'll make arrangements for you to see Paigo in Penatanguishene tomorrow morning."

"And I want to interview Adara."

LaCroix cocked his head and raised an eyebrow at Raven.

"Give me a chance, Sarge. I can probably get more out of her than anyone else."

"We've got a mountain of evidence against her, Rave. Most of it in her own handwriting."

"I know." Raven leaned forward, locking her eyes on his. "But, we don't know the ties between Paigo and Adara. Did she have any involvement in the abductions and murders of those girls? Did he have a hand in Ena's death? And I'm really freaked out about all of those pictures of me on that wall. Is something going to happen to me because he's cast some sort of spell. Or worse, is something going to happen to my –" She cut herself off there. She'd almost let it slip that was going to have a baby. "Is something going to happen to Riley? There's a reason he targeted women who looked just like her. He'd even been trolling her profile on the Dating Pool."

LaCroix sighed. "Fine. But, do it in the morning. Let's get the hell out of here for the night."

"Amen to that," Mick said.

Despite the fact that both Paigo and Adara were locked up, Mick insisted on staying the night at Raven's again. On the drive home, Raven said, "I'm starting to think you've got the hots for me, Warren."

"Well, you *are* hot," Mick laughed.

"Yeah, yeah." Repulsed, she thought. She was definitely repulsed Tate thought she was hot. And that wound her back to thinking about the one person she wanted to think she was hot. Was she working tonight or home sleeping? Was she thinking about her or had she moved on weeks ago? Considering Riley's profile was on a dating website, she had to assume she already moved on. She had to stop thinking about Riley.

When they got to the cottage, Raven locked up, set the alarm, and headed straight for her bed, crawling up the mattress and face planted into the pillows with a groan. And pictures of what she and Riley had done in the bed she was lying on raced through her mind. Red hot desire shot through her body, arrowing straight to her core. Every muscle in her body tensed. Damn Ena and her genes.

"I'm sorry," she whispered as a sob ripped through her chest. She couldn't regret the tiny life growing in her belly, but she regretted losing Riley with every cell of her being, regretted hurting her and betraying her trust. Could she have done something different, said something different instead of sending Riley away? Something to change her mind?

"I'm so sorry." Her shoulders heaved and she muffled her wrenching sobs in the pillow.

* * *

They got an early start in the morning and Raven let Mick believe her red, puffy eyes were a result of her morning sickness. She was good at keeping her thoughts blocked from Mick and at listening to others' thoughts now that she remembered all of Ena's lessons. She was also learning, thanks to advice filtered through Kiran from his mother, Rauri, how to control her psychic ability so that she wasn't picking up everyone's thoughts, just the ones she wanted. She was quick to pass on that advice to Mick.

They arrived at the jail in Penatanguishene and went through a number of security checks, including leaving their weapons. It was as if Raven was missing a piece of herself when she didn't have her Sig.

Paigo waited for them in an interview room with his hands in cuffs attached to a chain around his waist despite his right hand being heavily bandaged. That told Raven the guards thought he was a threat.

"Has he been cooperative?" she asked the guard escorting them.

The guard, a big burly man with rusty hair cut in a military buzz cut, let out a short laugh. "He's not exactly cooperative, but no major concerns. He's a puny little thing, but he's got some muscle in there."

Raven walked into the room ahead of Mick and a sleezy smile appeared on Paigo's face. They sat at the table across from him and Raven's skin crawled. No one creeped her out more than Gregor Paigo, but she needed to push all of that down and focus on what she was doing.

"Let's talk about your profile on the Dating Pool."

That dropped the smirk from his face, Raven thought with a tug of satisfaction.

He tilted his head to the side, squinted his eyes, and his lips pursed, lifting at one edge. "Dating Pool? What's that?"

She could have tried to read his thoughts to see if he was genuinely confused or not, but there was no way in hell she wanted to see inside Paigo's brain.

"The dating website?"

Paigo snorted. "Dating website? I don't even own a computer, why would I be on a dating website?"

"You could have used your phone," Mick said.

He snorted again and locked eyes with Raven. "You've seen my phone, Rave. You were the one who frisked me. I'm still enjoying the memory of that."

His creepy grin was back and Raven's stomach roiled. But, he was right. He had an old flip-phone which didn't have the capability to go online.

"I'm surprised you haven't figured it out yet, Rave. I thought you were smarter than that." His eyes traveled from her eyes down her body and back up again.

"Okay, let's talk about your dark magick room in your son's apartment." Raven expected the grin to fall from his face again, but it didn't. He continued to stare at her as if he was imagining … yeah, she couldn't finish that thought.

Paigo leaned forward, getting as close to Raven as he could

with the table between them.

"Think about it, Rave. Don't make me have to spell it all out for you. That would be really disappointing."

"Is it your room or Tate's?"

"Finally," he said. He raised his hands as far as they could go with the chain attached to them, the sound of metal on metal rattling through the air, and then dropped them to his lap again. "Now we're getting somewhere."

Raven's head spun. Was he saying it was Tate's room, that Tate was using his identity on the Dating Pool, that Tate was the one abducting those girls?

"You were at the old cabin. You were going there for the girl."

He cackled an eerie, sickening laugh. "There's no rules to say a man can't admire his son's work, now is there?"

It was like she was sitting inside a fridge, she felt that cold. Her body was trembling, her stomach churning, and she prayed to the Goddess she didn't boot all over the table. It was the image of puking on Paigo that settled her a bit. She needed to interview Sabrina O'Connor again.

"So Darren Tate abducted and killed those girls and you, what, stopped in to diddle with them?" She brought the image of puking all over Paigo back to her mind to block out the one she just voiced.

Paigo leaned forward again and sucked in a long, loud breath through his nose. "Ahh, that's nice. You still smell the same, Rave."

Raven lifted her right leg under the table and placed her boot between his legs, pressing down like she would on a gas pedal. Paigo froze, his face turning red and his disgusting grin no where to be found. The veins in his neck and at his temple bulged and pulsed.

"Enough of your bullshit, Paigo. Talk to me or we get up and walk out of this room right now."

His voice came out strained and high-pitched. "Darren. It was all Darren. He targeted those girls with the intention of working his way to your girlfriend. Those other girls were just a smoke screen."

"How is Adara involved in all this?"

Spittle flew out of his mouth with a grunt of pain. "Darren. He lured her in promising to give her Ena's coven."

Raven lifted her foot and Paigo's chair shot back, his hands cupping his groin as he doubled over.

"That's police brutality. You can't do that," he sputtered.

"Do what?" Raven asked. "Did you see any police brutality, Constable?"

Mick shook her head, looked up at the camera in the corner of the room. A tiny smile grew on her face. With the angle of the camera, there was no way you could have seen what Raven had done. "No, Detective. I don't know what he's talking about."

They didn't talk as they went through a reverse process to exit the jail. As soon as they got outside, Raven darted towards a garbage can and heaved. And heaved, until she was sure her stomach ended up in the garbage can. Mick handed her a bottle of water. God knows where she got it from. She rinsed her mouth and took a tentative sip, afraid to put anything into her stomach.

Raven got in the car, exhaled a rush of air and sank back into the passenger seat.

"You okay," Mick asked. She put her seatbelt on, but didn't start the car.

"I should have put it together. The pigsty at the cabin and the state of Tate's apartment. I should have known." She knew Mick was referring to her physical and mental health, but she ignored it. She needed to keep her mind on the case, not on her past.

"Do you think Adara was under Tate's control?"

"Let's go find out." Raven pulled her seatbelt on as Mick started the car.

Chapter 19

They briefed LaCroix when they got back to the detachment and he placed a call to the officer tailing Tate. He stayed the night at a friend's place as he couldn't get into his apartment with the forensics unit there and he hadn't emerged yet.

Adara was brought up from the holding cell and put in an interview room. Raven stood in the box watching her. One moment she could be sweet, innocent Adara and the next she could turn into an angry, hateful bitch. Raven didn't understand the transformation. She'd see how long it took for her to turn, she thought as she stared at the meek woman through the glass. But, she wanted to get to the sweet version of her before the angry one came out. She needed to speak to the Adara she knew.

"Ready?" Mick asked as she popped her head into the box.

Raven nodded. "Yeah, let's do this."

"How do you want to play it?"

"I'm going with compassion. I need to keep her from getting angry and defensive as long as possible." Adara was aware her plan to destroy the evidence against her went afoul. Raven opened the door to the interview room, focusing on the empathy she felt for Adara and pushing down the anger.

"Hey," she said softly as she took a seat across from Adara.

"How are you holding up? Are you okay?"

Adara's head dropped slightly to the side, but her sad eyes stayed locked on Raven's. "Oh, Raven. You must think I'm a horrible person."

"I've known you my whole life, Adara. You've been so good to me." She had to swallow and push back the thoughts of Adara keeping her and Ena from healing their relationship, thoughts of Adara forcing her to sleep with Jax. "I'm trying to understand all this. Can you help me understand?"

Adara sighed and looked up at the corner of the ceiling. "I don't know what to say, sweetheart. Grayson said they have enough evidence against me to convict me of murder."

"Tell me your version. I can't imagine you plotting to kill your best friend. I don't understand any of it, Adara."

Adara dropped her head, staring at her wringing hands on the table. There was a long moment of silence before she began talking in a voice that was barely audible. "I met Darren at Mystique." Mystique was a Wiccan store near Huntsville, affectionately known in the Wiccan community as the Mystique Boutique. Ena sold a lot of her potions through the store, owned and operated by a member of the Solstice Coven. "He seemed like such a nice, young man. He helped me to my car with my bags and we stood there talking for a while."

"When was this?" Raven asked.

"Oh, nearly a year ago, I suppose. It was early last summer. He told me he was interested in the Wiccan religion and asked me if I'd mentor him, but it was important that no one knew. He was worried about his job. He thought it might have a negative influence on his position if word got around." She took a deep breath and looked up at Raven. "Would I be able to have a glass of water?"

"Of course." Raven nodded at Mick and Mick left the room.

Adara watched her leave and then looked back at Raven. "It started innocently, I suppose. He'd say things like how I dedicated so much of my life to the coven and how loyal I'd been. Then he started saying that I really deserve to be more than a third-degree Priestess. Over time, I suppose I started to buy into it. I gave just as much to the coven as Ena. Why didn't I deserve to be the HPS? She'd had her time. She had everything and I had nothing, yet I'd given just as much of myself to the coven as she had. And at some point the talk turned to how I could become the HPS and Darren introduced me to black magick. At first, I was appalled, but he asked me if I wanted to be HPS like I deserved to be and, Goddess help me, I did. I wanted it more than anything." She bowed her head and wept.

Raven sat there with her fists clenched in her lap and her blood racing through her veins like hot lava. Adara hadn't been under any dark spell. She'd known exactly what she'd done. Mick came back in with a glass of water and set it in front of Adara. Then she left again and came back in with a box of tissues and sat them next to the glass before returning to her seat. Raven took slow, deep breaths trying desperately to calm herself down.

Adara took a couple of tissues and held them to her eyes. "I was heartbroken when Ena died." She hiccupped as she regained control of her tears. "She'd been my best friend since we were kids."

"But, you killed her," Raven said in as soft a voice as she could manage.

"Yes. And I'm so sorry. I don't know what got into me, Rave."

"And you tried to kill me."

Adara's eyes shot up to meet Raven's. "No, sweetheart. I just wanted you to stop what you were doing. You were getting too close to figuring out what actually happened and I just wanted to warn you off. I love you, Rave. You're like a daughter to me. I've always loved you."

"Like you loved Ena?" Raven expelled a harsh breath. "Adara, you don't hurt the people you love."

"I'm sorry. I just wanted to come out of the shadows and into the light. I don't know how it all got so out of control." She bowed her head and wept again.

Raven didn't have an ounce of sympathy for her. Her teeth were clenched as she tried to get her next question out without sounding like she felt. "You want to tell me why you put a spell on me so that I'd sleep with Jaxon?"

Adara's head shot up, as if she was surprised Raven knew about that. She must realize they had her Book of Shadows.

"Your relationship with Riley wasn't healthy, Rave. I needed you to see that. You weren't even coming by for breakfast anymore. It's not healthy to spend all of your time with one person, excluding all others, even your moth…even me."

Raven's eyes narrowed to slits. Her pulse throbbed in her neck, at her temples. Adara purposely tried to break up her relationship with Riley because she wasn't coming around for breakfast enough? Was she freaking kidding?

"You did everything in your power over the past twelve years to keep Ena and I from reconciling. You took everything in my life that meant anything to me - my mom, Riley. You may as well have raped me. You took my choice away, forcing me to sleep with someone I had no interest in." Her voice broke and a sob ripped out of her constricted lungs. "I hope you rot in jail. You are dead to me, you selfish bitch." She lunged across the table and Mick grabbed her around the middle, pulling her back.

The next thing Raven knew, LaCroix's arms were around her, leading her out of the interview room while Adara screamed behind her.

"Rave, please. I love you. I just tried to do what was best for you."

"Bullshit. You wanted me close so you could use my powers." Her chest heaved, the sobs coming fast and furious.

"Enough," LaCroix growled in her ear. "She's not worth it, Rave."

She completely humiliated herself in front of LaCroix. She'd sworn to herself she would never be a victim again after what Paigo did to her, but she felt like a victim. It would crush Jax to know the real reason she slept with him.

In the hall, she struggled to control her tears. "What she did with that spell, forcing me to sleep with Jax …" Saying those last five words in front of LaCroix was one of the hardest things she'd ever done, but what she had to say was too important. "It can never go beyond us, do you understand? Jaxon can never know what really happened." How could LaCroix ever respect her again knowing what she let happen, knowing she basically allowed Adara to rape her?

Grayson put a strong hand on Raven's shoulder and squeezed. "If that's what you want, Rave, I'll respect your wishes. But, you realize we won't be able to charge her for that particular crime."

Raven couldn't meet his eyes. She kept her head bowed as tears continued to stream down her face. She was surprised they didn't evaporate with the heat her face was giving off. She trembled all over and wanted nothing more than to run and keep running. "Mick? He can never know."

"Agreed," Mick said softly.

"Take a break," LaCroix said. "Then we'll meet in my office." He walked away and Raven was sure he was doing it out of respect, giving her a chance to pull herself together. She didn't know if she could pull it off.

By the time Raven made it to his office, Mick had managed to get Adara to write out a long statement. While Adara was writing, Raven placed a call to Sabrina O'Connor. The description Sabrina gave matched Tate, not Paigo.

"Do we have enough to arrest Tate?" Raven asked. Her head was so filled with what Adara had done and Tate and Paigo's involvement in it that it was all jumbled and confusing. She was tired, so tired. She'd tossed and turned all night, thinking about Riley while telling herself to stop thinking about Riley. Her lack of sleep was catching up to her.

"Yeah, we do," LaCroix answered. "Do you want in on the arrest?"

"Are you kidding?" She wouldn't miss it for the world.

LaCroix placed another call to the officer tailing Tate. He'd emerged from the friends house and gone to his own apartment. LaCroix, Mick, and Raven suited up in Kevlar vests and were about to head out when Raven got a call from Cheryl Danby, the forensic tech. She explained the prints they lifted from the spare room at Tate's apartment, which belonged to Gregor Paigo, didn't match the prints they lifted in the black magick room. And then she added that the prints they lifted from the black magick room matched the prints from the cabin Sabrina was found in. Those prints belonged to Police Constable Darren Tate. They ran DNA tests from samples collected from Gregor Paigo upon his arrest and they were not a match to the DNA evidence collected from the victims. However, Paigo's DNA showed the suspect was a close relative of Paigo's.

* * *

Raven let Mick drive again and they followed LaCroix's SUV.

"This is so messed up," Mick said. "I went out on that call with Tate when we found Emily McMurtrie's body and he was so cold. He took one look at her then sat in the car and waited for you to arrive. I figured he was squeamish around the body and didn't want me to know. I was so stupid."

"He had me fooled, too, so don't blame yourself. I let him go last night." Mick hadn't said a word about Raven sleeping with Jax and she was grateful. She didn't want to discuss it with Mick, or anyone else.

"It just really pisses me off. I can't imagine how you feel with all of this. I mean he conspired to kill your mother and was raping and killing girls because they looked like your girlfriend." Mick snapped her mouth closed. "Shit. I'm sorry."

"Don't be. It's true." Raven leaned her head back and closed her eyes. The sound of squealing tires had them flying open again. She looked out the windshield to see LaCroix's SUV pulling a U-turn. Mick slowed down and swung the car around to follow as Raven's cell phone began ringing.

"Bowen," she answered.

"Rave, put Mick on," LaCroix said in a crisp tone.

Why the hell did he want to talk to Mick and not her? "She's driving."

"Put her on."

Raven huffed, but handed the phone to Mick hoping she'd be able to hear LaCroix's part of the conversation.

"Yeah," Mick said.

Raven strained to hear, but couldn't make out LaCroix's words. Mick's eyes widened and she glanced over at Raven and winced. Shit, what was happening?

"Yep. I got it." Mick handed the phone back to Raven and hit the switch to turn on the emergency lights.

"Tell me for fuck sakes," Raven spat. LaCroix was driving pretty damn fast and he had his lights on now, too. She watched as LaCroix made a turn onto Riley's street and everything fell into place.

"Oh, fuck," Raven sat up straighter in her seat, no thoughts of being tired now. She wanted to be at the wheel, passing LaCroix to get there faster. They pulled into Riley's apartment building and came to a screeching halt in front of the main doors. Raven was out of the car before Mick had it in park. She pulled the outside glass door open and rushed past the plain-clothes officer, Christopher Matlock, standing at the intercom.

"I've been trying to get the super to open the door," he said in a panicked tone. "Tate followed a lady inside, but I didn't get here in time to catch the door. The super's not answering."

Raven stuck her key in the lock, threw open the door, and shot to the stairwell. LaCroix yelled her name behind her, but she ignored him, taking the stairs two at a time, pulling her Sig out of its holster. LaCroix, Mick, and Matlock's boots clambered on the stairs behind her, but she couldn't wait, not with the thoughts hammering her brain with what Tate might be doing to Riley. She ran down the hall to Riley's door, put her ear to it, and listened.

LaCroix, Mick, and Matlock approached the door. Raven's eyes locked to LaCroix's and he gave her a nod. She inserted her key in the lock and it wouldn't turn. Shit, had Riley changed the lock? Pulling the key out, she looked up at LaCroix again and he motioned for her to step aside.

Ena's words from her deathbed played in Raven's mind. *You have great powers, Rave. You've only to open yourself to them.*

"Wait," Raven said. She closed her eyes and reached out psychically, spreading further and further through the apartment, reaching for Riley. "She's not there. No one is in the apartment. Oh, my God. He's taken her," Raven wailed, collapsing in Grayson's arms.

"Hold on, Rave. Let me call Riley's cell." LaCroix pulled his cell off of the clip on his belt while continuing to support Raven and dialed Riley's number.

It was probably only a matter of seconds that passed while they waited for Riley to answer, or not, but it seemed like eons.

"Riley, it's Grayson LaCroix. Can you tell me your whereabouts?"

Raven couldn't hear Riley's response. LaCroix nodded as his eyes met hers. "I need you to stay there. I'm sending an officer over." He mouthed to Raven that Riley was fine. "I'll explain when I get there, okay?" He nodded again. "Yeah, everything's fine. I'll speak to you soon." He ended the call. "She's fine, Rave. She's at work. It looks like Tate pulled a fast one to drop his tail."

Raven took a step out of LaCroix's arms and leaned against the wall, forcing her lungs to take in some air.

LaCroix put a hand on Mick's shoulder. "Head over to emergency at the hospital and stay with Riley. I'll run Raven home and meet you there."

Raven was about to protest and insist she went to the hospital then thought better of it. She had to get used to not being around Riley.

* * *

As they approached Raven's cottage, Raven sat up straighter in her seat. Something was off. The cottage was shrouded in darkness.

"My porch light is on a timer. It should be on by now."

"Maybe the bulb's out," LaCroix said as he turned into the driveway.

"I just replaced it last week. And I always leave the stove light on. There's no light in the kitchen window."

"Power out maybe?" LaCroix put the SUV in park, turned it off and removed the key from the ignition.

The hair on the back of Raven's neck stood at attention and a chill ran down her back. "Something's not right."

LaCroix made no move to exit the vehicle. He turned slightly in his seat to face Raven. "Are you sensing something?"

"Something. Yeah." She opened her door and got out of the

car. LaCroix was beside her before she hit the porch steps. Raven got her key ready and reached out with her psychic powers, moving infinitesimally further out, testing the waters.

"Tate's in the woods. Watching," she whispered. She turned the key in the lock and opened the door, slipping into Tate's mind for a peak as she stepped into the foyer.

She didn't get two steps inside the house before she realized she'd made a huge mistake. She'd opened herself for Tate's attack. Sharp, searing pain stabbed into her head as if a knife rammed into each of her temples, over and over again. She sunk to her knees, bent forward, and dropped her head to the floor, her hands pressing against her temples. She knew how to block Tate's attack, but she couldn't focus on anything other than the pain. Sick. Goddess help her, she was going to be sick.

Raven barely registered LaCroix's movements beside her. She knew he was speaking, but had no idea if he was speaking to her or into his phone or police radio. She crawled along the floor on her elbows and knees, hands still firmly against her head as if it would explode if she didn't hold it together. She got to the powder room just in time to deposit the contents of her stomach in the toilet. Goosebumps prickled her skin as a bead of sweat trickled down her back. She curled onto her side on the floor. Focus. She tried to take deep breaths and relax her tense muscles, but the pain was unlike anything she'd ever experienced.

"Raven? For Christ's sake. Tell me what you need," LaCroix yelled.

Raven took another deep breath and threw up a block. It was more like an old, rusty gate creaking closed, but once it clicked into place, the pain ceased.

"Thank the Blessed Goddess," she groaned. "The bastard got in my head." She pushed herself to her feet and turned on the cold water tap, splashing her face and rinsing her mouth. Still bent over the sink, she asked, "Did you lock the door?"

"No, he didn't." Tate stood in the doorway, grinning, with a gun pressed to the back of LaCroix's neck.

Raven dropped her head. He wouldn't know she blocked his spell and that was to her advantage. With a flick of her hand, Tate's gun went flying across the hall into the living room.

LaCroix was quick. He spun around and grabbed for Tate's arm, but Raven flicked her hand again and sent Tate soaring across the living room. He landed with an *oof* on the floor in front of the sliding glass doors.

"What the hell was that?" LaCroix whispered.

Raven nudged by LaCroix, stalking her prey across the living room.

"Get her away from me," Tate yelled. He crab crawled backwards until he pressed up against the glass. "Sarge? Get her the hell away from me."

Raven wanted to laugh. He was a pathetic, cowering bastard. She reached down and grabbed him by the shirt front as his face paled several shades. Hauling him to his feet, her ice blue eyes pierced his. "You murdering, low-life bastard. You're no better than the creep you call a father."

"Rave," LaCroix said in a soft tone. "Let him go." His hand rested on Raven's shoulder. "He's not worth it."

He was right, but she wanted to make Tate hurt as much as the innocent women he violated. The rest of his life in prison didn't seem enough to pay for the lives he snuffed or ruined. She murmured a spell as she stared into Tate's eyes, repeating it three times.

"What did you do?" Tate asked with his eyes bulging from their sockets. "You put a spell on me. What did you do?"

Raven smirked. "Don't worry, Tate. It was just a simple three times three spell." She ensured everything bad he'd done would come back to him threefold. That would be a bitch while he was sitting in prison.

"Break it, damn you." His voice rose several octaves. "Break the spell, you bitch."

"Cuff him." She turned so that Tate's back was to LaCroix. LaCroix pulled his cuffs from his duty belt and braceletted Tate's wrists.

Raven released Tate's shirt and he staggered into LaCroix. LaCroix gripped his arm and led him out to his SUV with Tate quick stepping beside him, as if he couldn't get away from Raven fast enough.

Raven sank into her easy chair and dropped her head into her hands. Her head didn't hurt anymore, but it was like she had a headache hangover. Goddess, help her. She wanted so badly to hurt Tate, she could have torn him to shreds with her bare hands.

"You okay," Mick asked. She'd been halfway to the hospital when she received LaCroix's call and sped to Raven's with lights and sirens. She laid her hand on Raven's shoulder and squeezed.

"No," Raven croaked. Her chest heaved with the first gut wrenching sob. "I had the power to heal her," she wailed. "If I hadn't been such a selfish, judgmental brat and blocked my powers, I could have saved her." What she wouldn't give just to have Ena's voice back in her head.

Mick settled onto the couch next to Raven and pulled her into her arms. "It's not your fault, Rave. If you need someone to blame, lay it on Adara, Tate and Paigo."

"Adara was able to use my own powers against me because I allowed it, because I tuned out. How could I have been so unforgiving all these years? What happened to me wasn't Ena's fault. I blamed her for not seeing it, yet I was the one hiding it from her. If it wasn't for my own stupidity and selfishness, none of this would have happened."

"Shhh," Mick cooed, stroking her hand over Raven's hair. "If all of this didn't happen, you wouldn't have that beautiful baby girl in your belly."

Raven shook with the force of her sobs. "But, I'd have Riley."

"You have to tell her about the spell, Rave."

"You made me a promise. You can't tell anyone."

"Oh, Rave. Riley wouldn't tell Jax."

She never would have thought Riley would tell Kiran about Paigo raping her, but she had. "I can't take that chance. I can't."

Chapter 20

In a worn t-shirt and yoga pants, Raven sat in the lotus position on her deck facing the water. Her eyes were closed as she listened to the waves rolling into shore. Another few weeks and the leaves would fill out the trees and she'd be able to hear them rustling in the breeze. She imagined she could here them now. Birds chirped and whistled back and forth, calling to each other. Soon those playful calls would translate into nests of baby birds, mouths agape, waiting for their regurgitated meals. The thought nearly made her smile.

Seven days ago she cast a healing spell to mend her broken heart. It hadn't worked. It wasn't that she sucked at spells or that she was out of practice. The Goddesses simply wanted her to experience this pain. There was a lesson she needed to learn from this experience. The sooner she could figure out what that lesson was, the better. She even conjured a ball of healing energy and hovered it over her heart, to no avail.

Raven tilted her head back, enjoying the warmth of the sun on her face. It was surprising how much she missed Ena's voice in her head. Now, more than ever, she needed someone to talk to, someone to help her through this endless heartache. She understood now why Ena took so many lovers to her bed. She was trying to cope with her own heartache over losing Kiran. It wasn't how she would deal with the heartache, but she understood it.

She heard the tires on the dirt road long before they turned into her driveway. So much for her peaceful morning.

One car door opened, then another before they closed simultaneously. So, he'd brought reinforcements this time. Raven huffed out a breath and opened her eyes, staring at the sunlight sparkling off the surface of the lake, and waited. She almost laughed listening to him banging on the front door.

"Raven? Open the bloody door or I'll break it down, aye?"

Raven huffed again. It was a reinforced steel door. He'd probably hurt himself trying. She uncurled her legs, stood up, and walked over to the side railing.

"I'm back here."

Kiran rounded the corner with Simone close on his heels. His face was red, his eyes narrowed, but Simone was suppressing a grin, her eyes lit with a mischievous twinkle. Kiran marched to the base of the steps leading up to the deck and glared up at her. Raven's hands tightened on the railing, bracing for his wrath.

"You haven't been answering your calls or your door, haven't been into work all week, haven't bloody well been seen or heard from. Have you no respect for those who care about you?"

"I took some vacation time."

His hand shot through his ebony hair, leaving it askew. "Ah, well. That's fine then, aye? Do you not think we'd worry about you? Do you know how many times I've been over here?"

Okay, now she was getting pissed. "Yeah, actually, I do. I'm entitled to take some time out if I want it. I don't have to answer to you or anyone else."

"Kiran." Simone's hand slid down Kiran's forearm. "This isn't helping." She brushed by him, her lithe body rising up the stairs as if she was floating. When she got to Raven, she covered one of her hands on the railing with her own. "First and foremost, are you okay?"

"I'm fine. I just needed some alone time."

"You've heard about Riley?"

Odd that the sharp pain in her chest just wouldn't ease off. The mention of Riley's name brought it into crisp focus. "I heard." Of course she heard. Mick sent her dozens of texts every day, pleading with her to tell Riley about the spell. She'd even sent her a picture of the spell from Adara's Book of Shadows.

Riley was packing up her apartment. She'd taken a nursing job in Toronto and maybe it was for the best. At least Raven might be able to heal if she wasn't running into Riley on a daily basis. It was one of the reasons she hadn't left her cottage in a week.

"So, you still have some contact with the outside world then," Kiran said. He muttered something and stalked off to the back of Ena's car and opened the hatch.

"Why can't he just give me some time?" Raven asked.

"He knows you're hurting and that hurts him." Simone patted Raven's hand then placed both of her's on the railing. "He has the Hayes' psychic powers, but not the same way you experience them. He doesn't see visions or hear thoughts. He's an empath."

If there was anything worse than hearing what people were thinking, Raven imagined feeling their emotions had to be it. "That's gotta suck."

Simone laughed, a light musical sound that drifted away on the breeze. "I'm sure it does. I guess we all have burdens to bare."

True that, Raven thought. Some more than others. They stood there silently watching Kiran heft a large box up the steps. Raven raised an eyebrow at him. "Moving in?"

A low, rumbling laugh rose up from Kiran, easing the

tension between them. "I want to get to know my daughter, aye? But, I don't think us living together would be good for our health."

Raven resigned herself to having visitors and opened the sliding glass door for him. He set his box on the coffee table and asked if it was alright if he made coffee. Raven shrugged. "Help yourself." She made herself comfortable on the couch and Simone sat next to her.

"How's the morning sickness?"

"It sucks."

"Raven?" Simone sighed.

Raven rolled her eyes. "It's only first thing in the morning, so I can deal with it."

"That's good. Did you get the prenatal vitamins?"

"Shouldn't I make an appointment for this?" She knew she was being defensive and had no idea why, except that they were infringing on her personal time. "That way you can bill for your time."

It wasn't a glare that Simone gave her, but it was close. "Is it really so hard for you to let people care about you?"

No, but the one person she did want to care wouldn't. Or couldn't. "I'm not sure I'm worthy." Where the hell had that come from?

"Of course you're worthy, love," Kiran said as he carried a tray of coffee cups in and set it next to the box on the table. "You've been through a lot these past few weeks, but you needn't be so hard on yourself."

Raven was saved from this line of conversation by a knock at the door. "Don't answer it."

"Och, no," Kiran said, heading for the front door. "You're not going to lock yourself in this house and avoid dealing with the outside world."

Raven surged to her feet. "You have no right to decide how I live my life. No right. I'm a grown ass woman and I'll do what I damn well please. Do not answer that door." She charged down the hall after him, but wasn't in time to stop him from unlocking the deadbolts and swinging the door open. She could see the Purolator van in the driveway and studied the man standing there with a Purolator envelope in one hand and one of those electronic signature devices in the other. He had waves of sandy brown hair and a days growth of fuzz on his face. His hazel eyes were wide, flickering back and forth between Kiran and Raven.

"Raven Bowen?"

"Aye," Kiran answered, waving towards Raven.

She could have throttled him.

The man handed her the machine and a stylus pen. "I just need a signature."

Raven grabbed the device and the pen, scrawled her signature across the screen then shoved it back at the man. She took the envelope, slammed the door and turned, glaring at Kiran. "Do I come into your home and dictate what you do?"

"You're not doing yourself any favours by locking yourself away. You've had a week. Now you'll deal with what's bothering you."

"I'll deal with it in my own damn way."

"Oh, aye. You're like me alright. Stubborn as a mule."

They both ran their hands through their hair then stomped back down the hall to the living room. Simone stood at the end of the hall, smirking at the two of them.

"Are we ready to behave like grown ups now?"

Raven threw the envelope on the table next to the box. She just wanted them to leave her in peace. She sunk back down on the couch and buried her face in her hands. Maybe if she ignored them, they'd go away.

Kiran picked up a cup of coffee and settled into the easy chair. "You're filled with anger, Raven. It's seeped into your very bones. I ken why you've held onto it all these years, but it's time to let it go."

She could feel a trembling deep inside - the rage vibrating within. *It's seeped into your very bones.* Could her baby feel it? That couldn't be good. Most of her anger and resentment had been focused on Ena for the past fifteen years, but she didn't feel that resentment towards her mother any more. She made her peace with Ena. So, why was the rage still there?

"I have a therapist for that."

"You've made an appointment to see Dr. Shoal?" Kiran asked.

Of course he knew her name. They were all probably talking about it behind her back. She nodded in response with her face still buried in her hands.

"That fair pleases me, love."

Raven listened to the leather of the easy chair creaking then what sounded like paper being unfolded.

"There's something else," he said.

Raven scrubbed her face with her hands then wearily lifted her head to look at her father. He was holding a creased sheet of printer paper, his eyes tired and sad.

"I've been finding wee notes and letters around the house. This one was on Ena's laptop. It's addressed to you, love." He leaned forward, stretching the paper out towards her.

Raven took it and slumped back into the couch.

My Dear Sweet Angel,

I'm sorry. Please forgive me.

I'm still not sure what it was I did to anger you so, but I think it had to do with all the boyfriends I brought home over the years. I'm not sure you'll ever read this letter, so I'm just going to pour my heart out. The only man I've ever loved was your father. When he left, it broke something inside me and all the men I brought home were a sad attempt to ease the pain of losing your father. I'm not saying that's an excuse. I never should have exposed you to my promiscuous behaviour. I'm going to my death knowing I failed as your mother and my dying wish-

Eyes pooling, heart pounding, Raven crumpled the paper in her white-knuckled fist. "I can't do this right now."

"Aye. I understand. You'll want to do that in private. But, I think if you can forgive her for not seeing what was happening to you, love, it will go a long way to easing that anger."

But, she had forgiven Ena, hadn't she? And she understood the heartache Ena must have been feeling. She knew exactly how that felt, not that she'd use it as an excuse to bring home every woman willing to sleep with her. She couldn't even imagine sleeping with anyone other than Riley.

"That brings us to the next thing," Kiran said. He took a utility knife out of his pocket and cut through the tape on the top of the box on the coffee table.

What now? Why couldn't they just leave her be?

He opened the top of the box and pulled out a manilla envelope. "Here's another one of the letters I found. Would you like me to read it?"

"Do I have a choice?"

Simone wrapped her hand around Raven's, the one with the letter still fisted in it. "We think it's something you need to hear."

We? Were Simone and Kiran a team now?

Kiran sat back down in the easy chair and unfolded the letter. "My Dear Sweet Angel. For over one hundred and fifty years, a Bowen woman has headed the Solstice Coven. It is your destiny, Rave. It's who you were born to be."

Raven shot to her feet. "Oh, no you don't. The two of you think you can talk me into becoming High Priestess and you're wrong. I haven't had anything to do with witchcraft or Wicca since I was twelve years old."

"Is that so?" Simone asked, nodding to the altar Raven had

set up under the window facing the lake. The table was covered by a purple velvet cloth. White and purple candles sat behind three small wooden vessels placed around a pentagram - the one on the left contained water, the one on the right was filled with soil, and the one at the top of the pentagram contained salt. Various crystals and gemstones graced the purple cloth and a stick of incense rose out of its holder.

"That's ... I ..." She didn't want to explain she tried a healing spell or why she tried it. "That's different. I'm not practicing witchcraft. I was just trying something out."

Simone smirked and raised an eyebrow.

"Simone and I will help you. It will take some time, aye, but eventually you will be ready to take over the coven and Simone has agreed to fill in as acting High Priestess until you're ready. Ena was right, love. It is your place, your destiny. Your legacy."

For the past week, Raven had a chill in her bones she just couldn't shake, but Kiran's last comment filled her with warmth. Was that some kind of sign? Was she truly destined to take Ena's place?

"You don't have to decide right away," Kiran said, as if he read her thoughts. "Take some time and think about it."

Both Kiran and Simone rose to their feet. Kiran folded the letter and set it on top of the box then tapped it. "The rest of this is things Ena wanted you to have. There were a few other things - some drawings you made as a child and baby pictures, pictures of you growing up - that I wasn't able to put in the box. I guess I wasn't ready to let go of them yet." He smiled at her, but there was such sadness in his pale blue eyes. He was hurting, too. Not only for losing the love of his life, but for what he missed out on by not being there to see his child growing up.

Raven nodded. She was so tired all of a sudden. She

walked them to the door and Kiran turned, wrapping her in his warm embrace. Raven stiffened. The only person who'd hugged her in a platonic sense in the past fifteen years was Adara. She hadn't even begun to process Adara's betrayal.

"I love you, Raven. I'm here for you. You don't have to go through this alone, aye?"

The breath trapped in Raven's lungs released and she relaxed into Kiran's arms, hugging him back. "Thank you, but I really just need some time to myself."

When Raven hugged him back, Kiran tightened his hold then stepped back and brushed a kiss over her cheek. "Oh, aye. You're a stubborn one Raven Sage Bowen."

Raven closed and locked the door behind them then headed to her bedroom and crawled into the middle of the bed, Ena's letter still clutched in her fist as she dozed off.

* * *

The sun was beginning to set as Raven stepped out onto her deck. Oranges, pinks, and purples melded together across the sky and reflected brilliantly off the lake. Raven set her decaf coffee on the arm of a Muskoka chair and wrapped a throw blanket over her shoulders before easing down into the chair. She drew her feet up, hugging her knees and stared out at the lake.

"Hey."

Raven jolted, her head whipping around to see Mick sitting on the steps leading up to the deck.

"Holy shit. You scared the crap out of me."

"Sorry," Mick grinned, like she'd enjoyed scaring Raven. "I thought maybe if I sat here and waited, you'd come out eventually."

"How long have you been sitting there?"

Mick shrugged. "Only about twenty minutes."

"Well, now you can leave. I'm not in the mood for company."

Mick pushed to her feet and helped herself to the chair next to Raven. "You can't hide forever, you know?"

Raven leaned her head back and closed her eyes, trying to block Mick out.

"She's leaving in the morning, Rave. You're running out of time."

"Stay out of my business, Mick."

"But, if you just show her that spell …" Mick gasped and slapped her hand over her heart. "Oh, my God. It's not Riley not forgiving you that you're worried about. You can't forgive yourself."

Raven's fingers curled around the edge of the armrest and gripped tight. "Go home, Mick. And stay the hell out of my business."

"Rave-"

"Go home." Raven's tone left no room for argument.

Mick walked to the steps and half turned back to Raven. "There's a going away party for Riley at O'Donnelly's tonight. It would be nice if you came."

Raven listened to Mick's retreating steps. She waited until she heard Mick's car driving away then wrapped her arms around her middle, bent forward, and let her bleeding heart weep.

* * *

It was well past dark when Raven finally went back inside. She turned on a lamp and eyed the big box on the coffee table bathed in its soft glow. It would be full of Ena's tools of the trade, passed down just as she wanted to pass down the role of HPS. Maybe she would deal with it tomorrow. Maybe.

She picked up the Purolator envelope. She probably shouldn't put this one off. She pulled the tab, opening the outer envelope and pulled out a manilla envelope with a return address sticker that read Duvane and Duvane with a Huntsville address below it. Lawyers, she figured. Her name was handwritten across the front with a note that stated they had been unsuccessful at reaching her by phone and asking her to sign and return the enclosed documents.

She opened the envelope and pulled out a thick stack of papers. The letter on top identified them as having to do with Adara's estate. Apparently, Adara had singled her out as her power of attorney. Well, shit. The last thing she wanted was to be responsible for Adara's affairs.

She tossed the papers back onto the coffee table and went through to her bedroom, stripping down to her panties and a tank top as she crossed the room to her bed. The sheets were cold against her skin, sending a shudder through her body. She thought of Riley at O'Donnelly's pub and shuddered again, for totally different reasons. But, she'd found a way to tamp out her desire. She just had to think of her betrayal of Riley with Jax. That left her cold and shivering, but it was better than hot and bothered with no way of dealing with it. Well, not in the way she wanted to deal with it.

She could get up and go to O'Donnelly's, just to say goodbye. But, if she did that, the past week of trying to heal from the loss of her would go down the toilet and she'd have to start all over again. Riley was gone. She lost her the moment she got into Jax's bed. And Mick had been right on the money. She couldn't forgive herself. She'd done the one thing she abhorred most of her life. She'd given in to her sex drive, dropped her morals, betrayed the person she loved most in this world. It didn't matter that Adara hexed her. She was supposed to be this powerful, hereditary witch. Adara's spell shouldn't have been able to coax her into Jax's bed.

Raven shifted onto her side and curled into a tight ball. Her right hand extended to the cold, empty sheets next to her. "Goodbye, Ri," she whispered. "I love you forever."

Raven's fingers brushed something and she pulled Ena's letter out from under the duvet. Damn, she'd forgotten about it. She sat up in bed and turned on the bedside lamp.

My Dear Sweet Angel,

I'm sorry. Please forgive me.

I'm still not sure what it was I did to anger you so, but I think it had to do with all the boyfriends I brought home over the years. I'm not sure you'll ever read this letter, so I'm just going to pour my heart out. The only man I've ever loved was your father. When he left, it broke something inside me and all the men I brought home were a sad attempt to ease the pain of losing your father. I'm not saying that's an excuse. I never should have exposed you to my promiscuous behaviour. I'm going to my death knowing I failed as your mother and my dying wish is that you'll find it in your heart to forgive me. Not for my sake, Raven, but for your own healing.

You've been filled with anger since before your thirteenth birthday. For a long time I thought it was puberty and the rebellion of a teenager. It wasn't until the night you left home that I realized your rage was because of me. You said I didn't see you, but I did, my love. I saw you. But, it was through the veil of my own heartache. And for that, I am truly sorry. You deserved so much better.

My biggest regret in this life is sending Adara after you that night instead of having the courage to go after you myself. Adara has always wanted children. But, she wasn't able to have them, you see? So she kept my child instead of helping to solve our issues. That's not an excuse either. I have no one to blame but myself for our fractured relationship. In these last days of my life, I've been trying to forgive myself for that. Perhaps forgiving yourself is the hardest of all because I just haven't been able to get there.

So, here's a little life advice from your mother - be kind to yourself; don't let your fear keep you from repairing the damage in your relationships with those who matter; forgive those who have hurt you; and, most of all, forgive yourself.

Blessed be, my sweet angel. I love you to the moon and back.

Mom xoxo

Tears streamed down Raven's face. She related to a lot of what Ena said in her letter. She certainly understood the veil of her heartache. How could Ena possibly see what was going on with her daughter if she felt anything like Raven did now? Raven didn't even want to be around anyone never mind *see* what was going on with them. What scared her was the years never eased Ena's suffering. Was she destined to live the rest of her life like this? What would that do to her own daughter? One thing she knew for certain that she wouldn't be repeating - she wouldn't be bringing a long line of lovers home, parading them in front of her daughter. She didn't think she would ever sleep with anyone again because the only one she wanted to sleep with didn't want her.

She brushed her finger over the line *Blessed be, my sweet angel. I love you to the moon and back.* Ena had said that to her every night at bedtime, right up until the last night Raven spent at her mother's house. She'd been nearly sixteen at the time, but she still loved hearing Ena say those words. *Love you more*, had always been Raven's response and she whispered the words into the silence. "And I do forgive you, Mom. I never should have screamed at you and run. I wish I'd had more courage, too."

Raven curled back up on her side, clutching the letter to her chest, and cried silent tears into the night.

* * *

Raven spent half the morning running into the bathroom to dry heave. When she finally made it out to the kitchen, she set a pot of coffee to brewing and sat at the island to wait for it. She lowered her head to rest on her folded arms. Her abs felt like she'd done a million crunches and her throat burned after all of the wretching.

A knock at the door had her groaning. Not only didn't she want to see anyone, but she looked like hell. She'd brushed her teeth and washed her face, but her hair was all over the place after another night of tossing and turning and she desperately needed a shower.

She heard the dead bolt click and the door open. The only person who had a key for her place was Riley. She lifted her head and peered over her shoulder and there was Riley in all her glory - flaming hair curling loosely over her shoulders, skinny jeans and a tight t-shirt showing off her toned body, and those adorable freckles giving her a flash of innocence. Raven groaned again and lowered her head back down to her arms.

"Holy, shit. You look like hell. Are you sick?"

Yeah, she was sick. She was dying of a broken heart and so damn disgusted with herself she didn't know what to do. "Morning sickness," she groaned. The coffee maker gurgled the last few drops of water through the filter and Raven rose from her seat. "Coffee?"

"Yeah, sure. Should you be drinking coffee?"

"It's decaf."

"Oh, yeah, great."

Riley sounded nervous, piquing Raven's curiosity. "I thought you'd be well on your way to Toronto by now."

"I was." Riley slipped onto one of the stools at the kitchen island as Raven poured the coffee. "The more I drove, the more I thought about what happened between us. It was eating at me. We've known each other for four years. I *know* you, Rave. You're a lesbian. You're not bi. You've never been interested in men. And I know how you feel about casual sex and why you feel that way. So, it just doesn't make any sense, Rave. I guess I need to understand why you slept with Jax."

Raven placed the mugs on the island and sat next to Riley. With her hands cupping the mug, she stared into her coffee. "The why doesn't matter, Ri. I made the biggest mistake of my life. Believe me, if I could change what I did, I would." She listened to Riley sigh and shift in her seat. Then Riley's palm covered her cheek and she couldn't help but lean into it. Tears stung her eyes and her aching abs clenched. "Ri?"

"Rave? I can see it's eating at you. Sleeping with Jax goes against your core beliefs. There has to be a reason."

Raven got up, taking her coffee with her, and went through to the living room where she could look out at the lake. Rain drops danced over its surface, a dull grey today, reflecting the overcast sky. Sometimes it was as smooth as glass and others as choppy as a sea. Sometimes it was a deep blue and sometimes it was a depressing grey, like today. It seemed to be a reflection of her mood.

"If the why doesn't matter, Rave, then why won't you tell me?" Riley asked from a couple of feet behind Raven.

"Because it doesn't change anything," Raven said as her fist rubbed the searing pain over her chest.

An exasperated sigh blew over Raven's shoulder. "Humour me."

Raven turned and locked eyes with Riley. Her pale green eyes shone with unshed tears. "Why?" Did Riley drive all the way back here because she couldn't leave her? Was she ready to try to forgive her and put it behind them? Hope, bright and warm and beautiful, flared in Raven's heart.

"Because I need to understand what happened so I can move on. I need closure, Rave. I need to know if I made a horrible mistake so that I won't repeat it."

Just as quickly as that brief flash of hope warmed Raven's heart, Riley's declaration chilled her to the bone. She shivered and turned back to the window, hugging the warm coffee cup to her chest. She couldn't tell Riley the truth and risk her telling Jax because she was hurt and bitter. But, maybe if Riley figured it out for herself and had time to process it, she'd come back to Raven.

"I know how much I've hurt you, Ri. I know what it feels like to be betrayed by the one person you think you can trust.

All these years, I thought Adara had my back, but the truth of it was she did everything she could to keep Ena and I from reconciling because she needed to keep me close so she could steal my powers. And she used those powers to kill my mother. She used my own powers to put me in the path of Jax's truck, to nearly send me off the cliff at Ena's." Raven tried to hold back the tears, but they spilled out over her ebony lashes and dribbled down her cheeks. She turned and faced Riley again. "She used my own powers to make sure no one took me away from her, that no one came between us."

"I don't understand. What does that have to do with you sleeping with Jax?"

Raven's delicate nose flared and a deep line formed between her brows. Maybe on the drive back to Toronto, Riley would figure it out. She didn't know what else to say to get her thinking about it, so she rambled on. "She put a spell on the hospital staff so that you would let Ena lie there and die. She couldn't have done that if I hadn't allowed her to steal my powers. Don't you see? I'm responsible for Ena's death. I killed my mother by blocking my powers."

"Oh, Rave. You can't blame yourself for that."

Riley took a step forward and Raven flinched back. She couldn't stand for Riley to touch her right now. "You're better off without me, no matter the reason for my betrayal."

Raven turned back to the window and blew into her coffee. She could barely see the lake now through the thick curtain of rain. Riley's drive back down to Toronto was going to be a bitch if this didn't let up.

"So, that's it then? You're not going to tell me why you slept with him?

Raven squeezed her eyes closed and leaned her forehead against the cool glass. "There's nothing to tell, Ri. I don't know what you want me to say."

Riley's heavy footsteps echoed down the hallway, the front

door opened then slammed closed. The pressure in Raven's chest was almost too much to bear. Everything in her screamed for her to run after Riley and tell her the truth, to beg her forgiveness. But, Riley deserved better. She let her go.

Epilogue

December 21st

A light dusting of snow covered the clearing in the woods. Raven stood at the altar wearing the long black wool cloak Kiran bought for her in Scotland when he took her to meet his family. Her family. Aunts, uncles, grandparents. Cousins by the dozens. She wished Ena could have been there with them as Kiran's family shared their stories of the times they spent with Ena.

She sighed heavily as she replaced the items from the alter into a wicker basket.

"Alright, love?" Kiran asked as he slipped his arm around Raven's waist.

The edge of her mouth curled up as she glanced at Kiran and then looked up to the light blue winter sky. "It's times like this I wish she was with us." Kiran and Simone were grooming her to take over as High Priestess of the Solstice Coven. She hadn't wanted it at first, but that trip to Scotland with Kiran, getting to know his magical family, fired up her desire to return to her Wiccan beginnings. His entire family were witches. Some of them extremely powerful. Her psychic abilities came from her paternal grandmother, Ruari Hayes. In the two weeks she spent in Scotland, she learned more from Ruari about her psychic powers than she learned in her lifetime.

"Aye," Kiran said, so softly Raven barely heard him. His eyes moved up, scanning the sky as if he'd find Ena there.

Raven slipped her hand into Kiran's and gave it a squeeze.

* * *

The sun was setting over Fairly Lake as Raven stepped out onto her deck, breathing in the crisp air. She thought for sure she would have this baby today, on the winter solstice, but so far her daughter was being stubborn. As much as the baby inside of her filled her with love, Raven still felt two great, gaping holes inside of her. One left by Ena. What she wouldn't give to have her mother's voice in her head again. She laughed at herself because eight months ago she was willing to do anything to rid herself of that voice.

The other hole, the one that still tore her apart if she thought about it too much, was the one left by Riley. It still stole her breath away to think of her. She spent weeks hoping Riley would figure out Adara cast a spell, forcing her to sleep with Jax. But, in the seven months since her departure from Solstice, Raven hadn't heard from Riley. Seven months and she still thought of her every day, still reached for her in the night.

"Stop it," she told herself. Riley was gone and there was nothing she could do about it.

A flash of headlights in the driveway pulled Raven out of her reverie. It wasn't Jaxon. She would have heard his truck from a mile away. That left either Mick or Kiran, coming to check on her. She made her way towards the side of the house and stopped dead in her tracks as Riley stepped out of her little SUV, her breaths shooting out in little white puffs on the cold evening air. She stood in a steel blue down coat and skinny jeans, looking at the cottage for a moment before tucking that glorious red hair behind her ear, closing the car door, and starting towards the front porch.

"Hey," Raven said, finally finding her voice.

Riley stopped when her eyes found Raven at the side of the cottage at the deck railing. "Hey. It's a bit cold to be out here without a coat."

Raven had to smile. Still the nurturer, looking out for everyone's well-being. "I've only been out for a few minutes." She placed her palm at the base of her spine, rubbing absently. The sight of Riley standing there was too good to be true and she wondered if she was dreaming.

"Well, it's too bloody cold for me, even with a coat on. Are you going to invite me in?"

Nervous fingers found their way through Raven's thick black hair, leaving it sticking up on end. "Yeah, sure." She waved towards the sliding glass door on the deck.

Riley climbed the steps to join Raven and eyed the back of the cottage. "You've put an addition on."

The deck itself now spanned the entire back side of the house, but Riley was referring to the wing Raven added to the cottage over the summer to give her a sun room, office space, and a baby's room. She followed Riley into the cottage and took her coat as Riley went to stand in front of the fire in the living room.

"Can I get you something to drink?"

Riley turned, placing her back to the fire. "Coffee would be nice."

A little black kitten pounced across the carpet from Raven's room then chased her tail, running in a mad circle. Raven laughed.

"Oh, my God." Riley bent to pick the kitten up. She held it out in front of her to check it's gender then hugged it to her chest. The kitten rubbed its forehead against her neck and she giggled. Such a beautiful sound. Relaxed and laughing and … happy. Riley was happy. A sharp pain sliced through Raven's chest at the thought of Riley being happy because she was in a new relationship.

"Let me guess," Riley said as she snuggled with the kitten. "You named her Luna."

Raven smiled. Not an easy task when her heart was weeping. "No, that's too cliché. Guess again." She rubbed her lower back again. So many aches and pains. She wished her daughter would come already.

"Really? I was sure you would have named her Luna." She grinned, her pale green eyes flashing in the firelight. "I don't have any other guesses, Rave. What's her name?"

"She's Jet."

"I love it." Riley giggled, nuzzling her nose into the cat's fur. "Raven and Jet. You both have jet black hair."

"It was more because she darts around here at the speed of light."

Raven left Riley to play with the kitten and went into the kitchen and put a pot of coffee on. She felt awkward and nervous having Riley here which was so not like her. She couldn't let herself get her hopes up. The fall afterwards was too freakin' painful.

"So, you look like you're going to have that baby any day now."

Raven startled. She didn't hear Riley come into the kitchen, but she was directly behind her, bent over the island leaning on her elbows. With one hand still massaging her lower back and the other one circling her huge belly, Raven said, "Yeah, any day now." Glancing at the clock on the oven, she gave her daughter another seven hours. She could still be born on the solstice.

"You're back's sore." Riley straightened. "Why don't you go put your feet up and I'll make the coffee."

Raven dropped her hand from her back to her side. "I'm pretty sure I can handle making coffee." She waddled over to get a couple of mugs from the cupboard and set them in front of the still brewing pot.

Riley ran a finger down the leather bound Book of Shadows sitting on the island. "You're practicing witchcraft again?"

"Yeah."

"I had dinner with Mick and Jaxon a few nights ago."

"Yeah, I heard." Mick hadn't been able to wait to tell Raven all about it.

"They seem to be very happy."

"Yeah." Raven heard Riley's exasperated sigh as she poured coffee into the mugs. Her lower back was aching like a bitch and she didn't have the patience for small talk.

"I know why you slept with Jax, Rave."

Raven turned to face Riley. What was she doing here, rubbing salt in old wounds? "Is that so?"

Riley blew out a breath and her shoulders seemed to deflate. "Look, I'm not saying this very well. Just bear with me, will you?" When Raven only stared at her, Riley continued, "I thought moving down to Toronto would make it easier to get over …" She waved her hand between Raven and herself. "Us. You. I thought distance and time would be enough to allow me to move on."

"So, what? You came back here to ask me why again because you think that's what you need." *Blessed Goddess, please don't put me through this again.*

"Mick told me you haven't been with anyone since we broke up. And I don't get it. You're the type of person who needs a lot of sex. I was working a lot of shifts and when I was home I was too tired. So, in a way, it's my fault you slept with Jax."

"It wasn't your fault." Raven shook her head. It wasn't like she hadn't had the opportunity to date since Riley left, but she just wasn't interested in anyone other than Riley. Her belly tightened and her lower back spasmed, so she turned around, giving her back to Riley to hide her grimace. She rode the wave of pain then picked up Riley's mug and passed it over the island to her.

"You came all the way up here because you're worried I'm not getting enough sex?"

A nervous laugh escaped Riley's lips and her hand flew up to cover her mouth. "Sorry. That's not a sentence I ever expected you to say."

"Riley," Raven began, then braced her hands on the marble counter as her belly constricted again and she felt like her lower back was breaking. She concentrated on breathing in and out then stared down at the pool gathering at her feet as her water broke. *Oh, shit.*

"I miss you, Rave. That's why I came."

"Riley," Raven huffed. It suddenly occurred to her that the back pain she been having on and off since the night before was back labour. Her daughter *was* coming on the solstice, which both excited and terrified her.

"I haven't been able to stop thinking about you. I love you, Rave. I still love you. And I wondered if you haven't been with anyone because you still love me, too."

"Riley?"

"What?"

"I'm having a baby."

"I know."

"Now. I'm having a baby, now."

Riley looked startled for a moment then whipped into action. She got Raven into bed and checked to see how dilated she was and was shocked to find the baby's head crowning. "You don't have time to go to the hospital, Rave. We're going to deliver this baby right here."

"Call Jax and Kiran," Raven panted as Riley scurried around gathering supplies. She could hear Riley on the phone as she opened and closed drawers in the kitchen. What the heck would she be looking for in there?

Her belly tightened again and she grimaced in pain, trying to breath through it. She wanted to push. Her baby girl was right there. All she had to do was push and she'd be holding her daughter. She became so overwhelmed with that thought she forgot all about pushing. Was she ready for this? She was prepared. She had everything the baby would need. But was *she* ready? Would she be a good mother?

The next contraction had her crying out loud. She panted through it, then yelled, "Riiiiley!"

Riley ran into the room, panting herself, with her arms full of towels, wash cloths, bowls, and Goddess knew what else. Raven was sure she caught sight of a turkey baster in there somewhere.

"Everyone's on the way." She dumped everything on the end of the bed and checked Raven again. "Okay." She swiped some hair from her face with her forearm. "Shit, Rave. This baby is coming."

Riley ran into the bathroom and Raven stared after her in disbelief. "Where the hell are you going?" If Riley answered, Raven didn't hear it. She doubled over with another contraction and screamed bloody murder.

Riley was at the end of the bed again and Raven wasn't even sure when she came back. If she was at the damn hospital she could have asked for drugs.

"On the next contraction, I want you to push."

"What?" Raven tried to sit up. She was sweating like crazy, her whole body covered in a slippery sheen. No, she wasn't ready for this. Who was she to think she could care for a tiny little life? The kitten meowed from the floor just then. You're different, Raven thought. You're so much easier to care for than a baby. The kitten pounced off into the living room, seemingly happy with her answer.

"I can't have the baby yet. Jax wanted to be here." She bent forward in pain again and the urge to push was tremendous. Whether she was ready or not, her daughter certainly was.

Kiran stepped into the room just as Raven let out a growl and bore down.

"That's it, Rave," Riley cheered.

Raven flopped back into the pillows. It just began and already she was exhausted. She didn't know what Riley was doing between her legs and she didn't want to.

Kiran stood at the head of the bed and took Raven's hand. "What would you like me to do, love?"

"Get me some drugs," Raven panted. "Good ones. Try the main street in town. You should be able to get something there. Heroin maybe. That would be good."

Kiran laughed nervously. "Could you have a wee nip? Would that help?"

"No alcohol," Riley said from the bottom of the bed. "Sorry. No heroin either."

"Oh, fuck," Raven spurted as another contraction began. She squeezed down on Kiran's hand and he let out a yelp.

"Push," Riley commanded.

Raven sat forward and let out another rip roaring growl. Kiran slid in behind her, supporting her back as she pushed. Goddess, bless him. What other father would jump in and help out in a situation like this? Raven collapsed back into him and saw Riley grab the turkey baster. What the hell? There was a sucking noise - once, then again, and then the most beautiful little wail filled the air. She started laughing as tears streamed down her face. That was her baby girl crying. Oh, blessed be. She knew what true joy felt like in that moment. Her heart swelled with it.

Mick and Jax got jambed in the doorway with both of them trying to rush in at the same time.

"Am I too late?" Jax asked.

"No, no, come here," Riley said. "One more push, Rave."

Shit, she thought she was done. She didn't know if she had the energy for one more. Then the contraction was upon her and she bore down. Riley, Jax, and Mick let out a whooping cheer in unison. Riley tied off the umbilical cord and let Jax cut it. He was a trooper. He didn't even hesitate.

Riley held Raven's daughter, wrapping her in a receiving blanket. She brought her to Raven and placed her gently in her arms. Raven could barely see through her tears. The baby stopped crying and squirmed in her arms. She had a cap of dark hair and all of her fingers and toes. Tiny, but perfect.

"She's beautiful."

"Yep," Riley said. "Jax is going to clean her up and then you can feed her."

"I am?" Jax paled, his eyes wide as he stared at the tiny baby in Raven's arms.

Mick tucked her arm around his and leaned into him. "I'll help you."

Feed her? Life as Raven knew it was over. A whole new set of responsibilities had just been born. And Raven was okay with it. "Welcome to the world, Indigo Amaris Ruari Bowen. Blessed be," she grinned.

"Blessed be," Kiran repeated. "Ah, your mum would love that, Rave." Kiran leaned over and kissed her cheek and then, to the rest of the room, said, "Ena's middle name was Amaris, aye? And Ruari is my mum's name."

"It's beautiful," Riley said.

"Yeah, beautiful, just like her," Jax said, leaning over the bundle in Raven's arms. "God, Rave, she's your mini-me."

The room filled with laughter.

Raven grinned up at him. He'd been okay with her naming their daughter Bowen, knowing the family tradition and she loved him for that. "I'm sure there's a lot of you in there too, Daddy."

Jax's breath caught and a tear dribbled down his cheek. Her daughter was a very lucky girl. Raven would make sure she knew her daddy well.

* * *

The next morning, Raven sat in bed with her daughter suckling at her breast and Jet curled up beside her. She touched the tip of her finger to the palm of Indi's tiny hand and she curled her little fist around it, gripping tightly.

Riley poked her head in the door. "Could I talk to you for a minute?"

"Yeah, sure."

She came in and sat on the bed next to Raven and leaned over to watch Indigo, smiling down at her.

"She's gorgeous, Rave. She's got your hair, for sure."

Raven laughed, her eyes glued to Indigo. Her daughter's short black hair stuck straight up. Her delicate nose was Raven's, but she could also see some of Ena in her. "I just wish my mom was here to meet her." Raven bent her head, pressing her lips to Indi's silky hair and hiccuped. She squeezed her eyes shut, desperately trying to force back the tears.

"You don't still blame yourself for Ena's death, do you? It wasn't your fault, Rave."

Raven thought of Ena's letter saying that it was easier to forgive others than it was to forgive yourself. She was so right. "I'm working on it."

"Mick told me you've been seeing a therapist regularly."

Raven's shoulders tensed. "That doesn't have anything to do with our relationship." Damn Mick and her big mouth.

"Doesn't it though? Didn't your past cause you to be so insecure that you sought comfort in Jaxon's bed when I wasn't there for you."

In a way, it's my fault you slept with Jax. Riley's words from last night came back to her. "My behaviour wasn't your fault."

"No, I've come to the realization I have to take some of the responsibility for what happened to our relationship. I wasn't there for you when you needed me, Rave. And for that, I'm so sorry."

Tears pooled in Raven's ice blue eyes. "I'm sorry, too. I never meant to hurt you, Riley."

"I know," Riley said with tears forming in her own eyes. "I love you, Rave. I've never stopped loving you."

"You said to me once I was too closed off, that you couldn't be in a relationship that wasn't going anywhere."

"I think I understand now why you're like that. I didn't know about the trauma in your past when I said that."

"I'm learning to open up more. I'm trying anyway."

"But you still won't tell me why you slept with Jax?"

Raven sighed. "Do you remember what I told you the day you left for Toronto?"

"Yeah, I think so."

"I gave you the answer to your question that day, Ri. At least, I gave you enough to figure it out." She searched Riley's eyes for a sign she understood, that she figured it out, but it wasn't there.

"You told me a bunch of stuff about Adara and how you could have prevented Ena's death if you hadn't been blocking out your powers. I don't understand, Rave. Why can't you just tell me?"

Raven glanced down at Indigo when she stopped suckling and found her asleep. She moved Indigo to her shoulder and gently rubbed her back.

"Because if Jax ever found out, it would kill him."

Riley's mouth dropped open and her eyes narrowed. "All this time you've refused to tell me why because you're worried about hurting *Jax's* feelings?" She rose from the bed and took a step back.

That stabbing pain was back in Raven's chest. She couldn't take any more of this. "I couldn't risk you telling him."

"You think I can't keep a secret?"

"Riley, you told Kiran what Gregor did to me."

"That was different, Rave."

"Was it? Did you realize how much that might hurt Kiran, knowing if he'd come back a few years earlier that would have never happened to me?"

"Oh, my God." Riley's eyes pooled and she bent over, bracing her hands on her knees. "You said Adara wouldn't let anyone come between you and her. What did she do, Rave? Was I getting in the way? Is that it?"

Raven just watched her. Riley's eyes darted back and forth as if she was reading and then she sank to her haunches and covered her head with her arms. "She put a spell on you. That's why you slept with him."

When she lifted her head, Riley rubbed her hands over her face as tears spilled out of her eyes. "And I pushed you away. I left you alone to deal with all of the crap that was happening in your life."

"No, don't do that. I cheated on you. You had every right to push me away."

"If I'd known the reason, I would have been there for you, Rave."

"I didn't know the reason myself until just before we arrested Adara. I couldn't give you a reason because I didn't understand it myself. I couldn't figure out what the hell got in to me."

"Why didn't you just tell me when you found out?"

Indigo let out a dainty burp then snuggled into Raven's shoulder. Raven wanted to weep at the innocence in her arms.

"Think about it, Ri. If someone put a spell on you so you slept with someone you had no sexual attraction to, how would you feel?"

"I'd feel like I'd been … Oh, my God. You're worried Jaxon will feel like he raped you?"

"Why would I feel like I raped you?" Jaxon's voice was short, clipped. Raven and Riley looked up to see him standing in the doorway, hands fisted tightly at his sides and a scowl on his face.

"For fuck sakes." Raven scooted to the edge of the bed wearing just a t-shirt and panties and got up to lay Indigo in her cradle. She covered her with a blanket and then grabbed a pair of sweat pants from her dresser, shoving her legs into them and yanking them up. She would have stormed out of the room if she didn't have to walk gingerly. Riley and Jax followed her into the living room where Mick stood, wide eyed.

"Rave, why would I feel like I raped you?" Jax yelled.

"Shhh," Mick whispered. "You'll wake the baby."

Raven eased herself down onto the couch and dropped her face into her hands. "Fuck." Now she'd have to tell him. She had no choice. "The reason I slept with you …"

Jax took a deep breath and sat on the coffee table facing Raven. "I've known you most of your life, Rave. I know you have no sexual interest in men. I figured you slept with me because you wanted to get pregnant."

Raven's head flew up and she met Jax's eyes. "What? No."

"Then why?"

Raven closed her eyes wishing she could make them all disappear. "Adara's powers weren't very strong. She didn't have the power to do a lot of the things she was doing."

"So she was getting them from someone else," Jax said.

He was well-versed in witchcraft and Wicca. Raven didn't have to explain it all to him. "Yes."

"She was soaking up your powers."

"Yes. Probably for years."

"To do that, she'd need to be around you a lot. Is that the reason you and your mom never made up? Did she keep you apart?"

Dear Goddess, she loved that he got it. Raven nodded. "And I was spending too much time with Riley. So she did something that she thought would break us up."

Jaxon shot to his feet. Both of his hands sunk into his hair and he rubbed furiously. "Jesus H. Christ. She put a spell on us, is that what you're saying? Jesus fucking Christ."

His long legs took him to the front door and it slammed behind him. The baby began wailing as Mick took off after Jax. Raven started to push up from the couch, but Riley waved her back.

"I'll get her. Just breathe for a few minutes."

* * *

By the time Indigo was settled again, Kiran was in Raven's living room. She left him with Riley and took a long, hot shower. When she walked out of the bathroom, the first thing she noticed was Indigo was no longer in her cradle. She dressed quickly and found Kiran sitting in the easy chair, gazing lovingly down at the baby in his arms. Riley sat on the arm of the chair wearing the same dreamy expression on her face.

"You guys."

They both looked up and grinned.

"I want her to get used to sleeping in her own bed. I don't want to be one of these parents who ends up having their kids sleeping with them all the time." It was kind of like having a crate for your dog so they wouldn't sleep on your bed. Once they started, you were stuck with them hogging the bed and the covers.

"I couldn't help myself, love. I didn't get the chance to do this with you."

Raven couldn't help herself either. She sat on the other arm of Kiran's chair and joined them gawking at her baby. Kiran had retired from the Royal Navy when they travelled to Scotland the past summer. Not only did he want to get to know his daughter and his granddaughter, he wanted to be there to help Raven with her baby so she could continue to work in the job she loved. It hadn't take long for Raven to figure out her father was the best.

Jet sat at Kiran's feet, staring up at them like they were all nuts. Then she climbed up the leg of Raven's sweats and padded over to look down at Indigo. She nuzzled her cheek and purred.

"Aww," Riley said. "I think Indigo has a protector."

Kiran bent over and brushed a soft kiss over Indigo's forehead. "She's going to need it." He looked up at Raven. "And we need to make sure you're well protected."

Raven rolled her eyes. She understood why Ena had been concerned, especially after Adara stole her powers, but she could protect herself now that she knew there may be a threat. She couldn't see witches seeking her out to steal her power. Then again, she'd been out of the Wiccan loop for so long, she may be a bit naive. "I can cast some protection spells and I've got the talisman you gave me."

The door opened and Jaxon and Mick walked in. Jax pulled a watch cap from his head and wrung it in his hands. "Sorry about walking out. I needed some air."

Raven stood and faced him, unsure what to say.

"Could I have a word with you in private, Rave?" Jax asked.

"Yeah, sure."

Raven led him into the office then shoved her hand in her hair as she turned to face him. An antique mahogany desk sat by the window with a massive iMac centred on it. On the other side of the room, she'd set up her altar on a long table that resembled a hutch. Like the desk, it was antique mahogany with intricate carvings on the legs and sides. A purple altar cloth lay across its surface with her tools, candles, incense, and crystals.

Jax wrung his hat as if it was soaked. She half expected his eyes to start bleeding, they looked that hurt.

"Do you feel like I raped you?"

"No." She took a step toward him and stopped herself. "I feel like Adara raped us both."

His cheeks flushed bright red. "Well, it was no hardship for me, babe." He ducked his head as if trying to hide his smile. "It was my every fantasy come true."

"Jax," Raven huffed.

"Sorry. I probably shouldn't have said that out loud." Waving his hat towards her altar, he said, "You're really getting back into it, aren't you."

"Yeah." Ena had been right in that, too. "It's who I am."

"True that." Jax stepped towards Raven and brushed his knuckles down her cheek. "I'm sorry for what Adara did, Rave. But, I can't regret the result. We made a beautiful child together and for that I am forever grateful." He leaned in and kissed her cheek where his fingers had caressed her.

She had the sense it was a goodbye kiss. Not in the sense that he was leaving her, but in the sense he was letting go of his desire for her. He was, finally, ready to move on. With tears blurring her vision, Raven watched Jax retreat.

* * *

With Kiran, Jax, and Mick doting over Indigo, Raven stepped up behind Riley and whispered, "Let's go for a walk."

"Are you sure your up for that? You just gave birth."

"We won't go far. I need a little air."

A short walk in the cool air, surrounded by nature, was just what Raven needed to clear her head and tell Riley what she needed to say. They bundled up and headed up the driveway to the quiet road. Raven stuck her hands in her coat pockets and Riley slid her arm through Raven's, leaning into her. She'd longed for that connection for the past nine months. Now she finally had it, guilt ate at her over what she was about to do. They walked in silence for a bit as Raven tried to figure out how to start.

Before she got a word out, Riley asked, "Why is Kiran so worried about Indigo's and your safety?"

"Ah." It took Raven a minute to switch out of what she was thinking to figure out how to explain. "My heritage makes me one of the most powerful witches in existence. So they tell me anyway. It makes me a target for witches like Adara who want more power."

"And Indigo will have those powers?"

"We won't know until she's older, but it's highly likely she will have great powers."

"Like your ability to heal? I envy you. Do you know what I'd give to be able to heal like that?"

"Yeah, but you wouldn't be able to use those powers at the hospital. You can't draw attention to it."

"Why the hell not? You've got the ability to do so much good. Why should you have to hide it?"

"I think you know why. People don't understand it, so they don't accept it. They judge something they know nothing about. That's why I stopped using my powers when I was a kid. I could hear their judgements, their criticism, and I couldn't stand it. I just wanted to be normal."

"I get that, but it's sad."

"I've constructed so many walls around my heart that it's going to take some time to knock them down."

"I know."

"When I left Ena's, I wanted nothing more than for her to come and find me. I never stopped wanting that. The longer she didn't, the more resentful I grew. At the same time, I didn't want her to come for me because I was afraid she'd find out what happened with Gregor and he'd kill her."

"I can't imagine how hard it must have been for you, Rave. You were only fifteen."

"I felt like she abandoned me."

"Well, that I can understand." Riley's birth mother gave her up for adoption when she was born. She tried to find her biological mother after her adoptive parents passed away when she was in high school. It was what brought her to Solstice. She was born in the Huntsville hospital, but that was all the information she had.

"I thought Adara was the one person I could trust and she ended up being the last person I should have. I feel like I can't trust my own intuition, my own gut."

"Oh, Rave." Riley stopped walking, her grip on Raven's arm forcing Raven to stop as well. "You have great instincts. Don't question them because of that woman. I mean, she fooled everyone, even Ena."

"I know, logically, you're probably right, but I just haven't been able to get there yet. I feel guilty for Ena's death-"

"Rave-"

"No, please. Let me finish." She stared into Riley's eyes until she nodded. "What I'm trying to say is that I have a lot of work to do on myself, Ri. Before I can be in a relationship."

Riley's jaw dropped and a puff of air shot out as her warm breath met the icy air.

"Are you saying I'm too late? Are we done?"

Raven pulled her hand out of her pocket and cupped Riley's cheek. "No, I'm asking for time to get my head on straight. How can I be who you need if I don't love and respect myself first? I know the pain of losing you, Riley. I don't ever want to feel that again. I want to make sure that I don't screw it up this time."

"And if you meet someone else in the meantime?"

Raven couldn't help but smile as she brushed her thumb over Riley's cheek. "The reason I haven't been with anyone since we broke up is because I don't want to be with anyone but you. I love you, Ri. That's never changed. I just need some time to work on being a better person for you."

"You already have changed a lot, Rave. This is the most you've opened up to me in the four years we've known each other."

"I'm trying."

As they walked back to the cottage, Riley entwined her fingers with Raven's. In less than twenty-four hours, Raven's world had tilted back into sync. For the first time, she felt like she could be a good mother and maybe, if she worked hard enough at it, she'd even deserve Riley's love again. Her heart soared with fresh hope at the idea of raising Indigo with Riley at her side.

COMING SOON

Watch for ***Something Wiccan This Way Comes*** - Book 2 in the Solstice Coven Series, coming to your favourite online bookstore in 2020.

ABOUT THE AUTHOR

Wendy writes mainly crime fiction with a hint of romance featuring strong female protagonists. She brings a vast array of life experience to her pages having held jobs on cruise ships in the Caribbean, addiction counsellor at a private addictions treatment centre, and years of experience in the security field.

She enjoys learning and holds diplomas in creative writing, forensic sciences, and law & security, to name a few.

When Wendy's not writing, you'll find her engrossed in the pages of a good book, out riding her bike, or spending quality time with her family.

She aspires to empower and inspire women as well as foster their healing with her novels.

Other Titles from Wendy Hewlett

The Taylor Sinclair Series

(Must be read in order)

Saving Grace

Unfinished Business

Runed

Trafficked (Coming Soon)

Stand Alone Novels

Ailey of Skye

Visit the author's website at: wendyhewlett.com and sign up for her Monthly Newsletter to stay up to date on news, new releases, giveaways, and more.

Follow Wendy on:

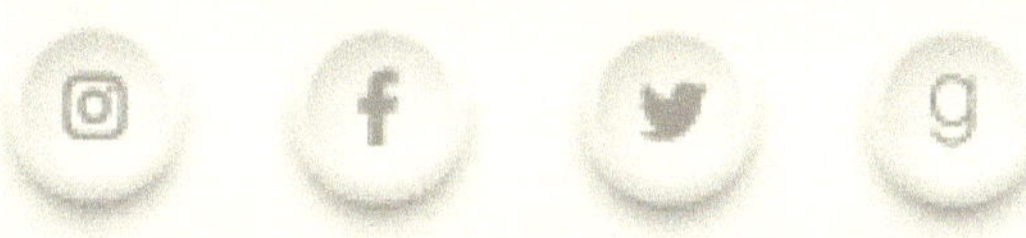

Reviews are the bread and butter of an Indie Author's career. Please take a moment to write a quick review where you purchased this book. It is greatly appreciated and allows Wendy to continue writing and publishing page-turning novels with wonderful, strong female protagonists.

9 781999 262617